GW01451573

Stacey Ennis-Theobald is an English author living in Berkshire with her wife and two dogs. She loves a good rom-com, Autumn afternoons, and hours in the bath. Stacey has always been interested in people. She has a history in social work and healthcare, and it shows in her writing. She loves to write about humanity, connections, day to day life, and things that almost everyone can relate to. *Sounds of the City* is Stacey's debut novel.

For Alice, and their invaluable support and belief in everything I've done.

For Polly, and her unwavering love and devotion.

For everyone who's ever searched for themselves in the pages of a novel, and not found it.

For me, because I can!

Stacey Ennis-Theobald

# SOUNDS OF THE CITY

AUSTIN MACAULEY PUBLISHERS™

LONDON * CAMBRIDGE * NEW YORK * SHARJAH

Copyright © Stacey Ennis-Theobald 2024

The right of Stacey Ennis-Theobald to be identified as author of this work has been asserted by the author in accordance with sections 77 and 78 of the Copyright, Designs and Patents Act 1988.

All rights reserved. No part of this publication may be reproduced, stored in a retrieval system, or transmitted in any form or by any means, electronic, mechanical, photocopying, recording, or otherwise, without the prior permission of the publishers.

Any person who commits any unauthorised act in relation to this publication may be liable to criminal prosecution and civil claims for damages.

This is a work of fiction. Names, characters, businesses, places, events, locales, and incidents are either the products of the author's imagination or used in a fictitious manner. Any resemblance to actual persons, living or dead, or actual events is purely coincidental.

A CIP catalogue record for this title is available from the British Library.

ISBN 9781035827886 (Paperback)
ISBN 9781035827893 (ePub e-book)

www.austinmacauley.com

First Published 2024
Austin Macauley Publishers Ltd®
1 Canada Square
Canary Wharf
London
E14 5AA

Writing wasn't my original dream. I grew up determined to help people. I didn't want to change the world, or save lives, or be a hero. I just liked people, and I wanted to help them.

I went to University, and spent four years training to be a Speech and Language Therapist. I graduated in the middle of a recession, and spent my time as a carer, and then a social worker.

And then I got lost. I floundered for a while, dipping into jobs that destroyed my soul, and my spirit, and my desire to help. I stared at screens all day, and cried all night because I wasn't doing what my heart wanted.

Only, I didn't know what that was anymore. I didn't know what the life I wanted looked like.

I had the perfect wife, the loveliest dogs, the safest home. But I didn't have the drive, or the sense of worth that I'd once had, and I didn't know how to find it again.

Until writing.

I began in fan fiction, like so many do. Typing away on my phone, late at night, building my little stories. And I posted them.

And the world opened.

People read my words, and they liked them. They sent me messages, and they left comments, and they shared my work, and they talked about it. They invited me onto podcasts, and Twitch interviews, and they showered me with love and gratitude and encouragement.

And it felt incredible.

I'd found a place I loved. A place I felt like a belonged, and something I felt good at. I'd found a dream, and a goal, and a purpose.

So I wrote, and I wrote, and I wrote. And as I wrote, I found myself again. I found my soul, and my spirit, and my people.

Then along came Alice.

Alice, and their belief, and their determination, and their investment. They opened doors for me, and handed me an opportunity I will never have the words to thank them for. I was able to stop working for a while - leave behind the anxious days and the tear-filled nights, and swap them for writing.

And that's where I am, as I sit and write this. In the library in Newbury, looking out over the canal, feeling indescribable gratitude for every step that led me here.

For Alice, and all they've given me. For my wonderful wife, Polly, and the way she's lifted me every single day. For my creative Brothers, for showing me a world I wanted to be a part of, and for reminding me to love what I do.

To the team at Austin Macauley Publishers, for getting this beautiful book into people's hands.

For everyone who is yet to read this. My first ever novel.

You have my unmatched love and gratitude.

# Chapter One

Finley shuffled in her seat, blanching at the click in her shoulders as she rolled them. She blinked rapidly, her eyes beginning to strain in the harsh light of her office, and the blurred glare of the screen in front of her beginning to reflect in the lens of her glasses.

She scanned her dual screens, weary eyes looking for the thing that had pulled her focus from her blueprints for the first time in hours.

She sighed, clicking on the flashing orange icon that told her she had a new message on the company's internal chat programme.

Lake, Noah: *Please tell me you're at least at home? It's embarrassing how much you work.*

Finley frowned.

She glanced at the time in the corner of her screen, wincing as she processed the numbers for the first time in hours. Nearing 10pm. Not the latest she'd been at the office this week, but close. She ran a hand through the thick, dark curls of her hair, pushing the wayward strands from her face as a wave of guilt washed over her at the thought of Peanut waiting alone at home.

Again.

Had she even remembered to leave on a lamp?

She sighed heavily, cursing herself for her neglect of the *one* thing she had waiting for her in her London apartment. She *knew* how bitter and sassy her cat got in the dark, and she knew full well that there would likely be a hairball on her pillow and a collection of wet leaves in her shoes if she didn't get home before the night set in.

Bennet, Finley: *Would you believe me if I said I'd had a home cooked meal, a long shower, and I'm in bed with a book?*

Lake, Noah: *Absolutely not. Get the fuck out of that office, immediately, or I'm coming for your cat in your sleep.*

Lake, Noah: *Poor neglected little Peanut.*

Finley winced again, her chest tightening a little with guilt.

Bennet, Finley: *Like you'd win in a fight against Peanut.*

Bennet, Finley: *I'm leaving now, I swear. The Bryce Ridge estate is breaking me, I can't get the licensing for anything they will sign off, and I can't get the sign off for anything I can get licensed!*

Lake, Noah: *Sorry, I didn't understand anything you just said, I don't speak architecture after 8pm in the evening.*

Bennett, Finley: *Then why are you even online?*

Lake, Noah: *Because my best friend is a workaholic, and I'm doing my caring duties, now go the fuck home, you're wasting both of our lives in that chair!*

Finley huffed out a laugh.

She knew Noah was right, and as much as it pained her to say it, she would a thousand percent be here until dawn if he wasn't around to bring her back down to Earth.

It always entertained Finley how the tables had turned. How they were now the stark opposite of how they'd once been, back when both had been fresh-faced university students. Back then, Noah had been the one to pull all-nighters on nothing but Red Bull and prawn cocktail crisps, and Finley had been the one to drag him from their digs and into the bars with all the strength she could muster.

But now, Noah had found his balance, and Finley was the one throwing her entire soul into the screen. And she was eternally grateful to her best friend for the way he clung to the last threads of her sanity, and kept her *just* about grounded enough to keep from snapping.

She pushed her chair back from her desk, her hands rubbing at dazed mocha eyes. Her bones and the stiff fabric of her shirt audibly creaked with the hours her tall frame had spent curled into the same position. She started to pack her belongings, her head still swimming with a million different things for her upcoming projects.

She blinked as her eyes landed on a brown paper bag and a thermos set to the side of her desk, a post it note stuck to the flask.

Then she cringed, her cheeks heating a little with shame.

*How* did she keep missing these being left there?

She plucked the note from the flask, already knowing what the words would say.

*I didn't want to disturb your phone call, but you looked like you could use some fuel and some caffeine.*

*Have a good evening.*

*Bella. x*


Finley shook her head, her lips curling softly.

Bella was sweet.

Maybe a little *too* sweet to really hold Finley's interest, but she had been a godsend for Finley's inability to remember to look after herself in the busy months before a project launch.

She was attractive, too.

Attractive enough for Finley to notice the way her patterned shirts cut just low enough over her chest, and the way she smelled when she leaned just a little too close over the briefing boards.

Though not *quite* attractive enough that Finley had ever thought twice about her once the office doors were closed behind her.

Finley blinked, her eyes catching movement in the only other light that remained on in the darkened office building.

"Bennett!"

She rolled her eyes a little, her back bristling immediately as the sharp voice called out from her boss's doorway. Demanding. Expectant. As always.

Before she could take a step towards the sound, Amelia appeared in her doorway, her crisp shirt and her jet black, pinned-back hair as immaculate as it had been when the day had begun fourteen hours ago. Finley could never understand how she did it.

"What's up?" Finley sat back on the edge of her desk as Amelia approached. "I was just about to head off."

"Co-Capita aren't willing to go ahead with the latest plans for the boarding house at Oak Hills."

Amelia held out a file, and Finley physically deflated, her stomach turning as she scanned the notes scrawled across the page.

"I need you to present all changes to them tomorrow at 10:30."

*"Seriously?"* Finley baulked. *"Why?* What happened, they signed this off three days ago!"

"*Co-Capita* signed it off, but the headteacher at Oak Hills has thrown her toys out of her pram and is insisting on a rework." Amelia shrugged, already turning on her heels. "We need this, Bennett. I trust you'll get this done?"

"I will, you know I will Amelia, I just…" Finley sighed, her tired eyes flicking once again to the clock, and to the brown paper bag in her hand. "I need to feed my cat. I'll take the work home, and I'll have the plans ready for you tomorrow by nine."

"Make it eight." Amelia eyed her knowingly. "You're a good architect, Bennett. My best. I wouldn't trust anybody else with this."

Finley gave a tight smile as she nodded, her mind already blazing with the changes that she would need to make tonight to what had already been hours and hours of work. She swallowed, her muscles already aching at the mere thought of the night ahead of her, and yet the fire of ambition in her belly just wouldn't let her say no. It never did.

Those two taunting words swam in her ears.

Her *best architect.*

Amelia had been saying those words to Finley for more than three years, and they were forever her driving point. The best. Finley wanted to be the best at what she did. She wanted to *win.* She wanted to reach her dreams, and Amelia really seemed to believe she could. It always felt so *close,* and yet she'd been overlooked time and time again when the company was considering promotions. It was no secret that a principal role was opening up in the coming months, and Finley was determined that this one had her name on it.

It had fucking *better* do.

Dan Myles was *so* sure it was going to him, but Finley put more hours in and everybody knew it.

It was her fucking turn this time.

She'd lost *three* promotions this past eighteen months, and yet she carried the biggest projects, she had the best proven record, and the best client feedback. She should be a shoe-in, and she knew it. All she had to do was get this pretentious-ass school under her belt, and she'd be a winner. She *knew* she would. She *had* to be.

Then she'd be one step closer to the ultimate dream of running the company.

The dream of standing on her own two feet and not *needing* anyone else.

Not needing anyone else's money, or their permission, or their goddamn fucking *approval.* Not Amelia's, or Jess's, or her father's.

And then, with a promotion, she'd have a team. More flexibility, more freedom to make her own decisions, the power to delegate. A little more time to herself.

Then maybe she wouldn't keep finding Peanut's revenge hairballs in her clothing.

She exhaled slowly, tucking her leather satchel under her arm and making her way towards the building's elevators. She turned the collar of her sharp, grey blazer up against her neck to shield the bite of the late English evening as she exited the office, and out onto the streets of London.

Even at the night hour, South Bank always had an aura of light, from the street lights and the buildings and the London Eye, and the ever-present glow of the Capital. It was never strange to find the street busy with the bustle of life and the sounds of the city.

Finley pushed her headphones into her ears, hitting play on her phone as *'girl in red'* began to block the sounds of the river, and the distant sirens, and the low bustle of the bars and the restaurants and the theatres in the city that never slept.

She kept her eyes low, barely sparing a glance at the pubs or the buildings, or the lights, or the buskers and the artists, or even the tree-lined banks of the river Thames as she trod the familiar walk to her home in Covent Garden.

She barely noticed the pubs that once would have called her in, fresh from a day in the office poring over blueprints with enthusiasm and juvenated energy, ready to take on the world with her friends and the girls of the city. Or the trees that held the flyers she would once have scoured, detailing music festivals and comedy nights and theatre shows that once upon a time she would have scrambled over her own feet to attend.

She wondered just how long it had been since she'd seen a live show.

Six months? More?

Her head still swam with work, the day's meetings and emails and phone calls playing over in her mind as she easily and habitually dodged the pedestrians and the buskers along the festival pier, and crossed the shimmering waters beneath Waterloo Bridge.

She could just about hear the rumble of the city over the music in her ears, and she turned the volume up on her phone as she made her way past the Lyceum Theatre, and the Royal Opera House, and the looming architecture of St Paul's Cathedral.

She barely noticed any of it. She barely noticed the people milling about around the Opera House, or spilling out of the streets of the tavern bar and restaurant on the corner of Floral Street.

She barely noticed the smells of garlic and ginger and beer and wine that floated across the evening air as she passed through the bustling streets that took her to the smart lanes of brick buildings that she called home.

And she barely noticed the life that still hummed around her as she punched her key code into her apartment building, and made her way through the bright hallways to her own front door.

Finley made it home in nineteen minutes.

She exhaled heavily as she finally closed her door on the sounds of the city, sinking to her knees on the hallway rug to embrace her disgruntled, skinny little runt of a tortoise-shell cat in a guilt-ridden cuddle.

*"Hey*, bub. Mummy's *so* sorry, Peanut."

She buried her face in the cat's weird, tufty fur, breathing in the comforting smell of the home she rarely got to see these days. She sighed, dodging the pissed swipe of a paw as the cat extracted herself gracelessly from her grip.

"I know, I know," Finley grinned, shaking her head as she followed the cat into the kitchen. "You've waited a lifetime already, I'm sorry."

She fought the fatigue in every one of her muscles as she dished up Peanut's food, grabbed a beer from the fridge, and flopped onto her sofa with her tablet and Bella Collins's brown paper gift.

She let herself sink back, the thick cushions of her teal corner sofa holding the heavy weight of her weary muscles for a relieving moment as she looked around her home.

She loved this apartment.

She loved the size, and the large glass windows that looked out onto the vibrant life of Covent Garden. She loved the way it always felt warm, nestled safely amongst the homes of other people around her. She loved the decor she'd spent so much time and money perfecting, all those years back when she'd first laid down her deposit, and hauled her life into the two-bed apartment.

She *loved* her home.

But she was *so* rarely here these days.

She couldn't remember the last time she'd even cleaned it. She dreaded to think of the layers of dust she'd find if she ran her finger over the shelves of her board games, and her DVDs, and her books.

Or over the arty greyscale prints, and the framed photos of her friends, most of whom she hadn't seen in months. Photos of her own smiling face on rooftop bars with Noah, and Harri, and Zayan. Fresh-faced and younger, in fields with a warm cider and a band playing on the stage behind her. On her own balcony, with a tiny barbecue and a homemade jug of mango daiquiri, with Kate sprawled across her lap and Peanut over her shoulders. Or in Noah's kitchen, with a Christmas dinner and a half-torn paper crown dwarfing her head over the pixie cut it had taken her three years to grow out. Photos from a calmer time, of the things she'd done before she'd let her job take everything she had.

She didn't even dare to think about the layer of dust that covered the sad and decrepit looking parlour palm in the corner of the living room, that she *really* should just throw away.

All her other plants were plastic.

For *great* reason.

She couldn't remember the last time she'd dusted or hoovered, but it never seemed to matter because she was just *never* here.

She lifted her arm, letting Peanut cuddle in beside her, before pulling the sandwich and crisps out of her brown paper bag gift. She still hadn't had the time or the heart to tell Bella Collins that she really *barely* tolerated pickle. Or that 'ready salted' was an absolute waste of a crisp flavour.

But really, who was she to be ungrateful?

She certainly wasn't whipping up steak bourguignon in the Crockpot these days, so this was the closest thing to fuel that Finley was getting.

She sighed, tucking her legs underneath herself as she flipped the cover from her tablet.

It was gonna be a long night.

~ ~ ~ ~ ~ ~ 🐾 ~ ~ ~ ~ ~ ~

Sophie clapped her hands gleefully as she stepped back to admire her work.

Her second degree now hung proudly on the wall of her small home office, in a matching frame alongside the first.

She felt the pride surge through every nerve in her body as she let her eyes roam slowly over the lettering.

*Sophie Cedars, BA.*

Two times over, now.

First History, and now Classical Literature. The history degree had taken her six passionate years to complete online via The Open University, the studying crammed between routine shifts at her sister's pub. Classical Literature had taken three equally ardent years.

And Sophie was *really* bloody proud of herself.

She knew she hadn't done this the conventional way. She knew she could have gone off to Uni, like Annie had, or Nikki, Ella, and Adam. She could maybe even have graduated and stayed in Oxford, Manchester, Bristol, or Brighton. She could have made a new life, built of her deepest passions, and worked every day in the field that she really loved. Somewhere like London, with galleries and *museums.*

Plural museums.

With artefacts from all over the globe, not just the ancient flint arrowheads of Carn Brea.

Sophie was vehemently aware of the poison side of that coin.

She knew the wrongdoings of British museums, in keeping artefacts that belonged to other cultures. She knew it well, and she understood the importance of repatriation, but she was a longstanding believer that exhibitions should *move.* Like they did in art galleries.

If Sophie ruled the world, historical artefacts would move around, under the ownership and subsequent loan of their rightful proprietors.

One day, when Sophie ran her own museum, that was how she would do things. She'd change the way curating worked, to include just the most *obvious* requirements of humanity and respect. She'd bring a little *ethics* into history. They didn't *need* to be mutually exclusive.

It was a hill that Sophie would die on. One day, when she had it her way.

But she certainly wouldn't just exhibit the grey flint and stone of the bloody Cornish coastline.

So, she knew. Sophie *knew* she hadn't done this the way that she *really* wanted to. She hadn't ever dreamed of studying in her own home in Polcarne, Cornwall for nine long years, but she was endlessly proud of the achievements she had been able to gain, and she couldn't *wait* for the years of hard work to finally pay off.

She grinned, her mind drifting as she allowed herself to indulge the fantasies. She indulged images of herself in sophisticated heels that clicked over the wooden floors of her very own museum in Oxford or London, or York. And images of herself in passionate discussions with archaeologists and historians as she curated her artefacts. Images of days embracing her passion with people who shared and understood it.

She caught sight of her reflection in the frame of her Classical Literature scroll.

Her tousled auburn hair was pushed back into the same messy bun she'd worn it in for *twelve* years, but the green eyes looking back at her sparkled with the shine of bubbling excitement. The spark of something new on the horizon.

Or at least, she *hoped* it was.

She knew, also, that beneath the fire and the determination that had pushed her through nine years of essays and exams, was a rippling stream of fear.

Fear that if she chased, she might never reach. Fear that the images in her mind might never be her reality, and she'd be left wiping down her sister's sticky bar, with two scrolls on her wall, and without a dream to carry her through her days.

But also, fear of what she would leave behind if the dreams *did* come true.

Sophie sighed, her giddiness wavering as she pulled the frayed hair tie from her russet bun, and ran her fingers through the messy waves.

Pulling pints in Polcarne, Cornwall's only bar was certainly not what Sophie ever *thought* she would be doing at the ripe age of twenty-six. But her sister owned the pub, and there was a very distinct lack of much else to do in their tiny hamlet town in the back end of nowhere.

It wasn't what she *thought* she'd be doing, but she did love it.

Most days.

She loved working with Bex, and with Bex's husband Pete. She loved working with the people of Polcarne, and seeing familiar faces every day.

She just wished they weren't *always* the same people.

Sophie spent every day serving the same beer to the same people she'd known all her life, and she couldn't help but watch the door sometimes, waiting for someone new to cross through the thick beamed archway.

She jumped, pulled from her dreams as Taylor Swift burst into song inside the pocket of her faded jeans. Her alarm made her jump *every* time, despite the fact that it had been the same song for five years. She chuckled, fishing the phone out and swiping the blaring tune away.

Time to relieve Bex for the last leg of the shift behind the bar at The Ship Inn.

She ran her fingers over the faded black uniform polo bearing the pub's name and sign. An enthusiastic insistence of hers back when she had tried to convince her sister that they should strive to increase their star rating. *More professional,* she had insisted, and Bex had distractedly agreed, her mind far more focused on trying to keep Drunk Dave from singing *'Brown Sugar'* on the ancient karaoke machine for the fourth night in a row.

Sophie had taken the song off the collection later that night.

That had been five years ago. Their rating had stayed the same. It had never really even been all that bad, but Sophie had just wanted *change.* She'd just wanted to prove that things in their tiny town *could* change, no matter how small it was.

But she had two degrees now. She was an *academic.*

Everything was different now. The world around her vibrated with possibility, and her dreams were but a hair's breadth away.

Everything was different. Sophie was sure of it.

It was just that everything *felt* exactly the same.

Her clothes, her hair, her job, her home, her dreams.

Nothing had changed.

She even had a third date tomorrow night with *Kyle-from-the-school-band,* and she couldn't help the niggling deflation in her heart at the thought that even a decade later, that was still how he was known.

Nine years, and two degrees, and all the passion, and the hope, and the vibrating possibilities of the incredible planet she lived on, and Sophie Cedars still wasn't making changes.

Her phone buzzed once more in her hand, and she smiled softly as Kyle's name and the new message icon caught her eye, and she flicked the screen to pull the words up.

Kyle: *Can't wait to see you tomorrow. I'll pick you up at 8.*

Kyle: *Got a surprise for you.*

Sophie shook her head, her lips curling into an amused smile. Kyle was sweet. She didn't get butterflies, or tingles. His kiss didn't really *spark* anything, and she didn't exactly get hot under the collar over his tweed cap or his talk of pilchard fishing…

But she had known him all her life.

So that was inevitable, right?

If she were *truly* honest, she had never *really* even gotten the hype back in 2008 when every girl she knew fawned over Kyle-from-the-band's quiffed blonde hair and ripped jeans, and his rock songs and his bass guitar. Let alone now that he was thinning on top and the holes in his jeans were a lot less deliberate.

But he was sweet, and she didn't exactly have a whole long line of options in Polcarne, Cornwall, where the men were all gamekeepers, fishermen, and farmers, and the women were all compulsory heterosexuals.

So *sweet* didn't seem all that bad. She could do a lot worse.

She bit her lip, the corners quirked into a smile as she cast her eye over her degrees once more before switching the light off in the little home office, and pulling the door closed behind her.

She had ten minutes.

She headed into her bedroom.

She loved this room. This was by far her favourite part of the house, with its bay windows and its views across the fields that she knew carried the ocean breeze. She could often smell the salt through her open window when the winds were high, and if she listened really hard, she could *just* hear the crash of the waves on the rougher days.

She turned to face her mirror. She grinned as she teased a brush through her hair, and the strands fell easily into soft waves, the colour shining different shades of red where the sun and age had caught it.

She eased the waves around her shoulders, spraying a little hairspray to keep the shape.

Everything around her might still be the same, but *Sophie* was different.

She was an academic now, and maybe she simply needed to drive her own change. And sure, maybe she couldn't increase the pub rating, or coax a stream of city high-fliers into Polcarne's little bakery, or bring the extensive world of arts and history into her own bedroom.

But she *was* in control of *some* things, and maybe the small changes were the key. Maybe the changes Sophie made in *herself* would open the doors she wanted.

And maybe they'd be a little less…*daunting.*

Maybe the changes Sophie *could* make would be the ones that didn't mean failure, and ones that didn't mean leaving her life and everything she'd ever loved behind.

And maybe someday, the small changes would bring the big ones with it. Maybe the Sophie Cedars with one degree and a messy bun was meant for Polcarne, Cornwall, but just *maybe* the Sophie Cedars with the two degrees and the perfect rippled waves would be the one brave enough to make the leap.

Maybe.

She grinned, spinning in the mirror with an animated flourish.

It was worth a try.

She skipped down the stairs, her heart feeling light and full of possibility as she hummed cheerily.

She grabbed an apple from the bowl in her kitchen, taking a larger than necessary bite as she bounced out of her house. She locked the painted blue door behind her, and made her way along her little flower lined path to her gate, and her chrome blue Ford Kuga.

Her light air stayed as she made the four-minute drive to The Ship Inn, manoeuvring the car effortlessly down the quiet, winding, bush-lined lane.

She still felt in high spirits as she pulled up to the car park of The Ship Inn, made her way up the gravel path to the heavy oak doors, and pushed it open. She always enjoyed her shifts with Bex, but today was extra special. Today they had a reason to celebrate, and if anyone was going to pop a bottle for Sophie and her achievements, it was her sister.

Today was the day. Sophie had two degrees now. Things were gonna change.

"Shit, Sophie, thank fuck."

Sophie frowned as her sister ran from behind the bar, making an immediate beeline for her the moment she was over the pub's threshold. She stuttered a little as Bex threw her tattered, grubby tea towel over Sophie's shoulder, and pushed the chain of keys and till fobs into her hands.

"Oh, hello to you too!" Sophie huffed, immediate disappointment surging her veins at the lack of a popping champagne bottle.

Or at very least, a banner.

Bex winced apologetically.

"Hi, I love you, I gotta go!"

Sophie's eyes widened, her stomach clenching and her degree instantly forgotten as she processed the unusual rush and the flash of flustered panic in her sister's eyes.

"I-is everything okay?" she asked, immediately nervous.

"Jack's been packed home from his sleepover, he's got the flu!" Bex spouted, her hands flailing a little in her hurried explanation. "But Pete's a wet wipe and complaining he hasn't had his flu jab, so I've gotta go rescue him!"

"Oh *no,* poor Jack," Sophie groaned. "What about Willow, is she okay?"

"So far." Bex leaned forward, planting a hurried kiss on Sophie's head. "Don't let Drunk Dave near the karaoke. He's been looking for *'Fat Bottomed Girls'* all afternoon."

Sophie rolled her eyes, her lips curling in amusement as her sister brushed past her and headed for the door.

"Do you need anything?" she called.

"I'll call you!" Bex shouted, her words just carrying as the door closed behind her. "Love you, Sis!"

Sophie sighed as she watched Bex leave, her spirits rumpled a little by her sister's unusual state of harassment.

Bex was the rock. The *solid* one. And when Bex got hassled, the world just immediately didn't sit right.

Sophie swallowed, her chest tightening as she watched the door swing closed behind her sister.

That wasn't true, really.

Not anymore.

Bex *had* been the rock. She *had* been the solid one. She'd been primary carer for Sophie and their mum for most of Sophie's life. But the past two years, since their mum had passed away, the cracks had finally split, and Bex's suit of unshakeable armour had crumbled. And it was Sophie's turn to step up to the plate, and hold the cracks together. For the one person she loved more than anything in this world.

And if that meant working alone instead of raising a toast to her own achievements, then Sophie could bloody well suck it up and do just that, and do it with a smile.

She pushed the rattled discomfort down, feeling it fizz a little in her stomach as she swallowed it. Then she turned towards the bar, and bit back a squeal so hard she tasted copper as she almost collided face to face with her most persistent regular.

"Afternoon Miss Cedars." The old man tipped a hat that did not exist, dipping his frail legs in a half bow. "May I buy you a drink?"

"I'm on the clock, Ern," Sophie chuckled, shaking her head in amusement as she stepped around the old man and made her way behind the bar. "You need a refill?"

Ern nodded, his completely unnecessary cane not touching the ground once as he crossed the room and propped himself up against the oak bar.

"I was once a young whippersnapper like you, you know," he chuckled.

Sophie grinned.

She had been serving Ern almost every day of her adult life, and almost every day the conversation went *exactly* the same way.

"Oh, I know," she agreed. "A very handsome one, I'm sure."

"I'm *still* handsome." Ern raised an eyebrow, grinning cheekily. He coughed, his eyes flying wide as his dentures popped out.

Sophie bit back a laugh as he pushed them back in.

"Of course you are," she chuckled. She rinsed a glass, pulling the lever of the only drink she'd ever served Ern Butterworth. She smiled widely as she pushed it across the bar. "One pint of Hicks with a small head! I'll put it on your tab."

Ern nodded. He lifted his pint slowly to his lips, his fingers trembling against the glass as he held it.

"I'm going away next week, you know." He grinned, his upper lip carrying a foam moustache that was just frankly *impossible* considering how small the head was on the beer.

Sophie chuckled.

*Every* day.

"Are you? Anywhere nice?"

She knew exactly what came next.

His caravan in Newquay.

Sophie was pretty sure that thing had been torn down for neglect more than twelve years ago.

"Yeah, me caravan in Newquay," Ern stated.

Sophie grinned. She usually answered this with the same question, day after day, and the conversation would follow the exact same path.

*Oh, you are? Well, that sounds very relaxing.*

*Put me feet up for a while. Do some fishing! Care to join me, Miss Cedars?*

*I wish I could, Ern, but I'm on the clock all week, I'm afraid. Maybe next time!*


Today was different though.

Sophie had two degrees now.

And a new hairstyle.

So maybe she could make another small change. Maybe *this* Sophie had a different answer.

She grinned.

"Yeah?" she chuckled, leaning her elbows on the bar as she watched Ern take another slow and shaky sip. "Gonna do a spot of surfing?"

Ern paused.

He furrowed his brow, lifting his beer in one hand while the other fumbled for the cane Sophie had never once seen him use.

He tutted.

"Don't be so *ridiculous*," he huffed. "I can't even get up me *stairs* anymore. Can't even *walk* without me cane!"

Sophie blinked. Well, that hadn't been the most successful change she'd ever attempted.

Then the intro to *'Fat Bottomed Girls'* began to play on the jukebox. She sighed.

Her high hopes played on a loop, a mantra circle around in her head as she watched Ern retreat to his armchair by the fire, not once touching his cane to the ground.

Today was the day. Sophie had two degrees now. Things were different, and Sophie was going to make a change.

If she dared.

# Chapter Two

Finley groaned as she stirred, the dull ache of a knot in her shoulder pulling her from her sleep. She blinked; her dazed eyes disorientated as she fought to process her surroundings. Her upright position, the absence of a duvet, the glaring overhead light and the persistent nudging of Peanut's head against the underside of her jaw were all stark indicators that once again, Finley had not made it into her bedroom before she passed out. She glanced at the clock.

5:02am.

*"Shit."*

She threw her arms over her face, exhaling heavily as she willed herself awake. She was exhausted, she hadn't had any real sleep, and now she knew she wasn't going to. She had to get up, eat something, make herself look presentable, and try to prepare at least a few notes on this *fucking* presentation before 7:30am when she'd have to leave for the office.

Though she knew she'd be fine.

She always was.

Finley Bennett had always had the gift of the gab. *'Charmer's chance'*, Noah always called it. But right now—her hair matted, her mouth so dry she really wouldn't be surprised if *that* was where Peanut had left today's payback hairball, and her clothes smelling like twenty hours of office work—charm wasn't even on the radar. She cursed herself for letting this happen.

Again.

Jess's words ran through her head *still,* every time that she did. As bitter to the taste as the day she'd uttered them.

*You give that job more than you give yourself, Finley. More than you ever gave me.*

It had been well over a year since Jess had left her.

Left her because Finley had *never had time* for her.

Because she *left the best of her behind those office walls.*

Because she *never put real life first.*

Bullshit.

Or so Finley had told herself.

She knew it was true. Every word of it.

But the job was her dream. Had been her dream since she was a teenager, and Jess just couldn't seem to understand that.

Or wouldn't.

Finley had *wanted* that time to herself. She had *wanted* time with her girlfriend, of *course* she had. But she had *needed* that goddamn promotion.

She had needed to reach her goals. Needed to keep climbing the ladder, further and further away from her childhood home, and the ever-controlling reign of her narcissistic father. Had needed to own her own life, and her own money, and her own decisions. Had needed to prove she didn't *need* the money or the roof or the rules that her father had lorded over her for her entire life.

Had needed to be free to live the life and the success that *she* wanted for herself, without having to answer to someone who held her down beneath the sole of a steadfast boot. Had needed it like *air,* and she had just never been able to make Jess understand that.

And she had always felt *so* close. Just *one* more push.

And one more.

And one more.

And Jess had tried and failed to accept the burden on their relationship.

She'd been a casualty, really. A heart that Finley had never meant to break. But in the end, it had been inevitable.

There weren't many people willing to come second to a suit and a salary, and it left Finley pretty lonely.

Finley sighed, scratching Peanut behind the ears as she hauled herself from the sofa. She needed to clear her head if she had any hope of nailing this presentation. She needed a moment to breathe. She was going for a run.

She grabbed her phone, shooting a text to Noah.

Finley: *Run?*

The reply was almost instant.

Noah: *Apollo in twenty?*

Finley grinned. She was ever grateful that she could rely on her best friend and colleague to be awake at *every* damn hour of the day, and always raring to go.

She felt the burn in her hips of a night slumped on the sofa as she made her way up the stairs and into her bedroom. She pushed past it, wincing only slightly as she stripped her aching muscles of her crumpled, sweaty shirt and fitted slacks, and swapped it for the soft, breathable lycra of her best running gear.

She breathed a sigh of relief, her mind already beginning to clear at the mere thought of a run along the river. She strapped her fitness tracker onto her wrist, tapping the screen until the stats she wanted displayed across it.

Noah teased her incessantly for the obscene value of Finley's running gear.

The lycra, and the tracker, and the trainers, and the hydration pack, and the weight bands, and the headphones.

It was all worth more than Finley's monthly mortgage, and she knew it was unnecessary, but running was one of the only hobbies she still found time for, so she invested in it.

And maybe if Noah invested in a slightly pricier pair of trainers, he'd be able to keep up with her pace.

Finley could still feel the deep ache in her muscles as she stretched, and she cringed at the thought of just how badly she'd treated her body lately. Expecting it to keep up her usual times and her distances with barely any fuel, more coffee and late-night beers than water, and next to no sleep.

None in an actual bed.

Really, she needed a duvet day. She needed a few extra hours of sleep, a home cooked meal with every vegetable under the sun, and a chance to switch both her brain *and* her body off.

But if she *didn't* run, her mind would ache as much as her body.

And so, her burning hips, and her weary legs, and the cricks in her neck and her shoulders were just going to have to push through it.

The slow jog through the early morning streets eased Finley in gently, and by the time she reached the corner of Rupert Street, she could feel the tension begin to lift in her muscles. She breathed in deeply, her eyes fluttering closed and her chest expanding in her appreciation of the morning air.

She loved the city at dawn. It was the one time, Finley ever really felt she acknowledged the world around her. She loved the familiar smells of fresh baking goods and heavy ground coffee beans as places began preparing for breakfast, and the almost dewy scent of the air in the early morning. She loved the odd sense of quiet. London was never truly quiet, but in the early hours the sounds were different. Fewer cars and buses and sirens, fewer people and bikes and phone calls and the muted hum of conversation.

Instead, Finley could hear clearly the calls of the stalls in Covent Garden as they began to set up for the market, and the hushed scuffle in the alleys as the shops and the restaurants took their morning deliveries. She could hear the low rumble of the tubes as always; London's hummed soundtrack. But it always felt more discreet in the quiet.

And the air was always clearer this time of the day, before the rush of the city awoke. Today's breeze was crisp between the height of the buildings, and the mist of a hot day brewed softly along the brickwork roads.

In the early morning, with the air fresh in her lungs and the day stretched out before her, Finley felt like the city was hers. Like London, and everything it held in its heart, belonged to Finley, and like she could stand atop it and be in *control.*

She still remembered the first time she'd felt that way. The day she'd snuck from her stifled prison when her dad had been asleep, and jumped the barriers at East Finchley tube station to go to a music festival with her friends from school. She'd been fifteen and stupid.

They hadn't even gotten in.

But the day they'd spent in the city, in the parks and the shops and the tubes and the museums, had been the freest Finley had ever felt.

It had been worth every second of the grounding she'd had when she'd returned that night.

And Finley still chased that feeling now, fifteen years later and long free of her father's reign.

Finley slowed her pace as she spotted Noah waiting for her outside the theatre, and she huffed in amusement at the clearly bed-headed state of his tight afro curls, and the grimace across his full lips as he stretched his calf muscles out ahead of him.

She wondered if he'd been awake before she'd texted him, or if he'd forced himself up at the sound of her message tone.

Noah was competitive.

Useless, but competitive.

He wasn't as fit, or as fast, or as strong as Finley was, and they both knew it. But Noah's determination and his sheer refusal to admit defeat left him forever breathless, and scrabbling to keep ahead of his best friend's trainer dust.

Which played out *very* nicely for Finley's inexorable desire to *win.*

"Morning," Finley greeted as she approached. She smirked, nodding her head in the direction of Noah's lean legs. "Careful not to stretch those things too hard, they might snap."

"And a very glorious fuck you too," Noah scowled, his own lips curling into a grin as he studied Finley in wry amusement. "God, you look like shit, Bennett."

Finley scoffed.

"Charming, as always."

"It comes from a place of love." Noah grinned, jumping on the spot as he shook out his muscles. He wrinkled his nose, taking a step back as he looked Finley up and down. "Seriously though. Are you even getting the basics? Eating? Sleeping?"

"I'm eating." Finley rolled her eyes. She knew she'd been caught. They'd had this dance before, and Noah could read her like an open book.

"Anything that *doesn't* come in sealed disposable plastic with a sugar tax?" Noah raised an eyebrow.

"I ate salad last night," Finley retorted.

"A single wilted lettuce leaf on the pathetic excuse for a sandwich in Bella Collins' little love packages does *not* count as a salad, Finley," Noah reprimanded. "God, your eyes look *purple.* Eat a vegetable. Are you even shopping?"

Finley grumbled wordlessly as she fell in beside Noah, the two setting off on their well-trodden path towards the river at an easy pace.

"Socialising?" Noah continued. *"Dating?"*

Finley narrowed her eyes.

"That is not a *basic.*"

"Wrong," Noah retorted. "We all have our *needs,* Finley. If the only company you ever have in that *obscenely* expensive bed of yours is that cat, then yours are *not* being met."

Finley groaned.

"My *needs* are *fine,* Noah!"

*"Are* they?"

Finley faltered, her mind flicking back to the last time she had tried to meet those particular *needs*. Five, maybe six nights ago, when she'd tried to watch porn and gotten almost immediately distracted by the interior design, and it had spiralled her mind into a series of ideas for an upcoming project. So instead of sending herself off to sleep with a blissful orgasm, she'd ended up scribbling notes onto her tablet with the video on mute until she'd finally passed out with her face buried in the pillow and 'Girls On Holiday' still playing on her phone.

She grimaced.

*"No,"* she grumbled.

"It's been like, two years, Finley," Noah panted, his voice more strained as they picked up their pace. "You've got to get back out there. Just do something for *you* for once."

Finley huffed.

It wasn't that she was specifically *against* dating. It was just that she knew how much she'd hurt Jess. She *knew* how little time she had to give to herself, let alone to give to someone else who needed her. Someone else who would *demand* things of her. Someone else to answer to. She knew how rare it would be to find someone who understood what she needed to do, and would tolerate it.

But even so, she had to admit she was a little lonely. And red-blooded. And she certainly wasn't adverse to the idea of a warm body in her, admittedly excessive, bed.

"It has *not* been two years, and it's not a deliberate *choice*, Noah," she retorted defensively. "I just don't have time to *meet* anyone!"

"Not true."

Finley shot her eyes to Noah's face, her eyebrow raised quizzically.

"It's not!" Noah continued. "We both know Bella Collins has been pining over those puppy peepers for the *entire* three years she's worked at Opal Arches."

"Oh my *god,* no-one is *pining."* Finley winced.

"I'm just saying, she's cute." Noah shrugged, eyeing his friend. "Despite her dire choice in sandwiches. Quit being a mardy moose, and ask her out."

Finley focused on her breathing as she let the words mull over in her brain. Maybe Noah was right. Maybe she *should* ask Bella out.

It wasn't like she'd *never* thought about it.

Besides, Bella worked with her. She knew how hard Finley worked, and she didn't seem all that deterred.

Where was the harm in one date?

She had nothing to lose. Not really.

She was deathly single, embarrassingly lonely, and Bella was sweet. And great to look at.

So, what was the problem?

Finley smirked, pushing her legs harder as her resolve spurred her on.

This morning, after her presentation, she'd find Bella, thank her for the coffee and the sandwich last night, and offer to take her out to dinner tonight to make up for it.

Decision made.

"Are you speeding up, or have I been eating too many filled yorkshires from Dougie's Pies?" Noah panted, his face drawing into a grimace as he fought to catch Finley's increase in pace.

"Never eat at Dougie's, Lake," Finley called, pushing just a little harder. "And you're slowing down!"

~ ~ ~ ~ ~ ~ ⏱ ~ ~ ~ ~ ~ ~

Sophie slipped her key into the lock on the door to the apartment above The Ship Inn.

She never bothered to knock anymore. Her sister almost never bothered to answer, and when she did, she simply berated Sophie for not using the key that she'd given her *'for a reason'*.

She crept quietly up the stairs and into the airy, spacious apartment that she almost knew better than her own. She'd spent so much time here in the twelve years since Bex had moved in, taking their mother with her. When she'd finally reached twenty-one, and secured the keys to the pub that would grant her adulthood and her independence, Bex had taken their beloved mum from the care home she'd been in for seven years, and become her primary carer.

In the early days, Bex had needed all the help she could get.

Sophie had been fourteen, and living with her aunt Linda, and she still remembered the ripple of excitement she'd felt in every one of her nerve endings as she'd watched her sister wheel their mother into her new bedroom, bringing her *home* for the first time since the accident.

The excitement that Sophie had felt over the idea that things would be normal again.

That they'd be a family again.

At fourteen years old, Sophie had spent many long but blissfully enthusiastic hours after school helping Bex to feed and change and care for their mother. Her homework had always been done by the light of her lamp beneath her sheets in the dead of night once Linda had retired to bed, but it had been worth it. Every tired morning, and every yawn hidden from a school teacher had been worth it to have their mum wake up with the people she loved, and not the starched blue tunics of the nursing home.

Then as the years had passed and Bex's family had grown, Sophie had learned just as eagerly to change nappies, and mix formula, and read animated bedtime stories between the administration of her mother's medication, and the cleaning of the lines of The Ship Inn's beer barrels. Her whole life, Sophie had cared for those she loved, and she didn't regret even a moment of it, because it had kept her heart whole. It had kept her going, when the town around her had expected her to fall apart.

Now, with her mother's old room vacant, and the commode and the hoist and the stairlift gone, the spacious apartment felt weirdly empty. Like, for the first time in Sophie's life, a *taunt,* almost. Like a reminder of all the things that Sophie could have been, if she'd had the time and the courage, and the *selfishness* to leave when her family needed her most.

Which she never, ever would have done. She never would have *wanted* to.

But this apartment liked to remind her anyway. Like some sort of ghost of her past, and what could have been her future, this apartment liked to tug on that buried, niggling part of Sophie's heart that felt so *shamefully* like resentment. The part that Sophie loathed with every fibre of her being, and she squashed it down with everything she had.

Because she *wasn't* resentful.

She wasn't.

She had loved her mum, and she loved her sister and her niece and her nephew, and she *didn't* resent a single one of them for the dream she hadn't chased because of them.

And the apartment *wasn't* a ghost. Or a shell. Or empty. It was a family home, full of beating hearts that Sophie loved dearly. So dearly, that even two years after her mother had passed, it kept Sophie here still.

"Morning, sleepy heads!" Sophie called, her voice barely above a whisper as she made her way up the stairs and into the hallway.

The place was dark, lit with the low white glow of an early morning through the cracks in drawn curtains. Sophie couldn't hear the sound of movement, and she knew that at 7am it was *highly* unlikely that Bex or Pete would be up yet. Nor Jack, if her nephew was unwell. But she did know it was pretty likely that little Willow would be around somewhere, reading her books in her bedroom, or colouring at her small table in the living room while she waited for the school rush to start.

She headed straight into the kitchen, depositing the small bag of groceries she had brought onto the counter.

This wasn't her daily routine, but it wasn't unusual.

Last night she had closed, and if she were truly honest, she was exhausted. She had an empty fridge, a floor in dire need of a mop, and an overgrown lawn awaiting her in her own home, but she had been unsettled after Bex's swift exit the night before, and she'd figured her family needed her more.

Her dirty floor didn't have a beating heart. It didn't come first.

And with Jack unwell, she'd thought Bex might appreciate the extra hands, and her niece might appreciate a little extra attention.

She grinned as the patter of small bare feet sounded along the wooden hallway, and she turned just in time to see a bedheaded Willow appear in the doorframe of the kitchen in her favourite pink nightie.

Seven-year-old Willow Arroway was the *exact* image of her mother at the same age.

Wide, curious green eyes that always seemed to glint with an endearing kind of mischief, and white blonde hair that stuck up at ridiculous angles, no matter how hard she tried to tame it.

And right now, after a night in Willow's unicorn printed bedsheets, the tufts were more outrageous than they'd ever been.

"*Hi,* Pickle!" Sophie whispered cheerily. "You're up and at 'em already? Is everyone else asleep?"

Willow nodded, shy and curious like she *always* was when Sophie arrived, despite the fact that she had seen her aunt every day for her entire seven years on the planet.

"Jack's all snotty and he's poorly," she answered.

"I know, honey," Sophie assured, her voice soft and gentle. "But you feel alright?"

Willow nodded.

Sophie grinned.

"You look like you need a little treat." She winked, grabbing her bottle of egg substitute, and her carton of oat milk, and holding them out to Willow with a flourish. "You look like you need *pancakes!*"

Sophie chuckled as Willow's toothy smile grew wide, and green eyes sparkled as she stepped into the kitchen.

"Can I do it?" Willow asked, her voice beginning to pitch in her eager excitement.

"Of *course,*" Sophie urged. "I need my sous chef, I can't do it all by myself!"

The kids weren't vegan, by any stretch, and Sophie would cook them whatever their mother asked her to if she had to.

But luckily for her, they both seemed to *love* trialling and tasting her vegan recipes for The Ship Inn's menu, and they *really* loved her vegan pancakes. Something not many in Polcarne did, and Sophie appreciated the little mouths of support in a town that spent far too much time slandering every effort she made to add vegan dishes to the favourites.

Sophie winced at the scrape of the heavy kitchen chair along the tiled floor as Willow dragged it back, clambering up onto it and folding her feet beneath herself as she knelt at the table.

She chuckled softly as she placed the ingredients, a bowl, a whisk and the small kitchen scales on the table before her niece.

"Mummy says you got a certificate at school this week!" Sophie praised, her voice almost sing-song as she set about measuring out the ingredients.

*"Yeah!"* Willow bounced on her seat a little in her enthusiasm. "It-it was the *star of the week* certificate and I-I got it because I—because I got *all* my spellings right in my *test!"*

"No *way!"* Sophie exclaimed, dropping her jaw in deliberate disbelief. *"All* of them? You did not!"

"Yeah, I did!" Willow giggled giddily, nodding her head. "There were *ten!"*

*"Wow,"* Sophie breathed. "You are just *so* clever!"

Willow grinned.

"Mummy throwed—threwed—frew me a *party,"* she exclaimed, bouncing a little in her seat as she pulled the bowl and the bag of flour towards herself. "To say how clever I was, and I got a cake."

Sophie flushed warm.

Partly with pride, for her niece and her achievements, and for her sister and the adorable parenting scene that *that* sounded like.

But also, partly at the humiliatingly ridiculous jealousy that surged through her stomach at Willow's words.

Jealousy that seven-year-old Willow had gotten a cake for her spelling test, but Sophie hadn't heard a *word* about her graduation from a three-year degree.

It was pathetic, and she knew it was, and she was immediately embarrassed by her own stomach's reaction. She pushed it down.

"Oh, *wow!*" she sang, her smile bright as she helped her niece to weigh out the flour onto the scales. "Well, you deserved it, you clever little pickle-bean. You'll have to teach me some of those spellings! What words did you have to know?"

Willow scrunched her face.

"It was...*school* and that's S, C, O...no *H*, O, O and L," she breathed, her face screwed tight in concentration as she considered the question. "A-and *triangle* and that's T, R, I, A, N, G, L, E...and I can't remember the others."

She turned her attention to the ingredients, shrugging softly as she began to pour the egg replacement into the bowl like Sophie had shown her countless times.

"Mummy says I must be like you," Willow stated. "Because I'm clever, and Mummy and Daddy aren't very clever, but you are."

Sophie laughed openly.

She felt her chest warm, her stomach almost flipping at the indirect praise from her older sister. Even at twenty-six years of age, she still felt like a giddy child whenever Bex's pride showed in her voice or her words, and it never failed to warm Sophie's heart to see just how much her sister *saw* her. Understood her, respected her, and was *proud* of her.

She'd always been proud of her, even on the days when Sophie struggled to feel pride in herself. It was always enough to keep Sophie going, even when the threads of doubt clawed at her own mind. And it had been for nine years, through two distance learning degrees on her own, even when so many of the other Polcarne residents had teased her for doing her degrees online, and not going to a 'proper' university. Bex had always pushed, and encouraged, and threatened anyone with a sour word with the water hose behind The Ship's bar.

And Sophie had *always* been grateful.

Especially when the people of Polcarne, Cornwall *knew* why she didn't go.

When they knew full well how much Sophie and Bex Cedars had needed each other, for nineteen long years.

Sophie had been just seven when Helen and Sam Cedars had lost control of their car on the icy roads from Truro to Polcarne.

She'd been just the same age that Willow was now, when her father had died, and her mother had lost her independence.

Bex had been fourteen.

And in one night, at seven and fourteen years old, Sophie and Bex Cedars had been left with each other, a room in their aunt's home, and a mother in the town's downtrodden care home. A mother who, for almost two years, couldn't recall their names.

They *loved* their aunt Linda. She had loved them, cared for them, and raised them.

But Bex and Sophie had been each other's rocks. The only people who truly understood the life that once was, and so even as the years passed and the future called them, Sophie hadn't wanted to move on. She hadn't wanted to leave Bex, or her mother behind.

She hadn't been ready.

She'd said some day.

But now their beloved mother was gone, and Bex was settled. She had a family of her own, and it didn't feel so much like Sophie was all she had anymore.

And now Sophie had two degrees. And a new hairstyle.

So just maybe *now* her new life was calling.

From London, or York, or Manchester, or Brighton.

Maybe one day *sooner* than some day.

If she dared to leave this one behind her.

"Mummy says Daddy is a blibbering idiot."

Sophie choked back a laugh. She had most *definitely* heard Bex call Pete a blithering idiot on more than one occasion.

She smiled softly as she watched Willow mix the batter, her tongue poking out at the corners of her lips in her effort and her concentration.

"I'm gonna go check on your brother honey, okay?" Sophie murmured. "You gonna be alright mixing that up nice and smooth for us for a minute?"

Willow nodded, her brow furrowed and her eyes not leaving her task as her little hands gripped knuckle-white on the whisk.

Sophie planted a kiss on the unruly tufts of Willow's hair, before heading down the hall to her nephew's room.

She rapped her knuckles lightly on the door, careful to keep the sound quiet enough not to wake Jack if he was still asleep.

She paused; her ear pressed to the soft wood as she listened for the sound of Jack's gentle little voice.

When she heard no answer, she pushed the door open quietly.

Like the rest of the apartment, the room was cast with the grey-white light of the early hour, filtering through the tiny gaps in Jack's space-themed curtains. *Unlike* the rest of the apartment, Jack's bedroom shone also with the green glow of his UFO-shaped bedside lamp, and the plasticky hue of his glow-in-the-dark ceiling stars.

Sophie smiled softly at the sight of the two large lumps she could discern curled beneath the star-littered duvet. One she knew was Jack, and the other she could only assume was his giant plush alien toy.

Sophie had won it for him at a fair in Truro two years ago, and thus her nephew's obsession with all things 'space' had been born.

Along with his dreams to become an astronaut.

Sophie was pretty sure nine-year-old Jack Arroway would be the first and *only* astronaut to ever be born of Polcarne, Cornwall, but *god* did she want him to do it.

She loved these kids.

She loved them with everything she had, and she wanted nothing more than for them to know dreams.

To know them, and to *chase* them.

To reach them.

Like Sophie was going to.

And she wanted to lead by example. She wanted Jack and Willow to see her fly. She'd taught them all their lives that if they loved something, they could work for it. Like she was doing, with her degrees.

But she had those now. She'd reached that step, and now she needed to show them how to chase that little bit further.

But if she was honest, now that she had the shiny certificates she'd worked towards for so long hanging on her wall, she didn't know where to start. And as much as she hated to admit it, she was scared to fail, and to find she really had been destined for Polcarne all along.

Sophie chuckled as the soft sound of Jack's snoring broke across the silence, and she tiptoed across the room in her efforts not to wake him.

She pulled the edge of Jack's duvet cave away just enough to run the back of her hand lightly over her nephew's forehead.

Warm. Clammy. But not too feverish.

Jack snored a little heavier at the touch, but he didn't stir.

Sophie brushed his sweaty blonde hair from his forehead, and carefully placed the edge of his cocoon in its rightful place before she crossed quietly back across the room, and closed the door softly behind her.

"Soph?"

Sophie jumped, biting back a scream so hard she tasted copper as her sister's hushed, sleep-hoarse voice sounded *right* beside her in the dimly lit hallway.

She hiccupped in her unnecessary fear.

*"Jesus* milk a badger, *warn* a girl!" she hissed.

"Well, that's a *very* questionable thing for a vegan to say," Bex croaked, shaking her head as she wrapped her dishevelled, faded blue robe tighter around her waist. "Do badgers even give milk?"

Sophie rolled her eyes.

She smirked as she looked at her sister's face; the same bleary green eyes and the same wayward tufts of bedheaded hair that Willow wore. An exact replica, save for the straight-cut neon pink fringe in contrast to the rest of Bex's bright blonde matted waves, the dark marks of a late night beneath her eyes, and the smattering of tattoo lines above the neck of her tattered t-shirt.

"Not willingly, I don't imagine," Sophie mumbled. "Pete still asleep?"

Bex nodded.

"He won't surface for an age yet, he was up 'til nearly 3am playing his pissing Scalextric," she moaned. "It is not 1990 and he is not fifteen, Soph, when will this end?"

Sophie grinned. She ushered Bex down the hall, away from the rooms where Jack and Pete slept, and towards where Willow was clattering around in the kitchen.

Bex halted the moment the sounds registered in her ears, and she spun to face Sophie with bright eyes and hopeful, parted lips.

"Is that my spawn making breakfast?" she hissed excitedly.

"Yeah," Sophie chuckled. "She was up when I came in, so we're making pancakes."

"I swear to Hendrix you are some sort of *angel,"* Bex groaned happily. "What did I ever do to deserve you?"

Sophie grinned, spinning Bex once more as she pushed her into the kitchen.

"You must be exhausted, Soph!" Bex breathed, guilty eyes finding Sophie's over her shoulder. "You know you don't have to do this, right?"

Sophie rolled her eyes.

"I know I don't *have* to," she murmured, "but I *want* to. You want a coffee?"

Bex spun again, grabbing Sophie's face with both hands as she planted a messy kiss on the side of her sister's head.

"You see, this is the shit that won you *'kindest girl in class'* at school, Sophie Cedars," Bex sighed as she released her sister from her grasp, and sank down into a chair beside her daughter. "Morning my future Jane Austen. How you gonna find time to be a famous writer *and* a famous chef, hmm?"

Willow furrowed her brow, one eyebrow raised as she glanced up at her mum.

"Who's *Jane Austen?"*

Bex frowned.

"Charles Dickens?"

Willow blinked.

"Roald Dahl?" Bex pushed. "Enid Blyton?"

Willow shrugged.

Bex winced.

"David Walliams…?"

"He's funny," Willow giggled.

"Wonderful," Bex sighed, her shoulders deflating a little as she shook her head in mock disdain. "Maybe you *are* your dad's kid after all."

Sophie giggled as she flicked the switch on the kettle, and set about making the coffees. She couldn't help the warm feeling in her chest, as she listened to Bex interact with Willow, instructing softly and calmly as she helped her daughter finish preparing the mix for their pancakes.

She couldn't help the way her heart tugged, her mind supplying her with memories of the way her own mother would do the same thing, mixing the batter for the fruit cakes she would bake with a tiny Sophie every Sunday morning. With the same soft voice, and the same calm eyes, while her dad would watch cartoons in the living room with a bleary-eyed Bex.

Bex wriggled her eyebrows, grinning mischievously as Sophie handed her a steaming mug of coffee.

"I would like to raise a toast!" Bex announced almost smugly, holding her steaming mug precariously in the air.

Sophie raised a quizzical eyebrow.

"To my baby sister, and her big, fat, *wonderful* brain!" Bex sang.

Sophie laughed, her stomach fizzing with the words of affirmation, and an obnoxious kind of *relief* at the *final* mention of her greatest achievement.

"I bought you a congratulatory bottle of champagne to pop at the pub last night," Bex declared. Then she sighed, screwing her face apologetically. "But then I had to run out and now it's 9am on a school day, so it feels a little inappropriate, but maybe tonight?"

Sophie's shoulders dropped, and she melted.

"Thank you, you're amazing," she sang earnestly, pulling out a pan from the cupboard beside the stove, and reaching for the oil. "But rain check? I have a date tonight."

Bex rolled her eyes.

*"What?"* Sophie laughed.

"Kyle Brown absolutely does *not* count as a date," Bex huffed.

"Of course, he does!" Sophie rebutted.

*"No,* he doesn't," Bex laughed. "The man has the personality of a wet fish, and he smells like one too."

Sophie rolled her eyes.

*"Rude,* he's sweet."

"Soph, no woman has *ever* had a fanny flutter over *sweet,* okay?" Bex retorted. "There's better out there for you."

"Oh, hardly," Sophie scoffed. "In Polcarne? They *all* smell like fish, Bex."

"You're not destined for Polcarne, Soph," Bex challenged, her tone softer. "And you're *not* destined for Kyle Brown."

Sophie faltered.

She dropped her eyes to her pan, watching as the oil began to bubble over the heat.

She knew Bex was right. *Wanted* her to be right.

But she still didn't know what to say when her sister called her out on it. She still didn't know how to admit that with the scrolls hanging on her wall and the reality ahead of her, she was far too scared to let go of the life she'd always known in favour of the one she'd always chased.

"Who knows," Bex laughed, lifting her mug to her lips. "Maybe you'll meet someone at Ern's caravan."

~ ~ ~ ~ ~ ~ ⟨♪⟩ ~ ~ ~ ~ ~ ~

Finley's presentation was a triumph, even by her consistently high standards.

Both Co-Capita and the head of Oak Hills had loved the plans, and they had hung on every word that Finley had spoken. By the time the clients exited the board room, Opal Arches had explicit sign-off on all of the plans for the entire school, and Finley's busiest project was finally on the downward slope to completion.

She exhaled slowly, physically feeling the stress of the past few days drain from her body as the room emptied, leaving her alone with Amelia and Dan Myles.

"Nice work, Bennett," Amelia grinned as they made their way to the door. "I never expected anything less."

Finley chuckled, shaking her head. She was feeling good. The endorphins of an early morning run, the elation of a job well done, and the apprehension in Dan's eyes as Amelia had praised her were all vibrating through her nerves like adrenaline, and she was feeling unstoppable.

"Yeah," Dan croaked, clearing his throat almost awkwardly as he offered her a stiff handshake. "A lucky win."

He grinned, quirking an eyebrow, and Finley bit back a scoff.

She hadn't needed luck.

She never needed luck.

She was good at what she did, and she knew she was.

And with that presentation done, she should get a Friday night off tonight for the first time in weeks.

Which meant now was the time.

She took a deep breath, clenching and unclenching her fists in an effort to dispel some of the lingering nervous tension from her presentation as she made her way across the hall, and into the open plan office.

It had been a *long* time since she'd asked anyone out.

She hadn't dated since Jess, and all that had taken was a few well-placed smiles and a couple of cheeky lines. But that was six years ago, when she was younger and cockier, and she'd been all piercings and quiffed hairstyles, with well-defined abs and nothing to lose.

Now she had aching bones, and dark circles under her eyes, and a date meant dinner and not throwing back six Skittlebombs in Heaven or GAY.

So, she couldn't deny she was definitely a little rusty.

*Confident.*

Definitely confident.

For all the rust in the world, she still knew the look in Bella's eyes when they met hers across the water cooler. And the little *'love packages'* were a fairly sure sign that Finley wasn't about to be rejected.

But she was rusty, all the same.

She rehearsed her words over in her head, pushing her shoulders back and her chest a little higher as she reached Bella's section of the office.

She had this.

Cool, calm, and confident.

Charmer's chance.

She approached the low partition wall around her colleague's desk slowly, giving the woman time to notice her before she interrupted her work.

"Hey, Bella…"

"Finley, hi!"

Finley couldn't help but notice the way the blonde's cheeks flushed just a little redder as her name left her lips. She bit back a grin.

"I hear congratulations are in order!" Bella gushed. "Claire says you really killed it in there. Like you always do."

Bella's blush deepened as she spoke, and the word *pining* flashed through Finley's mind before she could stop it. She shook it away, immediately uncomfortable with the feeling.

"Thank you." She smiled, brushing the compliment off the best she could. "Listen, I wanted to thank you for leaving me dinner last night."

Finley winced as she recalled the week, and the number of times those brown paper bags had appeared on her desk. She felt her own cheeks heat at the realisation that this was the third time Bella had left her food and drink this week, and she was pretty sure she hadn't taken the time to thank her for any of them.

"And er…the night before. And the one before that."

"It's really no problem, I know how much Amelia gets on your case." Bella shrugged, smiling shyly. "Someone's gotta look after you, right?"

"Right," Finley chuckled. The sound was a little hollow, and she felt the first trickles of nerves in her veins as she heard it.

The air felt a little stilted. A little awkward.

Presumably just because she was a little nervous, and Bella seemed a *lot* nervous, and they were in the office under several prying eyes.

That was all.

Plus, they really hadn't ever talked all that much, now that Finley thought about it.

She swallowed the nerves down before they filtered into excuses and second thoughts.

"Maybe one of these days you'll eat a hot meal!" Bella chuckled.

Finley grinned.

She forced her eyes to hold Bella's gaze, fighting to regain some of the confidence she'd felt just moments ago.

"Well," she murmured, leaning her elbows down on the low partition across the desk, in an effort to look as smooth as she hoped she sounded. "Maybe I just need someone to share it with."

Bella's throat bobbed, her cheeks flushed deep, and Finley's confidence soared.

"M-maybe!" Bella chuckled, a little shaky and a little hoarse.

Finley smirked.

Well-practised, and well-aimed.

"Maybe…you could join me for dinner tonight?"

Bella frowned.

"Like uh…a work thing?" she stammered.

Finley shook her head, her lips twitching at the corners in amusement.

"Like a date."

Bella's eyes widened, her breath catching in her throat in a choked sound that sent an immediate surge of confidence through Finley's veins.

Finley bit her lip through another deliberately charming smile.

Who needed Skittlebombs and abs?

"Y-yes!" Bella's voice almost squeaked, and her blush deepened even further at the sound. She cleared her throat. "Yeah! Yeah, that would be great, I…yeah."

"Great." Finley grinned, her confidence dangerously straddling the line of arrogance at the open display of blatant excitement. "Do you like French food?"

Bella simply nodded, her eyes a little misty with their awed sparkle, and Finley almost laughed with self-satisfaction.

"I'll make a reservation at Galvin." She winked as she backed away, knowing full damn well that the move was far cockier than was warranted, but she couldn't help it. She felt good. "Seven?"

Finley fought hard against her body's urge to fist pump as she retreated to her desk. Another win for the day's list, and things just kept getting better.

Her fingers almost shook with the adrenaline of success as she pulled up the instant messenger programme, and typed out her glorious update to Noah.

Bennett, Finley: *Guess who smashed their presentation, AND has a date tonight.* 💪

Lake, Noah: *Yes Fin!* 🎉 *I would expect nothing less from that charmer's chance.*

Lake, Noah: *What time do you want me for styling?*

Bennet, Finley: *Sir, I am a 30-year-old strong independent lesbian, I know how to look good without a man's input.*

Lake, Noah: *Please, we both know if I don't help you, you'll end up in a three piece.*

Finley blinked.

That was exactly what she'd been planning to wear.

Lake, Noah: *And brogues.*

Finley winced.

Bennett, Finley: *What's wrong with that?*

Lake, Noah: *Nothing, usually. But she's your colleague, it's all she's ever seen you in, and you need to set a new tone and a new aura between you tonight.*

Finley pursed her lips, nodding reluctantly.

That, surprisingly, actually sounded about right.

And was *not* something she would have even remotely considered.

Bennett, Finley: *Fuck, FINE, but if you make me late, you're paying for the meal.*

Lake, Noah: *You'd be lost without me and you know it.*

Finley grinned. She felt good, her mind sharp and her blood pumping strong in her veins as she adjusted her screens, and pulled up the Bryce Ridge blueprints.

She was on top form today, and she was *winning.*

And nothing was going to bring her down.

# Chapter Three

Sophie tried her hardest to listen to Kyle's rundown of his day. She tried her very hardest to focus on his words, and not to let her eyes dart disdainfully around the fish restaurant that her date had brought her to. But the smell was a little overwhelming, and she was finding it particularly difficult not to stare in horror at the whole-ass *octopus* on her date's plate.

She prided herself on her ever-present optimism, but even she had to bite back a grimace as she pushed her wet, barely-touched salad around her own oversized bowl.

The whole place *stank* of seafood, and even if the restaurant was in the *big city of Truro*, and it was *four stars*, she still couldn't think of anywhere she'd hate to be more.

She'd been vegan since 2012 and it was really beginning to test her well-practised patience that no-one ever seemed to remember this key detail.

And Kyle hadn't even *noticed* her new hair style.

She'd spent longer than usual getting ready, trying to embrace the changes she wanted to make. She'd swapped her usual jeans and boots for a soft, flowing dress and heels, and she'd curled her hair with her old straighteners until it sat in beautiful waves around her shoulders. With actual *definition,* not the usual any-which-way she let it fall.

She felt like a bloody Disney princess! Like *Ariel.*

Except with a little bit of thigh chafe, and a precariously wobbly ankle.

She was a new woman, with flair and grace and beauty.

And her date hadn't mentioned her appearance *once.*

*Or* her recent graduation.

Kyle had seemed so sweet and endearing on their last couple of dates, and Sophie really had wanted to give her old friend a chance. But under the sickly smell of the fish and the flickering lights of the candles, she was struggling not to find the wispy hairs over his widow's peak, and the yellowing collar of his white and green gingham shirt more than a little bit discouraging.

And he hadn't asked her a single question about herself.

"And then the net got caught around Dave's leg as we hauled it onto the boat, and he just *fell in,*" Kyle laughed, his eyes crinkling in watery amusement. "Right into the net. Just floundering about in a pile of pilchards for about five minutes. His mouth was going just as much as the fish! Tommo wanted to put a hook in it!"

Kyle laughed loudly, shaking his head at his memory as he dug his fork into his octopus, splattering god-only-knew what juice across the bed of vegetables and lemon.

Sophie fought a baulk, tasting bile as she fought to keep her eyes trained anywhere but on Kyle's meal.

"*Oh,* that reminds me!" Kyle blurted, his eyes widening as he spoke through his mouth full of tentacle. "I've got something for you."

Sophie's own eyes shot wide.

She watched as Kyle wiped his fingers half-heartedly on his napkin, and reached into the pocket of the jacket slung across the back of his chair.

Tweed, of course.

It was always tweed.

Even Kyle-from-the-school-band, who had once worn leather and ripped jeans and band Ts, had grown older, and swapped the metal studs for brown herringbone tweed.

And it wasn't that Sophie didn't *like* tweed. She actually thought it looked pretty sexy, on the right person. It was just that it was every man she knew's idea of dressing up *and* dressing down, and so it almost just felt like a uniform.

Like Polcarne was some kind of *really* budget *'Brave New World'*.

But Kyle was sweet. He was sweet, and Sophie was here for a reason, and she closed her eyes for a brief moment as she fought to push down the feeling of unease that bubbled in her chest.

She smiled softly, her eyes widening in anticipation as they flickered open and Kyle handed her a small, neatly folded paper bag.

"I saw this in St Austell market and I thought of you," he exclaimed, his cheeks reddening shyly under his sandy hair.

Sophie's smile grew wider, and a little more genuine. She felt her stomach flutter with unexpected excitement at the fact that Kyle had thought of her. The fact that he had seen something he'd thought she would like, and intentionally made a gesture.

The thought was *sweet*.

As always.

She bit her lip in anticipation as she peeled back the folded paper, and carefully tipped the contents into the palm of her hand.

She frowned.

The leather cord necklace was rough; hand braided and hand finished, with a silver pendant hanging from the centre.

Shaped like a fishing hook.

Sophie blinked.

"I thought you could wear it and it would make you think of me," Kyle explained.

Sophie flicked her gaze up.

Kyle seemed nervous; shifting in his seat as he watched Sophie with hopeful eyes, and her chest immediately clenched with guilt over the crease she could still feel in her brow.

She schooled her features, forcing her eyes and the corners of her lips to soften in an effort to appear a *lot* more appreciative than she felt.

The *idea* behind it was sweet.

But the *execution*…

"I-is this real leather?" she croaked.

"Of course!" Kyle exclaimed excitedly, pushing his chair back as he moved to stand. "No knock-offs for *my* girl. Here, let me put it on for you!"

Kyle was behind her before Sophie could even begin to protest, and she felt a wave of nausea as his calloused fingers swept her carefully styled hair over her shoulder, and wrapped the hideous necklace around her neck.

She failed to bite back her grimace at the feel of the leather against her skin, and she couldn't help but wonder how many vegan points she was losing for being in a seafood restaurant with a leather strap round her neck, a fish torture device sitting against her chest, and likely traces of octopus juice in her hair.

She wrapped her fingers around the pendant, holding it away from her chest instinctively as Kyle moved to sit back in his seat, uncomfortable with its weight there.

"Let me see, then!" Kyle urged.

Sophie dropped her hand, biting back yet another grimace as the heavy hook fell back into place against her chest.

She immediately felt bad once again as Kyle's eyes lit up, and he grinned satisfactorily.

"Beautiful!" he breathed. "Now you look like a proper fisherman's girl."

Sophie bit her tongue.

Why did those words feel so rough against her spine?

She wanted to rebuke them.

She wanted *very* strongly to tell him that they were on their *third* date, she was *not* his girl.

But she was all too aware of just how harsh that would sound, and she really wasn't in the business of breaking hearts. And also, she wasn't entirely sure it was true.

*Was* she his girl? Was a third date a sign she was?

And didn't she *want* to be?

Why was she even here?

"It'll be a reminder of where we came from, when we both make it big." Kyle grinned, leaning back in his chair. "And I think that might be coming sooner than you know."

Sophie blinked.

Why did that feel like something *very* questionable was coming?

"You remember I said I had a surprise for you?"

"Yeah…" Sophie nodded numbly, her mind beginning to swim with the spark of excitement in Kyle's soft blue eyes, against the uncomfortable anticipation building in her own stomach. "What is it?"

Kyle took a deep breath, and Sophie felt the nerves in her stomach plummet.

"I'm moving to London!"

Sophie's eyebrows shot up.

Well, that was *not* what she had expected.

To London? Kyle Brown?

Well, good for him!

She couldn't help but feel the slightest hint of disappointment. She might not have been head over heels for Kyle, but he was safe, and secure, and so she had *wanted* things to work.

Besides, that was a relatively cruel build-up for an *'I'm leaving'* announcement.

Also, she was undeniably *crazy* jealous right now.

"Kyle, that's incred…"

"I want you to come with me." Kyle's words cut her off as he practically jumped forward, his hands reaching for Sophie's across the table.

Sophie froze.

The words hung leaden in the air for a long, silent moment.

*What* did he just say?

And with so much unabashed *confidence!*

She stared, bewildered, at the excited flush over Kyle's cheeks and the spark in his eyes.

Had he hit his head? Swallowed too much sea water?

A hook necklace was one thing, but to *move to London* with him?

She had literally been on *two* dates with this guy, even if she had known him all her life, and he wanted her to move 300 miles away from home with him?

A move she hadn't dared to do in *nine* years, and he thought *he* was the push she needed?

She shook her head, her eyes fluttering closed in disbelief, and her sunny disposition struggling hard to stay lit beneath this absolute tidal wave of insanity.

"You want…*what?"*

"Soph, think about it!" Kyle's grin grew wider as he squeezed her hands. "We could get a place in Camden, a flat by the water."

Sophie faltered.

The thought was…*almost* appealing?

London.

Maybe not Kyle.

If she listened for even half a second to the screaming voice, she'd squashed as far down in her stomach as possible, she was well aware that Kyle was ridiculous.

But what he could offer her was appealing. London. And the history and the culture and the *opportunities.* The chance to finally follow her dreams.

Her stomach fluttered, a tiny little embryo of hope just starting to *think* about stretching its wings.

"We could make such a life of it, Soph." Kyle was speaking again before Sophie could even begin to form her thoughts into words. "I could work on my music, you could work in the bars, you could even get a real degree! We could…"

Sophie's stomach dropped, the embryo recoiling and the words flooding a sour taste through her mouth far worse than the fish in the stuffy air. She felt her chest close hard and tight, and her sunny disposition snuffed dark.

"Wait…" She closed her eyes for a moment, pulling her hands out of Kyle's clammy grip. "Wait, wait. I could get a *what?*"

"A real degree!" Kyle repeated enthusiastically. "You wouldn't have to get those online things anymore."

Sophie exhaled heavily. She clenched her jaw, her eyes fluttering closed and her fingers wrapping tight around her glass of wine. The words burned hot through her bloodstream as she brought the glass to her lips, fighting to keep a lid on the outburst of anger that bubbled below the surface.

Fighting not to react too strongly to the outright *audacity* of this guy. Fighting to keep that resentment down in the pits of her stomach with her other guilt-wrapped feelings.

But it didn't want to go.

Not this one. Not this time.

Kyle Brown had known her for twenty-six years. He had known her through every school lesson, and every field trip, and every exam. He had known her through her father's death, and her mother's change. He had known her through every minute of nine years of gruelling study, and he had known *exactly* how hard she had dreamed of her own heels clicking across the floor of a national museum.

He had known her through *everything,* and he still didn't understand her?

Nine years of blood, sweat and tears had gone into those degrees. Nine years of dreams and goals and aspirations.

And Kyle Brown the pilchard farmer had just dropped his threadbare tweed and shat all over them, and everything that Sophie had ever worked for, in one swift movement.

Something in her stomach flipped.

A switch, flicking for the first time.

And the current was *electric.*

She exhaled sharply, her blood pounding *molten* with the sudden understanding that she didn't owe Kyle-from-the-fucking-band *anything,* and she didn't *need* to keep a lid on her anger.

It was *liberating.*

"Are you *serious?"* She slammed her glass down, adrenaline coursing her veins as Kyle's eyes widened, his lip trembling and his jaw dropping open. "A *real* degree? What are the two I have to you, pissing *toilet paper?"*

"What? No!"

The genuine shock on Kyle's stupid face pissed Sophie off even more.

"Sophie, I didn't mean…"

Sophie cut him off. He'd said enough.

"You want me to *move to London* with you on our *third date,* but you can't even take me seriously?" She pushed her chair back from the table with an audible scrape. "I am *so sick* of not being taken seriously, Kyle."

"Sophie, I'm sorry, that's not what I meant," Kyle blustered. "Please, let me explain."

Sophie raised an eyebrow, folding her arms as she leaned back in her chair.

This should be good.

"Go on."

Kyle's eyes shot wide, his throat bobbing visibly as he realised, he was actually going to have to follow through on that half-assed excuse, and Sophie rolled her eyes as he stuttered.

"I-I just meant that if you want a museum, then a degree in London might make that dream more realistic."

Sophie scoffed.

Now that the switch had been flipped, she did not have the energy for this.

"Oh, save the shit for your shovel, Kyle," she snapped. She pulled her bag from the floor, swinging the strap over her shoulder as she stood. "You're a twenty-seven-year-old fisherman with a *music studio* in your childhood bedroom, you don't get to lecture me about what's a *realistic dream."*

Sophie only glanced back once as she flounced from the restaurant, leaving a very flustered Kyle bobbing his open mouth uselessly, like a floundering pilchard.

She felt guilty.

Of course, she did.

She knew she'd been harsh; knew the insult was *maybe* a little unnecessary.

And also, *not* what she really believed.

But Kyle had hit a sore point and she had finally reacted instinctively. Plus, she couldn't deny that it felt incredibly satisfying to walk away from the restaurant and leave Kyle-from-the-band scratching his receding hairline and wondering when the *'kindest-girl-in-class'* had grown a backbone.

~ ~ ~ ~ ~ ~ 🎵 ~ ~ ~ ~ ~ ~

Finley took a slow sip of her over-priced wine, fighting not to let the grimace show as she swallowed back the sharp liquid. She never had been one for white, but that had been Bella's preference, and she had wanted her date to have the best. She shifted slightly in her seat, exhaling slowly as she fought against the urge to fidget.

She was *incredibly* uncomfortable.

Noah had convinced her to wear the *tightest* wet-look jeans that she hadn't worn since long before Jess, and there was a damn good reason for that. They'd never really fit over the curves of her hips, and they chafed in *all* the wrong places.

Also, they were *really* warm, and the restaurant was practically fucking subtropical.

Bella seemed to have appreciated them, if the glint in her eyes as she scanned Finley's outfit was anything to go by, but the discomfort was enough that Finley had struggled to focus on a single word her date had said in the past fifteen minutes.

And that wasn't *quite* how she wanted this evening to go.

She leaned forward over the table, as if somehow, she could fix more of her attention on Bella if she were just a little bit closer. She bit back a muffled groan as the tight fabric of her jeans pinched her upper thigh, chafing hard against her most sensitive areas. She shifted, wincing as the material practically squeaked against the cheap pleather seat beneath her.

"You alright, Finley?"

"Mmhmm," Finley nodded, praying that the light sheen of sweat she could feel over her forehead wouldn't be visible to her date in the low lighting. She flashed a signature smile, hoping the resulting spark in her eyes would distract Bella just enough to avoid having to explain her embarrassing predicament. "Just a little warm. You really do look incredible tonight, you know."

She did.

She looked *great*.

Finley had obviously noticed her before, otherwise they wouldn't be here tonight, but she had never really noticed just *how* blue her eyes were, or just how thick her hair fell around her shoulders. And the way the emerald green material of her dress clung to her curves had ignited things in Finley's stomach that she'd been missing for a *long* time.

Things she was *very* keen to not be missing anymore.

It was just a shame that right now, the date felt a little bit...*flat.*

Nerves.

Finley was pinning it on nerves.

It was her first date in a long time, and Bella was clearly a little shy. It was endearing, and Finley wanted to give it a chance.

"Sorry, you were telling me about your..." Finley faltered as she tried to remember. "Life drawing class?"

"Pottery!"

Finley winced.

She *hated* herself right now for her complete inability to focus and the complete absence of her usual charm, but she really was uncomfortable.

"Right, shit. I'm sorry," she breathed. "I'm listening, I swear, I'm just nervous."

She smiled earnestly as she met her date's gaze, training her eyes in a way she *knew* always won her a blush.

She smirked as Bella reddened instantly.

At least the physical attraction was *definitely* there tonight.

Even if these goddamn trousers were playing utter havoc with any sexual desires she might have been having.

"Nervous?" Bella huffed, her blush deepening impossibly as she dropped her gaze shyly to her wine glass. "Finley Bennett? I find that hard to believe."

Finley chuckled.

"Well, my date is smart, beautiful, and dressed like a goddess," she flirted, smiling cheekily. "I can't be blamed for a few butterflies."

*"Oh,"* Bella laughed, her eyes shining and her blush spreading to her ears as she flicked her gaze back to meet Finley's, her fingertips tracing the rim of her wine glass. *"There's* that irresistible charm."

Finley chuckled, softening a little under the coy gaze and the gentle tease.

"That, and it's been a while," she admitted. She shrugged softly. "I'm a little out of practice, and I want to make a good impression."

Bella huffed a shy laugh, nodding gently.

"If it makes you feel any better, I'm *really* nervous too," she breathed.

Finley raised an eyebrow.

"Yeah?"

"Yeah," Bella huffed. "Which is *really* annoying because I've been hoping for a while that you might ask me out, and now that you have, I'm falling over my own feet and I can't find my words."

Finley laughed openly.

The air felt lighter for a moment, the quiet confession seeming to break through some of the tension that had built around their awkward nerves.

Finley studied her date.

The revered blue eyes, and the carefully styled blonde hair, and the *beautiful* dress, and the flustered nerves that all told her that Bella had invested something in this.

She'd made an effort, and she wanted this to go well just as Finley did.

The date was *nice*. Bella was nice, and they just needed some time and a little less pressure for the awkwardness to fade. Finley was determined to remain optimistic. Perhaps the busy atmosphere of the restaurant wasn't helping. She'd invite her date back to hers for some wine she could stomach, and maybe she'd be able to get a little more comfortable and a little less chafed on her own sofa.

Then she'd be far less distracted, and she could focus all her efforts on her date.

"Would you feel less nervous if we got out of here?" she murmured. "I have wine at home, and I'm pretty sure I have ice cream, so we could always…"

*"Yes."* Bella nodded, her eyes rolling in her enthusiastic agreement. "God, definitely. Let's go."

Finley smiled widely as she pushed her sour wine over the table, and raised a hand to call for the waiter.

She blew a breath out through her cheeks as they gathered their things to leave. She knew it might have been slightly too soon to invite a date back to her place, but Finley never had been great at the long game. She didn't pride herself on her patience, and frankly she just didn't like to waste her time.

And if this was going to *be* something, then Finley would rather start it off in a much more comfortable environment.

Despite the initial successful break in tension, the bitter evening air seemed to immediately cool down any warmth that had begun to spark between them, and Finley found herself once again awkwardly searching for words as they waited for their taxi.

They didn't speak a word as the black cab carried them the fifteen minutes through the streets of Central London, and back to Finley's home.

Finley considered touch.

She considered taking Bella's hand, or placing her own over her thigh, but the air still felt too stilted, and too unsure, and so she couldn't find the nerve.

She would have *sworn* the taxi driver shot her a look of *sympathy* as she paid him.

As she pulled back the door for Bella to step out of the taxi, Finley was beginning to wonder if she'd made a colossal misjudgement.

She was beginning to think that in her efforts to make this date less awkward, all she'd actually done was extend the discomfort into a situation it was now five times more difficult to escape from.

For *both* of them.

Until she took Bella's hand, holding her steady as she stepped out of the taxi, and those misted blue eyes met her own.

Bella smiled; a shy, flirty little quirk of her lips, her lashes fluttering in a cliché that Finley was frankly disgusted to admit made her blood a little hotter.

And the air shifted again.

Just a little.

Not unbearable heat. Not wanting, or desire-filled, or electric.

But *something* a little warmer. Something a little more hopeful.

Finley smirked, stepping back as she gestured towards the glass doors that led through to her apartment, allowing Bella to lead the way.

She chuckled under her breath as she watched her pass.

Bella's hips swayed with a purpose Finley was in no position to ignore, and she shook her head at the second flare in her own bloodstream at the movement and the implication.

She'd really thought she was a little harder to get than this.

But if *this* was the way this was going, then maybe they really did just need a little privacy and the space to get more comfortable.

Finley grinned as she made to move after her date. Then she clenched her jaw, her knees buckling and her throat tightening as her god forsaken trousers squeaked, pinching down on her upper thigh with her movement.

Yep, *definitely* the space to get a little more comfortable.

As Finley finally did close her front door on the city lights, leading Bella through the hallway and into the living room, the nerves immediately began to fade. The air was still a little stilted; uncertain; but Finley was already feeling much more confident on her own ground, and she was feeling far more sure that she could turn this around.

Until Peanut brushed up against Bella's legs, and Bella jumped a foot in the air, her scream peeling through the awkward silence.

Finley froze.

Nobody had ever had that reaction to her cat's presence before, and she flat out blanked on what exactly she was expected to do in this moment.

And so doing nothing seemed like the obvious choice.

"I-I'm sorry," Bella squealed, her cheeks tinting red with her blush as she shied away from Peanut's affections. "It's just...I'm *really* scared of cats."

Finley blinked.

Scared? Of *Peanut*?

But Peanut was pathetic. Her legs were too skinny for her body, her nose was not a shape Finley had ever seen on a cat before, her fur stood up at weird angles, and she made a weird buzzing sound when she breathed.

A little off-putting, sure, but to be *scared* of her?

*"Finley,"* Bella pleaded as Peanut persisted, rubbing her head over her legs. "Could it maybe...be someplace else? *Please?*"

"Right! Shit, sorry." Finley started, launching forward to bundle the cat into her arms. "I'm so sorry. Here, let me just put her in the bedroom. Please, make yourself comfortable on the sofa."

Finley exhaled slowly as she deposited a disgruntled Peanut into her bedroom.

"Sorry P, you've been banished," she whispered, planting a kiss on the top of the cat's head. "Not cool, I know, but Mummy's on a hot date right now, and you and I *both* know I need this so...*please* just stay in here for a while, k?"

Finley would swear the cat *grunted.*

She scrunched her nose, staring Peanut down for a long moment, before she finally backed away, pulling the door ajar.

She couldn't *quite* bring herself to shut her in.

It wasn't *Peanut's* fault. She didn't deserve to be imprisoned.

Finley took a moment to compose herself as she made her way back to the kitchen. She felt a little shaken, if she was honest, and she couldn't help the alarm bells that chimed in her mind at Bella's extreme aversion to her cat. She pushed it down as she pulled the cork of her favourite wine, pouring the deep red liquid into two large glasses. If she really wanted to get back out there, then she couldn't just write people off over the smallest of things.

She deserved to give this a chance, at least.

And she couldn't deny that the sight of a beautiful woman across her sofa, her dress hitched just a little higher over her thighs as she crossed her legs, definitely made it easier to do just that.

Bella still seemed nervous, and Finley's trousers were still pinching her clit like a vice clamp, but alone in the low lighting of her home, with the conversation flowing just *slightly* easier away from the bustle of the restaurant, the air was beginning to change between them.

Finley was undeniably more appreciative of her colleague's appearance than she had ever been, and *god* it had been a long time.

They still hadn't made huge progress in the formation of a substantial connection, but Bella's crystal blue eyes had darkened significantly as the wine had flowed, and they were no longer even trying to hold back their blatant appreciation of Finley's body.

It wasn't long before flirtatious fingertips were following behind, tracing lightly over Finley's forearms, and then her thighs.

Finley smirked.

With *good* wine in her bloodstream, and the decreasing space on the sofa between them, she was feeling more than a little bolder.

She grinned as darkened eyes flicked openly to her lips, and not for the first time this evening.

Fuck it.

Maybe this wouldn't be love, but they were both consenting adults, right?

She had *needs*, after all.

And Bella certainly *seemed* to be on the same page.

She leaned forward, a sure hand tracing slowly over the line of her date's jaw. She chuckled softly as Bella's chest hitched, breath catching audibly in her throat.

She closed the gap.

The kiss was…*good.*

It wasn't electric. Far from it. And there were definitely no butterflies, and definitely no desperate surge of arousal, but it was hot enough to scratch an itch, and Finley pressed forward.

For all of Bella's reserved shyness on the date, she was *far* from holding back now. Finley's tongue had barely graced Bella's lips before eager hands were roaming everywhere that they could reach, and she could barely keep up. Trembling fingers pulled almost frantically at the buttons of Finley's shirt, and she faltered for a moment under the keen touch.

She *knew,* realistically, that there was nothing substantial between them, and she couldn't help the wave of guilty apprehension that clenched in her chest over the fact that she hadn't actually clarified that Bella felt the same way. She couldn't help but feel like maybe this wasn't a great idea. Maybe this wasn't fair. Maybe she needed to take a moment here.

Then her *fucking* jeans pinched her clit *again*, Bella bit down hard on her lower lip, and Finley was completely unable to suppress the growl that rumbled through the kiss.

*Fuck. It.*

Bella seemed more than keen, Finley *needed* the goddamn fucking trousers off before she lost all circulation to her clit, and she'd be lying if she said she didn't want the touch of those hands over her chest to continue.

So *maybe* she should just shut her brain up and go with the goddamn flow.

With one more flick of that eager tongue over her lips, Finley let her restraint go. She tugged at the emerald green dress, sliding her hands beneath the material until it rose over Bella's head and away. She hoisted her date almost roughly onto her lap, trailing kisses over her neck and her jaw as Bella began to roll her hips.

Under the movement, the jeans claimed their victim.

Finley clamped her jaw down, *way* too hard into the heated flesh over Bella's pulse point, as what felt like her entire vagina was gripped mercilessly by the all-out *satanic* material of her goddamn jeans.

Bella yelped.

Finley wailed.

*"Fuck,"* she panted, squirming desperately beneath her date as she tried to free herself from her vice. "I'm *so* sorry, it's these trousers! They're *so* tight, it's like my vagina's in a torture chamber!"

All movement halted.

There was a long moment of silence as the words hung in the air, and Finley closed her eyes, pursing her lips as the humiliation began to burn from her chest and out.

Until Bella threw her head back, her laughter filling the awkward space, and the sound soothed Finley's racing mind for a moment. She took a deep breath, wondering once again if maybe this was a bad idea. If maybe she should take the mishaps as a sign that deep down, she knew she didn't want this.

But before she could form the words on her tongue, Bella was speaking. Her voice was low, and husky, and her eyes were hooded, and the red-blooded lesbian in Finley hung instantly onto every word.

"Well, then, why don't we get you out of them?"

Finley swallowed.

Yep.

Fuck it.

Fuck it three times.

She surged forward, all guilt and all sensibility forgotten as Bella's hands pawed at her thighs and her ass, and the button on the front of the godforsaken jeans.

Then finally, *finally* the material was being peeled away.

With extreme difficulty.

The persistent fabric caught over every single inch of Finley's overheated skin, and Bella's brows furrowed in concentration and frustration as she fought to pull the material back.

"Okay *hang on,* let me…" Finley huffed out a breath, her own impatient frustration getting the better of her.

She wriggled her hips, pushing desperately at the band of the jeans. Bella pulled, trying her hardest to keep the magic alive with soft kisses peppered over Finley's stomach at any feasible chance.

It all happened *so* fast.

Finley gave one almighty shove, Bella gave a hefty tug, and Peanut appeared out of goddamn fucking *nowhere.*

Bella screamed, Peanut yelped, and Finley's knee collided *directly* with Bella's nose.

The sound was horrendous.

*"Shit!"*

Finley jumped up instinctively, just as her dazed date moved to stand, and her forehead crashed straight into Bella's eye socket.

Bella staggered, her stumbling feet landing on Peanut's tail. The cat yowled, swiping reactively at the flailing bare legs, her claws leaving visible lines of prickled blood.

Finley panicked.

"Jesus Christ, just *sit down!*"

She felt *immediately* guilty for the outburst, but in her defence, she was flailing about with her jeans round her knees, her cat was still swiping at her bleeding date, and she just needed everything to fucking well *stop* for a moment so that she could make sure the poor woman was okay!

The universe was clearly sending them blaring signals to stop this charade, and as Bella whimpered softly in the corner of the teal sofa, Finley waddling awkwardly in the direction of her first aid kid, any hints of sexual desire immediately vacated the premises.

It had become bright-beacon clear that this was *definitely* not a potential relationship on the cards.

And now it definitely wasn't a one-night stand either.

And Finley knew that this was not the priority right now. She *knew* it really was the *last* thing she should be thinking about when her date was bleeding and in pain, and she knew she was a *terrible* person for even considering the idea.

But she wondered if it would be acceptable to go and change her trousers, before she dealt with this situation.

# Chapter Four

Sophie practically threw herself into her usual stool at the bar of The Ship Inn. She hadn't wanted to stew in her resentment alone at home, and she hoped Kyle would have enough sense not to head straight to Sophie's place of work to drown his own sorrows.

The guilt was still tugging at her chest, and she *hated* the niggling feeling crawling under her skin telling her she'd overreacted.

She knew Kyle would be confused. She knew he'd be *hurt,* and completely failing to understand what had just happened. And it made her feel guilty. It made her want to run back, and put the stupid smile back on his stupid face, despite the fact that he had insulted everything she was and stood for.

And that in itself was pissing Sophie off.

She'd had *enough!*

She'd had enough of putting everyone else's feelings before her own. She'd had enough of feeling like her own reactions were unjustified, but everyone else's were fairly excused.

She *hadn't* overreacted.

She had been fully entitled to feel every ounce of the anger that coursed her veins.

Anger she couldn't shake, and frankly she didn't *want* to. She had spent far too many years pushing down her ball of fire, and she was done holding it back. Maybe this would *finally* be the push she needed to make her own moves. For the *real* change to be happening.

For *today* to be 'someday'.

"Well, shit, I know that look."

Bex eyed her sister knowingly as she pushed a pint of Sophie's usual light ale across the bar, a grubby tea towel slung over her shoulder.

*"What* look?"

Sophie narrowed her eyes over the brim of the glass as she gulped back as much of the liquid as she could stand to without a breath.

Bex smirked.

"That's the look you get when Drunk Dave talks about deer culling. And when Tommo starts his yearly petition to bring a Costa to Polcarne."

Sophie narrowed her eyes further, but she couldn't help the amused twitch of her lips.

Her sister read her like a pop book for toddlers. Always had.

"Or when people think Amy Winehouse wrote *Valerie.*" Bex grinned. "It's the look of Sophie Cedars clinging desperately to shreds of her sugar-sweet exterior. What's happened, kiddo?" She grimaced. "Also, *what* is that thing on your neck?"

Sophie groaned, letting her forehead thud against the sticky surface of the bar.

"It's just *stupid* Kyle and his *stupid* bald spots and his *stupid* taste in jewellery and his *stupid* opinions."

"I don't even need to know what he did to know that kid is beneath you, Soph," Bex sighed.

"He called my degrees *pretend.*" Sophie dragged herself upright, tugging the shitty necklace off and pushing it over the bar before draining the rest of her glass in heavy gulps. "I don't even care what he thinks, honestly, but that hit a nerve."

"He did *what,* you said?" Bex's eyes darkened, flaring protectively as she studied her sister. She prised the empty glass from Sophie's hands, refilling it as she spoke.

Sophie shrugged almost guiltily.

"He said I should get a real degree," she mumbled, picking sheepishly at the beermat in front of her.

Bex practically glowered.

"Soph, those things have taken you a *third* of your life to achieve," she growled. "You've got the fancy scrolls of paper in your frames that prove they're every bit as real as the hours you poured into them." She pushed the refilled glass back over the bar, fixing piercing green eyes on Sophie's as she shrugged. "Why would you even *think* about letting a balding pilchard farmer with appalling taste in jewellery tell you otherwise?"

Sophie smiled softly, some of the tension in her shoulders dropping in her older sister's presence. She knew Bex was right, but she also knew that Kyle wasn't the problem.

Not really.

"Because I feel like he's onto something," she murmured, her voice almost wistful as she thought about the fact that Kyle-from-the-school-band was moving on, while Sophie was still stuck going nowhere.

Bex raised an almost angry eyebrow.

"You are not telling me you think your degrees aren't real?" she demanded. "Because I swear to god, Soph, I will drown you with the Hicks tap…"

Sophie grinned, rolling her eyes.

"*No,*" she breathed, trailing a finger round the rim of her glass. "But maybe they'll never *lead* to anything real."

She swallowed, dropping her gaze as the words sucked the moisture from her throat, forming a lump that ached in her lungs.

"Maybe I spent so long studying just so that I could keep the dreams ahead of me," she whispered. "So, I never really had to leave."

"Soph…"

Bex exhaled slowly, and Sophie swallowed the thick lump as she dragged her eyes back up to meet her sister's.

Sophie huffed a soft laugh.

"He asked me to move to London with him."

"*Jesus.*" Bex's eyes bugged. "That's creepy."

"As all hell." Sophie nodded, her lips quirking in amusement. "But it was appealing, for a moment."

"To let him take you where the lights are?" Bex smiled softly, her eyes earnest as they searched Sophie's face. "So, you wouldn't have to do it alone?"

Sophie breathed out a chuckle, her smile growing wide for the first time since she'd left the restaurant.

Her sister always understood her.

Always made her feel seen.

She nodded.

"To let him take me where the opportunities are, but to just take a small part of home with me," she breathed. Then she chuckled. "Even if that *is* a balding pilchard farmer with appalling taste in jewellery."

Bex nodded, leaning back against the bar as she cracked the cap of a beer bottle, taking a swig of the contents.

"Guarantee you could get a better lay than Kyle Brown there though, Sis," she chuckled. "You definitely don't want that widow's peak weighing you down when you finally make a bid for freedom."

Sophie grimaced. She hadn't slept with Kyle, but she didn't need to have done to know *that* was true.

"Why don't you just take a trip?" Bex suggested. "Just a short one. Test the waters. *See* those damned lights."

Sophie furrowed her brow.

"A trip?"

"Yeah." Bex shrugged. "You can go tomorrow, if you like."

*"Tomorrow?"* Sophie yelped. "But…but my shifts, and my lawn, and…and Jack's not well, how would you cope? Don't be so ridiculous."

Bex rolled her eyes, grinning knowingly.

"These all sound like more excuses to me, Cowardly Lion," she chuckled, shaking her head. "I am a grown adult, with a grown adult husband, and we will be fine. *You* have about a decade of annual leave stashed up, you've got more money saved than I'd know what to do with, and it's about time you explored life beyond the Cornish coastline. Figure out where you really want to be."

Sophie opened her mouth to retort. To scoff dismissively. To ask just what Bex expected her to do on a trip on her own anyway, even if she felt she *could* go.

Which she clearly couldn't.

She needed to do a food shop! And mop her floor!

But any words she could have formed were swiftly cut off by the opening notes of *'Dude (Looks Like A Lady)'* blaring from the practically antiquated karaoke machine.

Bex's eyes bugged wide at the sound, and she threw her grubby tea towel to the bar's surface as she moved swiftly towards the source.

"Absolutely fucking *not,* Drunk Dave!" she shouted. Her voice dropped lower as she followed it up. "We have *got* to start vetting this machine."

Sophie watched, both amused and disturbed as Bex wrestled the microphone from the protesting patron, muffled arguments sounding over the scuffles until the song that played over the speakers was considerably less offensive.

"Evening, Miss Cedars."

Sophie sighed, her lips twitching in amusement as she turned on her bar stool to face the already alarmingly close Ern.

"Evening, Ern."

"I couldn't help but overhear that you're having a little bit of *man* trouble," Ern croaked, his cane waving in the air as he gesticulated. "Maybe I can be of some assistance?"

Sophie rolled her lips, biting down on them to hold back the bark of laughter that threatened to burst from her chest.

"I was a young whippersnapper like you once too, you know!" Ern chuckled.

"Oh, I know, Ern," Sophie agreed. "A very handsome one, I'm sure."

"I'm *still* handsome!" Ern raised an eyebrow, grinning cheekily. "I'm going away next week you know."

Sophie took a large gulp of her beer.

"To me caravan in Newquay," Ern continued. "Why don't you join me?"

"I'm on the clock all week, I'm afraid Ern," Sophie sighed. "Maybe next time."

"Or we could even go to Sicily!" Ern persisted, leaning impossibly closer.

Sophie choked on her beer.

*"Sicily?"*

"I've got a lovely villa in Sicily. Lovely bit of sunshine will soon have you forgetting about that Kyle Brown."

Sophie blinked. She looked at Ern for a long moment.

At his huge glasses on his tiny face, and his wispy white hair, and his watery grey eyes, and the cane just waving precariously nowhere near the ground.

And for one moment of complete and utter raging insanity, she considered agreeing.

Then Ern burped, and his dentures popped out.

"You gonna get me a refill, love?" he mumbled around his dentures as he pushed them back in.

Sophie took a deep breath.

"I'm not working tonight, I'm afraid, Ern," she replied. "I'm off the clock. Besides, that pint's still mostly full."

She watched, shaking her head in amusement as Ern grumbled wordlessly, squinted at his almost full pint for a moment, then turned and made his slow retreat back to his armchair by the fire.

Bex's words mulled over in Sophie's mind as she turned her focus back to her sister's battle with Drunk Dave, and she took a deep breath as she considered the possibility. *Could* she just take a trip? Head to a big city, and explore the museums, and the sights, and the culture?

What would she have to lose, really?

It was only the UK; it would take nothing to come home if she really hated it.

She nursed her second beer slowly as she fished her phone out of her pocket, resting her elbows on the bar. She wasn't all too sure where to start, but a Google search seemed like the best bet.

She smiled to herself, butterflies beginning to flutter in the depths of her belly as she typed her search.

*Places to stay in London.*

The sheer volume of results gave her pause, then she nearly had a hernia over the prices of the places she selected.

Maybe Airbnb.

She choked on her beer.

That was the cost *nightly?*

The pub rent barely cost them that much a *month!*

Her finger hovered for a moment over the close button, the reality already seeming completely unobtainable mere minutes into her search.

Then a particular result caught her eye.

*MapTrade UK—find your perfect holiday home exchange, anywhere from Yorkshire to Cornwall, London to Dublin.*

A home swap? Staying in someone else's home, while they stayed here in hers?

There was something endearingly grounded about the concept, and Sophie was intrigued.

And it certainly looked a *lot* more affordable.

She felt the butterflies beat just a little harder as she clicked onto the webpage.

The browser was simple. Effective.

*My home is in _____*
*I want to go to _____*

Sophie grinned; her beer abandoned as she typed in her request.

*London, Central.*

~ ~ ~ ~ ~ ~ (♫) ~ ~ ~ ~ ~ ~

Finley sank back onto her sofa, the open bottle of red wine in her hand, and the humiliation still burning hot through her bloodstream.

She looked down over the ridiculous state of her current situation. She was sprawled upright on her sofa with her bedraggled cat under one arm, still in her unbuttoned shirt and her best black bra, with her devil trousers swapped for a pair of very loose, very faded boxers. She was pretty sure she had never looked so dishevelled, but she could finally feel the air on her bruised vagina, and frankly nothing had ever felt so good. She let her head thud onto the back of the sofa, both regret and relief coursing her weary body.

She had tried, relentlessly and desperately, to call a taxi and escort her date to the A&E, but Bella had insisted she was fine, and nothing was broken.

Finley hadn't been so sure, but after much back and forth and several ice packs, she'd eventually surrendered and called Bella a taxi home instead.

She only hoped to whatever sapphic deity was failing her tonight, that it hadn't been the same driver who had brought them here.

It had been pretty apparent to both Bella and Finley that this was not getting a repeat performance, and Finley was trying desperately not to think about the dejected look in bruised eyes as she'd closed the taxi door behind her colleague.

*Not* the finest of efforts at getting back out there.

She was pretty sure she deserved that cold bed tonight.

She sighed, fishing her phone from her pocket and scrolling through her notifications in an effort to repress every single memory of the past ninety minutes. She'd noticed the many messages when she'd called for the taxi, and she was dreading the sheer number of emails she'd seen in her work inbox.

She opted for the text messages first.

She frowned as she read the name on the first message.

Dan Myles: *Hope there's no hard feelings, Bennett. You were good competition and I'm sure the next one will be yours.*

Finley blinked.

The next…*what?*

Her blood ran cold, her stomach turning with nausea as the implications of those words sank in.

This had *better* fucking *not* be what it sounded like.

There was no way.

Not again.

Not this time.

It was just fighting talk, surely?

After the day she'd had? The presentation, the win, the praise?

The promotion wasn't even supposed to be *announced* for another month.

But this did seem out of character for Dan, and that was enough to set the leaden pulse of dread pumping through Finley's chest.

She pulled up her email app, her heart sinking as she scrolled through the subject lines of the most recent string.

*You were robbed.*
*Commiserations.*
*Patriarchal bullshit.*

And the one that sent red hot fury through every one of her veins. A bulletin from Amelia. At 8pm this evening.

*New Appointment—Congratulations to Dan Myles.*

Seriously?

Finley leapt to her feet, her blood pounding in her ears and her skin crawling with the fury and the agitation and the bewildered confusion over the fact that she had missed this fucking promotion *one more fucking time.*

She paced the apartment, completely unable to comprehend what she was supposed to *do* with herself right now.

She let her raging feet carry her, wandering aimlessly around the same thousand square feet of her home on autopilot as her brain tried to untangle its thoughts.

She didn't get it.

She *didn't get it?*

After *everything?*

*How* was that possible?

This was it. This was her breaking point.

She felt her chest tighten, her throat closing as her feet continued to pummel the wooden floors of her home. She blinked as she found herself back in the living room where she'd started, her mind and her body feeling like entirely different entities.

Was this panic?

Was she having a breakdown?

She couldn't do this anymore. She couldn't *keep* doing this over and over again. Couldn't keep giving this company *everything* for *nothing.*

Noah's name buzzed across her phone screen, and she immediately hurled the vibrating device into the sofa cushions. She could barely process her own emotions right now, and she could not face trying to explain them to another human being.

Particularly not one who had *known* how much this meant to her.

The vibrations rang out again, and Finley cursed her friend's persistence. She closed her eyes, taking a deep breath in as she fought to calm her racing emotions.

She knew, really, that Noah was the only one who could bring her down right now, and she was feeling pretty bereft of any other options, besides another pointless and uncontrollable lap of her apartment.

She exhaled slowly as she fished the still ringing phone from the sofa, swiped the screen, and brought the speaker to her ear.

"Hey."

*"Fuck* them, Finley."

The immediate words, and the unbridled anger spat behind them from her usually laid-back friend brought the first sting of tears to burn in the back of Finley's eyes.

"Noah…"

"No, I'm serious. *Fuck* them." Noah's voice was lower than usual. Almost cold, and Finley swallowed as she registered that this was the angriest she had ever heard him. "This was *yours,* Fin. It wasn't even a question. She doesn't deserve the effort you give, dude."

"I don't think I can give it anymore, Noah." Finley sank back onto the sofa, the tears falling freely at her friend's words. "How am I supposed to just turn up on Monday as if everything is fine, and give a million percent for another week?"

Finley winced as she thought also of Bella, and the humiliation and the guilt she would feel as she sat and watched her dejected colleague walk through the office doors in dark sunglasses with a swollen nose.

"Just don't," Noah posited.

Casual. As if it was that easy.

*"Don't?"*

"When was the last time you took a break?"

Noah's voice was softer now, his normal reassuring tone laced back through his words, and Finley let out a soft exhale of relief at the sound.

"A *what?"* she teased.

"A break. It's this thing people do where they *don't work* for a few consecutive days, or weeks." Noah paused, and Finley could *hear* his stupid grin. "You know, when they have *lives."*

"But that's just it, dude! I *don't* have a life!" Finley huffed out a laugh, wiping the back of her hand over her eyes to stem the flow of her tears. "I don't have anything that isn't this goddamn fucking job. I wouldn't even know where to start with a break!"

"You need to take a few weeks off. Go somewhere quiet, and away from everything. Preferably where your phone picks up no signal."

Finley scrunched her face.

"Like, South of the river?"

*"No,"* Noah laughed, and Finley could almost see him shaking his head in disdain. "Like the countryside. The Lake District. Or Shropshire, or Pembrokeshire."

"Pembrokeshire?"

Finley flopped onto her front, burying her face in the cushions. She knew she was struggling to keep up here, but frankly it had been a long day, she was emotional, exhausted, and a little tipsy, and Noah had moved *really* quickly from raging against her employer to reeling off names of places she barely even remembered existed most of the time, and she was sure she was suffering a little whiplash.

"Yes, Wales." Noah chuckled. "Sea air, and sand, and cliff top walks, and fresh fish, and men in flat caps with Welsh accents."

Finley baulked.

"I don't…"

*"Just* tell me you'll think about it? You deserve some down time, Finley."

"Do the women wear flat caps?" Finley mumbled into the cushions.

"I wouldn't know, what's a woman?"

Finley grinned, then sighed as she dragged herself upright.

"Yeah, alright. I'll think about it. Thanks, Noah."

Finley felt her resolve pull a little tighter together as she hung up the phone, her friend's words ringing in her ears.

He was right. She really could use a break, and she *really* didn't think she could face the office on Monday.

But she just had *no* idea where to start.

She took a swig of her wine, pulling Google up on her phone.

She figured *hotels in the countryside* was as good a place as any to start, but it rather quickly turned out that there was really quite a *lot* of countryside in the UK, and she would very probably need a narrower search criteria.

Who knew?

She tried 'hotels in Pembrokeshire', and quickly felt a little overwhelmed by the vast spattering of BnBs and seaside Inns.

Frankly, she really had no idea what she was doing.

She sighed as she scrolled aimlessly through her search results, her mind wandering over what she really wanted to find. She didn't want a basic tourist BnB on a windy British beach. She wanted something remote. Somewhere she could hide in the background. Something *real,* where the people around her were just living their days. Working, taking care of their families, walking their dogs. Not pandering to every whim of a Londoner on holiday.

There had been a film once. Some cheesy romcom she'd watched with Jess one Christmas after she'd reluctantly packed her tablet away for the night. Where two people on opposite sides of the world had swapped homes for their holiday.

That had always seemed fun. To not only get away, but to almost live someone else's life for a little while. Amongst local people, and not just tourists.

Did people do that in real life?

Finley took another swig of her wine as she tapped out the search, her eyes widening as the results returned.

*MapTrade UK—find your perfect holiday home exchange, anywhere from Yorkshire to Cornwall, London to Dublin.*

Well.

People really did do this in real life.

Finley settled back into the sofa; her entire attention now drawn to the site as she began to set up her profile.

According to the form in front of her, she needed photos.

She frowned, her eyes flitting around her living room.

The lighting wouldn't be great at nearing midnight, and she certainly wasn't prepared to go back out onto the street to take any of the building's kerb appeal.

But she would definitely make do for now. She could take some more tomorrow if she needed to, but right now it was all-in, or nothing.

She hauled herself up, grabbing her phone and flicking the camera app open as she began to make her way around her home.

She'd get its best features, at least.

The large kitchen, with the giant range oven she never used anymore, and the smartly tiled bathroom with the pressure shower. The living room with the large double French doors, and the giant smart TV and the electric fireplace. The bedroom with her obscene bed that just forever remained cold. She'd get the little balcony with the tiny BBQ-come-firepit and the hanging pod chairs tomorrow.

She flopped back onto her sofa, loading the photos onto her profile, and beginning to fill out the details.

*Two bed apartment in Central London. Amenities, culture and history on your literal doorstep.*

She exhaled heavily as she hit 'save and publish', and flopped back onto the sofa, pulling Peanut back under her arm.

"Mummy's sorry, P," Finley whispered, her fingers stroking gently through her cat's matted fur. "About tonight. Shutting you away, and then your little tail getting trodden on."

Peanut grunted.

"If it makes you feel any better bub, I'm pretty sure between us we made sure that lady won't ever be coming back here again," Finley sighed. "It's definitely a criteria for future dates: must like cats."

She let her head loll back against the ledge of the sofa.

She felt out of sorts, and she wanted to talk to someone. She wanted to vent, and she wanted someone to lift her up. To tell her she wasn't losing. To tell her this was a mistake, and she deserved to stand at the top.

That she deserved the city to be hers.

But she honestly didn't know who to turn to. Noah had said all he could tonight, and she knew that.

She pulled her phone into her hands, her fingers toying with her contacts as she considered her options.

She could call her dad. Tell him that she'd failed. He would be sympathetic for a while, and then he'd tower above her. He'd tell her what to do, and how to fix it. Grow *angry* when she didn't bow down, and kiss the ground he walked on. Tell her she owed him her gratitude for getting as far as she had, but that she only owed herself the blame for failing to get further.

Like he always did.

She sighed, scrolling further through her contacts list.

She could message her mum.

But she didn't know where she was this time. Somewhere in her van in Europe, with her toyboy and her tie-dye, and her lack of any regard for Finley's dreams.

She'd tell her it didn't matter. Tell her she should have run with her mother, all those years ago. Traded her shoes and her dreams for a life on the road with twenty-year-old Theo Dubois and his homemade deodorant.

She certainly wouldn't understand the churning anger in Finley's belly tonight.

She could message Zayan, or Harri, or Kate. But they'd be out, watching Wicked in the West End for the fifth time. And they'd tell her not to worry. That there was more to life than suits and blueprints.

They wouldn't understand.

None of them would.

Finley groaned, sinking further into the couch as she tossed her phone to the side.

Then she started, her laptop chiming loud and unfamiliar from the coffee table. Not a sound any of her usual apps made.

Which meant it could only be one thing.

She jumped up, almost squashing Peanut in her excitement and the butterflies that swarmed in her stomach at the sound.

*"Shit,* that was quick!"

Sophie: *Hi! I know it's a really long shot, but any chance you're looking to swap with someone in a hamlet town in the ass end of Cornwall? Not much happens here, but I can guarantee you a quiet and relaxing stay!*

Finley held her breath.

Cornwall?

*What* was a *hamlet?*

Finley clicked on the profile.

Well, fuck.

She huffed out an incredulous chuckle as she scanned the description, flicking through the small collection of photos of the modest country cottage.

*What* were the fucking odds?

For the first time tonight, it felt like the stars were aligned in her favour.

She grinned as she pulled the message box back up.

Finley: *It's like you read my mind. That sounds like a dream right now. Your place looks adorable.*

Sophie: *And yours looks like a historian's paradise! Are you really only a fifteen-minute walk from Westminster Palace?*

Finley had butterflies. Stronger butterflies than anything she had felt all day. A huge presentation, a first date, a horrific attempt at a one-night stand, a rage-inducing career low, and this house swap with this total stranger was the thing making her stomach swoop like a blender on a Ferris wheel.

She chuckled.

Finley: *Thirteen, if you power walk* 😌

Sophie: *When are you looking to swap?*

Finley: *I was thinking...like, now?*

Sophie: *It's midnight* 😂

Finley: *Right...rough day! Tomorrow?*

Finley held her breath as she waited for a reply.

It had been back and forth. Snappy, quick. This was taking a little longer.

Her heart lurched in her throat, and she drummed her fingers impatiently on the coffee table.

Maybe she'd pushed her luck. Maybe she'd sounded like a psychopath, and Sophie had noped out of it. Maybe she should just forget this whole thing and just crawl...

The screen chimed.

Finley exhaled.

Sophie: *Let's do it.*

# Chapter Five

"Am I insane, Noah?"

Finley's earpiece crackled as she turned Sophie's Ford Kuga out of the town and onto the quiet roads that would lead her out into the back end of rural nowhere. To Finley's great gratitude, the car had been left for her at St Austell train station, and the keys stashed with the barista behind the small coffee counter.

Finley was a Londoner. She didn't own a car, and Sophie had said she wouldn't get far around here without one.

Frankly it was a stroke of pure luck that she'd ever even learned to drive.

"Yes."

Noah's voice was just audible under the fickle breaks in Finley's phone signal, and she wondered how long it would be before she lost him altogether.

"Always so encouraging," she mumbled.

"Well, you asked."

Finley rolled her eyes.

"If it's any reassurance," Noah continued, "I think it's only because it's been three years since you took any time off, and a large part of your soul has died."

Finley sighed.

"*Why* are you so dramatic?"

The maps app on Finley's phone spoke out over Noah's call, and she paused to listen to the instruction.

In a complete contrast to everything in her character, Finley felt pretty chilled. The train journey had been easy enough, she'd managed to resist checking her work emails for the entire five and a half hours, and the first half of this twenty-minute car journey had been dead easy.

The car smelled nice.

Like cherry blossom, and honey. And faintly like hop.

Something about the smell was relaxing. Almost reassuring.

Was this how Sophie smelled?

Finley shook her head, kicking herself immediately for the ridiculous lesbian intensity of *that* thought train.

*God,* she needed to get laid.

"What?" Noah huffed. "I didn't say it was *irreparable,* you just need a little TLC!"

Finley took a deep breath.

That she did. And this was already seeming like a great way to start.

The air was clear, the sky was blue, the scenery was beautiful, and she was feeling pretty good about her decisions.

Until she turned off the main road, the lanes narrowed to a quarter of the size, and she nearly shat her own spleen when she found herself hurtling towards a carrier tractor that was *definitely* wider than the space between the hedgerows that lined the worn-down tarmac.

*"Fuck a mottled duck!"* she yelped, feeling *every* ounce of her relaxed attitude seep instantly from her veins as she slammed on the breaks.

Her lungs clenched and her eyes widened in horror as the tractor did not.

"Are you *mental?"* she screeched, fighting and falling to keep the threadbare band of her composure intact as the tractor continued its journey towards Finley's certain death. *"Where do you expect me to go, upwards?"*

She felt her face redden, and her spine tighten with a deadweight tonne of stress and anxiety as she awkwardly reversed the oversized car back along the tiny lane, the parking sensors screaming blue murder and the tractor happily still lumbering along *at* her fucking face.

This was surely a colossal town planning blunder.

How was anyone ever supposed to get *anywhere* if they had to drive fucking *backwards* every time, they met another vehicle?

The roads were *way* too small, the car was *way* too big, and within six minutes Finley had run out of fingers to count her near death experiences on.

And Noah's call had been cut off.

Because there was no signal.

Which also meant, no more magical talking map.

Finley had *no* idea where she was, every road was lined with hedges and fields that all looked identical, and there was a grand total of zero landmarks by which to determine which way was up.

She was, quite frankly, flat out panicking.

77

Her fingers trembled as she pulled the car to a stop in the entrance to a field, pulling the map up on her phone.

She took a deep breath.

She could do this.

She could work out where she'd been when the signal had dropped, and use the offline map to plan out where she needed to go to get to Polcarne. Simple.

Or it would be, if she could work out how to read a map.

She'd done orienteering at school once.

In ten acres of Hampstead Heath, on a warm Friday afternoon.

That was the same thing, right? How hard could it be?

She just needed to calm down.

If she was really honest, the huge cow staring at her over the gate beside her was particularly off-putting, but if she just turned her back a little, she could get in the zone.

Calm.

Zen.

*Jesus,* she really hadn't known they made *noise* like that.

The nursery rhymes always made that sound *far* more delicate.

They also really didn't smell all that great. She could smell the pungent scent of manure through the closed window of the car, and it wasn't sparking huge amounts of joy.

She closed her eyes for a moment, willing her anxious brain to focus.

"Evening, love."

The sound of a rap on the passenger window of the jeep sent Finley's heart leaping through her throat, and her jaw clamped so hard she tasted copper as she bit back a scream.

*"Jesus,* fuck my soul."

"Nice night for it, isn't it?" The cheery voice carried through the thin glass, and Finley swallowed thickly as she tried to calm her racing heart.

Nice night for *what?*

Sending perfectly healthy strangers into cardiac arrest?

She watched, bewildered, as the man leaned his arm against the doorframe of the car, grinning widely as he bent down slightly to meet her wary eyes.

Finley blinked.

She was not a fan of stereotypes.

Never had been.

But *this* was the most stereotypical thing of all the stereotypical things that she had ever seen in her thirty years on this planet, and she almost wanted to laugh.

The flat cap. The overalls. The wellies.

Was that a *pitchfork?*

"You lost, me cock?"

Finley frowned.

His *what?*

The man furrowed his brows a little as he peered through the glass, and the Londoner in Finley panicked immediately. She was alone, in the ass end of nowhere, with no phone signal and this guy had a *pitchfork* and was talking *way* too damn casually about his fucking *cock* of all things.

But also, she was lost, she was tired, she was anxious, and she really didn't want to die alone driving round and round the tiny roads of Cornwall for the rest of all eternity.

So really, she wasn't sure she had too much of a choice.

She wound down the window.

Just the slightest of cracks.

And hit the lock button on the dashboard.

"A little! Would you happen to know the way to Polcarne?"

"That I do, my lover, just a moment."

The man leaned his pitchfork back against the gate, and Finley tried very hard not to think too much about the idea of being this man's lover.

"Show us yer map then."

Finley exhaled.

~ ~ ~ ~ ~ ~ 🎵 ~ ~ ~ ~ ~ ~

Sophie inhaled deeply as she stepped off the train at London Paddington.

If she was honest, she was already feeling a bit overwhelmed.

Unfathomably excited! She'd practically vibrated in her seat for five hours of British countryside through a train window, and that buzz was yet to fade.

But she was definitely overwhelmed.

Somehow, in all the hours she had spent meticulously planning her journey the night before, it had failed to occur to her that in visiting the busiest city on the continent, she would quite obviously find herself amongst *huge* numbers of goddamn *people.*

Which was *fascinating.* Seas of new faces swarmed around her, and she was almost giddy in her excitement at how *different* they all looked. From each other, and from the flat caps of Polcarne. It was exciting to Sophie, how different their lives must have been, and she wanted nothing more than to watch each and every one of them, and play it all out in her head.

But also, it was slightly terrifying, and not one of them had stopped for anywhere near long enough for Sophie to even process their faces, let alone come up with any kind of back story.

She fought her way along the platform, her wheeled suitcase being jostled behind her in the heavy flow of people. She gripped the handle tightly, keeping her eyes above her on the signs that pointed her in the direction of London's Underground.

She'd planned this bit out.

She wasn't stupid.

She might have been from a back-end Cornish hamlet town, but she knew well enough to know that an amateur country girl could not expect to simply *'hop on a tube'.* And she had been far too terrified to even consider trying this raw.

But with all her preparation, she felt invincible!

She fumbled in her pocket with her free hand, fishing her map out of her bag. Finley had told her what she would need to do, and Sophie had neatly highlighted the journey onto her freshly printed tube map.

She thanked her lucky stars that this was a direct line.

One tube.

Bakerloo Line to Piccadilly Circus.

To ease her in gently.

Finley had told her the closest tube station was technically Covent Garden, but that would have required a change of trains for two stops, and the country girl in Sophie had deemed that utter insanity.

She was more than capable of walking for nine minutes; she absolutely did not need to pay a fare and leave a carbon footprint for the sake of half a bloody mile.

Sophie grinned as she descended the escalators that would lead her, for the first time, down beneath the city of London and onto the world-famous tube map.

This had been a source of pure fear for Sophie in the hours that led to her arrival in London, and yet she couldn't help the smug sense of self-satisfaction as she successfully navigated the tunnels with surprising ease. She felt oddly powerful as she quickly found the right twists of descending paths that would lead her to the platform she needed.

Brown.

Follow the brown.

She was, embarrassingly, slightly disappointed to be following the mundane brown lines, when the other options were so much more *colourful,* but she did accept the complete irrelevance, really. And she had this *down* so far.

What had she ever been scared of?

*This* Sophie Cedars had this London thing all figured out.

Though granted, the wind in the tunnels was wreaking all sorts of havoc with her new hairdo.

The underground platform was a little less empowering.

It felt impossibly busier than the overground had, and Sophie gripped tightly to her luggage handle as the bodies jostled and closed in around her. It was so much windier than she had expected down here, and there was something so stilted and eerie about the fact that there were just *so* many people, but not one of them seemed to be speaking. Every head around her faced down, reading newspapers or phone screens or tube maps, and the few that did speak did so in hushed tones. Like some kind of unspoken rule.

Sophie had the distinct impression of being in a library.

A very windy, very busy, very unsettling library.

And she was *fascinated.*

Slightly terrified. Completely out of her element.

But fascinated.

The rush when the train pulled in was incomprehensible. Suddenly *every*body within an eight-foot radius of Sophie seemed to be upon her— pushing, and pressing, and walking forwards into space that simply did *not* exist.

And *still* the *silence.*

Sophie had never been *touched* by so many people before. There was a ponytail tickling her nose, a chin hovering beside her left ear, a kneecap pressing into the back of her right thigh, and a briefcase *uncomfortably* close to her asscrack.

And all without exchanging such as a pleasantry!

It baffled her that she seemed to be the only person on this twenty-foot platform that found this situation unnerving, and she was beginning to feel like a herded sheep.

For want of any other conceivable option, Sophie allowed herself to be swept along with the muted stampede, and breathed a sigh of relief as she finally managed to cram herself and her bag onto the heaving train.

There were still *so* many people on the platform, but by a stroke of miraculous luck, Sophie seemed to have *just* managed to squeeze the last standing space, her nose right to the doors of the stifling carriage.

Or so she thought.

Until a bare minimum of at *least* twelve more people forced their way boldly into the carriage, and she found herself practically suspended over her luggage, pressed against the underside of a teenager's arm and the slightly sweaty chest of a stiff man in a stiff suit.

And the push just didn't seem to be stopping.

Sophie almost whimpered with relief as the heavy hiss of the doors rang out and they began to close, and the push of the bodies ceased.

Except.

*No!*

Sophie shrieked loudly as a man in a tight suit and way too much hair gel launched himself through the closing doors and into the sea of bodies, craning his head forward at an *inhuman* angle in a bid to avoid severance that Sophie was *certain* should *not* have been successful.

*"Holy shit,* do you not understand the laws of science?"

Sophie froze as her own panicked voice peeled across the silence, and what felt like fourteen thousand startled eyes turned in her direction.

She clamped her jaw shut, her eyes closing for a moment as she begged whatever deity was responsible for her existence to just take her now.

She'd broken the golden rule. And *not* quietly.

Or particularly calmly, for that matter.

And she'd also, quite possibly, inadvertently picked a fight with a man with the ability to fold himself into an origami octopus.

Twenty-six years of pushing her feelings down fairly successfully, but *this* Sophie Cedars with the two degrees and the new hairdo seemed to be incapable of keeping her mouth shut.

She held her breath as she let her eyes flutter open, exhaling slowly as she met a few smirks and stifled giggles, but predominantly reactionless zombies engaged once more in their Metro newspapers.

She shuffled slightly in her awkward position, managing to *just* secure herself enough space to avoid leaning dependently on anyone else's body.

Until the train moved, and her full weight was thrown abruptly and mercilessly into the armpit of the teenage boy beside her, her luggage cracking him audibly across the shins.

What was the rule in *this* situation?

Did she apologise?

That would mean speaking.

And she knew now that that was tolerated thinly.

But she couldn't *not* apologise for the literal bodily assault she'd just thrown at this boy!

She settled for apologetic eyes, and a tight-lipped grimace in his direction as she hauled herself upright the best she could.

With nothing to hold onto, she was acutely thankful for her higher-than-average core strength, for allowing her to at least prise her face from the boy's sticky t-shirt. She might have been softer around the middle than Bex was, but she certainly carried the physical strength in the family, and right now it was paying off.

The problem now was that she knew there were six stops between here and Piccadilly Circus, and she was *right* in the bloody doorway.

That problem was eradicated at Edgware Road, and then again at Marylebone, as the chaotic madness saw her pushed further back into the depths of the carriage.

She had no real idea how it was happening. It felt something akin to the motion of a rough sea, if she were riding it on a surfboard. The push would come from the back, the solid block of people rippling as commuters managed to force their way from the depths of the carriage and out onto the platform. And in turn, the stationary bodies would be carried back, filling the spaces left by those who had disembarked.

Only Sophie's surfboard was made of paper, and every shuffle and every jostle and every goddamn movement knocked her clean off her feet. If it weren't for the press of several unknown and unidentified bodies against her own, she would undeniably be riding this thing on her ass on the unseen carriage floor.

She couldn't even see her luggage. It was in her hand. But it was lost to her sight, buried beneath the suits and the denim and the many, many limbs around her.

Sophie's fingers ached, clenched hard around the handle for fear that if she let go, she and the suitcase would be swept apart, and she would find herself watching it leave the train long before she did.

And then, at Baker Street, she struck gold.

The suited man in the seat right in front of her gathered his things and stood as the train pulled to a stop along the platform, leaving an empty seat.

An empty seat that was *hers*.

She was *right* beside it. There was no question.

She squashed herself as best she could against the person behind her as the man squeezed past, and she almost giggled with relief as she turned to sit her ass down on the glorious empty seat.

And landed immediately on the unmistakable warm cushion of a complete stranger's lap.

Sophie squealed, her heart lurching through her throat as she hurled herself up and off the unexpected intruder.

*How?*

How had this person slipped in before Sophie had managed?

Was *everyone* in this city an origami octopus?

She jerked her head round, her baffled eyes making contact with the openly disgusted and openly unamused glare of a middle-aged, middle-class woman.

Staring Sophie down like she was mad.

As if the woman had *always* been there, and Sophie had lost her mind.

And frankly at this point, Sophie was so disorientated that she might bloody well have done for all she knew.

She sighed, turning her head back away from the disgruntled stranger as she clutched desperately at her luggage, and trained her eyes instead on the tube line map she could just about see printed across the side of the train.

She checked the last stops off in her head, counting them down with increasing panic.

Sophie's *new* predicament was rather suddenly the fact that she had three stops left, and she was now a jam-packed sea of bodies away from where she needed to be to stand *any* chance of getting off this train.

She tried fruitlessly to move closer to the carriage doors. She was quite certain that her feet were nowhere near the floor, and her luggage didn't move no matter how hard she tugged it, and so she really was completely at a loss as to how to proceed.

The sea ripples had made it look so easy.

*Uncomfortable,* and undignified, but fairly seamless.

But Sophie was clearly lacking in some sort of required expertise as she stumbled over her own feet, or someone else's feet, or maybe even her own luggage for all she knew at this point.

But by some miracle, the doors did seem to be getting closer.

She stood her ground at Oxford Circus. She clung to the nearest rail, white knuckles on both hands as she fought to keep a hold of her position, and her poor, battered suitcase.

But she struggled to get any closer, the heave of bodies impossibly thicker this much closer to the door.

Until the train stopped at Piccadilly Circus.

Sophie panicked.

She'd been on this train for six stops. She knew how quickly the doors opened, and closed, and the train hurtled on once again.

She knew she absolutely did not have enough time to politely excuse herself past each and every origami octopus cramming themselves into the tube at Piccadilly.

So, she went all-in.

She gripped her suitcase handle with brute force, simply praying all of her luggage was still attached to the other end, and she practically hurled herself into the wall of bodies between herself and the door.

And through some fate of miracles, the ripples moved.

She stumbled forward, tripping and stalling over feet and bags and a bloody *bike* of all things, until she fell gracelessly out of the sliding doors, narrowly avoiding a broken ankle in the precarious gap between the train and the platform.

The smug voice telling her on a loop to *'please mind the gap'* could take a leap.

*'Please mind the gap'* implied some sense of control.

And that, it turned out, was *arrogantly* presumptuous on the London underground.

Having 'please mind the gap' on a loop was like throwing someone off a first-floor balcony then telling them to *'please mind the drop'*.

Preposterous.

Sophie righted herself, her heart pounding in its bone cage at the combination of relief that both feet seemed to be firmly on the ground, and outright terror over the fact that the train doors were beginning to close, and Sophie was still clinging desperately to the handle of a suitcase that was still very much on the train.

She resorted to her primal basics.

She tugged, grunted, and screeched, practically feral in her frustrated panic, until someone took mercy and hit the button on the doors, throwing her battered suitcase out onto the platform for her.

Sophie stumbled backwards, her shoulders sagging with relief that she and her bag were both finally on the platform at Piccadilly Circus, in mostly one piece.

She'd earned herself a few questionable looks with her feral screech, but at this point she really didn't care.

Maybe now she'd get a little bit of a wider berth for a while.

She allowed herself to be swept away with the masses again as she made her way up the ridiculous windy escalators. She would swear she was further down beneath the ground now than she was when she started, but she couldn't really be sure, and frankly she was incredibly disorientated.

And her hair was *everywhere.*

When she finally emerged from the pandemonium of London's Underground, Sophie was a little dishevelled, a lot sweaty, and *very* grateful to see the sky.

And the great sodding city of *London!*

The sheer size of the buildings, and the white masonry, the columns, the statues, the domed roofs, and the countless visible signs of centuries of British history and arts and architecture.

*Right* there.

In all their glory.

With people just milling about around it, leaning casually against the walls of the Criterion Theatre, and lounging on the steps of the century old Shaftesbury fountain, as if they weren't chewing Big Macs and Greggs sausage rolls *right beside* some of the country's most incredible history.

And immediately, *every* stress of London's Underground was forgotten.

Sophie's stomach vaulted as she considered the fact that this was her world to explore now. She was here, in this *insane* city, for two weeks, and she couldn't *wait* to search and learn about every corner of this new adventure.

Suddenly every fear she had ever had seemed hollow. Insignificant and minimal against the backdrop of sheer opportunity before her.

And Polcarne, Cornwall, felt a million miles away.

Sophie's eyes glazed with wonder as she tugged her luggage almost aimlessly along the streets. Her steps led her almost intuitively in the direction of the distant flags that she *knew* belonged to the masts of Buckingham Palace, just mere minutes away from where she stood right now.

The thing she noticed more than anything else was the *noise.*

Sounds she could barely decipher—the rumble of the tubes beneath her feet, the honking of the traffic, the hum of phone calls and conversations, and the music of the buskers and the shops and restaurants.

The second thing she noticed was the smell. Petrol, and smoke, and so many kinds of foods that she couldn't tell where one ended and another began. And that kind of indescribable smell of *busy.* Of lots of people; of laundry detergents and shower products and perfumes, and sweat and must.

It all should have been invasive. It should have been a disorientating attack on Sophie's senses, that left her scrabbling for the tube back to the cows and the damp sea air of Cornwall.

But it made Sophie feel *alive.*

She was completely overwhelmed with the knowledge that her own humble two feet were really here; *really* standing amongst some of the most notorious historical sites in British history.

And she was amazed still by the knowledge that just a few minutes journey from where she stood were the arts and the music and the culture of South Bank, or Canary Wharf and the city's hub of business and money and high fliers in suits, or Westminster and the political centre of the only country she'd ever known. And she was utterly *incredulous* at just how *much* one city could hold.

The heavy suitcase was starting to become a little cumbersome as Sophie pulled it through the busy streets, and she hesitated in her step as she realised that she had let her excitement get the better of her, and had failed to follow her directions.

She stopped alongside the bronze Equestrian Statue of Edward VII, her eyes scanning her surroundings for a sign that would tell her whereabouts she needed to go. She knew she was heading for Covent Garden, and she knew Finley had said to follow Coventry Street eastwards, and it was almost a direct line from there.

But Sophie would have been lying if she'd said she had any idea which way was up right now, let alone which direction was East.

Well.

There were *plenty* of people around.

All she had to do was ask!

Sophie stepped toward a woman in a suit. Deliberately, one who did not appear to be carrying a map or a Polaroid camera.

She looked like she belonged.

She would be a good bet.

"Excuse me!"

Sophie plastered her widest, most endearing smile across her face as she spoke, holding her hand out in a half wave.

Which the woman *completely* ignored.

Sophie felt the whip of the wind in the woman's step blow across her face as the stranger stepped around her and away, barely even sparing her a glance, let alone the time of day.

Sophie frowned.

Perhaps she'd been deaf.

Or wearing headphones.

Or perhaps she hadn't spoken English. That was always a possibility, of course, especially in London.

She tried again. A man this time. In a fedora and a scarf that wouldn't hold up Sophie's jeans, let alone keep her neck warm.

"Hi, do you happen to know…"

Sophie trailed off as the man, too, brushed past her without a second glance.

She blinked.

*Wow,* she really *was* a long way from home.

Sophie tried three more times.

The only person she managed to strike a conversation with, asked her for loose change.

She gave them a tenner, and sank back against the walls of an excessively grand looking Chinese restaurant, *no* closer to knowing where she was supposed to go.

Until her hamlet-town brain remembered that she was in the *hub* of the UK now, and they *actually* erected phone masts here.

She sighed, pulling the maps app up on her phone.

Well, that could have saved her a tenner.

Finley really was right. It took her just twelve minutes to find the apartment building, and it was crazy to her how much the atmosphere around her changed in such a short walk.

Where Piccadilly had been all tall buildings and white columns, Covent Garden was all golden brick, and well-kept plants, and modern looking buildings contrasted with wrought iron lanterns and uneven brick roads.

Finley's apartment building was weirdly magical. The entrance was a sleek, black-framed glass door tucked between the golden brick of the surrounding shops and restaurants, and the exterior of the storeys above boasted sweet fairy lights and modern looking balconies that all looked *exactly* the same save for the differences in the flowers in the boxes hanging from the bars.

Sophie felt like she was in a film.

Finley had given her the key code, and she grinned giddily as she punched the numbers in, and followed the brass numbers up through the bright hallways to the door she needed.

The simple key was waiting under a simple, grey rubber doormat, and Sophie almost squealed in delight as she let herself into the property and closed the door on her very first experience of the city of London.

She practically skipped as she made her way around the apartment, squealing in giddy excitement as she took in the spacious rooms and the tasteful decor; modern greys and greens and soft neutral colours, and arty prints and simple soft furnishings, minimalist and yet somehow still cosy enough to feel homely.

The apartment was immaculate, and full of gadgets that Sophie would absolutely guarantee she would be no closer to identifying the purpose of two weeks from this moment. But she would enjoy trying.

She grinned as she entered the kitchen, her eyes landing immediately on a printed note taped to the front of the fridge.

*Sophie,*

*Welcome to London!*

*If you're reading this, you survived the tubes. Congratulations;) you passed the first test of a true Londoner.*

*There's a supermarket delivery arriving tomorrow afternoon, because I didn't have many vegan options hanging around in the flat—sorry about that—but please help yourself to whatever you do find.*

*In the meantime, please use the cash on the coffee table for tonight's dinner. If you're not up for exploring just yet, you're in one hell of a Deliveroo location!*

*And I hope you like wine? I've left you a bottle of red.*

*I've also left my Oyster card. So, you can feel like a real Londoner.*

*Always a call or a text away if you need anything!*

*07798136255*

*Enjoy your stay!*

*Finley*

Sophie grinned, immediately punching the number into her phone and saving the contact. She wondered if Finley was as immaculately presented as her home was.

She sounded nice.

She wondered if *she'd* call her online degree *'pretend'*.

# Chapter Six

Finley frowned as she turned the car onto what was, according to the half-hidden street sign buried in the overrun hedgerows, Polcarne High Street.

She had to admit, she'd expected a little more life.

She knew London was the anomaly. She knew most towns didn't have the energy and the bustle and the ridiculous overcrowding that the country's capital did, but she had anticipated a *little* more of a happy medium.

Polcarne High Street had a grand total of about six buildings, and not one of them looked the same.

The butcher's was whitewashed stone, with an arched porchway with a chimney that made it look more like a whimsical holiday home than a murderous meat yard, and the sign boasted a large emblem of a smiling cow.

Finley was by no means against her meat, but this did seem a little on the nose.

The newsagent was sandwiched between the butcher and the churchyard, ridiculously small in its bizarre comparison. The tiny brown brick cottage was almost dwarfed by the crumbling tower of the church, and Finley got the distinct impression of two different towns in two different eras fighting for dominance in this odd little hamlet in-between.

The pharmacy had a thatched roof.

Finley wasn't sure she'd actually known those still existed outside of The Globe Theatre.

She couldn't help the little quirk of her lips as she drew the car slowly along the narrow road. The buildings were all so different, and yet somehow exactly the same. Each one had different architecture, and different colourings, and different brickwork. But they all *felt* so quintessentially *English.* So born of the British countryside that Finley had always just assumed only existed in stories and in Poldark. Save for the Ford Kuga, Finley felt like she'd been propelled back to days of yore, and it was quite *exciting,* in a magical, whimsical kind of way.

She grinned widely as she reached The Ship Inn.

She knew this was where Sophie worked. She'd been told if she ever had any problems, this was where she could find help.

The pub looked a little dishevelled. Splintered wooden beams lined ancient-looking paned windows, thick moss clung to battered dark roof tiles, and winding ivy pushed its way through the cracks in the yellow rendered stone.

And yet somehow it looked so *cared* for.

The splintered beams were painted, coated in an aqua blue that was somehow both calming and invigorating. Boxes of well-kept flowers lined each of the paned windows, and the sign was clean and crisp and clear.

Finley made a mental note to visit soon, once she was settled in.

And if Sophie's house was as well-loved as this pub was, then Finley was feeling fairly confident that she'd made the right decision in this swap.

She chuckled softly, shaking her head as she turned her focus back to the road. This entire experience was already feeling more than a little surreal, and Finley was getting more excited by the second to experience this new world.

Finley's stomach fizzed as she reached the end of the high street.

Sophie had said she lived just down the road from The Ship Inn, and so Finley could only assume that meant she was *very* close to her destination.

Which was, frankly, a grand fucking relief, as she was getting *really* tired of the beep of the parking sensors in this *tank* of a car, when she really did see no choice *but* to drive into these overhanging branches and these hedgerows.

The fizz didn't last long.

Three minutes later, Finley was still driving the chrome blue tank down the winding lanes of back-end Cornwall, and she hadn't seen a single building since The Ship Inn.

*Surely* this wasn't right.

*Down the road,* Sophie had said.

Finley guessed she hadn't strictly *left* the road, but she had been driving for some time now, and the sheer number of fields and gateways and sheep she had passed were giving her more than a little pause.

She must have been lost, surely.

In London, she could get to another *borough* in this time.

And yet, how could she be?

Follow the road from The Ship Inn.

The instruction was *really* simple.

Unless Sophie lived in a sheet-metal cow shed, then Finley really couldn't see how she could have missed anything here.

And yet the cottage was definitely not in her sights.

Just as Finley was beginning to think she'd been stitched up, and was halfway through a heated monologue about the perils of trusting strangers on the internet, the view changed.

Amongst the hedgerows and the cow fields and the sheep eyes, stood a row of small, neatly-kept, white-stone cottages with painted picket fences and cobblestone driveways.

Like something out of a goddamn *fable.*

Finley whooped in triumph as she *finally* pulled the jeep into the driveway of the adorable country cottage, she'd seen in Sophie's photos.

This too, was thatched, and the architect in Finley bit back an all-out squeal at the faded straw and the chimney that protruded through it.

The house was *everything* she had hoped it would be, and then some. Beside the drive, a white wooden gate latched onto a cobblestone path, lined with solar lights and flower beds that ran through an *adorable* little front garden.

It was so *quiet.*

If she stilled the wheels of her luggage over the stone drive, all that Finley could hear were the faint sounds of nesting birds, and crickets, and wildlife.

*Real* wildlife.

Not the street rats and the gammy pigeons of London's Covent Garden.

Finley's stomach swooped a little in childlike excitement as she thought about the life that might inhabit a garden like this one.

Rabbits, and frogs, and squirrels, and maybe even *deer* or *foxes!*

Finley liked to think of herself as an animal person. But she'd always been drawn to the runty things. The *unique* things. She'd had Monkey, that three-legged hamster that time, when she'd first moved to London. Three legs, and it forever used one of them to hang from its bars. Hence its name. Then she'd had Catapult, the budgie with a clipped wing. Every time she let him out of his cage, he'd struggle to the top of the room, settle on the curtain pole for several hours, and then dive-bomb at the sofa at some unforeseen time that *always* made Finley screech irrationally.

And now she had Peanut. And she was bedraggled on the best of days.

So, she'd always thought of herself as an animal person.

But maybe it *might* be nice to see some animals in all their glory. In their natural habitat. She wasn't an ecologist, by any means, but she was pretty certain there weren't many animals evolutionarily bred for a two-tiered cage in a Central London apartment.

Finley smiled softly as she scanned her eyes along the path before her, and the flowers that lined the walkway and the little garden around it.

Finley knew nothing about flowers. When she'd bought her apartment, the box along her balcony had already been blooming, and by some miracle it had continued to do so each season.

For all she knew, they could quite possibly be fake.

So, she really knew nothing about flowers, but she couldn't help but wish she could name the vast array of beautiful blooms in Sophie's garden. The *colours* were almost enchanting. Reds and blues and purples and oranges and the kinds of tealy-greens that Finley had never even known a flower could be. *Jewels* almost, amongst the well-tamed leaves and vines.

Finley didn't know, and didn't much care for flowers, but she couldn't help but be *insanely* jealous of the way they shone against the cobbled stone, and she wished hopelessly that she could line her own home with these, and not just the begonias in her shitty painted balcony box.

The entire aesthetic was quaint, and gorgeous, and Finley felt herself relax immediately.

Until the minute she stepped through the gate, and a goddamned *bat* dropped from the cottage porch, hurtling itself erratically in the direction of Finley's face. She screamed, somersaulting over her luggage as she dived, admittedly a *little* melodramatically, from its wayward path. She groaned meekly as she landed spread eagled across the cobblestones.

Jesus. And she'd thought Catapult was terrifying.

She sighed.

"Sweeping me off my feet already, are we Polcarne, Cornwall?" she mumbled, begrudgingly extracting herself from the mess of luggage and limbs as she hauled herself to her feet.

She fished the key from its spot on the ring alongside the car key, and stepped onto the thick-bristled welcome mat at the blue painted wooden door. She grinned at the *'home sweet home'* printed into the fibres beneath her feet, and at the little doorbell tucked into the side of the wooden arched overhead porch.

The house was even more beautiful on the inside.

Finley had seen the pictures, but even so she was impressed. The small space was light and airy, despite its low ceiling and thick exposed beams, and a modern looking log burner sat in the old converted fireplace in the living room.

The kitchen was open plan, fresh bright paint and clean slate tiles making the small space seem bigger, and a wide French doorway filled the room with natural light from the garden beyond it.

Finley had stepped all of 30 feet into this house, and it already felt like a home.

The light, pastel-coloured walls were complimented with brightly coloured canvas paintings, and patterned rugs, and a collection of scatter cushions that Finley was certain could rival the Dunelm at Brent Cross. The tea towels and the appliances and the mugs on the mug tree all boasted the same kind of jewel-tone colours that Finley had seen in the flowers along the cobblestone path, and the windowsills were lined with pots and pots of the healthiest houseplants she had ever seen.

She cringed as she thought of her own decrepit parlour palm, and what Sophie must be making of that travesty.

The house felt *kind*.

Which Finley felt was an extremely weird thought process to find herself on, but something about the home felt welcoming, and gentle, and caring, and she couldn't help but feel like that *had* to be a reflection of the person who lived here.

She grinned as her eyes landed on the coffee table, and a handwritten note with her name on it.

*Hi Finley,*

*Welcome to sunny Cornwall! I hope you found the place okay. Though I guess if you didn't, you wouldn't be reading this!*

*Please make yourself at home. I stocked the fridge and the cupboards this morning, and I even sent my sister to the butchers for you. She tells me the beef, in particular, is good.*

*The ciders on the counter are local brews. Don't be tempted to put them in the fridge. They're better at room temperature. Let me know what you think of them!*

*Anyway, I hope you enjoy your stay, and I've left some emergency numbers on the pad underneath this.*

*Use the Wi-Fi. The code is on the router.*

*Mobile signal isn't a thing in Polcarne.*

*Kernow a'gas dynnergh!*

*Sophie*

*x*

Finley smiled softly at the sign-off, making a mental note to scan the words with her translate app once she'd connected to the network.

Sophie sounded nice.

Her handwriting was really pretty. All rounded letters, and looping joins, and neatly dotted *i*'s.

Far prettier than Finley's inept scrawl.

She wondered if the woman's face was as pretty as her handwriting.

Or as pretty as her house.

Or the way her car smelled.

She shook her head, putting the note down with a defeated sigh.

She clearly *really* needed to relieve some tension.

She wondered if this house had a pressure shower…

~ ~ ~ ~ ~ ~ ♪ ~ ~ ~ ~ ~ ~

Sophie turned the dial on the shower in Finley's immaculate bathroom.

She squealed, throwing her arms out in an effort to catch herself as an *insanely* heavy cascade of ice-cold water plummeted hard against her face and her chest.

She fumbled with the various controls, her feet slipping on the tile as the water pressure did its damned best to knock her off her feet.

She exhaled heavily, spluttering slightly as she finally managed to turn the power down.

*Jesus* Christ.

Who the *fuck* was showering in *that*?

She chuckled, shaking her head as the pressure and the temperature evened out, the soft flow of warm water easing the tension from her adrenaline-soaked muscles.

Was the arctic power hose method some kind of city thing? Some sort of sadistic treatment for the warped and beaten bodies of the origami octopuses, stiff and bruised from a day of bending and cramming themselves into the tubes?

She wondered if Finley was an origami octopus.

She grinned as she pictured the woman she imagined would live in a home like this. The central location, and the beautiful apartment, and the copious gadgets suggested money, and success on a level that Sophie's small town mind could only begin to comprehend. The kind of success that Sophie always associated with stiff suits, and tower block offices, and huge conference rooms with large glass walls.

She wondered what Finley did for a living. Stock market, maybe. Or some kind of corporate financial management that made Sophie's jaw ache with boredom just to think about.

But then the vibrant character of Covent Garden felt like an odd place for someone *that* square.

It was central, sure, and Sophie was aware that not every person within a three-mile radius of a bar spent their whole life in it, but there was just something a little bit more *lively* and a little bit more whimsical about the location choice than the persona she had just painted of Finley.

She made a mental note to look around the home a little more. Find the *character* in it.

She shook her head of her thoughts, picking her shower bar from the little alcove shelf in the tiled walls, and beginning her usual routine. According to the *miraculous* new app on her phone, she'd had approximately eighteen minutes from the point in which she'd entered the bathroom until her food order arrived, and she'd already wasted several of those in a daydream.

The concept of Deliveroo was *unreal!*

Any food, from *any* venue in the area, delivered to her door?

Who'd have ever thought it?

She'd gotten a little over enthusiastic, admittedly, and had ordered dishes from three different venues simply because she could, and if she was honest, she was more than aware that she would not be eating more than half of her haul.

But she was excited!

She was on holiday. It was allowed.

Sophie shivered a little as she switched off the dial on the shower, reaching for the deep navy bath sheet Finley had left for her. She groaned contentedly as she wrapped the soft cotton around herself, warm over her skin from the heated towel rail.

How was a towel so heavenly?

Thick, and unnecessarily large, and just the right side of course.

Sophie didn't even dare think about what the thread count in this thing would be.

And they *smelled* so good. Like jasmine, and cedarwood and something *intriguing* somehow that made her nerves tingle.

Sophie managed to get herself clean and dry, and bundled into a threadbare t-shirt and pants, with four minutes to spare on her Deliveroo app. She practically skipped into the living room, her entire body buzzing with her elation at the thought that she was finally here.

In London.

Elation, and *pride.* Pride in herself for taking the leap.

Sure, maybe she wasn't here indefinitely. Maybe the return date on her train ticket, and the stranger's name on the post in her accommodation wasn't quite the lifestyle move to London that she dreamed of.

But it was a damn site closer to it than she'd been just yesterday, and she was proud of herself for being here.

In. *London.*

In the city of her dreams, with a feast fit for kings on its way to her door, a huge plush sofa waiting for her, and a blanket that smelled as good as the towel had.

She wondered if this was what Finley smelled like.

Sophie knew Finley was supposed to be irrelevant on this trip. She knew she was simply supposed to be a name on a travel website and an emergency contact, but Sophie couldn't help the curious part of her soul that needed to form a picture of the person who lived here, and the life they led.

The apartment had seemed immaculate as Sophie had entered it for the first time, but as she wandered it curiously now, Sophie could see the subtle, tired signs of a home that was often left vacant. Empty cupboards and a bare fridge, and hastily wiped down windows that smeared as the light caught them.

She wondered if Finley had cleaned this morning, for Sophie's sake.

She picked a few dead leaves off the dilapidated looking parlour palm, and peered into the bottom of its deep blue decorative pot. She chuckled, lifting the drowning plant from its swamp, and carrying it into the kitchen for a little TLC.

No wonder the others were plastic.

Perhaps Finley worked away a lot. Or perhaps she spent a lot of time with a partner, or family. Sophie couldn't help but be intrigued. She wanted to know more, and that was a relatively unhelpful mindset when she was supposed to be here to learn about *herself*.

When the buzzer rang, and Sophie finally sank onto the couch with her blanket and her banquet spread across the coffee table, she was almost vibrating with her giddy excitement.

She was completely, elatedly overwhelmed with the sheer range of vegan options that Deliveroo in London had offered her. Sophie spent hours of her life putting together a vegan menu in The Ship Inn, but she had never seen anything like this. Tofu gyros, and jerk tempeh, and jackfruit pepperoni pizza.

She'd never even *heard* of jackfruit pepperoni, and frankly she was almost sceptical about its authenticity.

The pizza was *so* good.

Surely there was no plausible way that this wasn't meat and dairy cheese, and yet the little green 'V' printed onto the labels told her that it was completely vegan friendly.

It made her feel weirdly emotional. Going vegan in Polcarne had been far from an easy ride. Sophie had lived her whole life surrounded by farmers and fisherman and gamekeepers and rifle shooters, and every single one of them had looked at her in, at best confusion, and at worst utter disdain when at the impressionable age of seventeen, she had announced she didn't wish to be involved in the murder or the consumption of living creatures.

Like *Sophie* was the extreme one. Like Sophie was the one who should feel embarrassed, and remorseful, and push her beliefs down to suit those of the people who surrounded her.

But here in London, a colourful little app on her phone screen had immediately validated her, and *encouraged* her, without her ever even needing to speak to a person.

She giggled, taking another unnecessarily large bite of her pizza.

She was excited, and incredulous, and she felt the overwhelming need to share it with someone, but frankly she wasn't sure she knew anyone who would care remotely about a gyros and some jackfruit pepperoni.

Unless…

She grinned, grabbing her phone from the coffee table. She pulled up a new message, and snapped a photo of her feast.

Sophie: *Deliveroo is celestial! I'm in love with London. Hope you made it okay. Sophie x*

Sophie had taken three mouthfuls when her phone buzzed.

Finley: *That didn't take long* 😂 *all you need is a pizza and a gyros to feel at home, right?*

Finley: *[Image Attached]*

Sophie grinned through a mouthful of garlic bread as her screen filled with the image of the open bay window in her own bathroom, a local brew cider bottle on the windowsill beside her bathtub. The fields beyond her house almost seemed to glow in the twilight, and Sophie couldn't help but think how different the sounds of the bats and the owls in the Cornish evening were, compared to the weird silence in this London apartment building, with its quadruple glazing, or full sound proofed walls or something.

Finley: *Forget Cornwall, I'm never leaving this bath. Top marks on the cider—thought it'd be weird warm, but it's actually pretty damn good!*

Sophie was halfway through typing her response, her mouth *way* too full of jackfruit pepperoni pizza, when a brush of fur over her pyjama clad legs sent her heart through her throat, and she screamed so high she'd swear the quadruple-glazed windows rattled.

She recoiled, dropping several pieces of jackfruit and one rogue piece of jerk tempeh across the floor as she shot her knees up and away from the furry intruder.

The cat seemed completely unperturbed.

Sophie panted, her entire body almost aching with adrenaline as she fought to calm the living fuck down.

For someone who once had found a *very* upset badger in her kitchen, and been dangerously unphased, Sophie had to admit she had probably overreacted a little here.

She eyed the weirdly cute mangy furball suspiciously as she typed out a message to Finley.

Sophie: *There's a cat in your living room, is that normal?*

Finley: *Oh my god, I'm so sorry! That's Peanut. Or at least it better be…Tell her she's supposed to be with her uncle Noah!*

Finley: *She has a real tendency to sneak through open windows.*

Finley: *…you're not terrified of her, are you?*

Sophie blushed, feeling somehow caught out for her dramatic overreaction to Peanut's presence.

She grinned as the cat jumped up onto her lap, nestling her head under Sophie's chin.

"Hi, *Peanut,*" Sophie cooed. "Isn't your name just *perfect* for that unusual little nose!"

This cat was somehow simultaneously the ugliest thing she had ever seen, and the cutest. She was affectionate, and wide eyed, and impossibly adorable despite clearly being a bit tragic. Sophie grinned at the first of the flat's blatant indicators of its owner's persona.

The fact that *this* was the animal that Finley chose to love was incredibly endearing. The weird, tufty fur still shone with the healthy glow of a well-kept animal, and the skinny legs completely contradicted the comfortable fullness to Peanut's belly. That, and the fact that Peanut was so comfortable, and so affectionate, suggested that however much Finley may have neglected her house plant, she clearly didn't do the same with her cat.

"Of *course,* I'm not scared of you; am I baby? Cause you're so *gorgeous,*" Sophie cooed, scooping the affectionate cat up into her arms. "Come on beautiful, come join Auntie Sophie in the blankets."

Sophie nestled herself back, holding her phone up above her as she snapped a photo.

She grinned.

That was cute, even if she did say so herself.

Peanut's wonky, wet little nose was pressed up against Sophie's cheek, and her rough little tongue licked at her flushed face in a way she was absolutely *certain* a cat had never done before. Sophie's laugh was genuine, and her green eyes sparkled visibly through the small screen of her phone.

She wondered if Finley would mind if she set this as her Instagram profile photo.

Sophie: *How could I be scared of this? What a little sweetie! Making new friends already.*

She attached the image to her text message, and hit send.

~ ~ ~ ~ ~ ~ 🐾 ~ ~ ~ ~ ~ ~

298 miles away, Finley choked on her cider.

Sophie was *beautiful.*

Beautiful in a way that Finley hadn't seen in a long time. All auburn waves, and sparkling eyes, and tinted cheeks, and the soft hint of dimples.

And she was in Finley's blankets, looking more relaxed in Finley's home than Finley had been in a long time, getting kisses from her runty little cat.

Five and a half hours away from where Finley was lying alone in a free-standing bathtub with a bottle of local cider and a share bag of sea salt crisps.

*Bollocks.*

# Chapter Seven

Sophie ran her fingers absently through Peanut's fur, her eyes fluttering open as she flicked them to the clock on the bedside table.

7am.

She had been lying in bed awake for over an hour, just listening to the muffled sounds of London as it woke.

She was pretty sure Finley must have had quadruple glazing in this place, because the sounds were *so* quiet this side of the glass.

It felt *crazy* good to know what lay just the other side of her cocoon. To know that the world outside her window was *full* of possibility, and opportunity, and experience.

She felt her heart flutter as she imagined how it would feel to wake up with London *every* morning. How it would feel to build her life around the sounds of the city, and the air of potential.

She imagined how it would feel to wake up in this bed every morning, in this beautiful apartment.

It would need a little *Sophie-ing,* of course.

The consistent neutral themes would need a little shaking up. A few brighter, more complimentary shades would need throwing in.

And there were definitely *nowhere near* enough scatter cushions.

And she'd need a space-themed bedroom, for her future astronaut's visits. And a lot more books. And an overwhelming number of family photos.

But with her own personal touches, Sophie imagined she could get used to waking up with the city of London outside her window. She could see herself learning to use the obscene coffee machine she'd spotted last night, and maybe she could even see herself turning the pressure up just a little higher on that power shower.

The heat would have to stay.

Only a maniac would shower in *that* ice water.

But she could adjust to the absence of her bath, and her bay windows. She could learn to navigate the tubes, and the city above them. She could do it all, if at the other end of it, she would get to work in a museum, full of all types of exhibitions and all types of people.

She could do it all if she would get to live in the world that today she would see for the first time. She was sure she could.

Now that she was here, away from the clutches of Polcarne for the first time in her twenty-six years, she knew she could.

And that was liberating.

Sophie stretched, groaning as her muscles ached in satisfaction. She had planned to get up early and get out into the heart of London before the morning rush, but Finley's bed was a five-foot-wide paradise, and she was having a *very* hard time leaving it.

She stretched harder, forcing her muscles to shake off the sleepy satiation, and to resist the urge to cuddle further into the bedsheets, and Peanut's fur.

She was pretty sure this duvet was duck feather, and as a vegan, Sophie *really* couldn't get behind this. But right now, she didn't have much choice, and *god* she would be lying if she said it wasn't comfortable.

She had also discovered a sleek black remote control that tilted the head of the bed up, and raised a goddamn fucking 52inch TV screen from the footboard.

It was obscene, and Sophie loved it.

She had immediately switched it on, flicked onto Netflix, and had a cheeky look at the things Finley had been watching. She didn't know what she had expected from the person who lived in this apartment. Maybe documentaries, or dramas, or maybe even a few psychological thrillers. But what she certainly *hadn't* expected was the long list of cartoons, and not a lot else.

Sophie grabbed her phone, smirking as she pulled up a text message to Finley.

She didn't know why, but something just compelled her to talk to this woman. Perhaps it was that she was in Finley's home. Or perhaps it was the shared experience. The fact that only Finley knew what she was living right now, and vice versa.

Perhaps it was the way she knew Finley didn't come with the preconceptions that her lifelong peers in Polcarne did. That Finley was something fresh, and new. Just like London.

Whichever way, Sophie couldn't help but share her thoughts.

Sophie: *I've got a worrisome feeling that my house is a bit too low tech for you! This place is like Tony Stark's holiday home.*

Sophie: *Though your love for the animated Garfield series does make it feel a bit less Iron Man and more Peter Parker.* 😌 *Hope you made it out of the bath.*

She certainly hadn't expected a response so early in the morning, but she grinned as her phone chimed almost immediately.

Finley: *I'll be honest, I resented having to grind my own coffee beans this morning. Felt like a 19th century miller's daughter.* 😌 *But god, was the taste worth it. And Garfield is for Peanut!*

Finley: *Spongebob Squarepants is for me.* 🍪 🥠

Finley: *Begrudgingly, yes, I dragged myself out and slept like a baby in your marshmallow bed. Do you always sleep with seventeen blankets?*

Finley: *Have you got your Polaroid and your fanny pack ready for a day of sightseeing?* 💁 📷

Sophie laughed, shaking her head. She knew they had barely spoken, but she really liked something about the easy way that Finley talked. And the way she wasn't afraid to text like she talked, either. It felt natural, with no games.

She jumped as the shrill sound of the buzzer rang out across the hall, and she frowned as she double checked the time.

Who knocked on doors at *7am?*

Maybe Finley had a delivery? Maybe it was the food shop? Did they deliver at this hour?

She jumped from the bed, fumbling with the catches of her suitcase as she hurried to find appropriate clothing. She hadn't bothered to unpack last night, and had simply crawled into bed in the first flimsy tank and tatty briefs she could grab from the top of her bag.

And she wasn't overly keen on a delivery driver seeing the holes in her rainbow print boxers.

She pulled frantically at the clothes in her suitcase, grunting in frustration as every item she touched just seemed to get less and less appropriate, and more and more like something that would be sociopathic to answer a door in at 7am. Her swimsuit, her dress for the theatre, her one sharp blazer that she'd brought on a whim just in case she happened to get a miraculous interview for a London Museum.

Sophie's hand had just closed around the promising fabric of denim jeans, when the unmistakable sound of a fist rapping against the front door to the apartment sent her heart catapulting out of her ass.

She squeaked, slamming her jaw shut as she jumped away from her suitcase as if somehow that was the intruder in this situation.

Wasn't she in a second-floor apartment?

With a whole key code setup going on, that should definitely have been a barrier between the front door and complete strangers?

So, whoever was currently the other side of the thin wooden door was either an axe murderer with a high-tech ability to dismantle computer systems, or someone who knew the code and likely had a legitimate reason to be calling.

And neither one needed to see Sophie in her threadbare boxers.

She panicked.

She flitted her eyes around the room almost desperately, squeaking in triumph as she spotted a jet-black fleece robe on the back of the bedroom door.

She made a quick decision.

*God* this was soft.

And it *smelled* incredible. Jasmine, and cedarwood, and amber. The same scent that had captivated her on the towels, and the blankets. She'd noticed it on the sheets last night too, but it was duller there. Overpowered by the smell of lavender fabric conditioner.

She wondered, briefly, if Finley smelled like this.

The thought made her stomach feel a little strange.

Clearly it had been *way* too long since Sophie had been genuinely attracted to someone, if the smell of cedarwood on a complete stranger's robe was giving her butterflies.

Christ, she needed to get a grip.

Not least because there was still someone at the door.

She pushed the strange feeling down, rushing through the hall as the door rapped for the third time.

She flung back the door, recoiling as she was met with the drawn fist of a *very* anxious looking man. His curly dark hair clearly hadn't been tamed since he'd woken up, and his clothes hinted at the same state of 'thrown on in a panic' that Sophie's own attire was. His grey joggers were threadbare and far too long around his ankles, and his t-shirt had several moth-eaten holes that Sophie was *fairly* sure were not a fashion statement.

Although in London, who really knew?

Sophie might have recoiled at a strange man in the doorway of a strange place at 7am, with a full aura of sheer panic. But there was something so openly kind in his dark eyes, even through the anxiety, that kept Sophie's nerves calm.

"Oh thank *god!*"

The anxiety in the man's face dropped along with his fist, and he launched instantly into a sheepish apology.

"Sophie, right? I am *so* sorry to barge up here and disturb your holiday and *especially* this early and on your *first morning...*" the stranger groaned as he winced. "But I'm losing my mind, and I don't know what else to do. Is the cat here? Finley's gonna *kill* me if she's not, that thing is like her *baby...*"

Sophie beamed.

Awkward, rambling, endearing...

She liked this guy already.

She wondered what his relationship was to Finley. A brother, maybe? Or a friend? A boyfriend?

He looked about her own age, and it occurred to her in the moment that she actually had no idea how old Finley was. She had just assumed they were similar in age, but that was based on no foundation other than her own imagination. And a scattering of group photos she'd seen around the apartment, but she had no idea how old those were. Finley could just as easily have been a pensioner, for all Sophie knew.

A very tech-savvy one.

But maybe that was normal in London.

"Well, then, you're in luck!" She grinned. "You must be Peanut's uncle Noah."

The man's face softened, his lips quirking into an abashed, almost humbled smile.

"Did...is that what Finley said?" His smile widened, and he shuffled slightly, clearly fighting to hide the pride that Sophie's words had built. "She called me Uncle Noah?"

"She did," Sophie giggled, nodding her head. "Did you want to come in? I'm about to tackle the ridiculous looking coffee machine I spotted in the kitchen last night. If I can figure it out, you're welcome to stay for one."

"Ah, well now *you're* in luck!" Noah grinned. "I happen to be a *master* in that machine."

"Then you came at just the right time, and I would really appreciate your mastery," Sophie chuckled, stepping aside to allow Noah to enter.

Noah had no sooner closed the door behind him, when Peanut padded almost arrogantly into the hallway, digging her claws casually into the wooden floors as she stretched. Not a care in the world.

*"Peanut Bennett!"* Noah shrieked, making a beeline for the cat. "Do not *ever* do that to Uncle Noah again, I've been worried sick!"

Bennett.

Sophie grinned.

Finley Bennett.

It had a nice ring to it.

"Why did you do me like this, huh?" Noah huffed, scooping Peanut up and into his arms, his face nuzzling into the cat's fur. "I set all your favourite things up at home, I gave you a box, I put *'Top Cat'* on, I thought we had a bond?"

"So the cartoons really are for the cat, are they?" Sophie chuckled, gesturing for Noah to lead the way into the kitchen. "I figured that was a weak excuse."

"They're not *not* for the cat, but I don't think Finley really minds having them on." Noah winked, grinning cheekily. "I mean, Peanut got her love from *somewhere,* right? A street cat doesn't just spark up a love for cartoons without a little push."

Sophie laughed.

"A street cat?" she repeated. She glanced at Peanut, her skinny legs sticking out in all kinds of odd directions as she tried to roll onto her back in Noah's arms for him to stroke her stomach. Another act Sophie wasn't entirely convinced she'd ever seen a cat do. She chuckled softly. That definitely made some sense. "Was she a rescue?"

Noah nodded.

"By our very own Miss Finley Bennett herself, no less."

"Really?" Sophie raised her eyebrows, surprise and interest pooling warm in her stomach. "How?"

"Ah, it was *very* heroic," Noah chuckled. "Fin climbed down a disgusting mud verge on mile five of a *really* rainy run to rescue this thing that I was just…*so* sure was a water vole."

Sophie snorted.

Noah grinned.

"It just looked so...*bedraggled* and washed out," he laughed. "Fin was sliding down this verge like some sort of gladiator, and I was just *shouting* at her. It was wet, I had a stitch, the water vole looked dead, and I was convinced Finley was just gonna come back with ruined trainers and tetanus."

"Do you even *get* water voles in London?" Sophie laughed.

"I don't know, to be honest," Noah chuckled. "Anything with fur looks the same to me."

"Well, then," Sophie cooed, reaching forward to scratch Peanut's belly. "Sounds like *someone* is lucky it was their heroic mum who spotted them that day, not Uncle Noah."

"She definitely is," Noah laughed, nodding in agreement. "The rescue wasn't even the most heroic part. Finley reached the bottom of the verge, picked this half dead thing up, and then stripped her whole-ass shirt off in the middle of the rain to wrap it up in. Start of a lifetime of being *way* too pampered for your own good, wasn't it, Peanut."

Peanut grunted.

"Wait, what? She just got naked in the streets of London in a downpour, because Peanut was cold?" Sophie laughed. "You're right, that does sound *very* heroic, I'm impressed."

Noah grinned.

"Sophie, I don't think I've even *looked* at a woman since I was, like, twelve years old," he chuckled, "but even *I* will admit that it was pretty sexy watching my best friend carry a sickly animal out of a distressed situation, in a sports bra, several litres of mud, and a hefty soaking of rainwater."

Sophie quirked an eyebrow.

She had no idea what Finley looked like, but she was filling in some gaps, and she also had to admit the image was appealing.

Noah scrunched his nose.

"Then she fell, like, six times on the way back up, and it did get a *bit* less sexy with each fall," he sighed. "Turns out there is a line in how much mud can look appealing on a person. And the slow-ass walk home in a lycra t-shirt in the pissing rain was probably the least fun I've ever had."

Sophie grinned. She was warming to Noah incredibly quickly, and the simple story was only sparking her intrigue in her house host more.

"I'm also *pretty* sure that's half the reason Peanut is so…*misshapen,"* Noah winced. "But that was four years ago, and Peanut Bennett has been the most pampered water vole I have ever known ever since."

Sophie chuckled. She reached her hand forward once again, to scratch her nails over the back of Peanut's ears.

She jumped, her eyes flying wide and her cheeks flushing red as the ties around the robe grew loose, and the material began to slip apart.

She straightened instantly, her hands fumbling with the ties as she tried to adjust the material in time to protect her dignity, and the faded, moth-eaten rainbow boxers from this near stranger's view.

"Shit," Noah started, his eyes sheepish as he moved to place Peanut down onto the floor. "I'm *so* sorry, I've completely bombarded your morning! Go, you get yourself sorted. I can work my mastery on the coffee machine. Latte, espresso, or cappuccino?"

Sophie blinked.

"Uh…" she faltered, her brow furrowing as she studied the machine, she was suddenly *very* glad to not be battling alone. "Just, like…"

Noah grinned, making his way past Sophie and over towards the kitchen cupboards.

"A normal coffee with milk and sugar like everyone but Finley Bennett drinks in the mornings?" He laughed.

"Yeah!" Sophie breathed out a laugh. "If that's an option. But no milk, thank you." She winced apologetically. "I'm vegan."

"No big, I'm dairy free!" Noah shrugged, nonchalant and nonplussed as he reached into a cupboard above his head, pulling out two matching navy mugs. "Fin usually has long-lasting oat milk somewhere in the barren cupboards, so I'll dig about."

Sophie beamed.

For the second time in less than twelve hours, London and the people in it had effortlessly made her feel seen.

And something about that was *extremely* effective at ebbing away her lifelong fears.

She excused herself almost giddily, leaving Noah to navigate the coffee machine while Sophie took the time to get herself dressed in some actual clothes.

And type Finley Bennett into Instagram.

Obviously.

Sophie clicked on the first return, and promptly choked on her own tongue.

*Jesus Christ* in a Kit Kat wrapper, was *this* Finley?

There weren't a huge number of results, and the profile photo was distinctly London. A beautiful brunette straddling a pushbike over London Bridge.

*Wow,* she really *was* hot.

Sophie's mind flashed, a vivid image of the woman in this photo climbing a muddy verge, wearing a sports bra and carrying a drowning cat. And honestly, she was pretty certain *that* should have been a Diet Coke ad.

Sophie scrolled through the most recent posts, her stomach splintering into a thousand butterflies as she came across an image of the brunette spread across the sofa in this very flat in sweats and an oversized hoodie, Peanut curled in the crook of her lap.

She swallowed thickly.

Suddenly she felt *very* flustered, sitting half naked in this woman's robe after a night in her sheets.

Somehow the smell of jasmine and cedarwood was even more enticing in the new knowledge, and Sophie cringed as she processed how *sad* it was that no-one, she'd ever dated had given her butterflies quite like this one photo of this gorgeous stranger had.

Kyle Brown could only *wish.*

She kept scrolling.

Holy fuck, those *eyes.* Even through the small phone screen, the warm mocha seemed to sink right into her, and Sophie's spine tingled.

She closed her eyes, her skin prickling with heat and her pulse thumping in her throat.

Well.

*Certainly* not a pensioner.

She shook the adrenaline rush from her fingers, and replied to Finley's texts. Even that felt a little different now.

Now that she knew she was texting a goddamn fucking *goddess.*

She took a deep breath, taking a moment to pull her shit together before she got herself dressed and headed back out to her unexpected guest.

Who she would now need to find a casual way to grill for more information on her astronomically sexy house host.

~ ~ ~ ~ ~ ~ 🐾 ~ ~ ~ ~ ~ ~

Finley's feet pounded the sand as she ran along the dusty path to the beach, the early morning air fresher than she'd ever known as it blew across the sea that she was yet to glimpse.

She was no stranger to a morning run, but something in the clear breeze in the air, and the faint taste of salt in her lungs was invigorating, and Finley could feel every one of the past week's mortifying moments fade further away with every muted slap of her trainers against the soft ground.

Her runs in London were always predominantly flat. Even surfaces and long, straight roads that lent themselves to speed and distance covered. It had become very quickly apparent to Finley this morning that the Cornish coast was far from flat. The Cornish coast was less about speed, and more about *stamina.* The peaks and troughs of the hilly terrain were sparking a burn deep in the back of Finley's legs that she wasn't used to, and she liked it. She made a mental note to boast to Noah about it later.

Sophie had been right about the lack of phone signal. There were patches where it picked up, but the general lack meant that Finley couldn't stream her music, and her fitness tracker was being very spotty, and she was being forced to do this the natural way and enjoy the sounds and the scents and the breeze and the view instead of her usual technology.

Which was nice. It was refreshing, in a primal kind of way. But lots of the *view* was exactly the same, and contrary to rather popular opinion, Finley found it just a little on the boring side. She'd been running for over three miles, and all she'd seen were fields and bushes and winding roads, and *way* too many cows. Finley had never known there were different types of cows, but the things here all looked completely different from one field to the next. One giant horned thing had looked set for battle when she'd passed closely by it in the narrow lane. She wasn't even a hundred percent sure some of them were cows, if she were honest, but her city brain couldn't identify what else the hulking things might be.

And also, there were horses, and that was terrifying. Didn't horses need to be in stables, with saddles and shit?

In her fourth mile, Finley began to feel herself wane a little, with the extra effort of the hills, and without the distractions of her technology to keep her going.

And then she saw it.

The sea.

The Atlantic Ocean. Or the Celtic Sea. Or maybe even the English Channel.

Google seemed to think it was all three, and Finley wasn't entirely sure how it worked, if she was honest.

But either way, it wasn't the banks of the river Thames, and Finley would be lying if she said she wasn't a little overwhelmed by its presence.

Sure she'd seen the sea before, but not here.

Not in the UK.

The sea was something Finley associated with long ago trips to sunny coasts of Mediterranean Europe, and even those were a distant memory of a time before her office and her home were the only places she ever saw.

It was not something she associated with her home country.

She'd had no idea it could be so *beautiful* here.

The deep blue of the sea, against the greens and the browns and the whites of the hills and the sands were mesmerising in a way that Finley hadn't expected, and she felt all of the tension expel heavily from her chest as she watched the bob and the sway of the water.

The way the waves broke on the shoreline, the same wave never made twice. The way the shades of blues and greys darkened as the waters grew deeper, until they dropped off the edge of the naked eye. The way even the dull British sun bounced sparkling gems from the surface, dancing away faster than the eye could trap them.

And the *sounds.*

The gentle lap of the waves and the sweep of the wind felt so much more refreshing to her ears than the brash sounds of the city that she worked so hard to block out every night in London. And they seemed to *change* depending on the way she chose to listen.

She was entranced.

She slowed to a walk as she stepped from the pavestone and onto the sand, the need to run stilled in her veins now that the sea consumed her senses. The sand was soft beneath the rubber of her trainers, and she smiled softly to herself as she stopped to peel off her shoes and socks.

The feel of the sand in Finley's toes as she curled them through it was weirdly satisfying, in a way she would never have expected. The *cold* of it, even in the mild air, should have been a paradox. Sand and sea were things of heat and sunshine, and coconut lotion and bikinis. Not of running lycra, cold waters and grey skies.

And yet it felt somehow even more refreshing this way. More grounding, and less like a fantasy.

More *real*.

Finley's lips spread instinctively into a beaming grin as she made her way slowly along the beach, her toes curling with each step, and her eyes transfixed on the water. The tide was on its way out. Or in. Honestly, Finley didn't understand it for love or money, but either way, the shoreline was quite far down the beach, and the barnacle-covered rocks stood proud from the damp sand around them.

Finley grinned, childlike and almost giddy as she reached the clusters of rocks. They weren't high, by any stretch. The tallest barely reached Finley's chest, but somehow the thought of climbing them and watching the sea from above them felt weirdly empowering.

She shuffled, gripping her trainers in one hand as she stepped up onto the lowest of the seaweed-lined rocks.

She winced.

The rough edges, and the loose stones and protruding barnacles were deceptively painful beneath her bare feet, and she faltered as she processed that maybe this was a venture she should be taking with her shoes on. Alas, that wasn't a feasible option right now, as her feet were caked in cold, wet sand, and she didn't very much fancy wearing socks full of sea-sludge for her four-mile run back to the cottage.

Maybe she didn't think this all the way through.

She climbed as high as her protesting feet would allow her, before surrendering and sitting herself down on the driest patch of rock she could find, and turning her eyes back to the mesmerising sea.

She smiled softly, almost wistfully as she let her mind conjure the memories of the last time, she'd really taken the time to watch the sea.

The last time she'd seen her mother.

On the coast of Albufeira, in the summer of 2017. Finley had been holidaying with Jess. Her mother had been parked in Santa Luzia, in her weather-beaten van.

The same van she'd jumped into all those years beforehand, when Finley had been just twelve, and driven into the sunset with a new man and a new life, and broken Finley's heart.

Her mother had said a lot of things that night. Most of which were nothing but a blur in Finley's mind. But the last line had never left her.

*I'll come back for you, Bambi. We can be free together.*

Finley sighed, picking absently at the rock below her as she watched the ripples in the ocean.

April Ashlock had kept her promise. She had come back for her. Five years later, when Finley was seventeen and determined.

Determined never to live the life her father demanded of her, *or* the one her mother abandoned her for.

Determined to stand on her own feet, and need nobody but herself.

Finley had stayed, and broken her mother's heart right back.

The next time they'd seen each other, Finley had been twenty-five. She'd been sipping Douro Port on the beach of Albufeira, with just enough forgiveness in her heart to sit through one long and poignant evening meal, watching the waves crash on the rocks of Praia dos Arrifes. The night her mother had tried one more time to tell Finley there was more to life than suits and salaries. The night she'd tried to coax her one more time into a life of bare toes, and open-air breakfasts over gas stoves, and marijuana and the open road.

Finley had been tempted, for the briefest crash of the waves.

But she hadn't wanted it. Not in her heart. And the gentle move of the waves had been her guide that night. Kept her head calm, and quiet, and clear enough to see her own mind.

That had been the last time Finley had seen her mother, and the last time she'd let anyone rock the boat she'd built for herself. The last time she'd let anyone question her dreams.

Finley chuckled softly, shaking her head as the crash and lull of the waves soothed her crowded mind, bringing her back to the here and the now. Holding her grounded, just like it had then.

She thought of Sophie.

She imagined the russet-haired girl in the photograph standing on the water's edge, or sitting on the rocks with a book and a thermal flask. She imagined how it would feel to have this escape on your doorstep every time the world got too much.

Was the ocean as magical to Sophie as it was to Finley?

Did Sophie still come here and watch the waves in the same way, even after a lifetime by the sea?

Or would this too, grow old like familiar soil always did?

Finley sighed.

She was all too aware that it was *ridiculous* to be thinking about Sophie.

She didn't *know* the girl.

But she *was* gorgeous, she really did seem quite sweet, and Finley was *deathly* single.

So, to be honest, she was happy to have a pretty girl to think about for a while, even if it was based on one selfie, a few scattered photo frames and a smattering of text messages.

She pulled her phone from her running belt, checking her screen for the stats of her run.

The message icon was flashing.

Four new messages.

Sophie: *It's four blankets, drama queen. We don't all have duck feather duvets.*

Sophie: *Of course, but something's missing. You got an 'I Love London' t-shirt lying around here somewhere? I want to really fit in.*

Sophie: *P.S. Uncle Noah spoiled our fun. [Image Attached]*

Finley's stomach flipped as her screen filled with a photo of Noah holding a disgruntled-looking Peanut in her carry crate, Sophie pouting as she held the camera up above them.

*God* she was adorable.

And really *very* sexy.

Finley shook her head, a blush burning her cheeks as she hastily closed the conversation before she said something stupid, pulling up the message from her friend instead.

Noah: *So, Sophie's cute…*

Finley: *I am so painfully aware.* 🙈

Finley: *Did she say anything about me?*

Noah: *And why would she have done that?*

Finley: *I don't know, maybe she's wondering about me too?*

Finley was *so* aware of how ridiculous that statement was. She knew most people would not be doing that.

Sophie was absolutely not standing at the banks of the river Thames, staring at the water and wondering if Finley saw the same colours.

Because most people were not that irrationally intense.

For god's fucking sake.

But then, maybe…

Finley: *So, is that a no?*

Noah: *God you are so single.*

Finley sighed.

"Don't I know it," she grumbled, pushing her phone back into her belt.

She watched the water for a few moments longer, letting the lull of the waves calm her heartbeat. Then she sighed, heaved herself up, stumbled painfully down the rocks, and began to make her way back along the beach in the direction she'd come from.

She rinsed her feet in the sea, chuckling with satisfaction as the heavy cakes of sand washed away from her skin with the waves.

Then she frowned.

She was now several hundred yards from the pavestone paths, with nothing but sand between her and where she needed to be. But her feet were wet, and if she put them in her socks now then she would drench them. And if she didn't put them in her socks now, then she'd collect another sand cake by the time she reached the path.

How did beachy people manage this?

Also, the sand *looked* like it had all washed from her feet, but they still *felt* suspiciously grainy, and Finley couldn't help but feel like she was in a bit of a lose-lose situation.

She sighed resignedly, grimacing as she pulled her socks onto her sandy, wet, no doubt salty feet, and slid them instantly into her sweaty trainers. The audible squelch of the shoes as Finley took her first step over the sand wasn't overly promising, and she could already feel the grain rubbing around the edges of her trainers, so it seemed blisters were a blatant inevitability by the time she took them off again. But honestly, she couldn't pretend it wasn't worth it.

Finley chuckled, taking one last long, lingering look at the sea before she turned, picking up her pace once again as she started on the four-mile run back to the cottage.

# Chapter Eight

Sophie was pretty certain her entire body was visibly vibrating with excitement as she entered the grand foyer of the British Museum.

For almost all of her twenty-six years on the planet, Sophie had been obsessed with everything that had come before her. She'd been mesmerised by the lives that had been led and the paths that had been walked that would lead to the world she knew today, and she was *finally* going to get to see some of the most famous artefacts in global history up close and personal.

Even if they were mostly pilfered and stolen with long histories of violence and oppression. One day Sophie would change that. But for now, she was selfishly euphoric to get the chance to see them.

She bit back a squeal as she positioned the headphones over her ears, and selected the first exhibit from the list on the little device she had been given for the audio guides.

Egypt.

Ancient, and cultured, and otherworldly. Fascinating, in its architecture and its religion and its customs.

Unlike anything she could say for Cornwall, and those *fucking* arrowheads.

She squealed with giddy excitement as she approached the exhibition of Egyptian Sculptures.

She'd known this would blow her away, but she felt her throat close a little in her overwhelming awe at just how incredible the artefacts were to see up close. So weirdly abstract, alien and detached somehow in this huge marble room, with their glass cases and their pristine information boards. Yet the history behind them was so *real* and so *tangible*. The things they'd been, and seen, and survived. And somehow the custom-made replicas were almost as interesting alongside the real artefacts; fine details noticed and mirrored and honed until it was almost hard to tell them apart.

She almost felt wistful. She felt elated, unbridled excitement through every inch of her veins, and she wanted to *share* it. She wanted to squeal, and jump, and vent her excitement until she was blue in the face, to someone who would actually *care.*

But she wasn't sure she knew who that was.

Bex would listen. She always did. So would Linda. But they didn't *care.* Not really.

The only person Sophie had known in twenty-six years who had cared as much about history as she did was her father. And for nineteen years, Sophie hadn't been able to share the twinkle in her eyes with him, or anyone else in Polcarne.

But here in London, Sophie felt so sure that she was just mere feet from others who would care as much as she did. And that felt indulgently empowering.

She wondered, for the briefest of moments, whether Noah had seen this exhibition. Maybe she should have invited him.

Or whether Finley had. She wondered if her gorgeous house host had ever cared enough to bother.

She blushed immediately as she realised, she was thinking about this complete stranger again for the tenth time today, and right in the middle of living out one of her lifelong dreams, no less.

She winced.

Pathetic.

Finley Bennett was *just* a pretty woman. It wasn't like Sophie had never seen one of those before.

She grinned, her shameful thoughts breaking as a small group of children gathered around her, their excitable voices ringing out above the audio guide in her headphones.

*"Look!"* A little boy no older than eight or nine pointed at a block of hieroglyphics carved into the stone. "It's a secret code!"

Sophie opened her mouth.

She couldn't help it. It was instinctive.

"It's *kind* of like a secret code to *us,* but it was actually just their way of writing letters!" she explained, smiling brightly as four little faces turned to hers in rapt attention. "Just like any other language. These are called *hieroglyphs. "*

"Hi-ro-gliffs?"

Sophie smiled as a young girl in a green sundress tested the word out on her tongue, her eyes wide with eager curiosity and her brow creased in concentration.

"That's right. See this chart here?" Sophie pointed to the wall beside them. "That tells you what all the different letters are."

"So, we can work it out *like* a code?" the little boy exclaimed excitedly.

"Exactly!" Sophie grinned. "So that lion there is an *L*. And then those two lines there are an *I*. So, you can translate it into letters that you know."

"Wow, that's so cool!"

"Very cool," Sophie nodded.

Four sets of little fingers prodded and poked at the chart, and Sophie stepped back to allow the children the space to see the symbols on the stone.

She felt elated.

Her stomach was fluttering, and her chest was swelling with pride and passion for the thing that she had loved so much for all of her life. Here, in a city 300 miles away from where Sophie had learned everything she knew, she had been able to share something with someone who had wanted to listen.

Okay, so it hadn't *quite* been a discussion with an archaeologist, or a seminar on Mycenaean Civilisation, but those children had shown more interest in the hundred words she had said to them, than anyone in Polcarne had done in anything historical that she had tried to talk about in a *long* time.

And that felt amazing.

She imagined doing this every day. Leading people round the exhibitions, imparting her knowledge and watching bright eyes shine with the same enthusiasm that she felt in her own heart. Maybe even that could be enough. Maybe even simply being a tour guide somewhere like this could make her so much happier than pulling pints in The Ship Inn ever could.

Maybe she really *could* be a Londoner.

Maybe.

~ ~ ~ ~ ~ ~ ♪ ~ ~ ~ ~ ~ ~

Finley gritted her teeth, her abs clenching as the kayak wobbled precariously beneath her feet. This wasn't her first rodeo, but she was quickly finding that navigating the rock of the boat on the sea was *far* more demanding than the gentle banks of the Thames at Tower Hamlets.

As beautiful as it had been from the shore, at this proximity the sea was freezing cold, it was full of seaweed, and Finley really wasn't overly keen on the idea of wearing the slimy plants as a scarf, so if these waves could just *chill* out a bit while she climbed into the damn boat, that would be wonderful.

She hadn't planned this when she woke up this morning, but her run along the beach had left her mesmerised by the waters. So, when she had found a pile of flyers for things to do that Sophie had left on the coffee table, she had been instantly drawn to the kayaks along the quiet beach.

Well.

Not *instantly*.

*Instantly,* she had noticed Sophie's surname printed on the front of a brochure sent from the National Trust, typed it straight into her Instagram search bar, and promptly choked on her Weetabix over a photo of the windswept beauty on a paddleboard.

But once she had cleared her airways, stalked her gorgeous house host for an unacceptable length of time, deliberated for a painful minute over whether it was too soon to follow the account, and decided it was, she had *then* been drawn to the kayaks.

And so, she found herself on the water.

Despite the initial mistrust of the rippling waves, Finley quickly found herself relaxing into the ebb and flow of the blue around her. It felt different here. When she and Noah took to the kayaks on the Thames, it was a sport. A plight for speed, and grace, and distance covered and time achieved. Something she could *win*.

Here it was leisure. A chance to let nature take her for a while, and to go where the water wanted her to.

She couldn't help but think that everything in Polcarne felt a little like that.

Calmer. Slower.

None of the people she had seen on her journey or her run had seemed rushed. Even the farmers and the fishermen and the people in uniforms seemed so much less *uptight*.

She imagined her own life that way. The freedom she could feel with just a little less pressure. To go from not enough time to breathe, to just enough time to live.

She frowned.

What would she even *do* in a place like this?

Finley's whole life was driven by ambition. By swinging stubbornly from one goal to the next, fuelled by the incessant fiery need to be *good* at something.

She wasn't sure there was much here to fuel the fire.

Maybe Polcarne was a little *too* remote. But maybe there was a happy medium?

A bigger town. Smaller than the city she drowned in, but with life and prospects and the freedom not to have to choose between the two.

Or *maybe* she simply needed to learn to take a step back and fall in love with her own city again.

She let her mind relax as her body took over the work, finding her stride as she paddled her kayak around the rocky coastline. The tide was lower now, and the water flooded in around the rocks she'd climbed earlier that morning.

She was still astounded by just how beautiful it was. She paddled further out, finding little nooks of rocky caves, and trees growing at obscure angles from bizarre patches of green amongst the jagged brown, and quiet beaches at the bottoms of *very* questionable looking cliff paths.

And then, in a moment of utter bewilderment, she stumbled across an animal she absolutely had not expected to find sunning itself on the rocks off the Cornish coast.

She blinked, her heart lurching into her throat and her brain questioning everything she'd ever understood about the world as she squinted in confusion at the rounded shape at the edges of her eyeline.

Was that a *seal?*

Surely not.

Finley may not have been an ecology expert, but everything she'd learned from David Attenborough suggested seals lived in, like, the North Pole or some shit. Arctic temperatures, with snow, and ice, and cameramen in fur-lined parkas.

Not half-assed sunlight on the shores of England.

Was it *lost?*

Finley pushed her paddle through the water, her curious excitement getting the better of her as she tried to catch a closer glimpse of the sunbathing seal.

Until the seal moved, twisting its body to better catch the sun, and Finley faltered.

Was it…safe?

What if it was hungry?

Finley's muscles tensed, her *flight* instinct absolutely beginning to kick in, and knocking the curiosity way into the depths of her stomach.

She was confidently certain that seals ate penguins. Right? She'd seen enough *'Planet Earth'* to know that was a given. But she was also quite adamantly sure that there was *definitely* not a group of fucking chinstrap penguins lurking about off the coast of St Austell, so what if Finley was the next best thing? She'd also seen enough *'Planet Earth'* to know she and her kayak probably did not stand a chance in a face-off against a starving seal, and she honestly didn't fancy sticking around long enough to find out.

She panicked, her arms practically vibrating in her fruitless efforts to reverse her kayak back through the waves and away from the rocks. The seal hadn't moved again. Finley was pretty sure it hadn't even noticed her.

But what if that was just a ruse? Just a hunting tactic, and she was nothing but naive prey.

Finally took a deep breath, the rational side of her brain fighting in embarrassment to convince her nerves to just calm the fuck down. She forced her shoulders to drop, summoning enough strength to simply turn the kayak around in the water, and at least paddle in the correct direction.

With the seal behind her, Finley's panic settled, and she focused her attention instead on the ebb and flow of the water, and the warming rays of the sun above her.

She briefly considered an exploration into one of the many caves along the rocks, but her confidence was feeling a little bruised, and she didn't think she could take the anxiety of the risk. The seal had been quite adventurous enough for one day, and her entire education was in question. If there were seals out here, then there could be polar bears in there, for all she knew. So, she settled instead for paddling the waves a little further out, and watching the way the sun soaked the colours of the waters and the land's edge.

She couldn't hazard a guess at how long she rode the water, but as her weary muscles pulled the boat back up onto the beach, she felt more relaxed than she could remember feeling in a *long* time.

She let her toes curl in the sand once again as she made her way back up the beach, her mind refreshingly clear of any thoughts other than the squelch of her feet, and the lunch she had waiting for her at the cottage. She'd seen the fresh bread in Sophie's kitchen and the cured ham in the fridge, and she'd honestly been thinking about it all morning. Simple, hearty, local food.

That wasn't in a brown paper bag, laden with guilt and awkward affections.

*"Trixie!"*

Finley jumped at the sound of a gruff voice shouting across the sand, and she looked up just in time to prepare for the thud of a heavy, furry body against her thighs and waist, a lolling tongue determined to make her acquaintance.

*"Hey,* baby!"

Finley grinned, bending down to ruffle her fingers through the dog's fur. *Trixie,* she assumed, was a big fluffball goober of slobber, thick fur, and an almost human face; deep dark eyes set into chubby cheeks. Lumbering, rough around the edges, but *so* goddamn *cute!*

She kinda looked like she was *supposed* to be a Spaniel? But Finley certainly hadn't ever seen a Spaniel this beefy, or this dopey in any of London's well-kept parks.

Living in London had never really allowed Finley to have a dog, and frankly she was much more of a cat person anyway, but she did love a good pup cuddle.

"Trixie is such a big old *baby,* I'm in love!"

She beamed brightly as the owner caught up with his tearaway dog.

The man chuckled.

"She loves a new face, and I don't think we've seen you around before? You new to the area?"

The owner looked just like the dog. Broad and rugged and tough, but with something in his eyes that was warm and gentle, and Finley liked him immediately.

"Trixie is a *very* cute name for a *very* tough dog," Finley cooed, cupping the hound's cheeks with the palms of her hands.

"She's uh…"

The owner scratched the back of his neck.

"She's named after Trixie Franklin, the best of *'Call the Midwives'*…"

Finley laughed openly.

"You do have the glamour for it, don't you girl." She stood, turning her attention to the owner with a smile. "And to answer your question, yes and no. I'm new, but I'm temporary! I'm on holiday."

"In Polcarne?" The man raised an eyebrow, looking intently at Finley for a long moment. Then his eyes widened. *"Oh,* you're Sophie Cedars' home swap?"

Finley blinked.

*How?*

Christ, small towns were insane.

"I...*yeah!* Yeah, I'm Finley Bennett, nice to meet you."

"Trevor Shaw." The man held his hand out, and Finley shook it warmly as he continued. *"Ah* I've known Sophie ever since she was in nappies with my Annie. Godsent angel, that girl. Do you know every spring she takes the lambs from up on my farm that get rejected by their mothers? Nurses them herself until they're strong enough to stand alone."

Finley's stomach flipped, and her hand flew to cover it instinctively.

"Course she causes me all sorts of problems when the time comes for the market, mind, but that's another story," Trevor chuckled, shaking his head. "And *not* one for a sunny day such as this!"

Finley's stomach churned as the implications settled low, and she winced as she imagined the distress that Sophie must feel at that stage in what must be a *very* unpleasant process for a vegan to be privy to. She swallowed, not quite sure what to make of the surge of pride that she felt in Sophie for at least *trying* to fight for her belief.

It was ridiculous, the way she felt she knew this woman, simply from a night in her cottage and a few minutes of social media stalking.

"Come by the farm if you get a minute spare," Trevor offered, bringing Finley back from her thoughts. "I've got a peppercorn cheese I've been trying to perfect, and I think this batch is the one!"

"I might just take you up on that!" Finley grinned. "Thanks, Mr Shaw."

"Oh, please! Call me Trevor. Can't be having any friend of Sophie's calling me Mr Shaw!" Trevor chuckled warmly. "Enjoy your stay in Polcarne, Finley! Come on Trixie girl. Time for lunch and a catch up on *'Bake Off'*!"

"Have a good day, guys!" Finley bent down once more to fuss over her new furry friend. "Nice to meet you, Trixie!"

She sighed as she watched the man and his dog retreat over the beach, Trixie tearing through the sand after the little rubber ball that her human threw for her.

She imagined a life where everyone you saw knew your life story.

Where the man who made your cheese had changed your nappy.

She couldn't help but find it funny, the way a tiny hamlet town, with a smaller population than three streets of Central London, could seem so much less lonely.

~ ~ ~ ~ ~ ~ 🐾 ~ ~ ~ ~ ~ ~

Sophie leaned back against the tree, pulling her blanket tighter around herself as the cooler air set in. Hyde Park was still buzzing, a low hum of chatter and laughter ringing just low enough to be comforting, and Sophie felt invigorated by the atmosphere.

She had visited the Borough Market, and been astounded by the sheer number of food traders; artisanal, and organic, and sustainable, and *so* many vegan options. Sophie had bought and packed herself a picnic, and was currently enjoying it in the last of the city's light.

She grinned to herself as she thought back over her first day in London. It surprised her just how quickly she'd felt at home in the city, and the realisation shot a tiny pang of guilt through her stomach as she thought of Bex and the kids, and the fact that she hadn't even contacted her sister since she'd first stepped off the train at Paddington.

She winced, fishing her phone out of her pocket. Bex would likely be at work now, but it would be fairly quiet in The Ship for another hour or two.

She hit video call.

"Well, well, well, if it isn't Gulliver's great, great granddaughter."

Bex's voice was spotty, a little muffled by the clink of glasses and the chatter of the locals in the pub around her, but her eyes sparkled with amusement and her lips curled into a smirk in the frame of the screen.

Sophie wrinkled her nose at the words.

"What?"

"Gulliver. You know, like…the guy who travels? Cause you're on a trip, but you're not some guy from the 1700s, so…" Bex trailed off, rolling her eyes as she shook her head. "Never mind."

Sophie blinked.

"Come on, don't leave me hanging!" Bex urged, her eyes wide with intrigue as she leaned back against the wall of the bar. "How is London?"

"Incredible." Sophie exclaimed. "I'm eating a *vegan pork pie,* Bex! It's made of *pea protein!"*

"You have absolutely not called me in the middle of my shift, from the greatest city in the UK, to tell me about a pea pie," Bex challenged, waving a beer bottle in disbelief just to the side of the screen.

"No, it's not a pea pie, it's a *no pork* pie," Sophie rebutted. "It's just *made* of peas."

"How is that not the same?"

Sophie faltered.

She studied the pie in her hand, her nose wrinkling as she considered the question.

"I don't know," she admitted. "But it doesn't *taste* the same, it tastes just like a..."

*"Sophie!"* Bex yelled. "Tell me about *London!"*

Sophie grinned.

"It's insane, Bex!" she gushed. "It's so big, and so busy, and there's so much happening all the time. And nobody talks to anyone, and they barely even look at each other, and everything is so *expensive!"*

"You're not selling it overly well, Soph," Bex chuckled, her nose wrinkled in disapproval. "Sounds like my idea of hell."

Sophie shook her head animatedly.

"No, but it's *fascinating!* There's so many bars and shops and restaurants. And all the people look different. I thought you had a lot of tattoos, but today I saw a bald guy with a dragon tattoo on his *head!* And the museum was *amazing!"*

Bex grinned, her smile and her eyes softening as she watched Sophie launch into her explanation of the grand museum, and its exhibits, and the children she'd shared her knowledge with.

"All that on day one!" Bex laughed, her tone both soft and incredulous. "You'll come back a changed woman."

"I hope so," Sophie breathed.

She really did. She hoped that she could return home feeling as strong, and as powerful as London made her feel. She hoped that the Sophie with the two degrees, the new hairstyle *and* the ability to work a tube map and decipher Egyptian hieroglyphics could stay.

The Sophie who did things for *her,* and not just for the people around her.

"Have you met anyone?" Bex asked.

"I met Noah! He came round for the cat, and he..."

"Oooh, *Noah?*" Bex grinned wolfishly, her eyebrows wriggling as she lifted her beer bottle to her lips. "What's he *like?* Reckon he'd be a better lay than Kyle Brown?"

"Maybe." Sophie smirked. "If I were a gay man."

Bex deflated.

"Well, that's no fun," she grumbled.

"Have you, uh…" Sophie paused, her cheeks heating a little under the words she was about to say. She felt irrationally flustered, as if somehow this simple question would give away the ridiculous number of times she'd wondered about Finley Bennett over the past twelve hours, and the number of times she'd scrolled her Instagram page over the past thirty minutes. "Have you met Finley yet?"

"Not yet, but Trev did!" Sophie replied, calm and neutral and completely unperturbed. "Says she seemed sweet."

Sophie nodded.

Sweet. That was never a bad thing. Although she did immediately think of Kyle Brown.

Hopefully Finley Bennet would be sweet, *and* more.

"Did he say…"

Sophie trailed off, her eyes widening in anticipation as the familiar tinny chime of the karaoke machine kicking into life rang out, and Bex snapped her head in the direction Sophie knew the machine was set up in.

"Oh, no…" Bex muttered.

Sophie held her breath.

Then the music started.

"*No,* Drunk Dave!" Bex yelled, slamming her beer bottle down on the bar. "Do *not* make me throw you out!"

"Is…is that *'Blurred Lines'?*" Sophie gasped, sitting upright in her surprise. "Jesus Christ, he's fifty-eight! How does he even *know* that song?"

"Starting to think it might be time to take that machine down," Bex sighed, her jaw tight and her eyes tired as she glared at Drunk Dave and the machine. "That, or bar Drunk Dave. I've gotta go sort this out. Love you, sis. Enjoy your bean pasty."

"Pea pie!" Sophie corrected. Then she blinked as Bex smirked. "No, wait…"

Bex winked as she ended the call, and Sophie chuckled as she settled herself back against her tree.

It felt good to see Bex. It felt reassuring, in a funny way, to hear whispers of her life over the phone, but to still be present in this grand, bustling city with its pockets of beauty.

It felt…*combined.* It made the world feel smaller.

Like she didn't have to choose. Like she could be in London with its promises and its potential, and yet she could still leave a part of her heart in Polcarne.

Like it wasn't mutually exclusive.

It was crazy how serene it felt here, in the most famous park in England. So peaceful, despite the fact that there were so many people still around.

Her phone buzzed in her hand, and she grinned as she pulled up the message from Finley. Her screen filled with a selfie of Finley in a kayak, in the high sun of the earlier morning, the cliff tops spread above the coastline behind her.

Finley: *Is everything in Cornwall as beautiful as this?*

Sophie huffed out a laugh.

No, it damn well wasn't.

The particular beauty *she* was admiring was usually reserved for an apartment in Central London.

Sophie: *That is one stunner of a view.*

She smirked.

She wondered if Finley would see through her.

She doubted it. It was subtle enough, right?

She snapped a photo of her picnic, Hyde Park spread across the background.

Sophie: *Eating for two again tonight.*

She sighed contentedly, cracking open a can of cider as she leaned back against the tree.

It was highly unlikely she would ever meet Finley Bennett, but it was fun to think about for a while. Maybe even exchange a few flirty text messages until the buzz wore off.

The phone rang.

Sophie panicked.

She bolted upright, staring unblinking at Finley's name as it flashed across her screen.

This was an *accident,* right?

She shouldn't answer it.

It was *clearly* a pocket dial. Or a slip of the thumb.

*Wasn't it?*

It was still ringing…

Sophie swallowed thickly, expelling as much of her gay panic as she could in a harsh breath as she dragged the screen to answer, and lifted the phone to her ear.

"Hello?"

"Good evening, Sophie Cedars."

Sophie laughed.

"Has someone been rifling through my post?"

She felt immediately relaxed, Finley's voice softer in her ear than she had expected somehow.

"I've done my due diligence."

Sophie raised an eyebrow. She could swear she could *hear* the grin in this stranger's voice, and her stomach fluttered a little at the thought.

"And by due diligence, you mean you stalked me on Instagram?" she teased.

"I needed to make sure I wasn't staying in the home of a criminal psychopath."

"True, psychopaths *are* well-known for advertising their criminal behaviour on their Instagram stories." Sophie grinned as Finley laughed. "Does my home give you serial killer vibes, then, Sherlock Holmes?"

"Well, it's a dangerous world, and not all psychopaths are skinheads and old white men, you know?" Finley teased. "Sometimes they're beautiful redheads with homes that smell like cherries, I'm just looking out for myself."

Sophie blushed immediately.

The easy words made every inch of her body flood warm, and frankly she had no idea what to do with it.

Or how to respond to the soft flirtation.

"How're you settling in?" she diverted. "Trevor lured you in for cheese yet?"

"Is everything in this town this predictable?" Finley laughed.

Sophie grinned.

"Nothing ever changes in Polcarne, Finley Bennett."

*"Ooh,"* Finley sang, her tone *absolutely* bordering smug, and sinking effortlessly into a brazenly flirtatious hum. "Sounds like I'm not the *only* one doing a bit of social media stalking. Find anything you liked, Sophie Cedars?"

Sophie giggled.

This was a new experience for her. The fact that a gorgeous stranger she'd never met was charming her from the end of a phone line was new, and unexpected. Whenever Sophie had flirted before, it had been with people she saw every day. It had always been light, and sweet, and masked with an air of innocence because these people had known her all her life.

But this was different. This was someone new, and exciting, and exotic in a weird, sheltered kind of way. Someone she didn't have to pull a pint for the next day. And that, and the definite cheeky air to Finley's tone, sparked a playful confidence that Sophie wasn't used to feeling in her own veins.

And she wanted to *test* it.

She feigned nonchalance, despite the flustered amusement she felt in her chest.

"I just wanted to see if you were hot."

Finley laughed openly, the sound echoing slightly over the line.

Sophie's stomach flipped. That laugh was so sweet, and yet so dirty at the same time.

Like the part of Sophie that she kept pushed *way* down in her stomach.

"What was the verdict?" Finley murmured.

Sophie raised an eyebrow, smirking at the smooth, clearly well-practised tone to that flirtatious voice.

Like warm *butter* over her skin.

She grinned, shaking her head.

She was pretty certain in twenty-six years she had never had anyone flirt with her so casually and so *smoothly.*

Especially considering they'd never met, and this was their first real conversation.

It made sense. There was no way someone as blatantly attractive as Finley didn't *know* their own power, and so it was completely reasonable that she would know how to use it too.

Sophie only hoped she could keep up.

She nestled back against the tree, as if the solid trunk could hold her spine up and keep her new found confidence pushed inside it.

"Why do I get the feeling you don't need an ego boost?" she teased.

Finley chuckled.

"So that's a yes, then?"

Sophie shook her head again, her cheeks twitching with a cocky smirk that felt almost alien on her lips.

This was an addition to the new and improved Sophie Cedars that she could *definitely* get behind.

She felt oddly invincible.

Until she heard the distinct sound of sloshing water, her mind short-circuited, and every shred of her newfound confidence plummeted into her stomach.

She sat upright.

"Are you in my bath again, Bennett?"

Finley chuckled again, low and unnecessarily husky.

"This is mine now. You might have to get used to sharing with me."


*Jesus Christ.*


Sophie slammed her eyes shut, not entirely sure whether to entertain the delightful images her mind was conjuring, or whether to shut them down as quickly as possible on the horrifying chance she might say something highly inappropriate.

She blushed deeply, her prior confidence now beating in her stomach in a preposterous whirlwind of butterflies.

She was a complete novice in the world of cheeky flirtation, and she honestly wasn't sure she could trust the new Sophie Cedars *or* the old one to play this smoothly without *actually* painting herself as a psychopath. She cleared her throat, and took the power back in the only way she knew how.

She diverted.

"So did you just call to flirt with me, Don Juan, or did you need something?" she choked, breathy and flustered, and nowhere near as smooth as she'd been hoping for.

She blushed deeper as the responding soft chuckle clarified her suspicions.

Finley Bennet knew exactly what power she held.

There was a pause, and Sophie clenched her jaw as the line trickled with the sound of moving water once again.

When Finley spoke again, her voice was lighter. Still lilting, but a little brighter, and a little less like melted butter.

A little less blatantly intended to reduce Sophie to mush.

"I called to find out more about the angel of Polcarne who rescues baby lambs and has a borderline obsessive collection of scatter cushions," Finley chuckled. "It felt strange being in your home and knowing nothing about you."

Sophie giggled, her shoulders dropping under the lighter air. She leaned back against the tree, lifting her cider to her lips.

"What do you want to know?"

"Why London?" Finley asked.

Sophie exhaled slowly, shrugging softly.

She'd been prepared for small talk. She'd expected an exchange of what they did for a living, what their hobbies were, what music they liked.

She hadn't been prepared for Finley to dive straight for the big guns. Although there was no way Finley could have known that, really.

It was a fairly innocent question. It just had a loaded answer.

Sophie knew she could have diverted. She knew she could have brushed the question off with a generic song of big city culture, and landmarks, and tourist attractions. But she was very aware that Finley Bennet had abandoned her life on a very sudden whim to disappear for two weeks too. And something in that compelled Sophie to be honest.

Because *maybe* Finley might understand more than anyone.

"I wanted to see if I had it in me," she breathed.

She half expected a quick quip, or some kind of dismissive joke, but Finley was quiet.

Quiet in a way that felt comfortable, and easy, and Sophie knew somehow that whatever she said next would be listened to.

And maybe it was that. Or maybe it was the fact that she had never met Finley and likely never would. Or maybe it was that she couldn't see her face. Or maybe it was the confidence that London seemed to instil in her. Maybe it was all of the above.

But *something* made it feel *so* damn easy to open up.

"I've been in Polcarne all my life," she started, her voice lower now. "It's all I know, and everyone who lives there assumes that people will never leave. They assume everyone will settle and build a life of their own. There's just not much to build a life *of.* "

Sophie paused, collecting her thoughts. Finley stayed quiet, seeming to know somehow that nothing needed to be said just yet.

"London has opportunities and excitement and potential. I guess I wanted to see if I could be what it needed me to be."

"The beautiful thing about London is you can be anything you want to be," Finley murmured. "What *do* you want to be?"

"A historian." Sophie grinned, the passion seeping audibly into her voice. "A museum curator. I want to live my passion every day, and not pull pints for people I've known since they were wearing pull-ups."

"Well, for *that,* you're *definitely* in the right place!" Finley urged, the energy in her own voice picking up alongside Sophie's. Matching her stride for stride. "You're always welcome back, you know. After the swap. I've got the spare room. I figure commandeering the British History Museum might take more than one two week trip."

Sophie bit her lip, her chest spreading with a warmth she hadn't expected. She didn't even *know* this woman, and she was offering her home to help Sophie chase her dream.

Trevor hadn't been wrong.

Finley Bennett was turning out to be *quite* the sweetheart.

"Commandeering the British History Museum would definitely take me longer than it took you to commandeer that bath, that's for sure." Sophie teased.

Then she laughed as the splashing water got louder, and the squeak of the bath made it very clear that Finley was wriggling contentedly.

"This was vacant, it was an easy siege," Finley quipped.

Sophie grinned.

"What about you?" she asked. "Why Polcarne?"

"Well, Polcarne *specifically* was nothing more than fated happenstance, a beautiful stranger messaged me on the internet and invited me to steal her bath." Finley paused, and Sophie imagined that cheeky grin.

Then she sighed, soft and almost wistful, and Sophie felt the air shift to something more earnest.

"I guess I just needed...*air,"* Finley breathed. "I just needed to get away from the grind of the city before it broke me. I've spent a long time putting my career first, and I...I learned a hard lesson this weekend. And honestly, I ran. I just wanted to get away from it all, and be where life feels a bit slower for a while."

Sophie nodded. She could see that. She could definitely see the stress and the pressure and the burdens that sat on the shoulders of the suited origami octopuses cramming themselves into the tubes at ungodly angles, just for the chance to steal another few minutes of the day's time.

She wondered again whether Finley was an origami octopus. Something about the soft tone of the calm, confident voice almost seemed to suggest not, but Sophie was very aware that that was a very bold assumption, based on incredibly little information.

"What do you do?" she asked.

"I'm an architect."

*"Wow,"* Sophie breathed.

That explained…well, a lot, actually. The success explained the money and the wardrobe full of suits. But the creativity also explained the vibrancy of the location, and the softer air to the apartment.

"Does it make you happy?" she asked.

*"Yes,"* Finley chuckled, the sound almost bittersweet. "It really does. I work a lot, and that's maybe not that good for me, but…well, people think that because I work so hard that I must be miserable, but I'm *not*. I love what I do and I know that that makes me one of the lucky ones. I'm just *tired,* and…"

Finley paused, her breath hitching sharply.

Sophie waited.

"And lonely." The voice was softer now. Lower. "I've spent a long time putting my job first, and it hasn't left a lot of room for me. And that feels so weird here. Everyone here seems the complete opposite of lonely."

Sophie breathed a small laugh.

It was strange, the way the world worked. Finley was right, in one respect. It was hard to feel alone in Polcarne, where your next-door neighbour was also your doctor, and your old school teachers were now your patrons. And Sophie knew, really, that with Bex around her she had never felt lonely. Not in the way that Finley did.

But there was a different kind of loneliness in never branching out. Never meeting anyone new, or never meeting anyone with the same views on life, who understood her veganism, or her online degrees, or her bittersweet dreams. A different kind of isolation.

She wondered if Finley knew both.

"And they seem happier for it," Finley breathed. "Being here makes me think that maybe if I could learn to kick back a bit, and leave room in my life for things besides work, then maybe I could be a little *less* lonely."

Sophie let her body melt into the tree behind her as she soaked in Finley's words. It was interesting and endearing to her that Finley seemed to have opened up just as easily as Sophie had. She wondered if Finley was always this open, or if she was caught softly under the same spell that Sophie was under.

Something told her it was the latter, though she couldn't quite place her finger on what that something was.

But sitting in a strange place, with a strange view, and talking to a *complete* stranger, having a conversation that had taken a turn that she had *not* expected, Sophie couldn't help but think that just maybe they might both have found a way to feel a little less lonely.

# Chapter Nine

Finley's stomach fizzed a little as she walked along the harbour in Charlestown. She felt weird. Walking the scenes she'd seen on her TV screen wasn't exactly *new* to a Londoner, but something about this felt more *magical.* Like pirates, and treasure, and adventure. The Three Musketeers. Treasure Island. *Poldark!*

Like the tales of her childhood.

Like the games she'd played with her mother, back when Finley had been a child and they'd been a family. Finley had had a dress-up chest the size of a small horse, stuffed to the brim with just about every costume a child could ever wish for. Pirate hooks and eye patches, and princess dresses, and police hats and fireman hats, and superhero masks and capes, and at one point a full dinosaur costume complete with a fully inconvenient tail. And despite the fact that she'd spent her whole life around some of the most famous landmarks in British history, there was something about the magic in Charlestown that felt more *childlike,* somehow.

She was almost embarrassed by how excited the thought made her, and she fought hard to school her features as she made her way along the famous harbour walls, the water glistening in the sun below her. The harbour was strange; so brashly aimed at tourists, with its skull and bones flags, and its cannons, and its wooden stocks that dotted the walkway around the water, yet so authentic in the way the cliff faces loomed either side, and the way the stone sea walls curved to form the narrow waterway for small fishing boats.

The whole aesthetic made Finley feel like she did as a child, lost in a world of play pretend, and she couldn't help the overwhelming urge to take a photo with the cannons and the rows of rum barrels.

She almost wished she had her hook, and her eye patch.

She glanced around, checking for wandering eyes before pulling her phone out and snapping a selfie against the backdrop of the harbour, one eye squinted closed, and her hand over her brow as if looking out to sea.

She sent it to Sophie.

Something she had done almost every time she had found something worth sharing since their phone call. There was just something about Sophie that drew her in, and made her want to talk to her. Maybe it was just that she was in Sophie's home. Maybe it was that they were living each other's lives, and that no-one else in Finley's city circle would be able to relate to the experiences she was having.

Or *maybe* it was that Sophie was very easy to talk to and Finley was *definitely* attracted to her.

Who knew?

Her phone chimed almost immediately.

Sophie: *Are you an origami octopus?*

Finley blinked.

Finley: *What? No, I was being a pirate. Treasure Island? Because Charlestown?*

Sophie: *That definitely wasn't a pirate.*

Finley pouted.

It *would* have been, if she'd had her hook and her eye patch!

Sophie: *But no, on the tubes. Are you an origami octopus?*

Finley frowned.

On the tubes?

Why would an octopus be on the tubes? Blue-ringed or Origami.

And wasn't that paper?

She was pretty sure she was missing something here, but at this point she figured it was probably better just to go with it.

Finley: *No, I like to think I'm more of a napkin swan…*

The phone rang immediately.

"Hey," Finley started, almost cautiously.

"It's a genuine question, Long John Silver."

Sophie sounded out of breath, and a little hassled. Although the playful tease was still running clear somewhere beneath the flustered tone, Sophie's voice fell heavier and sharper than Finley had heard it before. Finley may not have known Sophie Cedars very well at all, but she got the distinct impression that this was slightly out of character.

And also, it made absolutely no sense.

"Soph, have you been ordering your Deliveroos from Dougie's?" Finley screwed her face in confusion. "Because I *really* think that place is lacing their pies..."

"Talk me through your tube process," Sophie demanded.

Finley frowned.

"Like...finding the right trains?"

*"No,* like...are you one of these *insane* transmorphic people who risk body parts to get a space?"

*Ah.*

Well, this made some sense.

Sophie was battling the tubes in rush hour again.

But *what* did that have to do with octopu...

*"Oh,* origami octopus!" Finley exhaled as the lightbulb flickered on, and she processed the bizarre analogy. Or at least, she *thought* she did. "Like a really flexible creature, all folded up?"

*"Yeah..."* Sophie sighed, her breath seeming to even out a little.

Finley grinned. She had certainly never *expected* the words 'origami octopus' to give her butterflies, but then she had never *expected* Sophie Cedars.

"Your mind is beyond adorable," she chuckled.

"I just watched a guy lose his *fedora,* Finley! *Crushed!"* Sophie squeaked, her voice pitching higher with each word. "It could have been his bloody *head!"*

Finley bit back a laugh.

Sure, she found the rush hour tubes a lot, but it had never really occurred to her just how baffling the entire concept must have seemed to someone who wasn't adapted to London's constant hurry.

"No, I am not an origami octopus. I hate the tube in commute time and I don't take it if I can avoid it," she assured. "Why is this so important to you, Soph?"

Sophie exhaled slowly, and Finley could almost *hear* the moment she regained her composure in the pause.

Her next words were softer, and the playful, teasing tone was much more distinctive.

"I needed to make sure I wasn't staying in the home of an impulsive sociopath."

Finley laughed openly.

"Unless they're hot, right, and then it's moot?" She grinned.

"Correct. *Especially* if they have whiskey eyes I can get lost in," Sophie flirted cheekily.

And *far* more brazenly than she had just days ago.

Finley's stomach dropped, and she blushed at the words, and the lower timbre to Sophie's playful voice.

In her early text messages, and in their phone call Sophie had seemed so softly spoken. She'd almost felt tentative, like she was testing the waters of the world around her, and Finley had put it down to a shy nature. The sweet innocence of a country girl, like a Hallmark cliché.

But there was clearly something beneath that softness that burned a little darker, and a little cheekier. Something that seeped out in subtle moments.

And Finley knew the thought was incredibly hedonistic, but she couldn't help but feel like it was reserved just for her.

She cleared her throat.

"What would you have said if I *was* an origami octopus?" she chuckled.

"Uh…"

There was a pause, and Finley wondered if Sophie would retreat. Divert onto safer ground, like she had just a couple of nights before.

Or if that flicker of dark playfulness would prevail.

"At least you'd be flexible?"

Finley's stomach flipped hard, her chest flooding instantly with an almost uncomfortable warmth, and she huffed a laugh from her chest both at the flirtatious insinuation, and at her own useless state.

Well. The darkness prevailed, and it was cheekier than ever.

"Sophie Cedars, are you *flirting* with me?" Finley teased, *just* the right side of dramatic.

Sophie hummed, and Finley held her breath.

Then Sophie giggled.

"Stop fishing," she teased. "Come on, tell me about Charlestown."

Finley grinned.

She inhaled deeply, a strange, unfamiliar sense of *giddiness* rippling through her at the taste of salt in the air, and the tug of excitement in her belly.

"Do you feel like a giant child here too, or is it just me?" she whispered, her eyes darting her surroundings to make sure no one else would hear her confession.

She didn't know why.

She didn't know *why* it felt almost shameful to feel a giddy wonder at a pirate ship and a coastal harbour, but it felt out of character, somehow. Like she should have been above it.

Maybe she should have been.

But she absolutely wasn't.

"Because there's a pirate ship and a cave?" Sophie whispered back, and Finley could hear the teasing grin around the hushed words.

Finley gasped.

"There's a *cave?*"

Sophie laughed openly, and Finley practically spun on the spot as she darted her eyes across the harbour in search of this cave.

"A *smuggler's* cave," Sophie declared.

"A *smuggler's cave?*" Finley yelped, all and any shame completely forgotten. "Can I go in it?"

"If you don't mind wet feet," Sophie chuckled.

Finley's giddiness surged into an all-out butterfly frenzy, and she let out a squeak of excitement that she was fairly certain she hadn't made since she was a schoolgirl in dungarees.

*This* felt like freedom.

This felt like the world was hers.

This was that elusive feeling that Finley had chased for fifteen years, with suits and blueprints and thirteen-hour days, and it was an almost dumbfounding surprise that *this* was what was making her feel it.

A fucking pirate ship and a cave, and the whispers of a beautiful stranger.

"Oh my *god,* I'm going on an *adventure,*" Finley hissed, her fingers closing tight over her phone as her excited adrenaline gripped her muscles.

Sophie giggled.

"From Long John Silver to Jim Hawkins in a nanosecond," she teased.

Finley narrowed her eyes.

"Are you *mocking* my inner child?" she demanded.

"Never. I bet you were the *cutest* child *ever,*" Sophie cooed.

Finley grinned, rolling her eyes.

"I'm the cutest adult ever."

"That's exactly what makes me say it," Sophie sighed, deliberately swoony. "The big Bambi eyes must have been *impossible* to say no to."

"I can guarantee you they still are." Finley grinned as Sophie giggled. "In fact, that's what my mum used to call me."

"Bambi?"

"Mmhmm," Finley hummed.

She kept her eyes peeled as she picked her way down the harbour and onto the beach, scanning the jagged greys and reds of the cliff walls for the entrance to the cave.

"Dad, on the other hand, found it a lot easier to say no to me," she chuckled humourlessly. "His loving nickname for me was *Lifesucking Leech*. Much less delicate."

Finley's chuckle warmed as Sophie huffed a laugh.

She didn't know what it was about Sophie Cedars, but something in the soft voice on the other end of the line made it so easy to talk without thinking.

Finley had dated Jess for four months before she'd spoken once about her mother. And even then, it had been because Jess had expressed a very clear dislike for the fact that Finley wouldn't open up.

For all of her adult life, Finley had talked of her family and her own crushing expectations *only* to Noah.

And yet this woman she'd never met, with the adorable little twang in her voice and the sheets that smelled like cherry blossom, had her chatting casually about her family like it was an exchange about the weather.

And it felt freeing.

"So, your dad isn't where you get your charm from then?" Sophie chuckled.

Finley smirked, her stomach warming and her eyebrow quirking. She let her voice drop, lacing with the subtle husk she knew always won her a blush.

"Find me charming, do you?"

Sophie hummed, and for some *obscene* reason, Finley held her breath.

"You have a certain…*allure,"* Sophie giggled.

Finley grinned.

"Oh, so you *are* flirting with me?"

"Shut up and go on your adventure, Bilbo Baggins," Sophie scoffed good-naturedly. "Watch out for the crabs."

Finley froze.

"The…" She blinked. "Wait, what?"

"Happy adventuring!" Sophie sang.

"Crabs?" Finley swallowed, her heart rate picking up and her chest rippling with an embarrassing tide of fear. She cleared her throat, her eyes darting warily across the beach and the little pools of water along the cliff wall. "C-crabs? Like, big ones?"

"Take a photo for me," Sophie sang, quite deliberately cheerful and blatantly ignoring the cold quiver in Finley's voice.

"Crabs?" she repeated, high pitched and low volume.

"Bye Fin!" Sophie called, audibly holding the phone further from her mouth before she hung up.

"Sophie?" Finley squeaked. "Big crabs? P-pincers?"

The beep of the ended call frankly mocked her.

She blinked, holding her phone out before her as she stared at her own background photo, and the absence of an active call.

She knew she was being teased. She wasn't dense.

But she was also in unchartered territories, and if Polcarne had fucking *seals,* then Charlestown *definitely* had crabs.

And Finley wasn't sure she was all that keen on that idea.

The phone in her hand buzzed, and she rolled her eyes immediately at the words over her screen.

Sophie: *You're a big brave adventurer, Finley Bennett. You've got this* 😿

Finley chuckled, her shoulders dropping a little and her blood thawing in her veins at the playful words.

She shook her head, pushing her phone into her pocket.

She'd never admit it out loud, but she felt weirdly bolstered.

She *was* a big brave adventurer.

And she was going on an adventure.

She grinned, picking her way across the rocky coastline until she found what she could only assume was Charlestown's smuggler's cave.

It was…pretty small.

More of a *chasm,* to be honest. Just a jagged hole in the cliff walls, with a healthy dumping of seaweed across the stoney bed.

Really, barely a cave at all.

Finley wasn't convinced it'd hide a smuggler.

Assuming that was what a smuggler's cave meant.

She felt disappointed for a few long moments as she peered inside the well-lit chasm.

Then she remembered the crabs, and the seals, and the seaweed, and she felt her disappointment wane a little as she figured it was probably a good thing.

Finley was on an adventure, and that meant she would have to go into the cave.

And really, there was only so much adventuring in sea caves a Londoner could cope with.

This little chasm felt a lot less threatening than she had expected, and that was definitely not a bad thing.

She grinned, thinking about Sophie's words as she stepped over the invisible threshold and into the smuggler's cave.

Sophie had humoured her, built her up, and effortlessly encouraged a playfulness in Finley that she hadn't felt in a long time.

So *easily,* and so casually.

Sophie Cedars, and everything she coaxed, was unexpected, and Finley liked it.

~ ~ ~ ~ ~ ~ ♪ ~ ~ ~ ~ ~ ~

Sophie beamed as she flicked a handful of coins into the open case laid out before the busker, fighting the urge to dance along as the smooth sounds of Ray Charles played from the booming saxophone.

She had been wandering along the Thames at Southbank for the past half an hour, and she was in love with the vibrant air of entertainment and celebration and life.

Sophie had always known that Westminster would feel like the heart of London. She'd rightfully assumed that the famous landmarks scattered about the river bank, the powerful presence of Parliament, and the proximity to Buckingham Palace and Trafalgar Square would make Westminster feel like the city's *heart.* Yet here, just across the river, beneath the London Eye, and the lights, and the upbeat jazz, Sophie was beginning to think she'd found the city's *soul.*

Her phone rang, and she grinned as she watched the now familiar name flash across her screen.

"Hey, Fin!" she sang. "How was…"

*"Sophie…"*

Sophie stopped walking.

Finley's voice was low. *Too* low. Her tone was hushed, her pitch tense, and Sophie immediately felt terrified.

"Finley, are you okay?"

"I…I don't know…"

Sophie's blood ran cold.

"What do you mean you *don't know?"* she shrieked.

Finley whimpered.

"Fin, *what's* going on," Sophie hissed. "You're *scaring* me!"

"There's a *thing* in your kitchen."

"A thing?"

"A *monster* with a stripey face." Finley squeaked, her terror audible in the high pitch of her whispered voice. "And really snarly teeth, Sophie, it looks so *angry."*

*Shit.*

Sophie exhaled heavily, her shoulders dropping.

She was most *definitely* relieved that Finley wasn't being hunted by some lunatic axe murderer, or haunted by the ghost of The Headless Horseman…

But this situation wasn't exactly *ideal* either.

Of *all* the times for this to happen again.

"Finley, that's a badger."

*"No,"* Finley huffed. "No, badgers are *cute* and they have glasses, and tweed coats and they *do not* look like they want to *kill* me!"

Sophie covered the mouthpiece to hide her giggles.

Was that a *'Wind in the Willows'* reference?

Christ, this woman was beyond adorable.

"I can *hear* you laughing at me, Cedars!" Finley hissed. "You'll feel bad when I *die here!"*

"Stop *hissing* at it, or you really *will* die there!"

Finley squeaked, then fell silent.

Sophie rolled her eyes.

Okay.

Clearly, she was going to need to walk Finley through this, and she needed to do so *fast* before her adorable house guest lost a limb to an angry badger.

"Do you have any fruit? Or…mouse carcasses?" She grimaced.

"I…*ew,* no." Finley audibly shuddered. "Should I have? Are there mice here too?"

"Very probably," Sophie nodded mindlessly. "In the garden."

"And you thought this was a good time to bring that up?" Finley squeaked.

"Well, it's not like you don't have them in London!" Sophie yelped defensively. "They're all up in the houses here, in those townhouse basements! And there are definitely rats along the river bank, and in all those back alleys by the markets…"

"Sophie!" Finley yelped.

Sophie winced.

"Right. The badger. Do you have fruit?"

"I have strawberries?"

"Leave her a trail of strawberries out the front door and just stand clear," Sophie instructed. As amusing as this was, she could feel Finley's genuine fear through the phone and she wanted nothing more than to take it away. "Badgers are scared of humans, so she's probably as desperate to be out of that house as you are for her to leave. She'll only hurt you if she feels threatened."

There was a thud.

Then Finley shrieked.

"Sophie, I *think* she feels *pretty* threatened!"

Sophie couldn't help it.

It was just too cute.

*Tweed coats.*

She giggled.

*'The Wind in the Willows'.*

Bloody *adorable.*

"Well, Badger *is* a hater of society, and dinner, and all that kind of…"

"Are you *sure* you want your potential last words to me to be *mocking my terror?"*

146

"I'm sorry," Sophie laughed. "You're just *so* very cute. Have you laid your trail?"

"Flirting with me is *not* gonna make this any less distressing, Cedars!" Finley huffed, though Sophie could hear the curl of the words as her lips twitched into a soft smile. "And yes, I've just…"

Finley cut her own words off with a high-pitched yell, and Sophie froze at the sound of a loud crash, the tinkling of broken glass following it.

*"What* the pissing hell was that?"

There was a moment of silence.

"Erm, I *may…*" Finley murmured, her voice sheepish, *"potentially* have broken a lamp jumping over the sofa."

"Why did you jump over the sofa?"

"The badger was coming."

Sophie sighed.

"Christ…"

"I'm *so* sorry," Finley whispered. "If I *live* long enough, I swear I'll replace it."

Sophie bit back a giggle.

"You're so lucky you're so cute, Bennett."

"That's the second time you've called me cute in the past five minutes Cedars, I'm beginning to think you…*holy fuck,* it's working!" Finley yelped. "Sophie, it's *working.* She's eating it!"

Sophie held her breath.

There was a long pause.

And rather a lot of shuffling.

And a few squeaks and squeals.

Then finally, the slam of the front door, and a heavy exhale.

Sophie grinned.

"Did you live to see another day?"

"Yes, thank you. My *hero,*" Finley gushed, and Sophie could hear the teasing smirk that wrapped around the words. "Tell you what, the animals in this place *really* don't seem to like me much. *'Percy the Park Keeper'* is a bunch of absolute lies."

Sophie giggled. Finley Bennett really was turning out to be a huge softie, and Sophie really could not cope with the fact that this big city, high-flying architect kept making cartoon references.

"They can *smell* the city girl on you." Sophie grinned. "Glad I could help. Let me know if you come across a toad in a flat cap now, won't you?"

"Oh, fuck off."

Sophie giggled, wiping at her eyes as she heard Finley's laughter catch with her own.

"You're very lucky you're cute yourself, you ginormous ass," Finley chuckled. "Come on then. Tell me about Southbank."

Sophie grinned.

*So* very cute.

~ ~ ~ ~ ~ ~ (♪) ~ ~ ~ ~ ~ ~

Finley frowned as another piece of sloppy beetroot slipped between the rungs of Sophie's barbecue grill. The handwritten recipe for vegan burgers that she had found in a binder in the kitchen had included a photo.

A photo of perfectly rounded, thick, juicy looking patties that had been delicately topped with onion rings and fresh lettuce.

A photo that looked absolutely *nothing* like the gooey pile of floury mess that Finley was currently trying to grill.

She poked the burger with her spatula, groaning as another chunk broke away. She had to admit, the watery mixture was not particularly whetting her appetite, and to her grumbling stomach's dismay, she was pretty certain Polcarne did *not* have Deliveroo.

Finley had always liked to cook. She'd never been overly fantastic at it, but she'd always enjoyed whipping up a steak stir fry in her overpriced griddle pan, or a Bolognese with a little red wine. It wasn't something she ever made the time to do these days, but she'd always found the process quite therapeutic.

This, however, was *not* therapeutic.

This was the stuff of a perfectionist's nightmare.

She jumped a little as her phone rang.

She sighed, abandoning the disappointing meal in favour of focusing her attention on the considerably *less* disappointing name that rolled over her screen.

"Hey, Soph!" She beamed.

"Am I cool enough to visit Pop Brixton?"

Finley chuckled. *Brixton?* That was a way out. There were many places she had expected Sophie to visit during her stay in London, but Brixton had most definitely *not* been one of them.

And *cool* enough?

Pop Brixton was a hipster collection of bars and eateries in a bunch of old shipping containers. It was *fun*, sure, but Finley had certainly never considered it particularly *elite.*

*"Anyone* is cool enough to visit Pop Brixton."

"I feel like you're lying to me. This place is made out of *shipping containers,* Finley! And all of the drinks here are craft and botanical, and the people are all wearing deep V necks and tiny scarves."

"Like I said, *anyone* can be cool enough," Finley laughed. "Besides, you're *very* cool, Soph."

There was a pause.

Then Sophie's voice dropped. Almost shy.

"You think so?"

Finley chuckled.

She really liked the snippets of tentative confidence that fell more and more from Sophie during their chats, but she couldn't deny she loved it when Finley could make her shy.

Which she knew she could do with just a few carefully chosen words, and a very specific tone of voice.

"Well, *no* actually," she teased. *"You,* Sophie Cedars, are *smoking hot. "*

"Charmer," Sophie muttered, but Finley could hear the soft smile in her voice.

"I'm just truthful." Finley shrugged.

*"You* are just a flirt!" Sophie laughed.

Finley grinned.

"And why can't I be both?"

"Quit flustering me, Finley Bennet," Sophie demanded. "I'm trying to appear *cool. "*

Finley laughed openly, shaking her head as she prodded once again at the beetroot mess spread in front of her.

"Just be you," she urged, softer and more earnest. "Now, explain to me why your beetroot patty pictures look incredible and mine are just disintegrating over your barbecue."

Sophie gasped.

"You're cooking *vegan?*"

Finley grinned, her stomach flipping at the excitement in the breathless voice.

"Well, I can't stop thinking about the lamb." She shuddered. "Besides, your recipes made it look *really* appealing!"

Sophie squealed.

"But right now, what *I* have produced does *not* look appealing," Finley whined.

"If it helps though, it's earning you *major* sexy points," Sophie murmured.

Finley dropped the spatula.


*"Really?"*


*"So* many," Sophie hummed. "Come on then, let's fix your dinner. Walk me through what you did."

Finley smirked, shaking her head.

It was getting *far* too easy for Sophie Cedars to push her buttons.

~ ~ ~ ~ ~ ~ 🎧 ~ ~ ~ ~ ~ ~


Sophie frowned, biting back a whimper of frustration as she pressed yet another button on the digital screen of Finley's oven, and for the thirteenth time the appliance beeped, but sweet pissing *nothing* happened.

She had been in London for five days, and she was growing tired of the junk food she'd been relying on up until now. Finley's online shop had been full of fresh vegetables, and Sophie was hellbent on cooking this bloody butternut curry if it killed her.

But the oven had other ideas.

And she was one more antagonising beep away from setting fire to a tea towel and just roasting her butternut over that like the primal country girl she clearly was.

The towel was saved by the ringtone of her phone, blaring out across the kitchen counter.

She grinned, her shoulders dropping slightly at the sight of Finley's name.

"Hey!"

"Does all Trevor's cheese taste like a damp sock?"

Sophie grimaced.

"Why do you think I went vegan?"

"Is it supposed to be *grey?*" Finley's voice was muffled, distorted as if she spoke around a mouthful of her food.

"Ah, the peppercorn, eh?" Sophie shuddered. "Are you eating it now?"

"Yeah…I was hoping you might *distract* me while I get through it."

Sophie laughed as Finley audibly bit back a gag, coughing slightly as she spoke.

"Are you trying to flirt with me with a mouth full of fusty cheese?" She quirked an eyebrow.

"Is that not doing it for you?" Finley coughed again.

"Weirdly, it almost is." Sophie grinned. "You know you don't *have* to eat it, right?"

"Really?"

"Of course not," Sophie laughed. "Trevor won't know! I'm pretty sure nobody ever does eat that stuff."

"Oh, thank *god.*"

Sophie giggled, shaking her head.

"Now, talk me through this oven, Bennett. Do I need a third degree to work it, or is there a hidden secret?"

"Not a woman of technology really, are you?" Finley chuckled.

Sophie smirked.

Finley Bennett and her bloody charm had a very embarrassing way of flustering Sophie into a blushing pile of useless mess. Which, if she were honest, Sophie kind of liked.

It made her feel alive.

And she *loved* the idea of tinting Finley's ears as red as she knew her own were. But Sophie Cedars was intuitive. She knew full well that no amount of smooth charm, or buttery words would fluster Finley.

She was too well versed.

Far too used to attentive eyes, and deliberate flirting.

So, Sophie had her own game.

She knew that to fluster Finley Bennett, she had to catch her off guard. Say things that sweet country bumpkin Sophie Cedars would never usually say.

"The most high-tech things in *my* house are battery powered and in a box under my bed," she retorted.

Finley choked.

"Now," Sophie continued, biting back her amusement, "which button do I press, Inspector Gadget?"

"Uh…" Finley cleared her throat. "I think you just pressed all of mine!"

Sophie giggled.

"Put it back in your pants, Casanova, and help me cook my dinner."

~ ~ ~ ~ ~ ~ (♪) ~ ~ ~ ~ ~ ~ ~

Finley closed her eyes, her entire body melting into the heated stone bed beneath her.

She could feel every ounce of tension drain away, pulled into the stone as if it were some kind of osmosis, and she had had *no* idea how much she'd needed this.

She'd been at the spa for two hours, and she was still struggling to comprehend how *quiet* the place was. It was smaller than the spas she was used to; the extortionate ones she had visited with Jess, way back before her career had numbed her mind to the meaning of the word *relaxation.* But even so, she had not expected to be the only person in the room for the entire morning.

She grinned as her phone buzzed beneath her, softly chiming the ringtone that she had set specifically for Sophie.

She slid the screen to answer.

"Hey, Soph, how's…"

"I am going to *kill* you, Bennett!"

Finley sat upright.

She had heard Sophie in a tube-fuelled state of fluster before, but she had never heard a bite like this in her voice.

And certainly not aimed at her!

"What?" She frowned. *"Why,* what did I do?"

The line was *very* noisy.

The wind sounded far stronger than anything Finley was used to in the city, buried amongst the protection of the tall buildings. Sophie's voice was practically screaming into the blustering abyss, and Finley held the phone a little further from her ear instinctively.

*"Climb up over the O2, Sophie,"* the voice on the line mocked, "it'll be *fun* and the *views* are so *worth it!"*

Oh.

That.

Finley bit her lip, stifling the amusement that threatened to make itself known.

Now the noise made sense.

If she had to hazard a guess, she'd say Sophie was already at least halfway to the dome's top.

"You didn't *have* to! Why didn't you just say you're scared of heights?"

"I'm *not* scared of heights!" Sophie yelled. "I'm pissing *terrified* of hauling myself over the roof of a 170ft high glorified shitting *tent* in *gale force winds!"*

Finley covered the mouthpiece as she giggled.

Okay, maybe she *was* at fault here. Maybe she *could* have warned Sophie that the weather was probably a pretty key factor in how enjoyable this particular activity would be.

And Sophie did seem genuinely scared.

Finley did feel *pretty* guilty.

But in her defence, she had genuinely thought Sophie would enjoy this.

"I'm sorry, Soph!" she pleaded. "You can yell at me the whole way down, if it'll make you feel better?"

Sophie was quiet for a moment, and Finley held her breath as she waited for the onslaught.

"I didn't call to yell at you," Sophie sighed.

Finley exhaled.

"I called so you can *distract* me while I risk my life to get *down* from this thing."

Finley grinned.

"It would be my pleasure, Sophie Cedars." She relaxed back against the heated stone bed. "How would you like me to do that?"

"Just talk to me. Tell me about your morning."

"I'm at the spa! I had a massage this morning from a *very* chatty lady called Gloria. Her eighteen-year-old son is at uni in London, so it took me most of the forty minutes to convince her that that did *not* mean I knew him…"

Finley grinned as Sophie laughed, followed instantly by a squeak of terror.

"And now I'm just lying around on a heated lounger, talking to this cutie who's doing a *really* great job of getting through something pretty terrifying."

"Don't patronise me, Bennett," Sophie huffed.

Finley rolled her eyes, her lips tugging into a satisfied grin.

Clearly something about this terrifying experience was dropping all of Sophie's people pleasing barriers, and Finley definitely liked it.

But before she could form the carefully chosen flirty words, and the deliberate husk in her voice to say as much, Sophie was talking again.

"You talk to me a lot when you're naked."

*"Wh*...I'm not *naked* in the spa, Sophie," Finley laughed.

"Shhhh, let me imagine."

Finley choked out a laugh, her cheeks colouring instantly. She knew the comment had been playful—a method of distraction for Sophie—but she just couldn't help the way her veins burned at the slightest hint of flirtation from this woman.

She glanced down at her bikini clad body, her cheeks burning hotter at the realisation that while Sophie wasn't strictly correct, she wasn't exactly far from it.

She raised an eyebrow, shaking her head in bashful amusement.

"Why, is it helping you?"

"Yes, now I'm in my happy place."

Finley chuckled softly.

God *damnit,* she was becoming *such* a gay mess for Sophie Cedars.

~ ~ ~ ~ ~ ~ 🎧 ~ ~ ~ ~ ~ ~

Sophie pressed her face to the glass of the London Eye pod, far too entranced by the view over the city to care how many strange glances the other occupants were shooting in her direction.

Funny how *this* height was fine.

Sophie was one hundred percent certain she was falling in love with London.

She was falling in love with the lights, and the variety of faces, and the vast array of different buildings and parks and theatres and shops and architecture and graffiti and artwork and everything that felt so different to the world she knew.

She was falling in love with the constant sound of life, and the rumble of the trains, and the buskers, and the market calls, and the snippets of different languages she heard every day as she wandered the city.

She had treated herself to an all-out tourist day, complete with an *'I Love London'* t-shirt. She had been to the London Bridge and Tomb experience, visited the dungeons, snapped selfies outside the Houses of Parliament and Big Ben, and been dramatically disappointed in the complete lack of anything to look at 10 Downing Street.

She'd even bought last minute tickets for a show tonight from a booth in Leicester Square.

She had splashed out on a very expensive, very indulgent lunch in a vegan restaurant, which she still couldn't quite believe existed, and now she was at the very top of the London Eye, looking out over the city she'd once thought would be a distant dream she'd never reach.

Six days in, and she just couldn't get over how incredible it was to have all of these amazing things on her doorstep, and it was *crazy* to her to think that Finley had gotten so lost in the pressures of the city that she'd grown numb to it.

She couldn't help but wonder if she herself had grown numb to Polcarne in the same way.

Was Finley finding the same incredulity there? Was she sitting now on a cliff by the sea, looking out over her own beautiful view and wondering how Sophie could ever want to leave there?

Sophie blushed a little, twisting her fingers over themselves in coy embarrassment as she realised that once again, Finley Bennett was occupying her mind.

She'd found this had been happening a lot, these past few days. The way Finley would just seep into her thoughts naturally, with ease and comfort as if she'd always been a feature. And each time she did, Sophie found herself wanting to hear the calm soothe of her voice.

It hadn't escaped her that she'd been so worried about leaving Polcarne and everyone in it, and the way she would miss them, and yet the person she found herself yearning for was a Londoner she'd never met.

She fished her phone out, her finger hovering hesitantly over Finley's contact.

She didn't even have a washed-out pseudo-reason to call this time.

She simply wanted to hear the voice that was somehow becoming the soundtrack of her trip, despite the 300 miles between them.

Was that weird? Was it too much?

Probably.

But for the first time in her life, she wasn't sure she cared.

She dialled the number.

"Hey!" Finley's voice sang out almost immediately. "I was just thinking about you."

Sophie's stomach plummeted.

"Y-you were?" She cursed herself for her stutter. She could feel the heat rising through the blush on her cheeks, and she found herself grateful that Finley couldn't see her face.

"I was looking through your books for something to read," Finley continued, "and now I'm accidentally-on-purpose halfway through your school yearbook."

"Oh *no!*" Sophie groaned, covering her face with her free hand. "I will get you back for this, Finley Bennett."

"This girl looks very cute! A Sophie Cedars, class of 2012. Do you know her? *Hugely* oversized blazer, really short, stubby tie?" Finley teased, her voice irritatingly mischievous *"Adorable,* though. All dimples and a straight cut fringe, and sparkling eyes."

Sophie grimaced.

*Why?*

Why her?

"In my defence," she grumbled, "I always had hand-me-downs, and Bex was a *lot* taller than I am."

"Yeah?" Finley murmured, her voice lower and darker in that increasingly familiar flirtatious hum that never failed to make Sophie's cheeks feel warm. "Are you as small as you are adorable?"

Sophie grinned, rolling her eyes.

"Will you *quit* flustering me in public places?" she chuckled.

"I make no promises," Finley murmured.

Sophie closed her eyes for a moment, her blood feeling warmer and her chest feeling *just* a little tighter.

She hated how easily she flustered when Finley flirted with her.

Hated how *inexperienced* it made her feel.

But she also *loved* the racing of her heart, and the flutter of her stomach, and that new and unfamiliar feeling of excitement and nerves and anticipation.

"Favourite quote…" Finley continued, reading the words Sophie knew were printed beneath her yearbook photo. Her voice was playful and soft, with no real mockery in the tease. *"'To live is the rarest thing in the world. Most people exist, that is all.'"*

Sophie blushed, groaning viscerally as she tipped her head back.

"Look, *all* teenagers are cringey, okay?" she huffed. "It's a rite of passage."

Finley chuckled.

"Besides," Sophie insisted, "I'm sure you were…"

"I don't want…"

Finley's voice cut her off. It was darker this time. Lower. A husk ran through it that was immediately captivating, and Sophie stopped talking.

*"'To be at the mercy of my emotions. I want to* use *them, to* enjoy *them, and to* dominate *them.'"*

Sophie swallowed.

Well, mother of patchwork elephants, *that* was *irritatingly* sexy in an *incredibly* cliché way.

And now she had goosebumps.

Which was pathetic, really. And she knew it was. But there was something about listening to this gorgeous woman with the silkiest voice she had ever heard, quoting lines from her favourite book—and seemingly off by heart—that was *doing* things to Sophie that she would never have anticipated that something this fucking *cheesey* would do.

Also, the way Finley's voice had darkened, and the specific quote she'd chosen was…*warming,* in a way Sophie hadn't felt in a long time.

*"Shit,* you goddamn cheeseball," she huffed. "That was *annoyingly* attractive."

Finley laughed.

"*Picture of Dorian Gray,* right?" she chuckled. "Would you believe me if I told you that was *my* yearbook quote?"

"No." Sophie grinned.

"You'd be right." Finley's smirk was audible. "Mine was *'I never look back, darling. It distracts from the now.'*"

Sophie blinked.

"Edna Mode," Finley stated.

Sophie blinked again.

"*'The Incredibles'? No capes?*" Finley pressed; her voice almost incredulous.

Sophie shook her head.

"You're an idiot, Bennett," she giggled.

"*Wow,* what happened to attractive?"

"You're an attractive idiot."

"Look, we all have our role models, Cedars," Finley deadpanned. "Sorry, did you need me for something, before I hit you with this tangent?"

Sophie faltered.

"Uh, no. I just…"

She trailed off.

Was this weird to say?

*Fuck it.*

"I just kinda wanted to…to hear…"

*Shit.*

Yes.

It was definitely weird to say.

Oh god, *how* was she going to dig herself out of this giant, awkward as *shit*…

"Yeah, I get it." Finley murmured.

*Oh.*

Sophie exhaled.

Finley's words were so soft. So easy. So instantly reassuring.

She melted.

"So, tell me about the tombs!" Finley pressed, genuine interest clear in her tone. "Did you scream?"

Sophie beamed.

She was really beginning to find it difficult to keep a handle on the feeling that bellowed at her from behind the wall she *tried* to build around it.

She *liked* Finley.

Liked her like she hadn't liked anyone in a *really* long time.

And that was frustrating as *shit*, because it was *stupid*.

She'd never even *met* the woman.

They were from totally different worlds, living totally different lives, 300 miles apart.

Or so she tried to tell herself.

But every time she supplied her niggling brain with that excuse, it gave her one simple response.

*For now.*

After all, wasn't that why she was here?

To test the waters? Make a change in her life?

Still, that did not change the fact that she had never *met* Finley Bennett.

She could not possibly like her.

It was ridiculous.

Wasn't it?

# Chapter Ten

Finley grunted, her jaw clenching as she shot a glare at her ringing phone.

For the sixth time, today.

She considered answering, just to stop the barrage, and the pressure, and the anxiety that crushed each and every time the ringtone had burst her little Cornish haven. Amelia's name was a taunt.

she had never expected, and she was somehow both proud and ashamed of the way she recoiled from it.

Ashamed because this was her career. This had been her dream since she was twelve years old and scribbling on a sketch pad by the low light of her bedside lamp in the small hours of a sleepless morning. A dream she had chased with fire, and passion, and *sacrifice.* She'd prioritised nothing but this, for as long as she'd known.

And one missed chance, and a week in a tiny hamlet town had made her shy away. Instead, of that fire, and that passion, and that sacrifice, she felt *resentment.*

And that made her feel ashamed, but it made her feel proud.

Proud that for the first time in her adult life, Finley knew that the freedom she needed right now wasn't in her suit or her salary.

She didn't understand it, but she knew it.

She swallowed, her shoulders sagging a little as the phone's screen fell dark and silent. She sank back into the sofa, her mind swimming with words she could barely decipher anymore.

Words she'd played in her head over and over and over again, for so much of her life.

Her father's brash demands for excellence, and their brutal contradiction against the narcissistic need to squash her successes. His heated insistence that she work harder, and longer, and never bring home anything less than the best. Nothing less than an A, or a record, or a win. But then the cold, indifferent dismissal when she met those demands and exceeded them. As if, somehow, it were simply the bare minimum to be the best.

Jess's heartfelt pleas for something softer than excellence. Her earnest urge for Finley to live her dreams, but to also live her life. The way those words had felt so demanding at the time, like a rein around Finley's shoulders, tugging every time she tried to soar higher. And the way that the niggling voice in Finley's mind had echoed them, and scolded her for not seeing their truth, and their value.

Finley's own words to Sophie. The almost promise that she would learn to kick back, and *learn* to be a little less lonely.

A strange, almost reluctant promise. One she knew all too well she needed, but she wasn't sure she knew how to want.

She sighed, her throat burning as the phone burst into life again, and she pushed it beneath the sofa cushions, as if somehow muting the sound would make the caller disappear. And with it, the decision to answer or ignore it.

She'd been ignoring Amelia's calls for seven days, and they were only increasing in persistence, and getting more erratic in their timings, and Finley's confliction was only growing stronger.

The first time she had declined Amelia's call, she had felt liberated. Like she was in control; taking charge of her life in her simple efforts not to let her boss dominate her time off and burst her newfound bubble.

The second time, she'd felt nauseous.

What if it was important? What if she was digging herself a whole world of trouble, and ignoring these calls were the nails in the coffin of her career?

But through a feat of sheer miraculous determination, she'd shrugged it off. She figured she was already in enough trouble for fucking off with zero notice for two weeks, so she might as well throw a little salt into the wound and at least make it worth her while.

This time she felt guilty.

Even if it was nearing 11pm.

But even so, there was something calming, and revitalising in the Cornish sea air that had made it far easier for her burdened mind to gain some perspective, and she was determined not to let this woman pull her back into her work and the mess that awaited her in London before she was ready.

She wondered, briefly, if Bella's bruises had faded.

Finley shuddered.

Amelia would survive without her for another week.

She hauled herself up from the sofa, leaving the phone buzzing beneath the cushions as she wandered out of the room, hoping that the more steps she placed between her and the caller ID, the easier it would be to ignore.

She thought about the past week. About Polcarne, and the sea, and the sand, and the farmers, and the sounds of the crickets. She thought about Trevor and Trixie, and the people she'd seen milling about the beach and the town. She thought about the calm way they seemed to stroll about their slower paced lives.

Then she thought about London, and the way Finley lived her own life.

Never seeing her friends, never taking breaks, never dating.

She hadn't lied when she'd told Sophie she was happy. She *was,* and she loved her job. And she had always strived for more. Strived for *better.* But she couldn't help but feel like maybe she'd been buried in her own metaphorical sand for too long, and that actually all she was really doing was cutting herself off from the parts of life that could make her feel more complete. Maybe there was a *different* better she should be striving for. A balance.

She thought about Jess.

Finley had always felt *so* guilty for the way that Jess had come second, every time. She had always felt so guilty for the amount that she worked, and her girlfriend had *tried* to understand, but she had never been able to cope with the hours that Finley put in. And Finley knew she couldn't blame her. She knew she could never have blamed Jess for feeling like her second priority, because Finley had known that she *was.* What Finley had wanted—*still* wanted—more than *anything* else was the role. Her dream. She hadn't wanted to distract her focus from that for even a moment. Even for Jess.

She guessed she should always have known, really, that Jess wasn't her future.

She thought about Sophie.

Finley had *really* liked the texts and the photos and the sound of Sophie's voice this past week.

She'd liked Sophie's open willingness to share her experiences, and her unabashed curiosity and enthusiasm about the world around her. She'd liked her sharp wit, and her soft nature, and the way she seemed to always have something to say to Finley. And she'd liked the way that Sophie always seemed to be thinking of Finley, just as Finley was thinking of her.

She was starting to think that maybe what she liked was simply *Sophie.*

And that was *stupid* for a whole host of reasons.

Namely, the 300-mile distance and the fact that she had never *met* the woman.

But even so, the one thought that stood out the most to Finley was that she wasn't sure she could be *enough* for Sophie Cedars.

What did she have to offer someone like Sophie? Someone so bright, and inquisitive, and so happy-go-lucky. All Finley knew was work. She couldn't even really show Sophie around the goddamn city that she fucking *lived* in, she'd been so out of touch with it for so long.

She hadn't managed to dedicate her time and energy to a partner who lived in the same room as her, let alone one who lived in a different county.

No matter how different Sophie felt in Finley's chest.

No matter how much that niggling voice in her head told her that she could be enough, if she just stepped back. Learned to live for *living's* sake.

Finley blinked, shaking her head of her thoughts, as she found herself in a room she had yet to enter in the time she had been in the cottage. She'd known it was here, obviously, but the small home office had reminded her too much of work, and so she had kept the door closed in a futile effort to forget that employment was even a thing.

But she found herself here now, and she cursed herself for the subliminal indication that Amelia was clearly getting under her skin.

Winning, without Finley even having to pick up the phone.

She let her eyes roam the room, taking it in properly for the first time. The walls were full on two sides with books; rows and rows of textbooks and biographies; of history, and languages, and binders of handwritten notes. The desk sat facing the window, looking out over the garden, and the remaining wall held just two items.

Two frames.

Two degrees.

Finley grinned.

She traced her fingers over the glass, her eyes widening as she took in the words and the logo across the top of the certificates.

*The Open University.*

Sophie had said that she had two degrees, but Finley hadn't realised that they were distance-learning ones. Online ones.

Something about that seemed *so* much more remarkable.

The determination, and the discipline, and the *love* that it must have taken for Sophie to do so many years of studying on her own agenda, without the rally and the drive of classmates around her to push her when things got hardest. The kind of *strength* and passion that Sophie must have had to have done that, not just once, but *twice.*

Finley was coloured well and truly impressed.

And the feeling lifted high in her chest, tapping into something Finley knew well, *so* very deep into her bones.

Sophie knew how it felt to *push* for something.

And something in that made this almost stranger feel so much closer. So much more *real* to Finley. More real than some of the people she spent every day with in their flesh and blood.

The windchime sound of Sophie's doorbell rang out through the quiet house, and Finley jumped, pulled instantly from her reverie.

She swallowed.

Sophie was away, Finley didn't know anybody in this *county*, let alone in this town, she was in the middle of no-one-will-hear-your-screams-nowhere, and it was dark.

She was pretty sure she could be forgiven if she was a *little* sceptical of a haunting fucking doorbell chime at 11pm.

That bell was cute and charming in the day, but somehow under the blanket of the dark, the whimsical little tune was straight from the goddamn horror films that haunted Finley's nightmares.

Kind of like how the films used ghost children and haunting nursery rhymes to strike fear, and it *always* impacted so much harder than it did when the ghosts were adults.

She considered ignoring it. Crawling under the sofa cushions beside her phone, and waiting for this, too, to go away.

But the rational part of her brain was aware, on some level, that if someone had made the effort to come to a remote cottage, in a hamlet town in the ass end of nowhere, at 11pm after dark, and ring the doorbell…well then, they probably needed something.

She took a deep breath, creeping slowly down the spiral staircase as she headed for the door.

Via the kitchen, where she grabbed the biggest frying pan she could find.

She considered a knife, but then she figured if it *was* someone in need of help on the other side of the door, then *she* would become the screw-loose psychopath in this horror film situation, and so she thought she'd better play it just a *little* less threatening.

Just in case.

She steeled her nerves, holding the frying pan tight in her clenched fist as she pulled back the door.

She blinked.

The unfamiliar tattooed woman on the doorstep was clearly a little worse for wear. Her green eyes were glazed and unfocused beneath her bright pink, straight cut fringe, and she leaned against the doorframe with a slump in her posture that suggested the structure was *probably* the only thing holding her upright.

"Hey…" Finley greeted.

The stranger frowned.

She stared at Finley for a long moment, before her glazed eyes scanned across the door and the pathway around her, as if checking her surroundings. Then those hazy eyes widened as they flicked back at Finley, and their gaze dropped slowly over her tank and PJ bottoms.

She let out a low whistle.

"Oh *shit,* Soph *really* scored this time!"

Finley smirked.

She was fairly sure she could take a *reasonably* well-educated guess at who this might be. And even without her instincts, the distinct resemblance to the smattering of photo frames across the walls of this cottage were enough to give her a justifiable confidence.

The hair was kind of hard to miss. She didn't imagine it was a common style in Polcarne, Cornwall.

"Sorry to disturb your late-night cooking, uh…*Sophie's conquest…*" the woman mumbled, waving a hand around Finley's middle.

Finley frowned, following the line of the gesture. Her eyes widened as she remembered the frying pan, and she blushed as she promptly hid it behind her back.

"But I could really use a seat while this room finishes just…" the woman slurred, gesturing wildly with her hands, "spinning around."

Finley chuckled, moving aside to let what she assumed was Sophie's sister stagger in.

Bex, if she remembered correctly.

"Where is my sister?"

Finley grinned.

"She's not here!"

Bex screwed her face.

"You were that bad, eh?" She shook her head as she let her eyes roam Finley's body once more. "Well, that's disappointing."

*"No,"* Finley laughed, putting the pan down as she followed Bex into the living room. "I'm not your sister's conquest, I'm…"

*"Really?"* Bex spun to face her, wobbling slightly on her feet. She furrowed her brow. "What a waste."

Finley blushed.

She was beginning to think the Cedars family didn't own filters.

"I'm Finley Bennett, I'm the holiday guest. The house swap, that you went to the butcher for?" She rolled her eyes in amusement as Bex flopped gracelessly onto the sofa, her face buried in the cushions. "Sophie, right now, is probably just leaving the night's production of *Wicked* in London's West End."

"Oh *shit* yeah, the trip!" Bex mumbled into the fabric. "Well, *not-conquest,* I'm very sorry to interrupt your *raving* holiday, but Sophie always lets me stay here when I've had a little beverage or two. Saves me mum duty at the ass-crack of dawn." Bex hauled herself around, flailing slightly as she propped herself up into a seating position. "You getting the drinks in then, or what?"

Finley bit back a laugh, silently amused by the fact that clearly now she was entertaining this unexpected guest.

"Uh…" She raised her brows. "I have wine? Or those Spurling local brews?"

Bex screwed her face up.

"Check the back of the second cupboard in from the left."

Finley headed to the kitchen, following Bex's instruction. She laughed, shaking her head as she pulled out a mostly full bottle of dark rum.

"Won't Sophie mind?"

"I doubt she even knows it's there, that's my secret stash," Bex dismissed. "She never keeps the good stuff."

Finley poured two glasses, handing one to Bex, and placed the full bottle down on the coffee table.

She raised her eyebrows in amusement as Bex immediately knocked the dark liquid straight back, pushed the glass onto the table, and proceeded to swig directly from the bottle.

Finley chuckled as she took a seat beside her new guest. She threw her own glass back, shuddering as the burn hit the back of her throat.

It had been a *while*.

And she didn't like to admit it in present company, but she definitely preferred a cola mixer with her spirits. And maybe a lime slice.

"So, I know why Sophie wanted a home swap. One night in London costs more than my life is worth, but what's *your* deal, Cheapskate Winslet?" Bex slurred slightly, waving the bottle in Finley's direction. "Why is a city high-flier like you in my sister's two-bed and not in a five star in St Ives?"

"Cheapskate Winslet?" Finley grinned, quirking an eyebrow.

Bex smirked.

"*Yeah,* you know, the *'The Holiday'*, the house swap…"

Finley shrugged.

"Maybe I was hoping to meet my very own drunken lady Jude Law on the doorstep of a country cottage after dark." She winked, tilting her glass at Bex cheekily.

Bex blinked.

"No."

Finley laughed.

"You're hot, Kardashian number six, I'll give you that," Bex smirked. "But you're not my type."

Finley scrunched her nose.

"Aren't there already six Kardashians?"

Bex blinked.

"I have no idea." She waved a dismissive hand. "Either way, I'm not about the pantie hamster myself, so you're shit out of luck."

Finley grinned. Bex wasn't her type either, but she was definitely shaping up to be someone she could enjoy being around.

"*Sophie,* on the other hand…" Bex slurred. "*She* would be *all* over you like a panda in a bucket of bamboo shoots."

Finley's stomach dropped.

She leaned back against the sofa cushions, trying desperately to hide the way her cheeks flushed and her heart pounded at the sound of her host's name, and the insinuation that had come with it. She bit her tongue, adamant that the '*I hope so*' that it seemed determined to shape would *not* reach Bex's ears.

She leaned forward, whipping the rum bottle from Bex's hand before she could take another swig.

She was *definitely* going to need a few more of these.

She poured herself another glass, downing it in one.

"Why would you need to come to *Polcarne* to meet a Jude…*ith* Law when you live in *London?*" Bex scoffed, grabbing the bottle back.

"Well, I was *joking…*" Finley started.

*"Flirting,* more like." Bex smirked.

Finley rolled her eyes.

"But you'd be surprised," she continued. "The last date I went on, I spent two hundred quid on shitty wine, bruised my own clit, and then broke her nose."

Finley paused, the reality of her words hanging heavy and embarrassing in the silence for a long moment.

Then Bex baulked.

"Kinky. Maybe you a*re* my type."

Finley laughed.

*"Then* I lost a promotion on the same night, had a practical meltdown, and promptly disappeared off the grid. And here we are."

Bex raised an eyebrow as she sat a little straighter, passing Finley the bottle.

Finley gave up with the glass.

She took a long swig.

"That not told you enough?" she chuckled.

"Nothing interesting *ever* happens in Polcarne, Bennett," Bex chuckled. "I'm definitely here for this story."

"Well, I've been an architect for nine years, and a senior at my company for three," Finley started.

"Shit," Bex breathed. "You really are a high-flier."

Finley chuckled through a large swig of rum.

"And my boss didn't give me a promotion that should *absolutely* have been mine," she huffed. "I work fifty hours a week, I smash my projects, and my clients love me."

"Is it because you're so humble?" Bex grinned.

"No." Finley narrowed her eyes, shooting a mock scowl in Bex's direction. Then she smirked. "It's because I'm charming as fuck."

"Clearly." Bex nodded "Did your date think the same?"

"She *did.*" Finley took another swig of rum, relishing the burn as it soothed the humiliating words. "Until I roundhouse-kicked her in the face."

Bex smirked, raising a single eyebrow.

"Humble, charming, and violent," she stated, counting each adjective off on her fingers as she said them. "Such a catch."

"That's what it says on my dating profiles," Finley quipped, smirking at the amused look on Bex's face.

"Just so we're clear…" Bex grabbed the bottle, waving it precariously in the air before her as she studied Finley in a glazed kind of amusement. "This was a kink thing, not a wife-beating thing, right?"

Finley groaned.

She let herself flop back, her head resting on the sofa cushion as she braced herself to tell the story she'd been trying to repress for a week.

"Ugh, *neither,* I was just *nervous,"* she confessed. "It had been a long time, I was wearing a pair of vice-clamp jeans I let a gay man coerce me into wearing, and I was really over enthusiastic about the idea of this girl getting me out of them." She laughed, letting her head loll to the side as she met Bex's gaze. "The jeans got stuck, there were a lot of limbs and a lot of wriggling, and I ended up kneeing her right between the eyes."

"I see." Bex nodded, pursing her lips. "A pathetic useless lesbian thing. Got you." She took another swig of rum. "Well, hey, we've all been there. What's life without the occasional sex bruise? Did you at least carry on?"

Finley grinned. There was something about Bex's brash, no-nonsense nature that made it feel *so* much easier to find the humour in the *incredibly* embarrassing situation that she had been trying to repress all week, and she felt herself relax into the woman's presence as she began to delve into the details of her story, the rum bottle passing seamlessly between the two.

~ ~ ~ ~ ~ ~ (♪) ~ ~ ~ ~ ~ ~

Sophie practically skipped down the stairs of The Apollo Victoria Theatre, and into the bustling foyer.

She felt *elated.*

The theatre had always felt like such a glamourous way to pass the time. The kind of thing people did when they had money, and sophistication, and class. And the small university-run theatre in Exeter served its purpose, but it didn't feel like the dream.

Not like the Apollo Victoria.

Not like *'Wicked'* in London's West End.

She felt so *immersed* in the art, and the culture, and the history, and the *life.*

She couldn't wipe the smile from her face as she picked her way through the animated crowds, heading for the bar. She had nowhere to be in a hurry, she had dressed up to the nines for her first theatre experience, and she was in far too good a mood to crawl home to bed just yet.

So instead, she figured she could sip on a Cosmopolitan and just be a part of the buzz around her for a little while longer.

*"Sophie?* Hey, Sophie!"

Sophie snapped her head round, craning her neck in search of the voice.

Surely they didn't mean her?

She didn't *know* anyone in London.

And it was a *pretty* common name.

"Sophie!"

The voice called again, and Sophie spun a full 360 as she hunted for any signs of familiarity. Surely, they didn't mean her, but they were being very persistent, and they *did* seem to be getting closer.

*"Soph…"*

The voice was right behind her now, a hand softly grasping over her shoulder.

She spun.

She gasped as her eyes landed on a friendly face she really did recognise, and a beaming grin that made her smile instantly.

"Noah! Hi!"

"How you doing, babes?" Noah beamed. "Good to see you again, how's London been?"

"It's been amazing! That show was incredible!"

"I *know* right?" Noah chuckled. "Six times and counting for us!"

Noah gestured behind him, and Sophie followed his gaze to a small group of people around her own age, who all waved enthusiastically.

"Hey, are you doing anything now?" Noah turned his attention back to Sophie. "We're gonna go and grab some drinks! Wanna join us?"

Sophie beamed.

*"Yeah,* actually! That would be *great,* if you're sure I wouldn't be imposing?"

"Never! We'd love you to come." Noah led her back to the group. "This is Harri, Kate, and my roommate Zayan. Guys, this is Sophie, she's staying in Finley's place while Fin is in Cornwall!"

*"Ooh* the house swap!" Zayan nodded enthusiastically, holding his hand out to meet Sophie's own. "Great to meet you Sophie, hope London's being good to you!"

"Come on then, let's get out of here!" Kate whooped, throwing an arm around Sophie's shoulders as she steered the group through the foyer and out of the exit. "It's *absolutely* 'She Bar' tonight gals, we have a *guest* to entertain! You ever been to Soho before, Sophie?"

Sophie grinned.

*No,* she had not, and she couldn't *wait* to set foot in a real-life gay bar!

Sophie was vibrating with both excitement and nerves as she followed the group into, *'She Soho'*, with Noah hot on her heels.

She wasn't *quite* raised in a barn, so she wasn't exactly alien to the concept of a gay bar, and as a bisexual child of the internet age, she definitely had her enthusiastic preconceptions about what she would find in here.

But she hadn't expected it to make her feel so *safe,* so *quickly!*

The moment Sophie passed through the doors and into the bar, she felt twenty years of small-town loneliness lift from her shoulders.

There were other members of the LGBTQ+ community in Cornwall, of *course* there were, and Sophie was absolutely not going to pretend she hadn't come across them on a reasonably regular basis. It was just that they all seemed to be in the larger towns and cities, and Polcarne always seemed to feel like a different world. A world where she was different to everyone else, no matter how accepting the people were of her.

But in here, Sophie was at home. She was amongst friends, and it was immediately *exhilarating.*

As the group crowded around the bar, Harri shouting drinks orders across the thumping music, Sophie snapped a selfie.

She sent it to Finley.

Obviously.

She grinned widely as Harri handed her a gin and tonic, and she took a large sip to calm her nerves as she scanned her eyes across the room.

She couldn't help but laugh at how different it felt in here to The Ship Inn, or any bar she'd been to in Truro. The people around her were all so different, some in suits and others in joggers and trainers. Some dolled up to the nines, and others in backwards trucker caps, and the many different hairstyles and colours and piercings and tattoos.

She felt…*vibrant.*

Not a word she'd ever felt explained an emotional state before, but she felt alive with promise and an odd sense of nostalgia for the parts of life she'd never lived before. London, and Noah, were presenting her with something freeing that Sophie had never known. She'd never drank, and danced, and let the night roll her with no cares. Not at eighteen, like her friends had.

At eighteen, Sophie had known hoists, and slide sheets, and wheeled commodes.

Not bars, and bottles, and a base that moved from her feet and up, and the writhing motion of a crowded floor of dancing bodies.

Sophie chuckled, shaking her head as she processed the sheer number of likely obtainable people in the room around her, and yet all she could think about was Finley Bennett, and whether she had seen her selfie from three hundred miles away.

Pathetic.

By the time the phone buzzed in her bag, Sophie was a few drinks in and was feeling *pretty* good about all things Soho, London.

She grinned as she saw the name across the message bar.

Finley: *Shit* 🤯 🤩 *!!! You look…*

Finley: *There isn't a word in the English language for* that, *Sophie Cedars!* 🔥 *You having fun?*

Sophie blushed, her blood heating with adrenaline and her stomach fluttering. Well, *that* was a little more openly appreciative than she had expected, and she *definitely* did not dislike it.

She wasn't sure if it was the alcohol in her veins, or the buzz of the bar around her, or Finley's unabashed appreciation, but she felt more carefree than she had in a long time, and she smiled openly as she typed out her reply.

Sophie: *Charmer.* 😁 *Yessss, but I definitely wish you were here.* 😚

Finley: 😳 *I wish so hard!*

Finley: *I'm so very jealous of every person who is in that room with you right now.*

Sophie: *I didn't peg you as the jealous type, Bennett.* 😌

Finley: *You look like FIRE and I'm 300 miles away getting emoji kisses.* 😖 *I don't think you can blame me.*

Sophie grinned, her butterflies beating harder.

She couldn't deny the buzz it gave her to be on the receiving end of a little bit of flirty attention, *especially* from someone as attractive and as likeable as Finley Bennett.

And the fact that she'd not stopped thinking about Finley for almost a week made every butterfly beat just that little bit harder.

Sophie: *You don't like my kisses?* 😳 😚

Finley: *That's the opposite of what I meant, and you know it.* 😚

Sophie: *Well, like I said…wish you were here.* 🚫

Finley: *You're a goddamn tease, Cedars.* 🚫

Sophie smirked. She was definitely laying it on thicker than usual, but Finley was also *definitely* a little looser-lipped tonight. She wondered if she, too, had been drinking.

Sophie: 😼 *What's your better offer tonight then?*

Finley: *Well, your sister's here!* 😌 *Do you know she keeps a rum stash in your kitchen?*

Sophie groaned.

If Bex was at her house, then that meant she was drunk. And a drunk Bex was *not* a golden keeper of Sophie's secrets.

So, the idea of her drunken sister spending an evening with her new, unconventional but definitely blazing crush could really only end in embarrassment for Sophie.

Shit.

# Chapter Eleven

"But then Drunk Dave was like 'you can't bar me, I've been drinking 'ere since before you were born! Ain't my fault you couple of snowflakes don't know good music'."

Bex waved the diminishing bottle of rum in the air as she talked animatedly, sprawled across the sofa opposite Finley.

Finley frowned.

"Didn't you say he sang *'Blurred Lines'*?"

"Yeah," Bex sighed. "That was unexpected."

Finley wrinkled her nose.

"Sort of sounds to me like *he* doesn't know good music."

Finley barely listened to Bex's reply.

She glanced at her phone; her eyes glued to the corner where the little light would flash if she had a message waiting for her.

She knew it was rude, but she was a little tipsy, and a lot distracted. Sophie was being *very* flirty tonight, and it was sitting very warm in Finley's belly. And it was all she could think about.

She winced a little as Bex pushed the rum bottle into her eyeline, and nodded at her to take it.

Finley had drunk more than enough now, and if she wanted any hope of getting through a night of Sophie Cedars' flirty text messages without embarrassing herself, then she needed to stop before the alcohol consumed her senses.

She was having a really hard time understanding how Bex seemed to be getting more coherent the more she drank. She seemed somehow more sober now than she had when she'd stumbled onto the doorstep, despite being a quarter of a bottle of rum *more* intoxicated.

The little light on Finley's phone flashed, and her stomach flipped as she made an almost frantic grab for it.

"Alright, eager beaver, who's got you fumbling with your trouser zip?" Bex scoffed, huffing out a laugh as she swiped the bottle back from Finley's hands. "Your date decided she *is* into a little pain play, after all?"

Finley baulked.

*"Fumbling* with my *zip?"* she laughed, shaking her head as she narrowed her eyes. "You genuinely have no filter, do you?"

Bex shrugged, smirking in amusement.

"Eh, what little I have is draining with that bottle."

Finley chuckled, turning her attention to her phone as she pulled up Sophie's text.

Sophie: *I have just been told, Finley Bennett, that you have some* very *unexpected Magic Mike moves.*

Finley blushed, huffing out a laugh at the unexpected words.

It had definitely been a *lot* of years since she'd done *that* in a bar, and she felt her cheeks heat in dark embarrassment at the drunken memories.

Sophie: *And as you* really *don't look the type, I think I'm going to need some evidence.*

Finley chuckled, shaking her head.

If she was going to be shamed, she might as well use it to her advantage.

She smirked, typing out her response.

Finley: *Sophie Cedars, are you asking me for a private demonstration?*

The response was immediate.

Sophie: *Are you offering one?* 😺

Finley bit her lip, her blush deepening as she let the words play out in her mind, Sophie's voice replacing the letters on her screen.

She took a deep breath, glancing up at Bex for a moment as she considered her options.

The way she saw it, she had two choices.

She could let this coast, and let the faux confidence of a little alcohol carry it on into dirtier waters. Test them out. Push Sophie's buttons.

Enjoy tonight, and possible spend tomorrow regretting her rum-weakened filter.

Or, she could pull it back just a little, and focus on the fact that Sophie's question meant something glaringly obvious, that spread butterflies through Finley's chest.

She grinned, settling for the latter.

Finley: *Talking about me, are you?*

Sophie: *Maybe.*

Sophie: *You intrigue me.*

Finley's stomach fluttered, and she swallowed thickly as she watched the little dots play out, telling her Sophie was still typing.

Sophie: *How's it going with my sister? Are you talking about me?* 😊

"Dude, your eyes are literally the shape of fucking *hearts* right now," Bex scoffed, swatting a foot blindly at Finley's phone. "Do you have *no* game?"

"Game?" Finley shot a sideways glance at Bex, her brow quirked in bemused question.

*"Game,* Don Lothario," Bex exclaimed. "Like, the ability to play it cool with the women!"

"Sorry, is it *1990* all of a sudden?" Finley retorted. "What are you suggesting, I wait three days, then tell her I think she's fat to get her attention?"

Bex smirked.

"Kick her in the face, that's your signature, right?"

Finley rolled her eyes, her lips twitching in amusement.

She turned her focus back to her phone, and typed out her reply.

Finley: *Maybe a little.*

Finley: *But I'm thinking of you more.*

"Does she at least like you?" Bex asked, her voice feigning disdain as she lifted the rum bottle to her lips.

Finley blushed.

"Uh…I don't know."

"What do you mean you *don't know?"* Bex choked, sitting upright as she swatted Finley's thigh with the back of her hand. "It's *midnight,* is that text *sexy* or not?"

"It's…" Finley scrunched her face, her eyes flitting back to her phone as she let Sophie's words play back over in her mind. "It's not *not* sexy?"

"Oh my god, give it here, I am a master at flirty text messages."

Bex swiped a hand at Finley's phone, and Finley's stomach dropped as she recoiled immediately.

"You are absolutely not having my phone," she scoffed, biting back a laugh.

*"Why?"* Bex whined, pushing the rum bottle onto the coffee table before making another unsuccessful grab at the phone. "Come *on,* I guarantee I will have that girl twisting her thighs together over you in ten words!"

Finley barked out a laugh.

"And *I* guarantee that you will *wilt* with regret if you have any part to play in that."

Finley's phone buzzed, and she turned the screen away from Bex as she pulled the message up.

Bex narrowed her eyes.

"Why?" She sat back, studying Finley suspiciously. "Why would I *wilt, Bennett?*"

Finley wasn't listening.

Sophie: *Oh?* 🙃 *Anything you care to share?*

"Finley Bennett, who are you texting?" Bex asked.

Deadpan. Cool. Almost *knowing.*

Finley faltered.

Bex raised an eyebrow.

"Give it to me," Bex demanded.

"No."

Bex lunged forward, her whole weight thrown in Finley's direction as she grabbed at the phone.

*"No,"* Finley yelped, twisting to keep her phone out of Bex's grasp. "What is wrong with you?"

"Who is it, Bennett?" Bex shrieked, practically climbing over Finley in pursuit of the phone.

*"Judith Law!"* Finley squeaked, bowling herself over and off the sofa in her efforts to escape Bex's grasp. *"Why* do you *care?"*

"Why don't you want my help, Casanova?" Bex grunted, throwing herself over Finley's back as she grappled for the phone. "Huh? Is it because we *both* know who Judith Law is? *Is it?"*

"I don't *need* your help, I am perfectly capable of sending my own flirty texts!" Finley choked, holding her phone high above her head as she clamoured to escape the ridiculous assault. "Get *off!"*

"I'm *so* right, aren't I Bennett?" Bex cackled, her limbs flailing as she finally managed to knock Finley prone, straddling her thighs as she pinned her down. "Panda in a bucket of *fucking bamboo shoots!"*

Finley huffed.

Bex had her pinned, the determined look in alcohol-glazed eyes was almost manic, and Finley was really beginning to see no way out of this.

She was well aware her next move was more than a little primary school, but frankly she hadn't been in a situation like this one since then, and so that was her brain's default response.

She shoved her phone down the front of her trousers.

Bex quirked an eyebrow.

"Is this your game?" She smirked. "Amateur."

Finley squirmed, squeaking in protest as Bex grabbed her wrists, pinning them down as she reached for Finley's trousers.

"We barely know each other," Finley yelped, wriggling as best she could under the restraint. "I thought I wasn't your type. You haven't even bought me *dinner!"*

Bex rolled her eyes, finally managing to grab the phone and pull it back into her grasp.

"It's locked," Finley panted, grinning smugly. "What a waste of your time and energy."

Then, as if by the request of fucking Satan, the phone buzzed, and the screen lit up.

"I *knew* it!"

Bex cackled manically, throwing her head back as she dropped the phone triumphantly onto Finley's chest.

Finley checked the screen.

One new message.

Sophie Cedars.

Finley groaned, resigned and breathless as she let her body flop onto the floor.

Bex patted Finley's chest, pushing herself up and off her thighs. She flopped back onto the sofa, grabbing the rum bottle and raising it to her lips.

Finley furrowed her brow.

"That's *it?"* she huffed. "You went full-scale *assault,* and now you've got nothing to say?"

Bex waved her hand dismissively.

"Flirt away, Cameron Diaz," she chuckled, shaking her head in amusement. "You have my full blessing."

~~~~~~ 🜂 ~~~~~~

"So, Sophie, what brings you to London?"

Sophie took another sip of her *very* elaborate looking gin and tonic, her hips and her shoulders rolling in time to the music in the bar around her.

Or as well as they could do, with the slightly restrictive proximity of the unfamiliar woman currently shouting in her ear.

She'd approached Sophie approximately eight minutes ago, with a swagger and a hooded gaze that in hindsight had made *no* attempt to hide her intent. But the Cornish innocence in Sophie had done her a disservice, and she had initially quite happily engaged in polite conversation.

Over the minutes since, the stranger had made her way further and further into Sophie's personal space, and Sophie was very quickly realising the error of her ways.

Now, the woman's hand was resting on Sophie's waist, and her breath was uncomfortably hot in her ear, and honestly Sophie *really* didn't know how to escape this situation.

It wasn't that there was anything *wrong* with the woman.

In fact, she was hot. *Really* hot. All smoky eyes and edgy grey-blonde hair, and displayed abs that made a washboard look bloated.

But Sophie's mind simply wasn't in it.

Sophie's mind was on her phone in her bag, and the charming stranger at the other end of it, and she *knew* how stupid that was.

She knew.

But she couldn't help it.

*"Soph!"*

Sophie yelped, almost choking on her gin as a firm hand wrapped around the crook of her elbow and tugged, and she found herself suddenly pressed up against Noah's side as he manoeuvred her through the crowds and away from her persistent admirer before she could even *consider* saying goodbye.

Which was probably for the best.

"You and me need a cheeky little shot, babes," Noah sang, linking his arm through Sophie's as he guided her towards the bar.

Sophie grinned.

179

She didn't particularly *want* a shot, but she could see the knowing glint in Noah's dark eyes, and the slight tension in his jaw, and she had worked a bar long enough to know that look anywhere.

It was a rescue.

Noah was saving her from her unwanted admirer.

She chuckled, shooting one sheepish, almost apologetic glance over her shoulder, before following Noah happily to the crowded bar.

"What shall we get?" Noah questioned, twisting his body to face Sophie as they leaned against the sticky bar. "Sambuca? Tequila? Ooh, have you ever had a Squashed Frog?"

Sophie wrinkled her nose.

"Well, *that* doesn't sound very vegan."

"Usually it's not, but this is a lesbian bar in London," Noah teased. "They have alternatives."

Sophie raised an eyebrow.

She wasn't overly convinced it sounded all that appealing, but she trusted Noah, so she reluctantly agreed.

She slipped her hand into her bag, pulling her phone out as they waited.

She grinned the moment she saw the name beneath the flashing icon.

Finley: *Well, I could share, but I guess it depends.*

Sophie smirked, typing her response out immediately.

Sophie: *On what?*

Finley: *On whether you're thinking about me.*

Sophie bit her lip.

She let her eyes dart around her at the bar, and the lights, and the dancing, and the people. She chuckled, shaking her head in amusement as she turned her attention back to her phone.

Sophie: *I'm in a lesbian bar in the biggest city in the UK, surrounded by the kinds of girls I've only ever seen on my TV screen…*

She waited a moment.

Just long enough for the little ticks to go blue.

*Just* to leave a moment of suspense.

Sophie: *And I'm spending my night texting you, Finley Bennett.* 😊

"So, who's the lucky Cornwaller you've been sexting all night, then?"

Sophie blushed, startling guiltily as Noah's voice snapped her from her trance.

"There is no…*Cornwaller,*" she tried.

It wasn't *strictly* a lie.

"And I am not *sexting!*" she huffed.

Noah rolled his eyes.

"Oh, come on, no-one gets gooey eyes *that* badly from a friendly text."

Sophie smirked.

Maybe she should have been playing it safer. Maybe this *should* be kept from the prying eyes and ears of Finley's best friend.

But Sophie was slightly intoxicated, and riding the high of an amazing day, her current great company, and Finley's surge of giddy butterflies in her stomach.

So, she wanted to play a little.

"I never said it was a *friendly* text…" she teased.

Noah raised an eyebrow.

"Are you single, Noah?" Sophie diverted, smiling deliberately sweetly.

"Deathly," Noah deadpanned. "Now don't you play this game with me, you said no Cornwaller, so is that a *Londoner?*" he squeaked, excitable eyes and curious fingers pointing to Sophie's phone. "Did you *meet* someone?"

"Not exactly…" Sophie drawled, deliberately honeying her voice in a way she *knew* would intrigue and frustrate her new friend.

Noah blinked.

Then Sophie's phone buzzed, and Noah's eyes fell instantly to the lit screen.

Noah gasped.

Sophie bit back a giggle.

"Yes!" Noah breathed, his eyes wide and his lips curling at the corners in incredulous surprise.

"No…" Sophie shook her head.

*"Yes!"* Noah hissed, gripping both of Sophie's shoulders as he shook her gently.

"Nope."

*"Sophie!"* Noah squealed. "Are you *flirting* with Finley Bennett right now?"

*"Absurd* suggestion," Sophie deadpanned. "I've never met the woman."

Noah grinned, raising an eyebrow.

"Oh, so you're just…free as a bird?" he teased. "No Cornwaller, no Londoner, just…single and ready to mingle tonight? So, you wouldn't mind if I set you up?"

Sophie winced.

"S-sure?" she stammered, fighting hard to ignore the bubble of discontent in her stomach at the thought of turning her attention away from her phone and onto an unfamiliar face.

Her phone buzzed again in her hand, and she cursed her own butterflies for the grin that spread instinctively over her cheeks.

Noah smirked.

"Sophie…" he whispered.

"Noah…" Sophie mimicked.

"Are you into my best friend?"

Sophie bit her lip.

The game was fun. But the alcohol, and the butterflies, and Noah's kind, excited eyes were always going to win.

She grinned.

*"Maybe,"* she whispered.

Noah hissed, high pitched and uncontrolled, and Sophie giggled as he practically squirmed on the spot in his excitement.

"Oh my *god,* this is the best day of my life," he blurted, his grip on Sophie's arms growing a little tighter. "Does she know? Do you need help? Cause you know, I can always guide you. What do you need to know? You wanna see her horoscope chart? What star sign are you 'cause I really think…"

"Hey, what can I get you guys?"

Sophie blinked, Noah's amusing barrage thankfully interrupted by the new presence of the bartender. A different one to the woman who had served them so far tonight.

*This* bartender was a broad, dark haired, muscular god of a human, who Sophie was fairly certain must have been photoshopped.

Honestly, that jawline was ridiculous.

But perhaps the most absurd aspect of the bartender's presence was whatever the *hell* was going on with Noah.

Noah's stance changed *immediately.*

His entire body stiffened, his chest puffed up and out in a way that made him look like a street pigeon, and his hands clenched in tight fists as he leaned *really* awkwardly against the bar.

"Oh, hey man. Just uh…" Noah croaked, his voice an unhealthy strained effort at a low timbre that frankly made Sophie feel concerned for his vocal cords. "Pint of Stella and a couple of whiskey chasers for me and my friend here, please, lad."

Sophie choked on air.

*What* was going on?

*Lad?*

The bartender frowned.

"You sure, dude?" he chuckled softly, reaching hesitantly below the bar for a glass. "'cause I've seen you tonight and I know you're on the Woo Woos."

"Uh…" Noah cleared his throat, his eyes wide with the first signs of panic, and Sophie intervened.

For safety.

"We will have two vegan Squashed Frogs please," she called, smiling sweetly.

"You got it," the bartender chuckled.

He grinned at Sophie, shot a smirk that should have been illegal at Noah, and then disappeared along the bar to fetch their order.

And Sophie turned immediately to dissect that display of utter lunacy.

"So, Finley…?" Noah croaked, his eyes sheepish as they searched Sophie's own.

Sophie was having none of it.

"Uh, excuse the *fuck* out of me, Vinnie Jones, but what the bloody hell was that?" she barked, her stomach beginning to shake with her giggles.

Noah blushed.

"What?" He tried.

"A pint of Stella?" Sophie laughed. "Noah, I've spent five hours in your presence and I've yet to see you drink anything that isn't 90% sugar."

Noah wilted.

"Well, I just…" he fumbled, wincing slightly as he fought to find his explanation. "Sometimes…when…I don't always…"

He glanced sheepishly around him as he stuttered, his pigeon chest caving into an awkward slump.

Until the bartender returned.

And he immediately tensed again, his chest somehow puffing impossibly further than before.

Sophie bit her lip to hold back her giggles.

"Cheers, man," Noah grunted, nodding his head in a manner that wouldn't have felt out of place at Danny Dyer's market stall.

Sophie's own eyes watered with amusement, and she let a small giggle slip as the bartender shot her a knowing look.

"No problem," the bartender chuckled softly. "For you, it's on the house."

Noah nodded, his lips parting a little as his façade slipped just enough for the surprise to flash in his eyes, and over his cheeks.

The bartender winked, shooting Noah a cheeky grin, before sidling along the bar to serve the next customer.

Sophie slapped Noah's puffed out chest as he watched the bartender go.

"Who *are* you right now?" she hissed.

Noah groaned.

He grabbed the drinks, his body deflating once again as he led Sophie away from the bar.

"He's just so *beautiful,* Sophie!" he whined.

"Right, and *clearly* into you," Sophie rebutted. "So, what's with the Mitchell Brothers act?"

Noah blushed.

Then immediately perked up.

"Wait, you think he's *into* me?"

"Noah, he knows your drink, gave your order to you on the house, and *winked* at you," Sophie laughed. "Nobody *winks* at *anyone!* So, *what* was *that?"*

"Ugh, I just…" Noah sighed, his head tipping back as he resigned himself to Sophie's questioning. "I see him in *The Village* bar every weekend when he's not working here, and he's always with these…*men,* and they're all burly and they drink pints, and go to the gym, and…"

"Okay…" Sophie drawled. "So, is he *dating* any of them?"

Noah furrowed his brow.

"I don't think so…?"

"So, then it's *irrelevant!*" Sophie exclaimed, swatting Noah's chest once again. *"Go* and be yourself, you giant dingbat."

"I can't just go up and talk to him!" Noah protested, his eyes wide with outraged panic.

*"Why?"* Sophie laughed.

"Because this is *London,"* Noah hissed, "I'll look like a psychopath!"

Sophie rolled her eyes.

She reached forward, swiping the first of the two shot glasses from Noah's hand, and threw it back. She frowned, shuddering at the pure taste of sugary syrup, before swiping the second shot and repeating her actions.

She pushed the two empty glasses back into Noah's hands, her brow raised in determination.

"I will have a Woo Woo and another one of those, please."

"But..."

"No buts!" Sophie interrupted. She grinned. "Come back with his number, and I'll tell you about Finley."

Noah's eyes widened, his lips parting as Sophie shot him a dirty smirk.

*"Ooh..."* Noah breathed, shaking his head. "You are a *dirty* hustler, Sophie Cedars."

"Go..." Sophie laughed, pushing lightly at Noah's chest in indication. "And no Vinnie Jones this time!"

"Alright!" Noah relented.

He took a deep breath, closing his eyes for a brief moment as he composed himself.

Then he puffed his chest out like a street pigeon.

*"No!"* Sophie scolded. "Put that away!"

Noah deflated, grinning sheepishly as he nodded in reluctant understanding.

Sophie sighed as she watched her new friend make his way over to the bar. She watched with bated breath as his chest puffed and unpuffed no less than four times, and she watched as the gorgeous bartender noticed every move.

She grinned at the subtle twitch in the bartender's lips, and at the way he made a beeline for Noah the moment he was free to.

She held her breath as Noah faltered for a moment, his chest puffed and his muscles tense. Then she beamed as he took a deep breath, and relaxed. He smiled naturally, if a little nervously, and then he was ordering, and the bartender was smiling with twinkling eyes.

Sophie hissed in satisfaction as she backed away, fishing her phone from her bag as she leaned back against the wall.

She unlocked the screen, her butterflies beating hard before she'd even pulled the message box open.

Finley: *I'm thinking a little about that dress, and a lot about that smile.*

Finley: *Wishing I was there so maybe I could be the reason for it.*

Sophie giggled, pressing the phone to her chest as her stomach jolted and her throat tightened.

The words were so very hammy, but they were *deliciously* successful, and Sophie was beginning to feel warm at the mere thought of Finley being in the same room as her.

And that was ridiculous.

Because it had never happened.

And it probably *wouldn't* ever happen.

*How* was Finley 300 miles away, having never *met* Sophie, and still making her stomach fizz with a few flirty words?

Sophie let her head thud back against the wall.

*God,* she was so done for.

~ ~ ~ ~ ~ ~ ♪ ~ ~ ~ ~ ~ ~

By the time Bex had passed out on the sofa, Finley was comfortably tipsy.

The time had flown, and she winced as she turned the screen on her phone and the numbers processed in her hazy mind.

2am.

She groaned, rubbing her eyes with the backs of her hands as she dragged herself, swaying ever so slightly, to her feet.

She tried waking her sleeping guest, and moving her to the bed in Sophie's spare room, but a loud snore and a few grunts later, Finley settled for covering the drunken mess in a blanket, and leaving a glass of water on the coffee table.

And taking a photo.

Of course.

And sending it to Sophie.

Sophie had been flirty this evening; even more so than usual, and Finley's blood had been running a little hotter all night as a result.

She wondered if Sophie was home yet. She knew she had been on her way with her last text message; a selfie with Noah in the back of a London black cab.

Finley smirked as she recalled the image. Sophie had acquired a trucker cap that she had most definitely not started the night with, and had somehow managed to make the thing look *adorably* sexy alongside her tightly fitted dress.

Bex hadn't said anything since the phone debacle but she'd looked at Finley way too smugly every time her phone had gone off since, and that had only added to the persistent deep flush in Finley's blood.

And by the time Finley had settled herself into bed, her phone was flashing once again with a new message.

Sophie: *I'm home, all tucked up in your bed* 😁

Finley melted.

She was honestly *one* more flirty message from Sophie Cedars away from a full-scale gay meltdown, and she really wasn't sure how many more of these late-night whispers she could take.

It had been a long time since her stomach had felt like this, and she knew she should be running. She knew that the Finley Bennett of London Central, senior architect and notorious workaholic would absolutely not be fawning hopelessly over a few cheeky text messages from a near stranger. *Should* absolutely not be this excited.

But the Finley Bennett that was *here,* in Polcarne, Cornwall, in a beamed cottage and seaside air, hundreds of miles from her laptop and her stale office…

Well, *she* was pretty smitten.

And she liked it.

Before she could even think about forming a reply, her phone buzzed again.

Sophie: *Well, that looks typical for Bex.* 😵 *I hope she played nice?*

Finley chuckled. She blushed, her mind spiriting her back to the floor of Sophie's living room, pinned beneath her house host's sister as she shoved her own phone down the front of her trousers.

She was fairly certain that would be too much detail to go into.

Finley: *She was a handful, but those are my favourite kinds of people.* 😌 *Fair warning though, she thought I was your latest 'conquest'.*

Finley: *I think she approved.* 😂

The phone buzzed almost immediately.

Sophie: *How does she make that sound like I have frequent 'conquests'?*

Sophie: *You've seen the place, I'm sure you can see how unlikely that is.*

Finley laughed openly. She thought about the farmer she'd met on her frantic route into Polcarne, and about Trevor and Trixie, and about the people she'd seen milling about on the beach and the roads through the town.

Firstly, there *really* didn't seem to be many of them.

Finley was pretty sure she could count on her fingers the number of people she'd actually seen since in Polcarne itself since she'd arrived. Most had been out in St Austell, or Charlestown.

And most had been older. Or families.

She certainly hadn't come across a huge number of potential conquests for a beautiful young historian.

She chuckled, typing out her response.

Finley: *It's not teeming with options, no* 😄

Sophie: *Although, there is one woman in Polcarne right now that I can't stop thinking about...*

Finley's stomach dropped.

Then she grinned, shaking her head.

She didn't know what it was.

The rum, or the late hour, or the flirtier tone of their messages tonight.

But she felt bolder. Braver.

Finley: *That's funny, because there's this woman in London who's been giving me butterflies with her texts all night tonight.*

Sophie: *Butterflies, eh? Sounds like you're pretty into her.* 😊

Finley: *Maybe I am. Do you think I should make my move?*

Sophie: *Absolutely. I'm sure you could charm her easily into your bed...* 😏

Finley: *Oh, I know it. I've got the adorable photographic evidence.* 🐾

Finley: *And there are so many things I want to do about it.*

Finley: *So, it is killing me that I'm 300 miles away, alone in hers.*

~ ~ ~ ~ ~ ~ 🎸 ~ ~ ~ ~ ~ ~

300 miles away, Sophie dropped her phone.

She exhaled heavily, every nerve burning with adrenaline at the implications of Finley's words.

Adrenaline and *definite* arousal.

It was not exactly news to her that there was a mutual attraction here, and she knew they had been flirtier than usual tonight, but this was the boldest thing Finley had said to her yet, and Sophie had been *completely* unprepared.

Her heart was thumping in her throat, her thighs were tighter than a bowstring, her stomach was freestyling parkour, and she had *no* idea what to say back.

Her fingers trembled as she fumbled for the phone, her mind completely blanking for any response that would sound even remotely smoother than '*holy shit, my body is yours*'.

She groaned, burying her head in her hands.

Why was this so difficult?

*How* had Finley flustered her *so* much with a simple text message?

She stared at the letters on her screen, her pulse racing as her alcohol-hazed mind filled with images of what those words meant.

Finley *wanted* her.

That was definitely what she was saying, right?

So many things Finley wanted to do about it?

Sophie's blood was burning, and her mind was swimming with an *incredibly* unhelpful sideshow of every possible thing that Finley Bennett might want to *do* about the fact that Sophie was in her bed.

The images made her more flustered, and more panicked, and now she really had *no* idea what she was supposed to say back.

Was this what it felt like? To flirt with someone she was genuinely attracted to?

Should she be *sharing* the images that flooded her mind?

Was she about to have the kind of text chat that she had only ever dreamed of?

With *Finley?*

Sophie's chest tightened, and she wasn't entirely sure she could breathe.

Then her phone buzzed in her hand, and her pulse skyrocketed as the words morphed into Finley's name over the screen, and the tone of an incoming call filled the room.

A *call?*

Were they going to have *phone sex?*

Sophie hadn't even had a chance to process the concept of sexting, and now she had to hear her crush's *voice?*

Jesus Christ in a Kit Kat wrapper, she was done for.

She took a deep breath, exhaling shakily as she lifted the phone to her ear.

"Hey…"

"Soph, I'm sorry."

Finley's voice was huskier than usual, and Sophie's thighs clenched instinctively.

She slammed her eyes closed.

*Jesus.*

"I've had a couple of drinks, and I got…*way* too cocky and ahead of myself," Finley murmured softly. "I hope I didn't make you uncomfortable?"

Shit.

Sophie shook her head.

The *last* thing she was right now was uncomfortable.

Perhaps with the exception of her rapidly dampening underwear.

She *really* needed to pull herself together.

"N-no, it's…" she chuckled, her cheeks burning at the hoarse husk of her own voice. "I liked it."

Finley exhaled heavily, and Sophie grinned at the audible relief.

"Yeah?"

"It's not often someone like you sends me flirty text messages after midnight, Finley, of course I liked it." Sophie grinned.

Finley's laugh was still huskier than usual, and Sophie swallowed as the sound flooded heat through her stomach and lower.

"Someone like me?"

Sophie bit her lip. With the voice that she had so quickly grown to *need* in her ears, with its added husk of a late night, and a few drinks, and maybe a little lust…she felt her nerves burn away into something a lot warmer.

"You know *exactly* what I mean, Bennett," she murmured. "Gorgeous. Funny. Charming. *Sexy.*"

Finley exhaled.

Sophie smirked.

"Shall I go on?"

"Only if you want to make me blush."

Sophie grinned.

"Oh, I *definitely* want to do that."

There was another exhale. Shakier this time, and Sophie shivered as the sound raised goosebumps over her skin.

"Can I see you?" Finley whispered.

Sophie knew that the hushed tone of Finley's voice was in part down to Bex's presence in the house, but the gravelly husk was causing *chaos* in her bloodstream and she was starting to feel *way* too warm under the thick duvet.

She hit the video call button, her stomach swarming with butterflies as her screen filled with the face she'd spent far too long staring at over social media for the past week.

*God,* Finley really was gorgeous.

All sparkling eyes, and tousled hair swept back from her face, and alcohol-flushed cheeks, and those *lips*...

Sophie bit back a whimper.

And it seemed she wasn't alone.

"Well, *this* hasn't helped," Finley groaned. *"Christ,* if you look this good on a front facing camera, then I think you'd kill me on a real date."

"A *real* date?" Sophie quirked an eyebrow, biting back her grin. And her butterflies. "So, this is a *date* of some kind, is it?"

Finley smirked.

Sophie melted.

"Of course not. You'd *know* if I took you on a date, Sophie Cedars."

Sophie giggled.

She nestled herself down into Finley's sheets, almost giddy with the pounding of her nerves. She grinned as Finley blushed at the action, her eyes glazing over.

"They smell good," Sophie whispered. "Do they smell like you?"

"I don't know," Finley laughed, the tips of her ears visibly reddening even over the tiny camera. "What do they smell like?"

"Jasmine." Sophie smirked. "Cedarwood. Amber. Intrigue. Excitement."

She stroked her fingers absently over the pillow, her eyes trained on the flushed face on the screen before her.

Finley had managed to light a fire in her bloodstream that Sophie hadn't felt in a *very* long time, if ever, and she wasn't sure she could even really put a finger on how.

She didn't quite know *where* this had come from, but the slightly taken aback, lust-glazed look in irresistible dark eyes had her hooked, and she wanted nothing more than to keep making those cheeks tint red.

She watched as Finley swallowed visibly.

"Butterflies," she murmured.

*"Sophie…"* Finley's eyes fluttered closed, and she inhaled sharply. "You're…"

A loud thump on the wall behind Finley cut the words off, and she visibly jumped, wide eyes flying open on the screen.

Sophie readjusted herself, suddenly feeling exposed in the burst bubble.

Despite the fact that she was fully clothed and 300 miles away.

"Bennett, you better not be having phone sex in my sister's bed."

Sophie rolled her eyes as the familiar sound of Bex's voice called through the thin walls of the cottage. Trust Bex to pull herself from a drunken stupor *just* in time to interrupt her efforts of seduction.

"You *know* it's your sister I'm talking to," Finley shot back, her face turning away to where Sophie knew the bedroom door was.

"And that's why you'd *definitely* better not be having phone sex in my sister's bed."

Sophie giggled.

Finley smirked.

"Wouldn't *dream* of such a thing." Finley grinned, turning back to face the camera. She paused. *"Unless…"*

She wriggled her eyebrows, throwing Sophie a lopsided, *dirty* smirk that sent goddamn fucking *flames* raging through her veins and *straight* into her underwear.

*Fuck.*

The goddamn smirk. The glint in those eyes. The *unfairly* low gravel of her voice.

Sophie shuddered.

This was getting dangerous.

She was *one* more of those irresistible smirks away from throwing all caution to the wind and telling Finley, *very* explicitly, *everything* that she wanted those lips to do to her.

And while that thought was appealing right now, she couldn't help but think it was probably not wise.

Not while they were both drunk.

And *definitely* not while her sister was listening.

She knew this needed to stop.

Well…to *pause,* at least.

But she couldn't help but tease just a *little* more.

"Speaking of *dreams…"* she feigned a subtle yawn, stretching her body in a way that she *knew* would frame her chest in the line of the camera. "Maybe it's time I caught up with mine."

"It is pretty late…" Finley murmured, her eyes hooded as they mapped Sophie's movement, entirely mesmerised.

Sophie grinned. Those eyes were fooling nobody.

"And this bed is *really* comfortable," she teased softly.

"Mmmm." Finley grinned cheekily as she buried herself down into Sophie's sheets. "I do kinda miss it."

Sophie swallowed.

She was beginning to understand why that had affected Finley so much.

Suddenly these 300 miles could go fuck themselves.

"Well, it's more than big enough for two," she husked.

Finley's eyes widened.

*"Oh,* are you propositioning me?" She smirked, her cheeky grin now bordering smug.

"What if I was?"

"Then I'd say I've got a long drive ahead of me." Finley winked. "But it would be *more* than worth it when I made it."

"I've no doubt," Sophie giggled. "Too bad you've been drinking then, isn't it, Bennett?"

Finley groaned.

"You're a tease, Sophie Cedars."

"You have no idea." Sophie smirked. "Night Finley."

# Chapter Twelve

Finley grunted in frustration as the shitty piece of shitty cardboard fell out of its supposed slot for the fourteenth time.

She had intended to be up early today and head out on a clifftop walk, following a map that Sophie had marked with various castle ruins.

But it was raining, and she was hungover, and so instead she was sitting at Sophie's dining table playing a stubborn battle of wills with a 3D jigsaw puzzle of a *'working windmill'*, which so far wasn't even fucking *working* as a jigsaw, let alone a functional turbine.

She was feeling a little antsy. She hated being cooped up, hated the heady feeling the morning after alcohol, and she *hated* the fact that she hadn't heard from Sophie bar a text first thing this morning, long before Finley had surfaced.

She was aware that Sophie was probably busy, and it had only been a couple of hours, and it wasn't like they usually talked *every* minute of every day. But Finley was feeling a little out of sorts this morning and she couldn't help but feel unsettled by the lack of the back and forth she'd come to crave.

She couldn't help but worry that she'd overstepped her mark last night. She knew Sophie had been as forward as she had, but the underlay of alcohol beneath the flirty exchanges had left a sour taste in Finley's mouth, and she couldn't help the crawling worry in her stomach that Sophie might regret it today. That it might have *just* been the drink for Sophie, and not the all-out raging crush that was practically vice-gripping Finley's chest.

Finley grunted. Again.

She knew she was starting to sound like a petulant chimpanzee, but it really was quite inconvenient just how much she liked Sophie. It was inconvenient, it didn't feel like she was winning, and this was *exactly* why she didn't date.

But she couldn't help it. Sophie made her feel things she hadn't felt in a long time. Made her feel freer. More in control.

Of the *right* things.

Or she did when she wasn't churning her stomach into a moth-eaten ball of chaos.

She grunted harder than she had yet as a whole wall of her jigsaw fell down.

Maybe she was a chimpanzee. With chimpanzee emotions and chimpanzee motor skills.

Her phone buzzed almost arrogantly against the wood of the table beside her, and Finley practically tore her own obliques as she dived across the fallen windmill to retrieve it, her heart in her throat and her breath trapped in her chest.

She sighed dejectedly, the name across her screen disappointingly not the one she was waiting for.

She pulled the message up anyway.

Noah: *When were you planning to tell me your charmer's chance crosses county lines?*

Finley blinked.

Finley:...*what?*

Noah: *Don't you play that game with me Finley Rae Bennett, there is a gorgeous girl in your bed* and *in your DMs, and YOU DIDN'T TELL ME!!!!*

Finley's heart thudded harder.

She gripped the phone tighter in her hand, her stomach swarming with butterflies as she typed out her reply.

If Noah knew about this, then maybe...

Finley: *Wait, did she say something?*

Noah: *Maybe.*

Finley groaned.

She was absolutely *not* in the mood to be teased right now.

Finley: *Noah! I am on a ledge right now and I swear to god, if you don't tell me what you know, I will put Peanut's hairballs in your coffee for a week!*

She stared at the screen, and at the little ticks that would tell her when her best friend had read her message.

The little ticks that just would not turn blue.

*Fuck.*

Finley was about three seconds from having the temper of a chimpanzee.

She knew she was dramatic and impatient at the best of times, but this truly felt like a matter of life or death, and she needed to feel back in control of things, before she surpassed chimpanzee and went full gorilla.

She typed out another prompt.

Finley: *Noah Henry Lake, don't you dare do this to me.*

She growled as Noah's status shifted to offline, the little ticks remained grey, and her messages remained unread.

What did this mean? *Was* Sophie interested? Or had she simply gossiped to Noah while she was drunk too?

Ugh, *why* did this feel so *weird?*

Finley sighed, flinging the piece of jigsaw she was holding onto the table and pushing herself up.

She was beginning to feel uncomfortably hungover, and she was in dire need of some caffeine and some grease. She hauled herself wearily into the kitchen, flicking the kettle on and dragging the ceramic coffee pot across the counter.

She lifted the lid, grunting with an admittedly unnecessary level of agitation as the bare base of the empty pot stared back at her.

She really was *not* in the headspace to be grinding more coffee beans like an eighteenth-century miller's daughter right now, and she was pretty damn certain Polcarne did not have a drive through Starbucks.

Or a *walk* through Starbucks, for that matter.

But maybe she did need to get out of the house. Maybe some air and a change of scenery would do her some good.

Bex had left this morning with a seemingly earnest urge for Finley to visit the pub for lunch, and right now that seemed like a pretty great idea.

~ ~ ~ ~ ~ ~ (🎣) ~ ~ ~ ~ ~ ~

Finley couldn't suppress the grin that spread across her cheeks as she pushed open the door and stepped into The Ship Inn for the first time.

The place might have looked a little downtrodden from the outside, but the other side of the painted white door was *everything* Finley's city mind thought a country pub should be.

And it *screamed* Sophie Cedars.

The candles on the tables matched the ones on Sophie's coffee table, and the lamps in the corners bore the same shades as the one that hung from the cottage's bedroom ceiling.

There was an impressive fireplace under a thick beamed mantle, and the slightly splintered old beams across the exposed brick walls and ceiling were brought to life with delicately placed fairy lights. The room was dotted with tables, and mismatched wooden chairs, and lumpy looking armchairs with threadbare arms, and the air was filled with the scent of roasting meat, and the slightly musty smell of hop and ageing ales.

Finley felt at home immediately, despite having never set foot in here, or in any other country local.

Except for the weird, awkward silence that she would *swear* had only fallen as she had stepped over the threshold.

And the fact that every set of eyes in the vicinity seemed to be focused on her.

And the whispered murmurs, of *new* and *who* and *house swap* that floated across the quiet pub.

Finley frowned.

Well, this was…*unfamiliar.*

In London, she'd be amazed if she recognised her own neighbour if she saw them anywhere but their own front steps. It would almost certainly be considered a sociopathic red flag if she noticed someone new walking into a bar in Covent Garden.

She took an uncertain step forward, trying her utmost best to avoid eye contact with any of the starey patrons as she made her way towards the bar.

She grinned, exhaling with relief as a familiar face nodded at her from behind the taps and the heavy oak.

"Evening Fidget Jones, how's the hangover holding up?"

"It's midday." Finley rolled her eyes. "And Fidget Jones?"

"Fidget Jones. Like Bridget, because you're deathly single, except you fidget so much you boot women in the face," Bex deadpanned.

"Bridget Jones had two men fight in a fountain over her, she was far from deathly single."

"And once you get within 300 miles of your latest crush, you won't be either." Bex grinned.

Finley blushed.

"You're losing your touch, Cedars," she deflected. "Cheapskate Winslet? Eight out of ten. Fidget Jones? Questionable four."

Bex scoffed.

Finley rolled her eyes.

"And the hangover is fine, but shouldn't *I* be asking *you* that?"

*"No,"* Bex scoffed dismissively. "If you're gonna date my sister, Bennett, then you're…"

Finley's eyebrows shot up.

"Bex, I haven't *met* your sister."

*"If you're gonna date my sister…"* Bex pressed, "then you'll learn very quickly that the Cedars do not get hungover. We own a pub; drinking is our number one skill."

Finley grinned.

"I thought Sophie's was history and classical studies."

"Wrong." Bex grabbed a glass, pouring a beer that Finley had never heard of from an ice-covered tap. *"Sophie's* is luring everyone into a false sense of security with her angelic smile, and then being freakishly deceptively strong." She pushed the full glass over the counter to Finley. "Closely followed by drinking, then by understanding old stuff and really complicated books."

Finley grinned, shaking her head. She wrapped her fingers around the glass, nodding her thanks wordlessly.

"So, it's just *your* number one skill then."

Bex narrowed her eyes.

"What can I get you, Bennett? Pete's special today is roast lamb and mint sauce, all the trimmings."

Finley winced.

She wondered if the lamb came from Trevor's farm.

The thought rose bile in her throat as she pictured Sophie nursing the weakened babies, and then fighting Trevor for their lives just months later.

She swallowed thickly.

Bex smirked.

"Do you want to see Sophie's menu?"

Finley exhaled.

"Yes please."

"You've changed." Bex grinned as she slid a laminated A4 page across the bar, and Finley relaxed as she let her eyes roam the meat-free options.

"Since last night?" Finley laughed.

"You mentioned the butchers in the first fifteen words you spoke to me," Bex scoffed. *"Yes,* since last night."

Finley baulked, her eyes widening with surprise.

"I was…*not* expecting you to remember that."

Bex grinned, shrugging almost smugly.

"Again, I'm a pub landlord. I can hold my booze."

"Right!" Finley laughed, nodding her head as she lifted her beer to her lips. "Number one skill, I got you."

She chuckled softly to herself as she scanned the surprisingly varied menu.

Or rather Finley guessed it *would* have been surprising, if she didn't know full well how much passion Sophie had poured into it.

Bex wasn't wrong.

Finley had always loved her steak and her greasy burgers. Until now.

How had Sophie managed to prise her from her meat without ever even meeting her?

She placed her order; a mushroom wellington roast that she remembered Sophie had raved about when she'd encouraged Finley to visit here, and Bex disappeared behind a wooden door to take it through to the kitchen.

Finley relaxed back in her seat, lifting her pint to her lips as she turned her focus to the people around her. She turned her head, fully intent on scouting the locals, and doing a little people watching that she would never have found the time for in London.

And found herself inexplicably close to the face of a very eager, very *old* stranger, leaning precariously towards her as he gripped the end of a stick that most definitely was not touching the ground.

She jumped, the gurgle of beer in her throat choking the all-out scream that would have escaped had she not been mid-swallow.

How the *hell* had she not noticed him approach her?

And how *long* had he been there?

"Afternoon, Miss," the man greeted, his watery eyes wide as he examined Finley closely. "I don't think I've seen you around these here parts before. Care to let an old codger buy you a drink?"

Finley blinked. She let her eyes focus on the stranger's face, and his pale eyes and his wispy hair beneath his oversized flat cap. And his dentures that were much too big for his face, and wobbled almost comically as he talked.

She had to admit, it wasn't the *worst* offer she'd ever had.

But she wasn't overly sold.

"Erm…" she croaked, her throat a little strained with a mouthful of beer that had almost definitely gone the wrong way. "Well, I…I already have one." She lifted her pint, offering the man a sweet smile. "But thank you."

"Perhaps a dinner then?" the man tried, giving a watery chuckle that almost shook his dentures from his mouth. He lifted a trembling hand forward, reaching for Finley's. "I'm Ern. Ern Butterworth. Pleasure to meet your acquaintance."

He lifted Finley's hand to his lips, placing a very shaky, unexpectedly wet kiss against it.

Finley fought the urge to snatch it back, squirming slightly in her seat.

The Londoner in her was finding the level of intimacy with this strange man more than a little uncomfortable, but she was trying her hardest to remember that she was in a hamlet town now, where people knew each other. And *wanted* to know each other.

She was pretty sure this man was harmless, really. No-one seemed to be paying him the blindest bit of attention. Besides, she was fairly certain she could take him if she needed to.

"Finley," she offered, smiling sweetly as she tried to politely extract her damp hand from Ern's grip.

Unsuccessfully.

For a frail old man, Ern really had some grip on him.

His wide eyes rounded impossibly further somehow, and he leaned ever closer to Finley as he waited, seemingly, for her to continue.

Though with what, was really anyone's guess at this point.

Finley took a blind stab.

"B-Bennett?" she tried, tugging a little firmer in an effort to reclaim her hand. "Finley Bennett. The house swap, I'm…"

"Ern, stop flirting with my patrons," Bex called across the bar, the door swinging closed with a thud behind her as she made her way towards Finley. She grinned. "I'm simply not sure this one's got it in her to keep up with you."

*"Oh,* balderdash," Ern laughed, finally releasing Finley's hand as he leaned against the bar, and pushed his empty glass towards Bex. "I was once a young whippersnapper like you two, you know."

Bex grinned, rolling her eyes in Finley's direction as she set about refilling Ern's glass.

"And I was a handsome one too!" Ern stated.

Finley chuckled, her shoulders dropping and her London panic relaxing now that Bex was beside her, and the air felt a little lighter.

"Oh, you're *still* handsome," she assured.

Ern coughed, his eyes flying wide as his dentures popped out.

Finley bit back a laugh, her hand flying to hide her grin as he pushed them back in.

"I'm going away next week, you know," Ern stated.

"Oh yeah?" Bex shot Finley a wink. "Your caravan in Newquay?"

"Sicily!" Ern declared. "Taking that lovely Miss Cedars on a jolly with me."

Finley choked.

Bex barked a laugh.

"Well, I'm sure you'll have a wonderful time," Bex chuckled, her eyes sparkling with amusement as she pushed Ern's pint back across the bar. "Might have to get in line though, Ern. Soph is developing quite the line of suitors."

"Ah, we're gonna put our feet up for a while. Do a spot of fishing!" Ern declared animatedly. He leaned back towards Finley, his pint spilling over the edges as he moved away from the bar. "Perhaps next time *you'll* join me, Miss Bennett?"

Finley pursed her lips, fighting an unexpected combination of laughter and bile.

"Perhaps!"

Finley let her giggles escape as she watched Ern retreat to his armchair by the fire, his pint spilling, and his cane not once touching the ground.

"Who knew you'd be such a hit in Polcarne, eh Bennett?" Bex laughed. "You're like fresh meat."

Finley grinned, rolling her eyes as she settled back onto her bar stool, letting her eyes wander the surroundings once again.

She couldn't help but watch the people here.

It was almost impossible in London. No-one ever stopped for long enough.

But here, in a sleepy little town in Cornwall, Finley found herself watching the lines in stranger's faces. Watching the colours of their eyes, and how far their smiles reached.

She imagined the lives they led, and how they entwined together. How the man in the corner with the weather-beaten hair and the dark stains on his fingers might farm the wheat for the bread baked by man by the bookcase, with the rosy cheeks and the shirt with the straining buttons. Or how the woman at the end of the bar with the bright eyes and the thick scarf might scan the groceries, or maybe press a stethoscope to the chest of the man by the fire, filling a goddamn *pipe* with handfuls of tobacco.

She could paint a story here. A real story, with lines and paths that twisted together. Not the broken fragments of society that London threw together, where the person who's underarm you rode your morning tube commute beneath was simply a needle in a haystack of people you would never see again.

Finley flicked her gaze to the door as it swung open, and a small group of men around her own age walked in. All flushed in the face, and wearing the same stained gingham, and the same worn jeans.

She wondered if they were Sophie's friends. She pictured them at school, with crested blazers and thicker hair, shooting paper pellets through a dismantled biro, and carving in the desks with the needle of a compass while a fresh-faced Sophie Cedars tried to focus on her work.

The men took seats at the bar, just a few feet along from Finley, and she tried not to recoil at the overwhelming smell of salt and sweat and fish.

She shuffled a foot further away.

"You heard from Sophie yet, mate?"

Finley's ears instantly pricked up.

She shuffled back a foot and a half.

The speaker's voice was hushed, sheepish almost as he looked around the bar, and Finley's stomach tightened at the assumption that he was checking whether Bex would hear him.

"Not since she went on her trip, but that's cool."

Finley couldn't help but turn her gaze to this speaker. She bit back a grimace. He was *definitely* the source of the smell.

If anyone had ever looked *more* like a fish farmer, Finley would lick a floundering trout.

She held her breath as he continued.

"We're just taking some space for her to work things out before the big move, you know?"

Finley frowned.

"Yeah, it's a big step I guess." The first man nodded. "Man, *Kyle Brown*. Moving to the big smoke with Sophie Cedars." He chuckled, shaking his head. "Who'd have thought it? You gotta tell us how it's done, dude."

Finley's stomach churned. She gripped the bar edge, her head feeling a little light and her throat closing just tight enough to make the air feel way too thick.

*What?*

She exhaled slowly, closing her eyes for a moment.

Even through the nausea and the rapid swimming in her mind, Finley knew full well that *that* sounded…*so* far from right.

She had never heard the name Kyle Brown. And *nothing* Sophie had ever said to her had even *remotely* suggested this.

If anything, everything Sophie had ever said to her had suggested *quite* the opposite.

The comments about the lack of options in Polcarne.

The flirting.

*Bex's* insistence.

*None* of it added up to Sophie being in a committed relationship with someone else, and yet here was Kyle Brown, with his fishy fingers and his fading hairline. Declaring openly in the middle of Sophie's workplace, that he was committed.

That *she* was committed.

Finley sighed.

*What* was she doing?

Even if Sophie *was* single, she lived 300 miles away and lived a life Finley knew nothing about. This was completely pointless, and the rational part of Finley's brain knew it.

She had come on far too strong last night, and she needed to step back. And *god,* she needed to reign in this rapidly growing crush. This *dependence.*

She was too busy, anyway. Even if Sophie did want her. She lived in *London,* for fuck's sake, and she had a career to work on.

She needed to give Sophie the space to enjoy her trip, and to focus her energy on building her life.

Alone, or with this wet wipe with a widow's peak.

Whichever she wanted.

She took a large swig of her ale, wincing at the bitter taste.

Okay.

This was it.

The resolve to leave Sophie Cedars alone.

It lasted three minutes.

Until her phone buzzed in her pocket, and her stomach flooded with a battalion of lit fireflies at the name that crossed her screen.

Sophie: *Managed to beat the morning rush today, and I'm in love with this place! [Image Attached]*

Finley sighed, all too aware that she was practically swooning as her screen filled with an image of Sophie's beaming face, the distinctly recognisable backdrop of Camden Market surrounding her.

Resolve.

She scoffed.

*What* resolve?

Finley: *You'd look great in a steampunk hat.* 🤩

Finley: *New city, new look, who dis?*

Finley cringed the second she hit send.

*Fuck.*

*Who dis?*

Who *says* who dis?

She sighed, dragging herself to her feet.

She shot a glance once again at Kyle Brown and his widows peak and his yellowing shirt. She winced, fighting a grimace at the smell, and at the fact that this complete stranger had made her stomach drop just with a few words that weren't even aimed in her direction.

*Pathetic.*

She clearly needed to address this with Sophie before her brain malfunctioned into dish soap and she lost every *sexy point* she'd gathered so far.

She pulled Sophie's contact up on her phone as she pushed through the doors and into the beer garden, taking cover under a weather-beaten marquee.

She hit the video call.

"Hey!" Sophie's voice sang out almost immediately. "Do you think I could get away with a clockwork wrist cuff?"

Finley chuckled.

"Soph, you could wear a trench coat of wilted spinach leaves and still be the most beautiful woman I've ever seen in my life. You do you."

Sophie blushed visibly, her lips curling into an abashed smile, and Finley immediately kicked herself.

Did she really not have *any* resolve?

She'd kinda thought she was stronger than this.

She took a deep breath, her stomach swarming as she tried to figure out how to broach the subject she needed to address, without coming across like an even bigger lunatic than she already had.

"You have a good night last night?" she croaked.

"Mmmm." Sophie's eyes sparked, a little playful and a *lot* flirtatious. She smirked. "I did. Did you?"

Finley's stomach flipped.

*This* was what she meant.

This absolutely did not scream 'committed to a fish farmer'.

This screamed 'interested', and it was too much for Finley's butterflies to take.

She stammered slightly, her words trapped somewhere down beneath the beating wings, and before she could answer, Sophie's eyes widened.

*"Oh,* shit," she gasped. "You know that guy, Cam?"

Finley frowned.

"Super-hot barman dude who turns Noah into Ross Kemp?"

"Yep." Sophie grinned, almost bouncing on the screen in her enthusiasm to share whatever was on her lips. "Guess who bagged themselves his number last night?"

Finley's heart sank.

"Oh…" she breathed. "I thought…" She swallowed thickly, bile rising thick in her throat as she fought to keep her disappointment hidden. "Isn't he gay?"

"I assume so?" Sophie chuckled.

Finley's frown deepened.

"But you got his number?"

"Not *me,* dingbat," Sophie laughed. *"Noah!"*

*"Oh!"*

Finley barked a laugh, relief flooding her veins far heavier than was really necessary.

Christ, she really did need to get a grip.

"Oh, that's *great,*" she breathed. Then she blushed, clearing her throat. "I mean, good. Nice work."

Sophie smirked, her eyebrow raising far too knowingly as she leaned a little closer into the screen.

Finley's blush deepened.

Then the words processed through her jealous, gay mess of a haze, and she gasped as she finally understood what Sophie was telling her.

*"Wait!"* she yelped. "Are you *serious* right now? The bar dude with the ear stretchers and the nose stud? And *Noah?"*

*"Yes!"* Sophie giggled. "Turns out he's more into Noah than he is Ross Kemp."

"Huh!" Finley huffed, chuckling softly as she pictured the scene in her mind. "Ten months I've been trying to get him to talk to that guy, but he'll do it for you in ten minutes?"

Sophie grinned.

*"Well…"* she husked, her voice dropping a little as she fixed her sparkling gaze on Finley's through the tiny screen. "I can be very persuasive."

Finley chuckled softly, shaking her head as her stomach clenched and her blood ran warm.

"I've *no* doubt," she breathed.

The air felt thicker for the longest of moments, and Finley's chest constricted with threads of desire as she watched the small smile toy with the corners of Sophie's lips.

*God,* she liked this woman.

And it really felt like that might be mutual.

But Kyle Brown's words echoed over in Finley's mind, and she winced as they cooled her blood way too fast.

"Listen, Sophie…" she started, taking a shaky breath in an effort to steel her nerves. "I-I'm sorry if I overstepped last night. I really didn't mean to make you uncomfortable, or to be inappropriate, and I…well, I guess I just wanted to know if I crossed a line?"

Sophie raised an eyebrow, her soft smile ticking into a knowing smirk.

*"No,* Finley. You didn't." She chuckled softly. "I told you; I liked it."

Finley exhaled, her shoulders dropping.

*"Oh…"* she breathed. "G-good. Me too."

"I uh…" Sophie shrugged, her cheeks tinting with the most adorable blush Finley had ever seen as she dropped her gaze from the screen for a moment. "I-I kinda like *you."*

Finley's heart stopped.

"You *do?"*

"Yeah," Sophie chuckled shyly. "Kinda."

Finley blew out a shaky breath, her lips pulling into a grin before she could even process their movements.

She bit her lip, her chest hammering hard as she tried to fight the exhilaration for just a minute longer.

Just enough to clarify.

"A-and I'm not erm…I'm not stepping on anyone's toes?" She cringed. "F-for want of a better…"

"Who do I need to beat with a stick?"

Sophie cut her off, her eyes flashing with something dangerously fiery that Finley had yet to witness in them.

She laughed, instantly remembering Bex's comments about her sister's deceptive strength.

Suddenly every tension she had carried all morning had melted, flooding her chest and her stomach instead with a warmth that she was *completely* unfamiliar with. She grinned, shaking her head.

*"Well,* the Polcarne rumour mill says Kyle Brown is moving to the big smoke with Sophie Cedars."

Sophie's jaw dropped.

"Oh, my *god,* is he *telling* people that?" she gasped, scrunching her face in shocked disbelief. *"Wow,* that's humiliating for him."

"I sense it's not quite true?"

"We had *three* dates. The third of which is a story for another time. Maybe on a…" Sophie dropped her voice, throwing a cheeky wink in the camera's direction, *"bath time* call tonight?"

Finley raised an eyebrow.

"How are you making a conversation about a date with a man who smells like fish sound like I'm gonna need a cold shower?"

Sophie blinked.

"Didn't think it all the way to the end." She shuddered. "Oh, and smelling like fish is not even his worst fault. He called my degrees *pretend!*"

Finley baulked.

*"What?"* she spluttered. *"Pretend?* Why the fuck would they be pretend?"

Sophie shook her head. Her face scrunched, her lips curled in irritation and disgust, but the soft, almost anxious light in her eyes betrayed her.

"Because I did them online," she murmured, quieter and less confident.

And Finley didn't understand *at all.*

"Are you *kidding* me?" she barked, animated and almost aggressive in her urgency and her honesty. "I thought that was *incredible!* Christ, a degree is hard enough when you're surrounded by peers and tutors and support, let alone on a laptop in a hamlet town! And you've got *two!"*

Sophie inhaled sharply, her eyes softening to something almost like awe as she let a small smile grace her lips.

"You thought it was incredible?" she whispered.

"Well, yeah." Finley urged. "It screams passion, and drive, and determination. *I* felt proud when I saw your frames, and I didn't even earn them!"

Sophie bit her lip, her smile almost coy, and her eyes sparking with something *warm* that made Finley's bones heat.

"Hmmm," Sophie hummed, her voice a little huskier and a little quieter than it had been. "You are earning so *very* many sexy points right now, Bennett."

Finley blushed immediately.

"And *no,"* Sophie chuckled. "I am not going *anywhere* with Kyle Brown."

Finley huffed out a laugh.

"Gotta say, I'm a little relieved."

"Yeah?" Sophie murmured. "Why, were you jealous?"

Finley smirked.

"Kinda," she nodded, her stomach flipping with nerves and excitement at the sound of her own words. "I kinda like you too. Except…you know, without the *kinda."*

Sophie giggled.

"Have we lost the plot?"

"Oh, absolutely." Finley nodded, grinning widely. "Feels pretty good though, doesn't it?"

"Mmm."

Sophie bit her lip, her eyes dancing with that same warm something that burned directly through Finley's bloodstream and into the gymnasium that was her stomach.

Finley's breath hitched.

Sophie grinned.

"Know what else feels pretty good?"

Finley laughed as the camera panned back, and Sophie lifted the phone to allow her to see the clockwork lined top hat and goggles that dwarfed her head.

"See, you look hot!" She grinned. "Now you just need a corset and some thigh highs."

"Down girl." Sophie winked playfully. "You're giving away your secrets."

Finley sighed.

"Can I take you on a date tonight?"

The words were out before she could even taste them on her tongue, and her own eyes widened as they filled the air around her.

"Wh-what?" Sophie's brow furrowed in confusion. Her eyes flew wide, nervous anticipation dancing behind them. "Why, are you coming home?"

"No, I uh…"

Finley paused.

*Could* she?

She closed her eyes for a moment.

*God,* she needed to chill out. Three words of encouragement from this girl and Finley was ready to move mountains. She let her eyes flutter open, her words strained with her nerves.

"I-I mean on a video call."

Sophie was quiet for a moment.

Finley immediately descended into a state of panic and regret.

"Is that stupid?" She winced. "That's stupid. *Please* forget I said anything."

"No, Finley…" Sophie chuckled, her eyes misting as they searched Finley's face. "That's adorable. Yes, *please* take me on a date."

Finley exhaled.

"Yeah?"

"Yeah," Sophie giggled. "What should I wear?"

Finley grinned. She might not have known the words were even in her mind until they were on her tongue, but she did already know *exactly* how this video date was going to play out.

And she had some planning to do.

"I'll text you," she murmured. "Let me iron out some details."

Sophie bit her lip, her giddy grin not quite hidden behind it, and Finley's stomach flipped for the thousandth time.

"Okay," Sophie breathed.

"Okay." Finley grinned.

"I can't wait."

Finley was in a complete and entire state of giddy gooiness as she hung up the phone, and she didn't think she could have wiped the grin from her face if she'd tried.

She almost rolled her eyes as she glanced at the screen, finding a new message from Noah plastered across it.

Noah: *Oh, just that she's got a big fat giant crush on you.*

Noah: *No big.* 😌

Finley: *You're an assbag, you know that?*

Finley: *Call me on your lunch break. I have news, and a favour to ask.*

Finley felt like she was floating as she pushed her way back into The Ship Inn. She couldn't wipe the smug smile from her face as she slid into her stool beside Kyle Brown and his fishy fingers and his little widow's peak that was kind of cute in a small-town farmer kind of way. She couldn't blame him really. She was as enamoured with Sophie as he was, and she'd never met the woman.

"What's got you grinning like a dopey Cheshire cat?" Bex shot, pushing a *delicious* smelling plate and another full pint glass across the bar to Finley.

Finley bit her cheek in an effort to stem the beaming grin that threatened.

"I have a date tonight," she teased, deadpan and nonchalant.

Bex gasped.

"With *Ern?*"

Finley narrowed her eyes.

"Sicily was *very* tempting," she laughed. "But no. With your sister!"

Bex grinned, wriggling her eyebrows as she leaned across the bar.

"Need some advice?"

Finley almost scoffed.

She *almost* scowled, a sarcastic quip burning *just* on the end of her tongue.

But actually, for what she had in mind, maybe she could use a little assistance.

"Maybe, actually," she admitted.

Bex smirked.

Then she stood upright, cupping her hand around the side of her mouth as she called out across the quiet pub.

"'Ere, Ern!" she yelled. "Finley here needs a bit of help *wooing* Sophie. You're the man for the tips, right?"

Finley barked a laugh, shaking her head as she shot her gaze to Ern and his wobbly dentures and his unnecessary cane. She grinned as he hauled himself to his feet, the cane not even in his hand as he made his way excitedly over to the bar.

Frankly, she wasn't even embarrassed.

She felt nothing short of pride as Kyle Brown flushed a *very* satisfying shade of red, and his gingham friends began to mutter and splutter amongst themselves in baffled outrage.

She couldn't quite believe the turn of events, and she refused to let her mind even consider the fact that this entire thing was utterly ridiculous and *completely* unsustainable.

Because it didn't matter.

Not right now.

Sophie Cedars liked her back.

She grinned, turning her body willingly to face Ern this time as the old man leaned against the bar beside her, his watery eyes sparkling with earnest seriousness.

"First things first, me cock," Ern stated, "you're gonna need a caravan."

# Chapter Thirteen

Sophie was pretty sure she had never felt so giddy as she rounded the corner, her eyes flicking between her surroundings and the words of Finley's instructions on her phone.

The message she had received shortly after their video call this afternoon would forever go down as the *cutest* thing she had ever read, and she was fairly certain she'd looked like a deranged Cheshire cat every time she'd looked at them since.

Which had been a *lot*.

She scanned the words again.

Finley: *Pack a picnic tonight, dress warm, and follow these instructions. I'm sending you to my favourite spot.* 😵‍💫

Finley: *I'll call you at 8* 🤍

Sophie melted again.

For the thousandth time.

She felt her stomach flutter with excitement as she reached the last of Finley's steps.

*The corner where Upper Ground meets Coin Street.*

She frowned as she scanned her surroundings. Was this it? Was she supposed to find a seat here for a video call?

It didn't particularly *seem* like a date space, particularly given the whole video call aspect, but she supposed she could be open minded, and sit on a fence, or a step, or…

"Sophie!"

She started at the familiar voice, and she spun in time to see Noah jog across the road to meet her.

"Hey!"

"Evening!" Noah grinned. "I'm here to escort you to your *date,* Miss Cedars. Consider me like a *chauffeur* for the evening. Except, I don't have a car…"

Sophie giggled as Noah extended his arm. She shook her head as she looped her own through it.

"You look *beautiful!"* Noah nudged her with his hip. "Finley's going to be *utterly* useless when she sees you, I don't know how much sense you'll get out of her tonight."

"Is everyone in London this charming?" Sophie laughed.

"None are *quite* as charming as Finley Bennett, that's for sure." Noah chuckled.

Sophie took a deep breath, calming her nerves as Noah led them up to a glass fronted building, scanning a key card to let them in. The building was quiet, and as they entered the foyer Sophie craned her neck in an effort to catch a glimpse of where they might be, and why she might be here.

Was this an *office?*

Was this Finley's office?

She frowned.

She knew Finley worked a lot, but if she was about to have her dinner date in her office chair then it really might be time to suggest that Noah perform some kind of intervention.

She felt the nervous anticipation seep into her bones as Noah led her into a lift, and hit the button for the top floor.

"Are you nervous?" Noah whispered.

Sophie raised an eyebrow.

"I'm more nervous that you're whispering, why are we whispering?"

Noah laughed.

"I don't know, it just felt atmospheric."

Sophie nudged him with her shoulder.

*"Yes,* I'm shitting myself!" She blushed as Noah chuckled. "First dates are terrifying enough when you're doing it with someone else, let alone when your date is 300 miles away and you've never met!"

Noah nodded, his smile curling a little softer.

"Fin *is* doing this with you though, Soph. She's doing the same thing, right?"

Sophie nodded, her own lips quirking into a soft smile.

That she was. She wondered briefly if the help *she* had recruited had done what she'd asked them to.

"And I know you haven't stood in the same *room* as Finley, but you've already connected with her in a way that I don't think I've ever seen *anyone* do," Noah assured, his tone almost awed. He shrugged. "If you ask me, I'd say you've met. In a funny kind of way."

Sophie's shoulders dropped, and she blew out a nervous exhale.

Noah was right. It wasn't like Finley was a stranger. She certainly didn't *feel* like one.

Her excitement buzzed through her veins again as they exited the lift, and Noah led them through a door to the stairwell. She grinned as they started to climb.

"The roof?"

Noah winked.

He tapped his key card over the last door at the top of the stairwell, and stepped back for Sophie to walk through.

She gasped.

"Oh my *god.* Th-the…"

She trailed off. She wasn't sure what to gush about first.

The *view* was incredible. The Thames, and the skyline of London over it, the lights beginning to sparkle over the evening sun, dancing over the water below them.

But the rooftop itself was *adorable.* A little table had been set up by the roof's edge, with blankets and candles and fairy lights, and a bottle of her favourite wine that she had *no* idea how Finley would have known to choose. Or Noah? Bex, maybe…

A laptop sat propped open on the centre of the table; the screen already open with a video call programme that Sophie didn't recognise.

"It's so the screen is bigger. And so, you don't have to hold your phone," Noah explained. "Finley set the call details up, all you'll have to do is answer when it rings."

Sophie huffed out a breathless chuckle, her eyes misting at the beautiful scene and the effort that had so clearly gone into it.

For a first date, no less.

"Thank you, Noah." She turned to face him, gripping his shoulders gently. "This is amazing."

"Don't thank *me!"* Noah held his hands up in rebuttal. "I followed *very* specific instructions." He rolled his eyes. *"So* specific. Like…*military."*

Sophie laughed.

"Thank you anyway."

"Have a nice night, Sophie," Noah grinned, handing the key card to Sophie. "She likes you. Treat her right!"

Sophie exhaled shakily as she settled herself down, her eyes wide as they mapped the scenery around her.

The bustle of London lifted her up from beneath her; the life and the lights and the scents and the sounds. And yet up here, just that little bit higher, Sophie felt secluded. Like she could watch the bustle from her own bubble, and something in that felt *powerful.*

For the days that Sophie had been here, London had swept her away. It had carried her, no matter how willingly, and it had thrust her into its highs and its lows and its character.

But here, above it all, on a quiet rooftop, Sophie felt in control. Like she was carrying *herself* through London's character, for the very first time.

Was this what Finley felt?

Was this why this was her favourite place?

Sophie checked the time.

7:55pm.

She hoped Finley was finding *her* spot okay.

~ ~ ~ ~ ~ ~ 🎵 ~ ~ ~ ~ ~ ~

Finley's stomach flipped as she turned the Ford into the estate marked on Sophie's instructions. She drummed her fingers on the steering wheel, her knee practically vibrating, she was jostling it so hard.

God, *why* was this date making her so *nervous?*

Sure, it was an unusual situation, and that in itself was enough to make the butterflies flutter, but it was more than that and Finley knew it.

She had a sneaking suspicion that really, it was because it *mattered.* As ridiculous and as unsustainable as it may be, Finley *liked* Sophie, and it mattered to her that this went well.

She frowned as she pulled the car up alongside a heavy wrought iron gate, an electronic lock-pad, keeping it secure. She checked her instructions. Sophie hadn't sent her a code, and this was the last point on the list. Was this where she was supposed to be?

She climbed out of the car, jumping almost immediately as she heard the heavy clang of the gates being drawn back, and grinned as Trevor Shaw's familiar face appeared behind it.

"Welcome, Miss Bennett." Trevor grinned, holding his hand out for Finley to shake as the other gestured behind him to a small utility buggy. "Your vehicle for this evening."

Finley chuckled, her eyes widening in surprise.

"Is this place part of your farm?"

Trevor shook his head.

"Technically, it's part of the estate my daughter owns, but the *orchard* still belongs to Sophie Cedars and Rebecca Arroway." He smirked as he tossed Finley the keys to the cart. "As does *this.*"

Finley furrowed her brows, her eyes flicking from the cart to the keys, and back to Trevor's.

"How do I know where to go?"

Trevor winked.

"Follow the lights."

"Th-the lights?"

Trevor smiled softly, clapping Finley broadly across the shoulders.

"Pete Arroway was here for two hours this afternoon." He chuckled, squeezing Finley's shoulder. "I'd say Miss Cedars likes you, Finley. You treat her well, mind."

Finley blinked, her mind spinning into overdrive as she watched Trevor retreat, climbing into an SUV she hadn't noticed when she'd first arrived.

"Oh, and Finley," Trevor called through the open SUV door. "Wi-Fi details are on the keyring." He chuckled, shaking his head. "Sophie Cedars spent many an hour studying in that summer hut, so we had to *modernise* the place."

Finley grinned, thanking Trevor almost sheepishly.

She felt giddy, and her nerves had only increased, and now she was also slightly concerned she might get herself lost in the middle of a slowly darkening estate in what appeared to be some kind of golf cart, and miss her date altogether.

If she could even figure out how to *drive* the thing.

She settled herself into the buggy, slotted the keys into the ignition, pressed the pedal, and promptly shot 15ft forward at breakneck speed, losing her picnic out the side of the cart in the process.

She slammed on the brakes, *just* catching herself before she flew through the open frame of the vehicle, and took a moment to calm the living fuck down.

*Christ.*

She retrieved the picnic on foot.

She wasn't quite ready to negotiate reversing this thing just yet.

She found herself grateful that at least this time, she wasn't wearing those *fucking* trousers.

Once she'd managed to control the buggy speed, Finley followed the stake lights that lay every few hundred yards, the glow not yet visible in the evening sun, but the shapes clear enough to point her way. She knew she would be grateful for those later on when she needed to make her way back.

She felt her breath catch as she finally pulled the cart into a large orchard in bloom, a running stream weaving through its centre. The scent of the pear blossom, and the trickling sound of the water was *beautiful,* and Finley found herself surprisingly overwhelmed.

A little bistro table and chair had been set up for her beside the water, complete with lanterns and blankets, a mini outdoor heater, and a bottle of her favourite red. She grinned at the assumption that Sophie had consulted Noah on her preferences in the same way that she herself had asked for Bex's advice.

Finley settled herself down at her spot at the table, her eyes roaming the area in awe. Sophie had called this her *second* favourite spot, saying her favourite couldn't be trusted not to wash Finley away with the tide at this time. Finley couldn't help but feel somewhat glad. She couldn't imagine a more perfect setting than this one, with the late sun's rays sparkling through the blossom trees and onto the rippling water.

And the *sounds.*

When Finley had first arrived in Polcarne, Cornwall, the quiet had been almost overwhelming. Deafening, somehow, in the way it could make her feel so exposed. So vulnerable with nothing to hide behind. No sharp suits, and no tall buildings, and no crowds of people or rumbling tubes or honking horns or lights or constant low buzz of human life.

But here, with the trickle of the water blending so softly with the chirps of crickets, and the faint song of twilight birds, and the occasional rustle of the wind and the wildlife in the leaves, Finley felt safer than she ever had.

It didn't feel like vulnerability here.

It felt like *freedom*.

She chuckled, shaking her head in disbelief.

This entire thing was *insane*.

Utterly insane.

She had well and truly lost her mind. Sitting in a remote orchard in God-Only-Knows-Where, Cornwall, *completely* on her own, dressed to impress, and about to have a fucking *date* with her laptop screen.

Preposterous.

And yet *somehow* it was already the best date she had ever been on.

She checked her phone, taking a deep, shaky breath as the numbers ticked over.

7:57pm.

Her message tone chimed.

Noah: *The cat is in the cradle.*

Finley rolled her eyes.

Finley: *That is not a saying.*

Noah: *Operation Bunny in the Burrow is ago.*

Finley: *Have you hit your head?*

Noah: *Your date is ready, ass. Have fun.*

Noah: *She looks stunning. Don't blow it.*

Finley: *Thank you Noah. I owe you one.*

Finley took a deep breath, checking her reflection the best she could in the screen of her phone. She smoothed down the collar of her shirt, changed her mind twice about how many buttons to leave open, and then finally propped the laptop open in the centre of the table, logging into the call she had set up earlier that afternoon.

She hit the call button.

~ ~ ~ ~ ~ ~ ♫ ~ ~ ~ ~ ~ ~


Sophie topped her wine glass up just a little more than necessary. She took a long gulp, in a fruitless effort to settle her wayward nerves.

She fidgeted with the laptop, tilting the screen, moving it back, changing the position, changing that back…

And then it rang.

She bit her lip, her stomach swooping as she pressed the button to accept.

"Hey."

Sophie bit her lip harder.

Oh, *god,* how was this woman so gorgeous?

She didn't know whether it was simply the bigger screen, or the angle, or the fact that Finley was wearing a goddamn *shirt* with *just* enough buttons undone to send her into meltdown. But whatever the reason, she looked about a million times sexier than Sophie had seen her yet and it was doing *nothing* to calm her racing pulse.

"Hi," she breathed. *"God,* you look good."

Finley laughed, her eyes sparkling.

"You look *beautiful* yourself. Noah warned me, but…" She inhaled sharply, chuckling softly. "I underestimated."

Sophie blushed.

"This *place* is beautiful! The view is amazing," she gushed. "Tell me then, why is this your favourite spot? Am I at your office?"

"I hate that the answer to this is yes, but yes." Finley winced, almost apologetically. "But that isn't why. Well, not *explicitly."* She scrunched her nose.

"I'm not judging, Fin," Sophie assured. She smirked. "Well, I *did* for a moment when I thought you were sending me to your desk, but *this* is amazing."

Finley laughed, shaking her head.

"That would have deserved judgement!" She grinned. "No, it's just…I don't always take a lot of time to myself, and I spend more of my life than is reasonable really in that office. But when things get a bit much, I steal myself away up there and it feels a bit less for a while. I can look out over London and over the river and remind myself where I am. Physically and metaphorically. That I've reached the dreams I wanted when I was a child, and when I stand where you are now it reminds me that that's enough. That my life is good. It's my happy place."

Finley's voice was so soft, so earnest that Sophie's chest swelled at the sound.

She'd never known this.

Never known such a seamless connection with someone, where something so vulnerable could be said just minutes into a conversation and feel so *natural.*

So *easy.*

She was entranced.

"What dreams did you reach?" she murmured. "To be an architect?"

"Sort of." Finley nodded her head. "To stand on my own."

Sophie stayed quiet.

She could see the unfinished words in Finley's eyes, and she knew they needed an outlet. And she knew Finley just needed a moment to form them.

She watched quietly as Finley took a steady breath.

"I don't like to play the victim. I wasn't, really. A lot of kids have it worse. I was just…I always *owed* my dad something. Mum left, and in his eyes it was my fault. Not his anger, or his need to control, or his narcissism. Mine."

Sophie swallowed as Finley's eyes dropped, the pain flashing clearly behind them for a moment.

"I was twelve. And from that day on, everything he ever did for me was a favour I owed him for. And I made a promise to myself that one day I wouldn't need him. Or my mum. Or anyone."

Sophie's stomach flipped. She'd appreciated the larger screen before, but she was sure she would have missed the look in Finley's eyes now, had she been watching through her phone screen. And she was *so* grateful for the chance to see it. The flicker of *steel;* the drive and determination that Sophie had always assumed must fuel Finley, but until now had lay hidden beneath the soft sparkle of her eyes.

Was it normal to feel this *proud* of someone you'd barely known a week? For something they did long before they knew you existed?

"Well, then you didn't just meet your dreams, you *exceeded* them!" she exclaimed. "About five times over!"

Finley's eyes dropped to her glass for a moment, her cheeks tinting subtly with a graceful blush.

Sophie took a sip of her own wine just to hide her swoon.

"That's what makes that place feel so good," Finley breathed. "I can stand there and know that no matter how hard that job gets sometimes, it's *mine.* And I earned it. And I *deserve* it. And I'm worthy of it."

Finley exhaled heavily, a *finality,* almost, in the breath, and Sophie got the distinct impression that this was not the first time Finley had spoken those words.

She pictured them on a mantra, falling from a younger Finley's lips in the mirror over and over again as she fought for her dreams. Fought to earn her place.

Sophie swallowed thickly.

"What about you?" Finley quirked an eyebrow, her eyes almost reverent as they scanned her surroundings. "Why is this your *second* favourite place? Besides the obvious fact that it's incredibly peaceful and beautiful."

Sophie smiled widely.

"My parents owned that estate when I was a child. It was home for a while, and I loved it. *God,* I loved *them.* "

She huffed a soft laugh, her heart flooding with a strained kind of warmth as it always did when she spoke of her parents. Or when she thought of her dad's soft smile, and her mum's tight cuddles.

"And when I was seven, they had an accident. My, uh…my dad died, and my mum suffered severe head and spinal trauma," she murmured, her eyes holding Finley's through the screen.

Finley's breath hitched, her eyes soft and her lips parted. But she held Sophie's gaze, strong and steadfast, and she didn't say anything.

There was no awkward drop of eye contact. No uncomfortable shuffle, no meaningless *apology.*

And Sophie fell a little bit harder in an instant.

"They lost control of their car on the ice one winter night, and…that was it," she breathed, shrugging softly. "Dad was gone, and Mum was…different. Bex and I were swept off to live with our aunt Bea, and the estate was sold to pay for Mum's care."

"Except for this," Finley whispered, her eyes finally breaking from Sophie's just long enough to sweep reverently across her surroundings.

"Except for the orchard." Sophie nodded, smiling softly. "My dad's ashes were scattered in the stream through the pear trees, and it became our sanctuary. Mum passed away last year, and her ashes joined his."

Sophie bit her lip, her chest tightening with affection as she watched Finley's eyes drift across towards the stream, and her lips curl into a soft smile.

There were people Sophie had known her whole life who didn't see the beauty in that.

There were people she had been friends with since her parents were alive, who wouldn't visit that stream because they *feared* it. As if her parents' ashes haunted the stream like some sort of hammy ghost story. Finley Bennett had never been within 300 miles of Sophie, and she was managing to demonstrate a deeper understanding through glass and fibre than some of Sophie's oldest friends.

Sophie huffed a laugh, her butterflies taking off to Polcarne, Cornwall as she leaned closer into the screen.

"After Dad died, Bex took on a lot. She was a parent at fourteen, really. To me, and to Mum. But every now and then, whenever things got hardest and she needed to breathe, she would whisk me away in the gator and we would go to the orchard, and play in the stream. And it would feel, for just a few hours, like we were a whole family again. And ever since then it's been where I go every time I'm really happy."

Finley was quiet for a moment, her eyes misting as they found Sophie's once again through the screen.

"Every time you're happy…?" she whispered.

Sophie huffed a laugh.

"You seem surprised?"

"I…" Finley chuckled softly; her voice almost dazed. "The way that story was going, I was expecting you to say when things get hard now."

Sophie shrugged, her lips curling into a soft smile.

"There's a reason I sent you there. That's a *happy* place. I like to keep it that way." She blushed, dropping her eyes to her finger as she trailed it round the rim of her glass. "Maybe that's weird, I-I don't know, but I…I like the idea that it's somewhere that *only* holds happiness for me. Like it's the place where things feel less dark."

"That's not weird. It's…it's beautiful." Finley smiled softly. "And *smart*. And kind of amazing, really."

Sophie flicked her eyes back to the screen, her lips curling into a smirk at the all-out *heart eyes* her date was throwing her.

It had been a long time since someone had looked at her that way. She wasn't sure they *ever* had, really. Not truly seeing her, like Finley seemed to.

It felt *good*.

"Still talking about the happy place?" she teased.

"Maybe not…" Finley smirked.

Sophie's thighs clenched.

"Bennett, we need to talk about that smirk."

Finley quirked an eyebrow quizzically.

222

"It's dangerous, you really can't just whip that out without warning."

"Dangerous?" Finley laughed. "What's the hazard?"

"The things it does to me," Sophie murmured.

Finley swallowed visibly, the light tint of a blush creeping over the skin of her neck and her ears.

"Good things, I hope?" She raised a brow, mocha eyes darkening as they mapped the screen.

Sophie smirked.

"The *best* things."

~ ~ ~ ~ ~ ~ 🔥 ~ ~ ~ ~ ~ ~

Finley had barely touched her food.

She was completely and utterly entranced in everything that was Sophie Cedars.

Noah hadn't been wrong. If anything, he had dramatically undersold just how stunning Sophie looked tonight, and Finley's mind was in a constant battle between the eternal gratitude that she felt over the *insane* fact that she was somehow lucky enough to be sitting here on a date with this woman, and the frustration of *every* goddamn fucking mile that lay between them.

The date was everything that Finley believed a date should be. The way the conversation flowed so easily, from hopes and dreams, to favourite memories, to which Tamagotchi animal they'd owned and how long it had lived, to the flirty tease that Sophie Cedars seemed hellbent on breaking her with, and never seeming like the switch was unnatural.

Finley had never felt so safe in someone's company, and she was hooked on the feeling.

Honestly, it was weird how much she was willing to give. She wasn't sure she'd laid herself this bare to Jess in over four years of their relationship. And despite every part of Finley that screamed that this was bad—that she didn't date, that she'd only hurt Sophie, that she shouldn't fall…

She found herself falling anyway.

"If you could have a superpower, Sophie Cedars, what would it be?"

Finley grinned as Sophie giggled.

"You're adorable. Time travel. But…" She placed her glass down on the table, her hands flying up to gesture emphatically as she spoke. "And here's where it gets complicated…"

Finley laughed.

God she was falling *so* fast.

She knew she needed to get a grip, and quickly, but it was just *so* hard to care when her date was *this* fucking cute.

"I want to remember *nothing* about my real life while I'm there, but then remember *everything* about the trip when I come back."

Finley let her eyes drift as she contemplated the statement.

"Why wouldn't you want to remember while you're there?"

"'Cause then I'll experience it properly!" Sophie exclaimed, her pitch rising with her enthusiasm. "Not all tainted by my modern eyes, and the things I already know. I'd want to travel back to 1860, live life as a proper Victorian person who knows nothing of life in 2021 for a week, then come back and remember everything."

"So that you truly understand the way things were for them?"

*"Exactly!"*

Finley sighed.

The sheer *thought* behind that answer was everything. Sophie Cedars was incredibly smart, incredibly insightful, and incredibly astute, and Finley was finding it *incredibly* attractive.

"Your mind is honestly the *sexiest* thing I've ever encountered," she sighed.

Sophie's hands dropped, and misty eyes widened as she processed the words. She fell quiet, and Finley bit her lip as she allowed the moment to settle.

It hadn't passed her by that Sophie would always respond to a physical compliment with a smirk and a cheeky quip, but to one based on who she was as a *person* with a blush and a shy retreat.

Finley was beginning to think that not enough people in Sophie's life appreciated her mind and the way that she thought, for the sheer *magic* of it.

That maybe the small town of Polcarne, Cornwall simply didn't understand how brightly their diamond in the rough shone.

There was a moment of revered quiet, and then that cheeky smirk spread across Sophie's lips and Finley grinned in anticipation.

"Yet." Sophie winked.

Finley raised her eyebrows.

"Yet?"

"It's the sexiest thing you've encountered *yet.*"

Finley's stomach dropped.

How did *that* alone make her skin feel a little too warm?

"Confident you can exceed it, are you?" she teased.

Sophie leaned forward, the camera framing the way her hair fell around the curves of her chest, and Finley's stomach flooded instantly with a heat she had *no* hope of quelling.

"I'm 300 miles away and I can see the way those eyes are darkening, Fin," Sophie murmured. "I've *no* doubt of the things I could do to you with a little less space between us."

Finley shivered.

She closed her fingers over the tops of her thighs, as if somehow, she could ground herself and stop them from tightening. She could feel the goosebumps prickle over the skin of her arms and the back of her neck, and she hoped to whatever sapphic deity had landed her this date, that Sophie couldn't see just how *much* her words had affected her.

"A-a *little* less?" she croaked.

Sophie smirked.

"A *lot* less."

Finley shifted in her seat.

Her tongue darted out to wet her lips as she let her eyes drop to Sophie's. She wondered if her date would notice, the other side of the screen.

"What kind of things?"

Sophie grinned.

"This is a *first date,* Finley Bennett, I can't *possibly* say those things out loud on a first date."

Finley chuckled, her eyebrow raising as she mirrored Sophie's stance, leaning in a little closer to the screen.

"But you're *thinking* them?"

"Oh, I'm thinking them alright," Sophie husked, her playful eyes dancing with mischief. "I'm thinking them *so* hard."

Finley bit her lip as she huffed out a laugh, her cheeks burning at her own increasingly flustered state.

God, this was *dangerously* easy for Sophie.

She shook her head.

*"Such* a tease from safe behind your screen, Cedars." She smirked. "Would you be saying this if you were sitting beside me?"

"I think I'd be doing a *lot* less talking if I was sitting beside you."

Finley's body flamed, and she bit her lip, nodding her head with a chuckle.

"What's *your* superpower then?" Sophie honeyed, her smile a picture of innocence despite the spark that still burned in mischievous eyes.

Finley huffed.

"Right now? Teleportation."

"Smooth." Sophie grinned.

Finley sat back, flexing her fingers in a desperate effort to relieve some of the tension Sophie had so easily wound tight through her muscles.

"Seeing the world through someone or something else's eyes. Like a…a clairvoyant meets a Bran Stark style warg. Imagine the things you could *see,* and the experiences you could have!"

Sophie rested her chin on her hands, intrigue clear in her eyes as she searched the screen.

"Whose eyes would you look through now, if you could?"

"I already *have* the best possible view right *now,"* Finley winked, throwing her best cheeky grin. She frowned. "Unless there's like…a bird, or a bug or something somewhere close to you. Then, that."

Sophie giggled.

"You are *so* cute." She shook her head, her eyes glinting with something that made Finley's chest swell. "This *whole* thing. This whole date. You're adorable, Finley Bennett."

Finley huffed out a laugh, her stomach twisting and her veins *burning* with everything that Sophie Cedars made her feel.

This was *crazy.*

*How* was she feeling like this over someone 300 miles away, who she'd never shared a room with? How was a couple of hours in a darkening orchard, with a stream and a computer screen, shaping up to be the best date she'd *ever* been on?

She shook her head.

"This is insane. I've never…" she trailed off, her words tangling on her tongue as she tried to find the ones that would make sense. "I've not felt…I…"

"Yeah…" Sophie breathed, wrapping her arms around herself in a move that made Finley's entire body melt.

"We're gonna meet, right?" Finley whispered. "In person?"

Sophie grinned.

"You asking me on a second date, Bennett?"

*"Absolutely."* Finley smirked. "Preferably one 300 miles closer to you, where I can…"

She trailed off, catching the words on the tip of her tongue before they fell.

Was that too forward? Too much?

Sophie had definitely been *more* suggestive, but she'd let the tease hang around the edges. She hadn't stated things so openly.

Finley swallowed, the air around her thickening as she watched Sophie do the same.

She wondered if the air on that rooftop in London felt this tight.

"Where you can *what?"* Sophie whispered.

"Where I can kiss you."

Sophie's eyes fluttered closed, and Finley felt every ounce of breath in her lungs expel as she watched her date's lips part, and the tint of a blush spread over the exposed skin of her chest and her neck.

Then those irresistible lips quirked into a soft smile, and Sophie chuckled shyly.

"Yes please. I *really* like you, Fin."

Finley beamed, her stomach erupting into a carousel of butterflies as darkened green eyes flickered across the screen, mapping the blush that she knew would be set deep into her own cheeks.

"I like you too," she breathed. "Like, a *lot."*

And that was unusual, and crazy, and terrifying. But it felt good, and for once in her life Finley felt happy to let something else carry her.

# Chapter Fourteen

Finley groaned, her eyes screwing tighter shut as the sound of her ringtone blasted through her sleep for the third time that morning.

She had been ignoring it for the past few minutes, knowing full well *exactly* who was calling her this early, the morning after her date.

She buried her face in the pillows, letting sleep pull her back under as the ringing died out.

Then it started again, immediately.

She grunted, hauling herself up against the headboard and begrudgingly pulling the screen to answer the incoming video call.

"This'd better be important, you persistent ass."

"It's 7 am!" Noah exclaimed.

"I have an alarm, Noah," Finley grumbled. "I don't need a wake-up call."

"It's *7 am,*" Noah squeaked. "I've been waiting for *eleven* hours."

"Honestly," Finley sighed, running the palm of her hand over her barely-awake face. "Don't you have better things to…"

*"Finley!"*

Finley rolled her eyes, though she couldn't fight the first tugs of a smirk at the corners of her lips.

"Just *ask,*" she huffed, biting back her amusement.

"Are you in love?"

Finley narrowed her eyes, shaking her head.

"You're an idiot."

Noah raised an eyebrow.

"So, yes?"

Finley stared at the screen for a long moment, at the stupid excited look on her ridiculous best friend's face, and the way he held his breath as he waited for her to answer his melodramatic question.

She sighed heavily.

"I want to marry her and have all of her babies," she mumbled.

*"Yes!"*

Finley groaned, slumping down into the bed and pulling a pillow over her face.

*"What?"* Noah scolded. *"Why* are you being a drama pyjama, Finley she's *amazing!"*

"I *know* that, but she lives *five and a half hours* away!" Finley threw the pillow off her face. "I haven't even..."

"Do *not* say *met her.* Yes, you damn well have." Noah pointed a finger at the camera, his body almost vibrating with his enthusiasm. "And Fin, you *know* she's here because she wants to move! Give her another reason to!"

"Noah..." Finley tried.

Fruitlessly.

He had a point, and she knew it.

"Besides, the Americans would drive that for a bagel." Noah shrugged.

Finley's phone buzzed in her hand, and she was powerless to stop the smitten grin that spread across her face at the name that flashed in the message bar.

"I don't own a car, and the American's drive *way* too far *way* too often," she mumbled, pulling the message up. "Besides, that's not the point. The point is that I could not expect..."

Finley froze.

Her words blocked like lead in her throat, her mind blanking immediately as she stared at the image that filled her screen.

Sophie Cedars had sent her a selfie that had broken her brain in milliseconds.

And she wasn't even all that sure why!

Sophie was nestled back against Finley's pillows, her shoulders bare above the hem of the duvet that wrapped *just* low enough for the curves of her chest to make Finley's blood burn. Green eyes glittered with something that sparked tight in Finley's stomach, and the heat in that playful smirk trickled torturously between her thighs.

Finley swallowed.

"Finley?"

Noah's voice barely grazed the edge of her consciousness, and she blinked as she fought for the words, she'd been trying to say.

"Uh…I…"

*Jesus.*

Why was this *so* hot?

Noah baulked.

"Okay, ew."

"Wh…?" Finley blinked, shaking her head in an effort to bring her focus back to her call and away from the wandering thoughts of Sophie Cedars and what lay just beneath the hem of those sheets.

Noah wrinkled his nose.

"Bennett, I know sex eyes when I see them and I *know* you're not making those at me."

"What?" Finley cleared her throat, closing the image down. "I-I'm *not* making…"

"Your face is red."

Finley's phone buzzed again.

Sophie: *Woke up thinking about you this morning* 🌿

Finley's stomach dropped, every nerve in her body burning. She clenched her jaw, her thighs tightening instantly.

"*Okay,* and I'm out." Noah shuddered deliberately, throwing Finley a cheeky grin and an awkward finger gun. "Use protection."

Finley sighed with relief as the call rang off, and she let her head fall back against the pillows.

She grinned, shaking her head as she pulled the image up once more, not even *wanting* to fight the heat that prickled beneath her skin. She typed her message.

Finley: *And now I'll be thinking about you all day!* 💧

Sophie: *We both know you would have done anyway* 😌

Finley chuckled.

Finley: *Oh, undeniably, but* this *sets a tone I've no* hope *of coming back from*
😼

Sophie: *Who needs to come back?* 😼

Sophie: *I hope your day starts as pleasantly as mine did.* 😊

Finley groaned.

Sophie was *barely* straddling the line of explicit, and she was doing things to Finley that she hadn't felt in a long time. *'Girls On Holiday'* hadn't managed this, and neither had her tryst with Bella Collins.

But *Sophie...*

Finley was certainly no stranger to a few flirty words here and there, or to a teasing photo or two, but she could absolutely say without a shadow of a doubt that *no-one* had ever made her this wet with something so delicately teasing.

She squirmed a little under the sheets, her simple white tank and her boxers suddenly feeling incredibly restrictive against her flushed skin.

She smirked. She couldn't deny that she *loved* the way that Sophie could push her buttons so easily, but she really needed to take some control back here.

She positioned herself back, deliberately tousling her hair enough to splay across the pillows. She pulled the white material of her tank tight around her chest, letting the fabric frame the curves enough to tease. She bit her lip, her eyes *just* dark enough as she snapped her own photo.

She sent it to Sophie.

Finley: *Thanks to you, there's a very strong chance it will.* 😼

Sophie: *Jesus Christ.* 💧

Sophie: *There's just no way you look that sexy in the mornings, Bennett.*

Finley: *Maybe you should wake up with me one day and find out.* 😊

Sophie: *I woke up in your bed, you're the one who wasn't in it.* 👾

Finley chuckled, shaking her head.

Sophie had a point.

She was in Finley's home, in Finley's bed, and Finley was 300 miles away practically vibrating with the urge to close the gap.

What was stopping her?

Why couldn't she just go home, and make the most of a few days with Sophie in person before the real world came crashing back down around them both?

Nothing, was the answer!

The sole reason she was still in Cornwall, was the niggling fear that maybe going home would just be too forward. Maybe if she did, she would simply be gate-crashing Sophie's trip, or maybe she'd even drive her out early, and she *really* didn't want to do that.

231

Partly for Sophie, and partly because she just didn't think she could handle the rejection right now.

She scanned the texts again, heat flooding her core once more at the photo and the suggestive words that had accompanied it.

The phone buzzed against her fingers, the image that filled her screen this time sending her into nothing short of a meltdown.

The camera was further back, showing more of Sophie's body across the screen. The sheets were draped loosely across her torso, leaving her bare thighs and those teasing curves of her chest free to taunt Finley into an overheated frenzy.

The image was still chaste. Still *tasteful.* Still barely grazing the line of dirty. But the tease in green eyes was enough to show it was definitely intended to work Finley up.

And it was *shamelessly* working.

The accompanied words did absolutely nothing to calm the all-out tornado in Finley's stomach.

Sophie: *And I really wish you were...* ☺

Finley exhaled heavily.

She pulled her own tank over her head, the material far too suffocating over the surge of heat in her bloodstream.

She fired a response back, her mind quickly beginning to fog with arousal as she let her eyes drift back over Sophie's words and her images.

Finley: *You're far too aware of your own power, you know that?*

Sophie: *What power is that?* ☺

Finley laughed, shaking her head.

She was fairly certain there was no way to answer this, without outright declaring the state of writhing arousal that a couple of flirty texts and two suggestive photos had pushed her into, and she wanted to at least show a *little* more decorum than that.

So, she opted to show, not tell.

She knew her cheeks and the now exposed skin of her chest would be flushed. She knew her eyes would be dark, and glazed, and lidded. And she knew her parted lips would be reddened.

And she knew Sophie would see that, through the tiny lens of Finley's camera phone, and *know* the effect that she was having.

Finley snapped her photo, and sent it.

She held her breath as the ticks turned blue.

The little dots that indicated Sophie was typing played out almost immediately.

Then they stopped.

Finley bit her lip, watching with bated breath as the dots started and stopped no less than three times, before finally the phone buzzed, and Sophie's reply flickered onto the screen.

Sophie: *Fuck.*

Finley huffed a half laugh and a half groan as she let her head fall back and her phone fall to the side.

She couldn't remember the last time she'd felt the ache this strongly between her thighs, and she let her eyes flutter closed as she allowed her mind to wander over every one of Sophie's teasing words, her flirty smirks, and the fire in those irresistible green eyes.

She slipped her hand beneath the waistband of her boxer shorts, her entire body melting as her fingertips found her clit for the first time in weeks.

Her back arched, her fingers tracing their skilful patterns instinctively as she imagined the way that Sophie would feel if she were the one beneath them.

*"Fuck."*

~ ~ ~ ~ ~ ~ 🎵 ~ ~ ~ ~ ~ ~

Finley's feet pounded the uneven tarmac as she ran along the road that led to Polcarne High Street. She'd forgone the beach this morning, hoping instead that she might find the little hamlet town alive with the bustle of the early morning.

She knew it was a long shot, really.

But she was beginning to tire of her own company, and she figured if she ran past the corner shop, and the bakery, and the school, that maybe she might feel at least a *little* less isolated for a few moments.

She was amazed at how fresh the air still felt here. Even four miles from the sea, she could still taste the salt and that indescribable tang that she had learned to associate with the ocean breeze.

Sure, it permeated slightly too much with the fresh scent of manure in way too many of the fields she passed, but even that felt cleaner, somehow, than the smoke and the fumes of Central London.

She slowed her pace as she entered the high street, and she couldn't fight the curl of a grin at her lips as she began to pass actual signs of human life.

Just as she'd hoped, she passed an unfamiliar woman setting a specials sign outside of a small café, and a red-faced man lifting the shutters on the butcher's window, and a slow but steady stream of pushchairs, and little bikes, and uniformed school children skipping and running ahead of their parents in the direction of the town's tiny primary school.

And she didn't recognise many of the faces, but everyone she saw offered her a smile, and a wave, and a cheery greeting, and Finley's chest expanded as she felt the small hamlet town welcome her with open arms.

Which was why, when she rounded a corner and almost collided with a barely awake Bex Arroway and two small children, Finley was beaming ear to ear.

"Okay, *ew,*" Bex groaned, blinking as she stared blearily at Finley's grinning face. "Why do you look like you got laid last night?"

Finley barked a laugh.

"I have never got what that means!" She scrunched her nose. "How can someone *look* like they got laid?"

"You look all giddy and you're like, fucking *glowing* with something," Bex grumbled, rubbing at her eyes. "And at 8am there's only ever one reason for that."

Finley grinned, rolling her eyes.

"You know full well I didn't get laid," she chuckled. "My date was 300 miles away, and I spent the night alone in your sister's bed."

"What does get laid mean?"

Finley blinked.

She looked down, her eyes widening and her lips rolling as she met the curious green eyes of a very small, very blonde little girl, with hair that stuck out at all kinds of angles.

And the bemused glare of a slightly taller, equally as blonde little boy, with floppy hair and dimples that made him look far more innocent than the fire in his brown eyes might have suggested.

"Erm…" Finley paused, her mind blanking slightly under the inquisitive little stare. "It…it means you get a really good sleep?"

The little girl frowned. Her eyes drifted, creasing delicately in the centre as she considered Finley's words, and Finley held her breath. She shot a glance at

Bex, whose eyes sparkled with amusement as she pursed her own lips in anticipation.

Then the little girl turned to Bex, those curious eyes still creased as she spoke.

"Why do you tell Daddy he's gonna get a good sleep when he does the cleaning?"

Finley bit her cheek to stifle her laugh.

"Yeah," the little boy chimed in. "And why do you say Auntie Sophie never gets a good sleep these days?"

Finley's eyes shot wide, and an outright giggle burst from her chest.

Bex groaned.

Finley choked on her giggles, her eyes beginning to water as she watched the weary embarrassment in Bex's eyes.

Bex scowled.

"Well, Finley here is gonna help Auntie Sophie get her good sleep, aren't you, Fin?" she goaded, smirking almost smugly as both sets of innocent eyes turned back to Finley.

Finley scowled right back.

Then she turned her attention to the children.

"You must be the very clever niece and nephew that your Auntie Sophie has told me all about?"

The little girl beamed.

"I'm Willow! That's Jack."

"I'm Finley. I'm staying in your Auntie Sophie's house while she's in London."

"Is Auntie Sophie staying in *your* house?" Willow asked, her wide eyes somehow even wider as they fixed on Finley's face.

"Yes, she is!"

Willow's eyes drifted once again in thought, for the briefest of moments.

"Will she get laid there?"

This time Bex barked a laugh, and Finley choked.

"I *hope* not," Finley mumbled, low and under her breath.

"She will if you go home," Bex retorted, just as low and just as mumbled.

Finley shot her a glare.

"Shut up!" she gritted. "Why do you hate me?"

Bex smirked.

"Do you have loadsa money?" Jack asked, bold and shameless, and completely out of left field.

Finley blinked.

She didn't have a huge amount of experience with children, and she was beginning to wonder how parents didn't suffer constant whiplash.

"Jack, *how* many times do I need to tell you that's *not* how we ask that question?" Bex chided, her eyes both apologetic and amused as she nudged her son lightly on his shoulder.

"Right, sorry." Jack nodded, sheepish and guilty as he tried again. "What do you do for work?"

Bex grinned.

"Better, thank you," she praised.

Finley laughed.

"I'm an architect."

Jack frowned. He shot a sideways glance at his mother, his eyebrows raised in question as he waited for confirmation of what he was really asking.

"Yes." Bex winked.

Finley grinned, shaking her head.

"Cool," Jack breathed, his eyes brighter now as they fixed back on Finley. "I'm gonna have loadsa money one day too, cause I'm gonna be an astronaut."

"And *I'm* gonna be a writer *and* a chef!" Willow piped.

Finley raised an eyebrow, shooting Bex an impressed glance.

"You sure these are your kids?" she teased.

"Drunk Dave says nobody from Cornwall is ever an astronaut," Willow stated. "Especially Polcarne."

So casually. So nonchalantly.

So *brazenly,* and Finley's chest crushed tight at the implications.

At the apathetic parroting of an adult's unwarranted opinion, like it wasn't a complete disregard of a little boy's dream.

"Drunk…" Bex spluttered, her eyes closing for a moment as she processed the words. *"When* have you been talking to Drunk Dave?"

Willow shrugged.

"He showed me a song on the jukebox when I came to the pub when Jack was ill," she explained.

Bex heaved a sigh, her thumb and her forefinger pinching the bridge of her nose.

"I'm the worst mother in the world."

"Well, that's definitely not true," Finley chuckled, shaking her head in assurance. "You're the mother of the next Neil Armstrong and Virginia Woolfe!"

Bex huffed a laugh, and Finley turned her gaze to the small children in front of her.

She let her eyes scan their faces, and the steadfast fire in eyes that looked *so* much like Bex's.

And *Sophie's.*

The spark of drive and determination that Finley *knew* was the same one she felt in her own stomach, and had done for so long.

Since the first time her father had told her she was a leech.

Since the first time she was made to feel less, or unimportant.

Finley might not have known Willow and Jack Arroway, but she did know that she didn't ever want the spark in those young eyes to dull.

She wanted them to know they *could.*

"Let me tell you something," Finley murmured. She squatted down to her knees, bringing her eyes level with the small gazes. "How old are you?"

"Seven," Willow declared.

"Nine," Jack stated.

Finley smiled softly.

"Well, when *I* was seven and nine, nobody thought I could be an architect," she breathed. "'cause I was a bit naughty at school, and my d…"

She trailed off, clearing her throat gently.

Maybe this wasn't quite the right audience for a childhood trauma dump. Maybe she should keep this directly relevant.

She changed tact.

"Some people in my town thought I wasn't smart enough. Or good enough."

"But you are an architect anyway," Jack exclaimed.

Finley grinned.

"Of course!" she laughed. "'cause those people don't get to tell us what we're gonna be. They don't know. How would they know? They can't tell the future."

Willow giggled, and Jack grinned, and Finley's chest spread warm.

"If you wanna be an astronaut, you just gotta work hard," Finley murmured. "Pay attention in maths and science, and just keep trying."

"Like Auntie Sophie?" Willow whispered.

Finley beamed, her entire body flooding with butterflies and something that felt a lot like pride.

"*Just* like Auntie Sophie," she chuckled.

"And *definitely* don't listen to Drunk Dave," Bex interjected. "In fact, please *never s*peak to Drunk Dave again."

The kids giggled, nodding their heads, and Finley grinned as she pushed herself back to her feet.

"Thanks, wise one," Bex murmured, shooting Finley a wink as the children began to talk animatedly amongst themselves. "See you tonight for a drink at the Inn? On the house?"

"Sounds good," Finley agreed. She stepped back, giving Bex and the kids the space to move past. "Bye kids, have a good day at school!"

She chuckled, shaking her head as both children ignored her entirely, their focus switched to the screen of a phone, and an animated argument over something that sounded suspiciously like Pokémon Go.

Finley grinned, shooting Bex one last wave as she took a deep breath, and set off to complete the last of her six-mile run.

~ ~ ~ ~ ~ ~ (♫) ~ ~ ~ ~ ~ ~

"I *knew* you'd be all up in her business like Pepe Le Pew."

Sophie rolled her eyes as Bex's voice rang out from the video call propped against the mirror she was using to apply her mascara.

"Granted I assumed you'd have to *meet* her first, but clearly her charms extend beyond physical barriers."

"Bex…" Sophie tried to warn, but she couldn't fight the smile that pulled at the corners of her lips.

"I'm just saying, I *get* it!" Bex exclaimed around a mouthful of bacon sandwich, waving the remains in the direction of the camera as she spoke. "When're you gonna meet her?"

"I don't *know,"* Sophie groaned. "She lives so *far away* and I…"

"Right, for now!" Bex cut her off bluntly. "Thought you wanted to be a city girl?"

"I can't just *move across the country* for a girl I've *never met."*

"You're wouldn't *be* moving for the girl, Bruno Mars, you wanted this before you even knew she *existed,"* Bex retorted, her exasperation clear in her tone and the roll of her eyes. She winked. "Bennett would simply be a *delicious* bonus. Besides you're getting *way* ahead of yourself! Just meet her. Ask her to come home, have a date in the city lights!"

Sophie threw her hands in the air.

"I cannot just *ask* her to drop her holiday to come home and take me to a rooftop bar, Bex."

*"Yes,* you *can!"* Bex insisted. "I'm telling you, that girl is *one* heart emoji away from packing her bags already, Soph." She scrunched her nose, shovelling another mouthful of bacon sandwich into her face. "Besides, how many clifftop walks does a person *really* need in Polcarne?"

"Enough that…"

Sophie's rebuttal halted, her brow furrowing as an abrupt knock rang out across the front door of the flat. Clearly someone who knew the building door code!

She checked the time.

8:46am.

A little early for unexpected visitors, but it wasn't exactly the first time.

She hoped it wasn't Noah. Peanut definitely didn't seem to be in the flat this time!

Before she had even managed to climb to her feet, the door knocked again. Louder, and sharper.

On the phone screen, Bex wriggled her eyebrows.

"Bet you my bacon that's Raggedy Don Juan now."

Sophie rolled her eyes.

"You saw her forty-five minutes ago!" she huffed. "I'll call you later, 'kay?"

"Love you, sis!"

Bex blew a very greasy looking kiss as the call rang off, and Sophie grimaced.

She pushed the mascara stick back into the tube, and hurried to the door before another angry sounding rap could ring out.

She frowned as she pulled back the door.

The woman on the doorstep was beautiful, her crisp shirt and her pinned-back hair immaculate.

And she did *not* look impressed.

Sophie's eyebrows shot up as the woman's gaze dropped over her body, as if somehow scrutinising her very being, before she smirked, pushing her way past and into the hallway.

"Where's Bennett?"

Sophie frowned.

"Finley's on holiday." She stood a little taller, her defences tingling under the woman's unabashed confidence. "I-I'm sorry, *who* are you?"

"I'm the woman whose calls she's been ignoring for over a week now."

Sophie blinked.

The woman bit her lip, visibly suppressing a tight smirk.

Sophie raised an eyebrow, folding her arms in defiance.

The woman rolled her eyes.

"Amelia Roscoe. I'm her *boss.*"

Sophie's stomach dropped.

*Shit.*

Her *boss?*

"Though the way she's been acting lately, you wouldn't think it," Amelia muttered. "Who are *you?" she* demanded.

"Uh…I'm just staying here, while Finley is away."

"Like a house sitter?" Amelia scoffed. "As if Bennett is ever home anyway?"

"No, more like a…"

Amelia wasn't listening.

She pushed her way through the flat, and Sophie panicked. She scurried hastily after Amelia as the woman pushed her way into the kitchen, narrowed eyes scanning the cupboard doors as if Finley might suddenly emerge from the fridge with a flourish.

"Please tell Bennett to stop playing games, stop ignoring my calls, and to get back to me immediately. I'm running out of patience, and she's running out of time."

Amelia made her way far too casually, far too *arrogantly* through Finley's home as she spoke, running her fingers along the edges of the furniture as if checking for dust.

And the action, quite frankly, pissed Sophie off.

Then Amelia absently picked up the pile of post Sophie had been collating for Finley's return, and began to leaf through the envelopes.

And Sophie saw red.

She closed her eyes, shaking her head as the cold panic in her veins thawed into the very heated burn of irritation.

Boss or no boss, *who* did this woman think she was?

Finley was on annual leave, it wasn't even 9am, and this was her *home.*

The *audacity!*

The words were out before she'd thought them through, and certainly before she'd had time to remember she was a people pleaser who detested confrontation.

"I'm *sorry,"* she spat, snatching the letters from Amelia's hands and placing them just out of the woman's reach. *"What* makes you think you can waltz in here like this?"

Amelia's lips twitched at the corners; an annoyingly amused smirk *just* hidden beneath her daggers as she held Sophie's unwavering gaze.

"Probably the same misguided sense of entitlement that makes Finley Bennett think she can disappear off the grid for a week and ignore my phone calls," she sniped.

Sophie almost laughed.

What kind of a Disney villain *was* this woman?

"Finley doesn't owe you this right now, you know," she stated darkly.

Amelia's eyebrows shot up.

*"Excuse* me?"

Sophie couldn't have held it back if she'd tried.

"She's entitled to her leave. She doesn't owe you her availability right now."

"Who are you to tell me what my employee does and doesn't…"

"I mean, there are *literally* workplace rights and policies that tell you that," Sophie interrupted. "You don't need me to do it for you."

She was pacing a little now, and she knew it, but there was something about that smug smirk and the demanding expectation that was *really* grinding Sophie's gears.

Amelia chuckled coldly, her eyebrow quirking in disdain.

"Need I remind you that there are also *workplace policies* about not fucking off for two weeks without adequate notice for your employer!"

Sophie halted.

*That…* wasn't untrue.

Amelia had her there, to be fair.

"You really shouldn't take Finley for granted, you know." Sophie dropped her tone, exhaling slowly in an effort to keep the building anger from showing in her voice. "You need to be careful."

Amelia's jaw tightened instantly.

"I need to be *careful?* Is that a *threat?"*

"No, it's an observation," Sophie stated, flexing her fingers to keep herself calm. "Finley works her *ass* off to get where she wants to be, and you keep her static because she's right where you need her."

Amelia shook her head, her eyes flaming with something Sophie couldn't quite identify.

This woman was pissing her off something *chronic,* but there was also something softer in the quirk of those lips that just didn't *quite* add up.

And somehow that was even *more* annoying.

"What is *that* supposed to mean?" Amelia snapped.

"Well, she's your best architect, right?" Sophie was pacing again. "If you promoted her, you'd need someone else to fill her shoes and you know no-one else would give what she does."

Amelia scoffed.

"You have *no idea* what you're talking about. You really have got some nerve…"

"Then prove it," Sophie shot.

*"Prove* it?"

"Prove it. Put Finley where she deserves to be."

Amelia's eyes flashed, her cheeks reddening in anger, but the corners of her lips quirked *again* and she dropped her gaze once more over Sophie's body.

"Tell Bennett to call me. *Immediately."*

# Chapter Fifteen

Finley sighed contentedly as she ground her coffee beans for her post-run breakfast.

A week ago, this had been a slightly archaic waste of time, but somehow this morning it felt almost therapeutic. She was on cloud nine, and she was pretty sure nothing could burst her Sophie Cedars shaped bubble right now.

She grinned as her phone buzzed across the counter with an incoming call, and she felt almost high with the endorphins of a run and a raging crush.

She frowned as she read the name across her screen.

What did Bex want? Bex did not strike her as the 'call for a chat' type. Besides, she'd *just* seen her.

"Miss me already?" Finley teased, hitting the loudspeaker button as she began to make her coffee. "Let me guess, can't stop thinking about me in lycra?"

"Finley!" Bex cried through the tinny speaker. "Help me, please, please tell me you're free?"

Finley abandoned the coffee immediately, grabbing for her phone.

Bex sounded strained, and panicked, and everything in it made Finley's blood run cold.

"You have nothing else going on in this podunk town, I'm begging you," Bex pleaded, the fear in her voice even clearer now as Finley lifted the phone to her ear.

"Hey, hey…Bex," Finley assured, fighting the shake in her voice as she focused her whole attention on her friend's voice. "I'm listening. What's going on?"

"It's Jack!" Bex exhaled, her voice hoarse with the recognisable strain of a person fighting their emotions. Fighting to stay calm, and not particularly achieving it. "School sent him home, he's woozy, and sick, and he looks like Trevor's cheese…Fin, I have to take him to the hospital but Pete's out and he isn't answering his *fucking* phone, and…"

Bex cut her own words off with a choked sob, and Finley's spine stiffened.

She'd *just* seen Jack, not even an hour ago. And he'd seemed fine! Full of beans, and inappropriate questions.

But Trevor's cheese was *really* grey.

"And I can't go on my own, Fin," Bex breathed, quiet and almost secretive. Pleading. "I…I can't face a hospital on my own. I can't be strong for him on my own."

Finley's instincts took their hold. She headed instantly for the door, grabbing her coat and Sophie's keys with her free hand.

"Get his things together," she instructed calmly. Mainly to keep Bex occupied, and breathing steadily. "Water, snacks, layers, comfy clothes in case it takes a while. I'm on my way."

"Finley…" Bex whispered.

Finley paused; hand raised to the door handle.

"Yeah?"

*"Please* don't tell Sophie."

Finley's chest tightened.

That felt uncomfortable. It felt *really* uncomfortable, and the lie already tasted like bile in her throat before she'd even told it. She opened her mouth to say as much. To tell Bex that Sophie needed to know. But before the words had even formed on her tongue, she understood. She knew, without a glimmer of a doubt, that if Sophie Cedars knew her nephew was hospital bound, she would be on the next train home.

Putting her own life on the back burner, like she had her whole life.

And Finley may have only known Bex and Sophie a matter of days, but she was already fairly certain she understood that Sophie's trip to London right now was a big deal. And not one that Bex would be willing to jeopardise.

So as uncomfortable as it felt, she pushed the bile down, and nodded slowly.

"Yeah," she breathed. "Yeah, you got it."

She hung up the phone and swung the door open, barely remembering to lock it behind her in her haste as she rushed to Sophie's Ford.

She practically swerved her way around the narrow, winding road to The Ship Inn. Quite frankly, fuck the tractors. *She* was hurtling at *their* faces this time, and they were just going to have to deal with it. She had the life of Polcarne's first astronaut to save, and she was hellbent on it.

Bex and Jack were already outside when Finley careered into the car park and skidded to a halt in front of them. Finley had been relatively calm, manic driving aside, but she couldn't help the shiver of shock as her eyes landed on Jack. Bex hadn't been wrong, he really was grey. And kind of waxy. And he was trembling, sweating visibly, and clearly struggling to stay awake. A far cry from the bouncing little boy Finley had seen just an hour before now.

Jack didn't even look at Finley as Bex bundled him into the car, and Finley's chest tightened with a sharp stab of fear.

Finley exhaled slowly, flexing her fingers over the steering wheel in an effort to force the calm back into her muscles. Jack needed his mum's attention right now, and Bex needed Finley to hold her shit together.

She glanced at them in the rear-view mirror, Bex in the left-hand corner, with Jack wrapped up tightly in her arms. She caught Bex's eye, asking unspoken questions with the raise of her eyebrows.

*Are we ready?*

Bex nodded.

"Thank you," she whispered. "I can give you directions. Head right out of here, and along the high street for now."

Finley simply nodded her head, her hands still tight around the wheel as she began to follow the instructions.

Her chest *ached* at the undisguisable worry in Bex's face, and the tightness of her muscles. Finley had only ever seen Bex laughing and joking, and being a general smart ass no matter who she was talking to. But now, she could see the lines around her eyes and her brow, and the slight sink of her eyes, that showed her ghosts. She looked vulnerable and scared, beneath something harder.

Like, Finley understood, a parent trying her hardest to hold her shit together for the sake of her child.

And Finley felt the back of her eyes burn hot as the image in her rear-view mirror shifted and changed. Morphing to that same face in fourteen-year-old Bex Cedars, pulling seven-year-old Sophie into that same protective hug.

*I can't face a hospital alone.*
*Please don't tell Sophie.*

Finley swallowed thickly, forcing her eyes back to the road.

It wasn't even a question. Those ghosts, those *demons* in her sister's eyes were why Sophie found it hard to leave.

And Bex knew it.

The hospital was just fifteen minutes away but it felt like a lifetime. Bex's voice grew softer, and weaker as she guided Finley closer. As though she almost hoped Finley wouldn't hear, and they'd never make it.

Finley was around and at Bex's door before the engine had finished rumbling, and she draped her own coat over Jack's shivering frame as Bex lifted him out of the car.

"I've got you, Stink," Bex whispered, planting a kiss on Jack's clammy head. "I've got you."

She looked as pale as he did as they approached the hospital doors.

Finley placed a reassuring hand on Bex's shoulder as the glass doors slid open.

"And I've got you," she murmured.

Bex's eyes misted for the first time as they met Finley's, and she gave a small, weak smile.

The first thing Finley noticed as they stepped through the hospital doors was the smell. It always was. It was always the thing people hated the most about hospitals, wasn't it? The potent antiseptic smell, and the dizzying lights, and the blinding amounts of white. So bright, and so brash, for a place that held so much darkness.

Hospitals always felt to Finley like she'd already died.

She wasn't the biggest fan, but she was fairly sure no-one was, and this was absolutely not about her.

Beside her, Bex's trembling hand reached for her own, and Finley took it firmly.

She held on as Bex checked Jack in at the reception desk, and she squeezed a little tighter each time the fear bled a little stronger into Bex's voice.

She held firmly as they led Jack into the waiting area, and found him a row of seats to lie him across.

She let go only to call for help as Jack's eyes glazed, and he passed out.

~ ~ ~ ~ ~ ~ 🎵 ~ ~ ~ ~ ~ ~

Sophie's throat burned as she paced desperately across Finley's bedroom floor.

She couldn't remember the last time she'd felt this on edge, and she had no idea where to put the uncomfortable surges of energy in her veins.

She'd tried frantically for the better part of two hours to get hold of Finley, but honestly, she had no idea what she would say to her once she did.

How did a person *start* something like that?

*Hi, I know you've not actually met me, and I really have no involvement in your life whatsoever, but I've just threatened your boss and quite possibly destroyed your career, how's your morning going?*

Sophie groaned, throwing her head back as she clenched her fists. *Why* had she opened her mouth? Sophie had spent twenty-six years being painfully polite to everyone she ever met, even to her own detriment. Like the time she'd sold her entire collection of Pokémon cards to a stranger for a fiver because she hadn't wanted to say no. But *now? Today?* Faced with her new, giant, raging crush's *boss? That* was the time she'd decided she was some sort of bloody *mobster?*

She wailed, throwing herself onto the bed with considerably more force than was required. She hit Bex's number again. If she couldn't get hold of Finley, she could at least vent a little with her sister.

She groaned, flinging her phone across the bed as her sister's voicemail greeted her for the third time that morning.

*Why* was no-one answering her?

Suddenly, in a rack of shaking sobs, Sophie felt *really* alone. Not in life, but in London. She'd been yearning for so long to be a little fish in a big pond, but now that she was here and she needed someone, and no fish would answer her calls, the pond felt terrifying. She felt like she was floundering, drowning in a way that she hadn't since her dad had died. And suddenly she wasn't sure that she could do this.

She had just *shouted* at someone. Someone *important.*

First Kyle Brown, and now this Amelia? *What* had gotten into her?

She rolled, rather dramatically, off the bed, groaning once again as she landed in a crumpled heap on the rug beneath the bed. She whimpered pathetically, shame beginning to grip her as she thought about what Finley would think if she could see her now.

Lying in a heap on her bedroom floor, staring unseeing at the dusty variety of objects shoved haphazardly beneath the bed.

Then she blinked, staring again with seeing eyes at a binder labelled 'Finley Childhood Photos'.

She sniffed. Well. She felt guilty enough already, she might as well add a *little* fun into the list of reasons why.

She brushed the dust off the deep red, faux-leather cover, and began to slowly flip through the pages of the photo album. The first photo was a baby scan, the name in the corner reading 'April Bennett'. Followed by a photo of a tiny newborn, cradled in the arms of a young, tired woman, with rosy cheeks, and a beaming smile, and a hell of a perm. Sophie smiled softly. Finley certainly had her mother's eyes.

The photos were arranged meticulously in age order. Through toothless grins, and chubby-faced toddles, and first school uniforms, and birthday parties and Christmases and summer holidays. Sophie wondered if they'd been placed as they were taken, or if someone, maybe Finley, had organised them all at a later date.

Sophie's tears welled in her eyes again as the photos waned. April Bennett stopped featuring, and so did the light in Finley's eyes. The photos were fewer and further between, and Finley's cheeky grin shifted first into something muted, and then later into something steelier.

The album ended on Finley's last day at school. In a shirt covered in scribbled messages and signatures, with tear-stained cheeks and red-faced friends. And a determined smile.

Sophie sobbed.

Finley had worked so hard, all her life, to be who she was. To feel free, and stand alone and successful.

And now Sophie had ruined it for her.

~ ~ ~ ~ ~ ~ ♪ ~ ~ ~ ~ ~ ~

Finley tried her hardest to take in everything the doctor was saying.

Mainly because she wasn't convinced Bex was absorbing a word of it.

Bex's hand was still gripped tightly around her own, and Dr Lamott had made more than enough references to alert Finley to the blatant assumption that they were co-parenting.

Correcting her wasn't really the priority right now, but it did feel a little weird.

Finley focused hard on Dr Lamott's explanation, picking out key words she knew she could Google later.

*Diabetes. Type 1. Hypoglycaemia. Insulin. Injections. Glucose Levels. Counting carbohydrates.*

Her free hand was wrapped around a handful of pamphlets, and Bex's gripped tightly to a printed copy of a referral to a specialist, and Jack slept beside them with an IV tube in his hand and a *much* healthier colour to his skin.

But this sounded like it definitely was not a one and done.

This sounded like Bex's time as a carer was not as over as she'd thought it was.

This sounded a *lot* like something Sophie would come home for.

Finley had had a colleague once, with Type 1 Diabetes. He'd had a pump in his arm, controlled by his phone. Finley knew very little about it, but she did know it was complicated to manage, and dangerous if you didn't.

By the time the doctor left Jack's bedside, Finley's head felt as woozy as Jack looked.

She squeezed Bex's hand, watching her new friend carefully.

"You okay?" she whispered.

Bex breathed a long sigh.

"I have no idea," she admitted, her shoulders sinking for the first time since Finley had picked them up from the Inn.

She looked exhausted. Her eyes were dark, the past five hours having drawn lines of black beneath them. Her pink fringe that usually sat straight down over her forehead was pushed back, sticking up in tufts that showed the dirty-blonde roots beneath it.

Pete was on his way. He had finally called back, panicked and apologetic, just as Jack had been having his bloods taken. Willow was being packed off to a school friends for the night, and Finley couldn't help but feel relief at the idea. She imagined her wide, curious eyes on the hospital ward, inspecting and listening and absorbing more darkness than any child should have to know.

"Did you process any of that?" she murmured to Bex, easing her hand gently away with the sudden need to stretch it.

"I got *he's okay* and then *he's got a lifelong illness."* Bex breathed a laugh that didn't quite reach humour. "That about right?"

"Pretty much, I think," Finley breathed.

"How am I gonna do this again, Finley?"

The words were calmer. Free of the strain and the panic that had laced it earlier that morning. Instead, they were an uncomfortable kind of resigned. Powerless, and helpless. And something in it felt worse than the fear.

Finley shook her head, shuffling forward in her chair as she turned her body to face Bex fully.

"Because it's not the same," she stated simply.

Bex's brow creased in the middle, her eyes watching Finley in a hopeless kind of confusion.

"It's not, okay?" Finley urged. "Yes, this will be a lot to learn. It'll be scary, and it might drain you for a while, but it's a tunnel with a light at the end. Your mum was…"

Finley took a moment before she spoke her next words. She knew she knew nothing, really, of Bex's mum or of the care that Bex had given her all her life. But she was certain of one thing, and she was sure Bex needed to be certain of it too.

"Look, I don't like to be blunt but I feel like you're someone who will appreciate me saying it as it is?" she tried.

Bex nodded.

Finley took a deep breath.

"From the little that I know, your mum was surviving. Just surviving. Your job was to keep her alive, keep her existing."

She paused, her eyes flicking between Bex's for any sign that she'd overstepped the mark. Bex's eyes misted, her hands beginning to twist over themselves as she chewed her lower lip. But she didn't object. So, Finley pressed on.

"Jack isn't just gonna *survive,* Bex. He's gonna have a whole normal, independent life, and do great things, and be an astronaut. Your job is to help him learn to manage this, so that one day he won't need you. That's the same role any parent has, right? To teach their children not to need them?"

Bex's nose wrinkled, and her gaze dropped as her chest hitched, and Finley pursed her lips in fear that she'd said something wrong.

"Oh god," Bex sniffed. "People with Type 1 Diabetes can't be astronauts."

250

"Oh." Finley sank back into her chair. "Shit."

Somehow that felt like the worst part.

Which was ridiculous. Jack Arroway was nine. Every nine-year-old boy wanted to be an astronaut. Next year he'd want to play football for Arsenal or something, it wasn't likely to be his lifelong dream.

But right *now,* it meant he had another strike against him. Something else for Drunk Dave to tell him would hold him back.

And somehow that felt worse than injections, and pumps, and carbohydrate counting.

Finley shook her head, her own determination beginning to burn in her veins.

"Okay, but Jack is nine," she argued. "There's time. He'll be the first astronaut from Polcarne, *and* the first one with diabetes. He's smart, Bex. He'll figure out this shit first, and then he'll figure out how to rule space. He's *not* going to need a full-time carer. Not forever. You've got this."

Bex sniffed, the corners of her lips tugging into a soft smile as she wiped at her eyes.

Then she lunged forward, throwing her arms around Finley in a bear hug that almost knocked Finley's plastic chair over backwards.

Finley chuckled softly, wrapping her own arms around Bex and squeezing her tightly.

"You'd *better* date my sister, Bennett," Bex stated, her voice close to Finley's ear as they released their hold on each other.

"Why?" Finley laughed.

"She deserves you."

Finley's eyes widened, her stomach flipping a little with the unexpected compliment. She swallowed the lump in her throat, unsure what she was supposed to say to that.

"You have to tell her," she deflected.

"That she deserves you?" Bex smirked.

"No." Finley narrowed her eyes. Then she blinked. "Maybe, actually. But I mean about Jack."

"I know," Bex sighed, rubbing her hands across her tired face. Her fringe stuck up in two new angles as a result. "But she'll come home, Finley. I don't want to hold her back anymore."

"Then stand your ground," Finley stated. "I've been on the receiving end of your persistence, I know full well how many lengths you'll go to get your own way."

Bex grinned, her eyes sparking with subtle traces of their usual easy humour, and Finley's chest felt a little lighter with her next breath out.

"*Or* maybe…" Bex wriggled her eyebrows. "*You* should go home and *distract* her."

Finley rolled her eyes.

"It's cute that you think she'd stay for me," she huffed.

Bex raised an eyebrow, staring Finley down.

"It's cute that *you* think she *wouldn't*"

Finley stared back, until Bex relented.

"No, you're right," Bex sighed. "She wouldn't, she's a people pleaser. But she *should.* And you should go home and show her that."

"Go *home?*" Finley baulked. "I don't know what you think is happening here, but *look* at this situation. A few hours ago, you called me and begged me to bring you here because you couldn't do this alone, you think I'm gonna jump on the next train back to London and abandon you in your time of need?"

"I called you because my twat of a husband wouldn't answer his phone," Bex insisted. Then she softened, her eyes earnest as they urged Finley to hear her. "But he *is* here, Fin. I'm not alone. I have a family, and a whole pub of friends. I spend enough time convincing Soph of that, don't make me convince you too."

Finley let the words wash over her. Bex was right. And if Sophie was ever going to believe that enough to have the chance to leave and make her life, Finley certainly needed to believe it too.

"Okay." She nodded, her stomach fizzing even at the mere mention of seeing Sophie. "I'll think about it. But *tell her* about Jack, okay?"

"You got it."

# Chapter Sixteen

Finley breathed deeply in the steam that filled the bathroom. She was usually a fan of a cold shower, but there was something about the smell of a hospital that warranted heat. Like she could burn the scent and the memories from her skin if she turned the heat up *just* bearable enough to stand beneath.

She didn't really know how she felt.

She felt weird. Like she was lying. She hadn't even spoken to Sophie since the dash to the hospital, but that in itself felt like a lie. She knew it wasn't her place. She knew Bex held the cards, and Finley really ought to stay out of the sisters' affairs, but she couldn't help but imagine the hurt in Sophie's chest when she found out they hadn't told her. She knew Sophie well enough now to know that she wouldn't agree with Bex. That she would categorically *not* accept that her trip to London was more important than being by her nephew's side.

So, Finley was fairly sure that this lie would hurt Sophie.

Or at very least, anger her.

Finley sighed, running her towel through her damp hair as she made her way across the hall and into Sophie's bedroom.

She'd had a few missed calls from Sophie through the afternoon, and she'd tried to call back once Pete had taken her place at the hospital.

The line had been busy.

Finley hoped it was Bex telling her everything.

She finished towelling herself off, and had just managed to throw on a t-shirt and pair of pyjama bottoms when her phone rang out, Sophie's video call incoming.

She took a deep breath, tentatively swiping the call to answer.

"Hey, baby."

She bit her tongue, her entire body tightening as the words slipped out before she could stop them.

She opened her mouth to dig her hole a mile further, but before she could speak, Sophie was spilling frantic words.

"Finley, oh my god. I've been calling you all day! I am *so* sorry! Fuck, I'm so sorry, I don't know what I was thinking, she just *showed up,* and…"

Finley frowned.

Sophie's eyes were misty, the edges red with a visible effort to hold back tears, and her voice shook as it spilled breathlessly through the speaker.

"A-and she was so *abrupt* and I-I just saw *red* and, and *shit,* I am *so* sorry, I…"

"Soph, breathe!" Finley cut her off. She smiled softly as Sophie's eyes traced the screen almost desperately. "Take a breath. 'Cause right now it sounds like you've killed someone and I'm *so* sure that isn't what happened."

Sophie inhaled slowly, pursing her lips as she blew a shaky breath through her cheeks.

Then her eyes widened.

"Wait, did you just call me *baby?"*

Finley blushed.

Crap.

"Uh…" She smiled sheepishly, her hand coming up to rub awkwardly at the back of her neck. "I was hoping you didn't hear that."

"I-I liked it," Sophie whispered, her lips curling softly.

*"Oh,"* Finley breathed. She cleared her throat, fighting the swoony smile that tugged at her lips. "Good."

Sophie bit her lip, and Finley's chest tightened for a moment in the almost giddy silence.

Then she started, shaking her head as she remembered the slightly more pressing issue.

She had answered tentatively because she had expected tears and difficult decisions about Jack, but this sounded like something completely different.

"What happened, Soph?" she urged. "Did someone do something to you?"

Sophie's eyes filled with tears, and Finley's heart sank.

Whoever it was. Whatever they did. She was gonna *lynch* their ass.

"No, it was *me!"* Sophie whispered. Her hands flew up to cover her face, and her voice strained as she continued. *"Shit,* Finley, your *boss."*

Finley's heart dropped, her blood somehow both cooling and heating simultaneously in her veins.

*Amelia?*

*What* on God's green earth could *possibly* have gone down between Sophie and *Amelia* that would leave Sophie so shaken?

She felt the hairs on the back of her neck stand on end, her jaw tightening with the surge of protective fire that raged unexpectedly through her nerve endings.

Her boss had *better* not have tried anything.

"She just showed up at your home and she was going through your things like she *owned* the place, and making these *demands* that you contact her," Sophie sniffed. "And she was just so *presumptuous* and rude that I couldn't help it!"

Finley sat forward, her fists clenching with her sudden irritation with Amelia's temerity, and with the desperate urge to reassure Sophie. Once again, she found herself hating *every* mile that lay between them.

"You couldn't help what, baby?" she murmured.

Sophie sighed, her eyes misting with a coy kind of awe once again.

*"Baby…"* she whispered, her cheeks flushing and her lips curling back into a soft smile.

Finley chuckled.

"So *did* you kill her?"

*"No,"* Sophie giggled softly. She winced. "But I'm *really* scared I might have killed your career."

"Huh?" Finley frowned.

She didn't *quite* see how *that* could be possible.

Sophie groaned, her head slumping back onto her shoulders.

"I told her you don't owe her your annual leave time. Oh *god,* Finley I told her she keeps you *static.* I told her she needed to be *careful!* Like I'm some sort of fucking mafia boss."

Finley's jaw dropped.

Wait, *what?*

That was *so* far from anything she had considered.

"You *said* that?"

Sophie groaned again, the tears welling visibly in her eyes.

Finley swallowed.

Well, this was unexpected.

And frankly, for her part, she had *never* been *more* damn attracted to Sophie Cedars.

She knew how intimidating her boss could be when she played it up, and if she knew Amelia *at all,* then she would *definitely* have played this up to get what she wanted.

And Sophie had stood her ground. Had defended Finley, when *nothing* had obligated her to.

And that was *damn* sexy.

And now Sophie was in tears?

"Wait…" she closed her eyes for a moment, the cogs turning way too slowly. "Wait, you're worrying about this because you *stood up for me?"*

"I'm worrying about this because I said things to your *boss* that were *not my place!"* Sophie threw a trembling hand in the air, the first few tears finally falling over her cheeks. "I'm *so* scared you're gonna get in trouble for it Finley, please can I have her number so I can apologise?"

Finley almost laughed, her racing heart trapping the sound in her chest.

Instead, she shook her head.

"No."

Sophie's eyes widened.

"N-no?"

"No." Finley shook her head again. "Whatever the consequences are, I'll deal with it, Soph. It's about time I stood my own ground. Let Amelia stew. You don't owe anyone an apology."

"I feel like you're wrong…" Sophie laughed weakly.

Finley grinned.

"Okay, so *maybe* it wasn't your place," she chuckled. "But so what? Waltzing around my house wasn't *her* place! I'm not mad. If anything, I am *crazy* attracted to you right now and I've never wanted to jump in a car and drive five and a half hours more."

Sophie huffed out a laugh, her eyes sparkling through the mist of her tears.

*"Really?"*

*"Really,"* Finley assured. "In part, because I need to make sure I still have a *job…"* she teased, laughing as Sophie groaned. "But *mostly* because I just really want to see you."

Sophie chuckled, her shoulders dropping and the tears ceasing to fall under Finley's reassurance.

"You're looking at me now," she grinned.

Finley shook her head.

"But I can't kiss you from here," she murmured. "And *god,* Sophie, I *really* want to kiss you."

Sophie's breath hitched, her eyes widening and her lip catching subtly between her teeth, and Finley would swear she could feel 300 miles of air thicken.

She watched as for the second time in as many days, Sophie's eyes fluttered closed at the thought of a kiss.

It was almost physically painful that she couldn't touch her.

She swallowed thickly.

"Would...that be okay?" she murmured.

Sophie breathed a laugh, her eyes as revered as Finley felt as they flicked back open.

"It'd be really, *really* okay," she whispered.

Finley bit her lip, her own bashful, giddy laugh breaking through it.

"Good *god,"* she groaned, grinning as she rolled her eyes back deliberately in an effort to pull herself together. "Come on, Cedars," she sighed. "Stop making a mess of me from way too far away to do anything about it."

Sophie giggled.

Finley pulled herself up from the bed, needing to walk just to do something with her crawling muscles. Something to shake the tension.

She headed down the stairs, making a beeline for the kitchen, and the Spurling ciders she knew were on the counter.

"Have you...spoken to Bex?" she tried softly, wincing as the blatant sound of nerves crept into her voice.

Sophie frowned immediately.

"Yeah...?"

Finley chewed her cheek.

It was already *very* apparent that Sophie had not been told the news, and that Finley had put herself in a position she now was not getting out of without breaking it herself.

Shit.

"She said Jack's been ill again," Sophie answered, nerves creeping into her own voice. "But you look a *lot* more worried than she made it sound like I should feel, what's going on, Fin?"

Finley blew a breath out through her nose.

"What did she tell you?" she asked.

She felt guilt surge heavy through her chest as Sophie's brow creased, and her skin paled in visible apprehension.

"She said he's been ill, and he's home from school..."

Finley groaned.

"Finley, please stop treading on eggshells and tell me what she's not saying!"

"She's ignoring my advice, and putting me in a very uncomfortable position, that's what's going on," Finley grumbled, running a hand over her face.

"Has something happened?" Sophie demanded.

"She asked me not to tell you..." Finley tried, knowing full well it wasn't going to fly.

"Which is an immediate sign that you *absolutely* should be telling me."

Finley closed her eyes for a moment as she tried to find the right way to approach this. She was going to have to answer, that much was clear. But what were the right words to say?

She opened her eyes, watching the screen and Sophie's worried eyes, and figured calm and open honesty was the only valid option.

"Jack has Type 1 Diabetes."

There was a moment of pause, and Sophie's face didn't change. Her brow stayed creased, and her eyes stayed wide, and her skin stayed pale. And for a brief moment, Finley wondered if they'd lost connection.

Then Sophie blinked.

*"What?"* she whispered.

"He had a hypo," Finley explained. "We took him into A&E, and the tests said he has Type 1. He has to have insulin injections, and..."

"Oh my *god,*" Sophie yelped, her body seeming to kick into gear as Finley spoke. *"Shit."*

The screen dropped back, Sophie's face replaced with a dizzying flurry of fabric and odd angular shots of Finley's bedroom as Sophie scurried about the room.

"Soph..." Finley tried.

"I'm coming home!" Sophie insisted, and the dizzying scrabble worsened. "Now. Fuck, *where* is my phone?"

"In your hand," Finley stated calmly. "Sophie, breathe."

"Breathe? *Breathe?*" Sophie snapped. "Thank you, Dalai Lama, but this is quite urgent and I need to get home, and I do not need the pitiful advice of someone who doesn't even *know* my neph…oh my *god,* people with Type 1 Diabetes can't be astronauts!"

Finley shook her head, knowing full well Sophie wasn't watching her.

"Don't come home," she instructed.

The scrabble stopped.

Finley took a deep breath, composing herself the best she could as Sophie's fraught face appeared back on the screen.

*"Excuse* me?" Sophie simmered.

"Sophie, this is why Bex didn't want me to tell you," Finley explained, keeping her voice low and steady. "She doesn't want you to come home."

"She says that, but she doesn't mean it," Sophie huffed, propping the phone up on Finley's beside table and beginning to haul her suitcase out from beneath the bed.

"She does, Soph," Finley urged. "She's tired of being the reason you aren't chasing your dreams. Imagine, just for a second, how that must feel?"

Sophie frowned.

"What?"

Finley swallowed. She really hadn't wanted to insert herself into Bex's business with her sister, as if she in any way knew more about their lives than they did. But Sophie seemed…*half* willing to hear what Finley had to say, so she figured she had to seize the opportunity while she could.

"I think she feels like your ball and chain. Like your *burden,* " she explained. "Like this thing that holds you back all the time. Just this once, let her feel like something more?"

Sophie's shoulders dropped, and she sank down onto her heels beside her suitcase as she blinked back the first signs of tears, and Finley's heart ached.

Ached for the girl who had spent her whole life trying to help a sister as stubborn as she was, while dreaming of something different and new and exciting. Always having to choose between the two.

The girl who sat now, half in an empty suitcase, with the same decision to make once again.

"I…" Sophie started, her voice beginning to wobble with the tears she tried to fight. "You *cannot* just drop a bomb like this on me and then expect me to stay on a jolly jaunt 300 miles away! I can't just *ignore* this!"

Finley didn't say anything. She couldn't help but feel maybe she'd said enough. Maybe this was down, now, to Sophie, and to Bex.

"I have to go, Fin," Sophie sighed, wiping at her eyes with the sleeve of her jumper as she reached for her phone with her other hand. "I have to call Bex."

Finley nodded, feeling her own throat burn with sadness for the girl she liked so much.

"Thank you, though," Sophie sniffed. "For telling me."

Finley sighed as the phone rang off, and she sank down onto the sofa in Sophie's living room.

Well.

Bex was going to get an earful now. Which meant Finley would probably get one from Bex very shortly.

Great day.

~ ~ ~ ~ ~ ~ 🎵 ~ ~ ~ ~ ~ ~

Sophie shoved another of her jumpers haphazardly into her disorganised suitcase as she dialled Bex's number for the fifth time.

The first three times it had gone to voicemail.

The last time, Bex had screened it.

Which meant she *knew* why Sophie was calling, and her refusal to answer was royally pissing Sophie off.

She was half a second from screaming into her ringing phone, when her sister finally answered.

"I don't want you here."

"Tough shit," Sophie grunted as she shoved her makeup bag into the scrunched pile of clothes in the case.

"You'll be in my way," Bex deadpanned.

"Not hearing it," Sophie gritted out through clenched teeth.

"I don't even like you."

Sophie growled, throwing her head back, and her toothbrush in the air.

"Rebecca Margaret Arroway, will you *stop* being such a stubborn martyr for once in your life!" she snapped.

Louder than she'd wanted to, but her sister was *really* trying her patience, and nothing would fit properly in her suitcase, and she truly wanted to scream.

"No, Sophie," Bex yelled, anger and frustration hoarse in her voice. *"You* stop being so fucking stubborn."

Sophie flinched, halting her frantic packing immediately.

Bex had practically been Sophie's parent for half of her youngest years, and she had never once shouted at her like that.

Bex sighed, pinching the bridge of her nose between a thumb and a forefinger.

"Look, I get it. I know how much you love Jack, and I *know* this is a big deal, and I *know* you want to be here for him as much as for me."

Sophie swallowed, her eyes filling once again with tears as she watched her sister over the screen, the familiar white walls of the hospital hallways visible in the background.

"But all your life there's been *something,* Soph." Bex's voice was softer now. Calmer, and quieter. But no less earnest. "Some reason not to do it, and most of them have been me."

"No..." Sophie tried.

"It's not a debate right now," Bex ordered. *"I'm* talking, *you're* listening."

Sophie shut up.

"Life is never going to stop and wait for you, Soph," Bex implored. "Polcarne is never going to press pause, and leave a little space in the timeline for Sophie Cedars to explore new worlds. *I* am never going to do that. Life is going to move on, and you are gonna miss a couple of spelling tests, and a few bouts of headlice, and the occasional A&E trip."

Sophie sniffed, no longer bothering to fight the steady flow of tears as they filled her eyes and streaked her cheeks.

"But you'll be here for the birthdays, and the Christmases, and graduations, and the big summer barbecues. You're not leaving us, Sophie. You're just making something for you!" Bex urged, her eyes kind, despite the determined steel, and the worried exhaustion behind them. "Jack is fine. We have some things we need to learn, and we have to be careful, but he is *fine."*

"You know I'm only meant to be here another week anyway, right?" Sophie huffed, dropping her gaze as she picked absently at the zip lining the edge of her suitcase. "This isn't my new life, it's just a trip."

Bex chuckled, shaking her head as she eyed Sophie knowingly.

"You and I both know that if you choose to come home now, you will never go back."

"Maybe it's not the right time," Sophie whispered.

"Or maybe it's *exactly* the right time," Bex coaxed. "Just tell me you'll stay the week. If anything dramatic happens, I *promise* I will tell you."

She held her hand up to the camera, her little finger poised upwards in a pinky swear.

Sophie grinned, despite her tears and the feeling of reluctance that still sat heavy on her shoulders.

"You'd better. I'm still mad I had to hear that from Finley."

"Yeah, she's clearly shown her alliance today," Bex teased, rolling her eyes. Then she chuckled. "Call that woman back, and tell her to get her ass to London and sweep you off your feet."

Sophie laughed.

She wouldn't be doing that.

But maybe she'd stay, just tonight.

"Can I talk to Jack?" she whispered.

"You can." Bex nodded.

Sophie watched, her stomach churning a little with nerves as Bex made her way back onto the ward, and through the door of a side room.

She plastered the warmest smile she could muster over her face as Bex passed her phone over to Jack, and his drawn little face appeared on the screen.

"Hey, Stink!" she breathed. "Mummy says you've been poorly?"

"Yeah, I just had an incident," Jack replied, his soft voice weak, but steadier than Sophie had been expecting.

She laughed at the words, and the nonchalance in Jack's eyes.

"An *incident?*" she chuckled.

Her nephew really was nine going on thirteen.

"I'm alright though. I just have to have some injections." Jack shrugged. Then his eyes sparked brighter for a moment, his cheeks dimpling with his smile. *"And,* now I'm gonna be the first astronaut from Polcarne *and* with diabetes!"

Sophie's heart clenched, and she pressed a hand over it as her eyes prickled with tears she fought back.

"Is that right?" she murmured.

"Yep." Jack nodded. "I heard Finley say it."

Sophie's heart melted.

~ ~ ~ ~ ~ ~ (🜂) ~ ~ ~ ~ ~ ~

Finley was in the garden, slumped in a bistro set with her feet up on the table, when her phone rang again with Sophie's video call.

She sat forwards, preparing herself for an emotional rollercoaster as she slid the call to answer.

"Hey," she murmured.

It had been an hour or so since they had spoken last, and Finley could see the tracks of dried tears over Sophie's cheeks.

She'd had a text from Bex, simply reading:

*I see how it is. Pretty girl trumps traumatised friend. Asshole;)*

The addition of the winky face had her believing she wasn't in too much trouble.

"You okay?" she asked.

Sophie nodded.

"Thank you."

"What for?" Finley creased her brow.

"Being…" Sophie took a deep breath, her lips curling into a soft smile as she let it out. "Well, perfect, honestly."

Finley blushed deeply, swallowing thickly under Sophie's gaze.

"I spoke to Bex. You were right."

Finley felt her heart flutter, hope blooming in her chest.

"You're gonna stay?" she breathed.

"Hmmm. We'll see in the morning." Sophie smiled softly, leaning forward into the screen as she watched Finley closely. "She said *you* were amazing."

Finley grinned.

"She's not wrong," she teased.

She settled herself back into her chair, lifting her cider to her lips and her feet to the table as she let her eyes cast across the garden for a moment. She was sure she could never grow tired of the way this garden felt under the setting of the sun. Streaks of golden orange shone through the smattering of trees, landing almost ethereally on the blues and the reds and the yellows of the wildflowers in Sophie's flower beds. The air was filled with soft sounds, of crickets chirping and the rustle of birds, and rabbits, and mice in the hedgerows. Finley knew it was unlikely, given the miles of fields and winding roads, but she always felt as though she could hear the sea when it was this calm.

She let her eyes drift through the trees, and into the field beyond Sophie's low picket fence.

She froze, cider halfway from her lips and her phone gripped tightly in her hand as her eyes caught something she wasn't sure she'd ever seen.

Not here, and certainly not in London.

A *deer*. A small one. Staring back at her from between the trees, golden orange streaking off its back. It was a little stranger looking than Finley had expected. Sort of weirdly squat, and a bit hunched. Its antlers looked nothing like any photo of a deer Finley had ever seen, but she was still fairly sure it was one.

She laughed openly, the absurdity of just how different Sophie's life was to her own washing over her once again.

"What's funny?" Sophie asked.

"There's a deer looking at me," Finley chuckled. "I...think."

"Is it wearing wellies and a gilet?" Sophie teased.

Finley narrowed her eyes.

"You're an asshole, you know that?" she huffed playfully.

"I'm cute though, so you let it slide." Sophie batted her eyelashes, and Finley grinned, shaking her head.

"You're adorable," she chuckled, her lips curling into a smirk as Sophie blushed. "And *no*. But it's just...there."

She turned her phone screen, pointing it at the supposed deer in an effort to share the image with Sophie.

"That is a deer, right?" she asked. "It looks a bit...*squished?"*

"It's a muntjac," Sophie laughed. "It is a deer, just a different type to what you're probably used to."

"I'm not really used to any!" Finley laughed, turning the camera back to her own face. "I mean, I know London *has* deer. And badgers, and squirrels, and foxes. But under all the lights and the noise and the constant rush it's just so easy to forget that we're not the only ones there. You know?"

Sophie exhaled softly, nestling herself back in Finley's sofa. And not for the first time, Finley's stomach flipped at the sight of Sophie so comfortable in her home.

"Yeah, I can see that," Sophie whispered.

"But here, in the quiet, it kinda feels like a fairy-tale," Finley breathed, letting her eyes flick back to the deer. It had clearly decided she was safe, and was happily chewing something on the hedgerow lining the field. "Like I'm being let in on a secret little world that humans aren't supposed to see. It's kinda humbling."

Sophie hummed, her eyes soft and adoring as she watched Finley, listening intently.

And for reasons Finley couldn't explain, she suddenly understood.

She understood her own life, and what she really wanted. She understood the mistakes she'd made, and the things she'd thought she knew about herself. She understood the things she had and she understood the things she didn't.

And she needed, for reasons she didn't yet know, to make Sophie understand too.

"Listen, Soph…" She took a deep breath. "Last night. On our date. We-we talked about me reaching my dreams, and I…I feel like I need to explain."

Sophie's eyes widened, apprehension and worry flicking across them for a moment.

"My ex-girlfriend, Jess…" Finley continued. "She left me because I gave more of myself to my job than I did to her. And she was right. I did."

She didn't know why the need to explain this burned so strongly, so suddenly, but she needed to say it. She needed Sophie to understand.

"It was my priority, my-my *everything* for so long. I've fought for *so* long for the career, and-and the *independence* I dreamed of, and actually…it's like it never ends. Every time I reach one dream, a new one is born. I think I've always focused on work because it's the thing I felt was best in my life, and…"

"You don't have to explain this, Finley. I understand what your career means to you." Sophie's voice was so soft, and so calm. So understanding. "That's why I need you to let me apologise to Amelia, I can't ruin…"

"No, Soph. It's not that, it's…" Finley blushed, her eyes fluttering closed. "I pushed others…I pushed Jess away because I didn't want to need her. I didn't want to put her first, because it would mean I wasn't standing on my own."

Sophie's face shifted, something unreadable in her eyes for a moment, but it still wasn't a challenge. She was still listening.

Finley took a deep breath.

"I guess I just want you to know that if I had…if I *really* wanted to be with someone, I'd make the time. I'd find that balance. I'd put them first, I'd chase a different dream. A different priority."

Sophie was quiet for a moment, almost revered eyes searching the screen.

When she spoke again, her voice was softer than ever. Low, and uncertain, an almost vulnerable husk running through it.

"Would you have made the time for me?" she whispered. "I-if things were different?"

Finley huffed out a laugh, her chest soaring at the sparks in Sophie's eyes that matched the ones in her own veins.

"Soph, I think what I'm trying to say is I'm pretty sure I'd make the time as things are now."

Sophie's breath hitched.

"What about the distance?"

"I'd make that too." Finley grinned, raising an eyebrow. "The Americans would drive further for a bagel."

Sophie laughed, something that sounded a lot like giddy surprise in the sound.

"The Americans drive too much," she teased.

Finley blushed, knowing instantly that she wasn't the only one Noah was gossiping about this with.

"Agreed," she chuckled. "But some things are worth the journey."

Sophie's lips parted, and she watched Finley with sparkling eyes for a long, quiet moment.

Then she exhaled heavily, tipping her head back against the sofa.

*"Okay,"* she groaned. "You are *one* adorable remark away from pushing me onto the next train from Paddington, and that would undo *everything* you and my sister have fought for tonight. So, I am gonna go, and I am gonna order copious amounts of food on Deliveroo while I have the chance, Bennett."

Finley grinned, her stomach fizzing with butterflies that she didn't even try to fight.

"And after that," Sophie murmured, "who knows."

Finley's mind was clearer than it had ever been by the time Sophie's voice rang off the line.

She liked Sophie in a way that she couldn't remember ever liking anyone.

And yes, it was *very* early days.

And no, they hadn't met.

And yes, it was highly unsustainable.

But it was also simple.

Finley wanted to be around Sophie Cedars.

Even without physically being in it, Sophie was managing to make everything in Finley's life seem *fresher* somehow. Finley wasn't even *there,* and yet London seemed new and exciting with Sophie in it. She couldn't even hear them, and yet those sounds of the city that Finley had spent years closing the doors on felt softer through Sophie's ears.

Polcarne was beautiful. It had opened Finley's eyes to so many parts of life that she had missed for so long, and she loved it here. But she couldn't help but feel like right now, what she wanted most was still in London.

She laughed as she replayed Sophie's words in her head. The things she had said to Amelia.

Admittedly they had been pretty bold, and Finley could only imagine the slightly amused disdain that her boss must have felt at the accusations, but the fact that Sophie had spoken with such *conviction* about it made one thing impossible to ignore.

Sophie understood her.

She understood her goals, and she understood her challenges, and she had done so in a week of phone calls when Finley had *never* been able to make anyone else in her life understand.

And Finley wanted to see her.

# Chapter Seventeen

Finley woke with an odd sense of discomfort.

Nothing was particularly unusual. The light was the same as it had been all week through the curtains, and the early morning birds were no louder than usual.

But something felt off-kilter, and she couldn't place her finger on it.

She grabbed her phone, her brow furrowed as she swiped to unlock the screen.

Six missed calls. All from Amelia. All within the last hour.

Finley sat upright, rubbing at her eyes as she willed them to adjust quickly. It wasn't unusual for Amelia to bombard her, and certainly she'd been doing exactly that this whole holiday. But in the stress of Jack, and convincing Sophie not to race home, Finley had almost forgotten her boss's run in with her current house guest.

She sighed, her thumb hovering over Amelia's call button, as she prepared herself for the inevitable battering she was about to receive over all of this.

But before she could muster the courage, her text chime rang, and Finley's blood cooled.

Shit.

Amelia *never* sent text messages.

She called. Always. Or she emailed. But she never sent text messages. It was notoriously *not* a good thing when Amelia texted, and now Finley's stomach was in full panic mode.

Finley swallowed, her nerves flaring thick in her stomach as she pulled up the message.

Amelia: *Bennett, we need to discuss your future. We've crossed some wires, and you need to hear me out.*

Finley's heart lurched.

Crossed some wires?

Hear her out?

What did *that* mean?

This was either very good, or very, *very* bad.

She hit the call button immediately, her feet pacing the floor beneath her instinctively as the dial tone rang.

She groaned as the call rang to voicemail.

She tried again. And twice more.

Then she sent a reply.

Finley: *I'm available. Call me.*

She growled, her fist clenching around her phone in frustration.

The woman had *just* sent the fucking text, and *now* she disappears?

Typical. When she'd been *hounding* Finley for a week.

Her pulse thumped in her ears as she pulled her suitcase from underneath Sophie's bed, haphazardly beginning to throw her belongings into the empty compartment.

It was no longer a question.

She needed to be in London.

And she *knew* it wasn't the job, but it gave a damn good excuse for being so forward.

She pulled Sophie's contact up as she locked up the cottage, her phone pressed between her ear and her shoulder as she hoisted her bags into the car.

She frowned as that too, went to voicemail.

Was *everyone* ignoring her this morning?

She took a shaky breath as Sophie's cheery voice sounded out the mailbox greeting, her entire body crawling with nervous butterflies.

She wouldn't normally leave a voicemail, but she had no idea how long it would be until she would get signal again, and she needed to know that Sophie had had a chance to say no. She needed Sophie to have had the opportunity to leave, or to ask her to stay away should she not want this.

The tone beeped.

"Soph, hey, it's me. I uh…I'm coming home. I need to see you." Finley closed her eyes, her nerves gripping tightly on her tongue. "I-I *want* to see you. And also, I'm either losing my job or getting a promotion, but mainly it's you."

She winced. Jesus, why was she being so *intense*? And so floundery? "I'm sorry, I'm…I'm nervous. I hope this is okay. *Please* just let me know if it's not, and I'll get a hotel room. Or-or turn around."

She exhaled slowly, letting her eyes flutter open as she sank into the driver's seat of the Ford.

"I'll see you in a few hours…I-I hope."

# Chapter Eighteen

Finley had managed to somewhat calm her racing nerves as she wound Sophie's Ford down the country lanes, thankfully more familiar to her now than they had been just nine days ago, but she could still feel her heart racing harder than it should be in her chest. But as she threw the car into a parking space at St Austell station, and hauled her suitcase from the boot, her nerves crept back into her stomach with force.

Was she really doing this?

Was she really racing half the length of the country to appear on the doorstep of a woman who right now, didn't know she was coming? Granted, it was her own doorstep, but that didn't feel like it made it much less insane. Besides, that wasn't what she was going for. She was going to save her career.

Sort of.

Well.

Not at all, really. But it'd be the story she'd tell, if anyone asked.

Finley skidded across the epoxy flooring as she darted through the station, in the direction of the self-serving ticket machine. She punched her order in, then gritted her teeth, resisting the urge to scream as the machine whirred painfully slowly in its leisurely attempts to spit out her ticket.

She was antsy, and on edge, and practically vibrating as she finally made her way onto the platform that would take her to London. Which wasn't ideal, considering at no point had she even *thought* about checking the train times, and she had completely overlooked the fact that St Austell station was not London. Trains outside of London didn't pass every two minutes, and she should definitely have done a little more preparation for this absurd dash.

She glanced at the departures board, her shoulders dropping a little as she read the numbers. Fifteen minutes to wait. The next train after that was in seventy-five minutes. So really, she'd nailed it.

Surprising, considering she'd barely used a single brain cell this morning, and considering it wasn't even 8am.

She stared at her phone screen as she paced the platform, barely aware of the scrape and the roll of her luggage wheels along the brick and tarmac as she dragged it behind her. She stopped only when she tripped over her own bag in her efforts to spin, and almost face planted the rails.

She took a deep breath, counting to four in her head as she exhaled it slowly. A technique she'd seen on a Tik-Tok video once, that frankly was doing absolutely nothing for her right now.

Maybe it had been count to eight.

Four in?

Who knew.

Either way, she'd never felt like such a livewire, and she needed to calm herself down before she imploded. She pushed her phone into her pocket, and glanced around the station in search of something to distract her mind. She considered buying a coffee, but she was jittery enough as it was, and she had no idea how she was supposed to survive a five-hour journey with this amount of adrenaline coursing through her veins.

She halted, squinting her eyes in bewildered confusion as she spotted a familiar figure, sitting hunched on a bench on the platform, with a suitcase at his feet. A figure she'd kind of just assumed was a permanent fixture on the inside of The Ship Inn.

"Ern?"

Ern looked up, his watery grey eyes finding Finley's as she approached his bench.

"Oh, 'ello me cock!" he greeted, his dentures wobbling as he smiled. "Nice morning for it, 'ent it?"

Finley huffed a laugh. She made a mental note to ask Sophie just what that meant. Whether there was some sort of secret activity that Cornish people did every day that required a specific type of weather.

"I'm worried I might regret asking this, Ern," she sighed, watching his wavering teeth warily. "But what are you doing here?"

"Heading to me caravan in Newquay," Ern declared. "Put me feet up for a while. Do some fishing."

Finley blinked. She'd always got the impression that wasn't something that actually happened.

"Alone, or…?" She shifted her wary gaze, flicking her eyes around the station as if some kind of carer or nurse might appear from the rails.

"Unless you'd care to join me, Miss?"

Ern shot her a very questionable effort at a wink, and Finley laughed.

"Ern, I am about to jump on a train, high-tail it to London, save my career, and profess undying love to a woman I've not yet been in the same room as," she sighed. "But maybe if it all goes wrong, I could run away and join you?"

"It would be my pleasure, my lover."

Finley grinned, dragging her suitcase to the end of the bench, and flopping down beside Ern.

She slipped her phone out of her pocket, resting it against the bench beside her as she shot a subtle text to Bex, out of Ern's eyesight.

Finley: *Ern's at the station with a bag. This normal, or is there some kind of dementia hotline I ought to call?*

"It won't go wrong, though," Ern stated, clear and earnest. "Lord knows that Sophie Cedars has waited a long time for someone like you."

Finley's entire brain short-circuited.

She turned her gaze slowly to Ern's face, her brows creased in the middle and her lips parted in her shock. She was *completely* taken aback. She'd fully written Ern off as only having about a quarter of his marbles, but that was a weirdly astute comment.

"Y-you think so?" she choked.

"Oh, I know so," Ern chuckled, nodding his head as he stared out across the train track. "What's she got 'ere? An old codger like me, an' a slimy fish farmer 'oo don't know 'er worth?"

Finley laughed. She had definitely underestimated Ern Butterworth, and she wondered if she was the only one.

"You weren't rooting for Kyle then?" she teased.

"That lad needs a clip round the 'ed with me stick," Ern barked, stamping the end of his stick on the ground in demonstration. "But *you*. You like 'er. You *see* 'er."

Finley was beginning to think this might be some sort of apparition.

This was, quite possibly, the most surreal experience she'd ever had. Including the badger.

She shook her head, almost a little dazed as the train pulled into the station, and the doors hissed as they swung open.

"Thanks, Ern," she chuckled. "That was…oddly insightful."

She turned to face him as she stood for the train.

"You coming?"

Ern shook his head.

"This 'ent me train, Miss."

Finley had no idea if that was true or not, but she got the feeling that maybe even if it wasn't, Ern wouldn't be getting on the train.

She felt weirdly calmer with Ern's words in her ears, and she could feel her muscles jittering slightly less as she boarded the train, and settled herself into a window seat opposite Ern's bench. She tried waving at him, but his watery eyes were closed, and his chin rested gently on his chest.

As the train pulled away, Ern's dentures fell into his lap.

Finley grinned. She reached into her pocket for her phone, to inform Bex of the latest developments.

And to stare obsessively again until either Sophie or Amelia replied to her.

She froze, her blood running cold as her fingers closed around nothing but fabric.

Then she flat out panicked.

She scrabbled frantically, her hands tearing at the pockets of her jeans and her jacket in a desperate search for the one thing she absolutely could *not* survive a five-hour journey without.

She felt *insane.* Her eyes bulged, and her hands shook as she tugged at the zip of her suitcase, hauling her clothes out shamelessly in search of the device she *knew* wasn't in here.

She knew it wasn't in here because she had stared at it solidly as she'd paced the station platform, and she had used it to message Bex when she'd been…

*Fuck!*

She practically roared with panicked frustration, her eyes prickling with frenzied tears as she processed her reality. Her phone must have been sitting on a bench in St Austell, alongside Ern Butterworth and his dentures.

Shit! Fuck! Bollocks! *Wankstain!*

She wailed, slamming her clothes back into her suitcase with more anger than was really necessary. *Why* hadn't she brought her laptop? Or a burner phone? Or simply been less of a fucking idiot in the first place?

She couldn't do this. She needed her phone. She needed to hear from Sophie, and from Amelia.

She shot her eyes around the train, searching desperately for someone she could borrow a phone from. She didn't know what for, to be honest. She didn't know Sophie or Amelia's numbers off by heart, but even if she did, her entire predicament was that they weren't answering her anyway. Even so, the train was *deathly* quiet, and Finley couldn't see a single soul in her carriage or the adjacent one.

She practically forced her way through the unsteady, slow-moving carriage doors, racing from car to car until she came face to face, rather abruptly, with a very unimpressed looking ticket guard.

"Sir!" she yelped, her hands coming instinctively up into a prayer pose, and she flushed red as she realised how *mental* she must have looked. "I-I left my phone on the last platform, and I *really* need to go and get it."

The guard raised an unamused eyebrow.

"Oh sure, I'll just turn the train right around, shall I?" he gruffed.

*"Please,* Sir, you don't understand," Finley panted, trying her hardest to put her shit back into some kind of sane presentation. "Is there no way we can get the phone onto the train at the next stop?"

"Are you asking me to source a member of Great Western Rail Service to fetch your phone, and *race a train* fifteen miles so that you can make a phone call?"

Finley winced.

She was so aware there was nothing that could be done here, but she felt sick with her anxiety, and she didn't know how not to try.

"Yes?" she tried.

"Absolutely not," the guard huffed, visibly already bored with Finley and her antics. "I would suggest getting off at the next stop, and going back. Now, ticket, please?"

Finley groaned, relenting as she pulled her ticket out of her jeans pocket, and sank down into the nearest seat. She really didn't want to get off the train, especially when they only seemed to run every hour. But she also really wasn't sure that she could cope without her phone. Without even the possibility of getting answers for over five hours.

She didn't even know if Sophie was still in London!

What if she'd come home for Jack? What if they passed each other on the tracks, and all Finley could do was wave dolefully out of the rain-streaked window like a 1920s war wife?

What if Sophie had heard her voicemail and was heading home *because* of Finley? What if she simply didn't want to see her, and had run?

Oh god, five hours was so *long!*

She was definitely going to burn a hole in the train floor with her bouncing leg.

And lose her mind.

It was inevitable.

~ ~ ~ ~ ~ ~ 🎸 ~ ~ ~ ~ ~ ~

As soon as the train stopped at Paddington, Finley threw herself through the doors so fast that she fell face-first over her own luggage, and landed in a cripplingly humiliating heap on the platform in one of London's busiest stations with an obnoxiously loud huff.

She groaned, her cheeks and her chest flaming beet-red as she fought to haul herself to her feet amongst the rushing, ever-silent crowd, and she exhaled heavily as she sheepishly brushed herself down.

That was quite enough.

She was behaving like an unhinged sociopath, and if she wanted any hope of either Sophie or Amelia seeing something good in her, then she needed to *calm* the *fuck* down.

She took a few steady breaths, clenching and unclenching her fist around her luggage in an effort to control some of the tension as she pushed her way through the crowds of Paddington underground. She could still feel the jitters, and her legs still fought to move a *lot* faster than she would have liked them to, but she managed to stay mainly in control.

Although she was *definitely* about to become an origami octopus for the first time in her life.

She gripped tightly to the hand rail, to stop herself from flying down the windy escalators as she made her way beneath the city. As the familiar metallic scent of the underground hit her nose, and the blustery sound of the wind whipped through her hair and her open jacket, Finley realised for the first time that she had a slightly onerous decision to make.

Go and lay her heart on the line to a woman whose eyes she'd never looked into, or go and get the bollocking of a lifetime from the woman with her career in her hands.

Honestly, one of them was quite considerably more terrifying than the other.

The thought that Sophie wouldn't be there because she didn't want to see Finley was spine-chilling.

*Far* scarier than whatever lay waiting for her in Amelia's office.

She took a deep breath, gripped the handle of her luggage a little tighter, and made her decision.

~ ~ ~ ~ ~ ~ 🦊 ~ ~ ~ ~ ~ ~ ~

The sounds of the city felt different to Finley as she emerged onto the busy streets of Embankment. She was more aware than she'd been in years of the soft rumble of the trains beneath her feet, and the whir of the traffic, and the gentle lap of the river Thames before her. She was more conscious than she'd probably ever been of the thousands of feet that scurried either side of her as she picked her way over the river and along Southbank, her luggage almost lost in the crowd of the lunchtime rush behind her.

She half laughed, shaking her head as she watched a gammy pigeon dart beneath the sea of shiny black shoes, and suits, and briefcases.

She wondered why it felt so different.

Was she seeing it through Sophie's eyes? Or had she simply opened her own, with just a few days of space and clean air?

She brought herself and her luggage to a slow stop across the road from the Opal Arches office building. She closed her eyes, tilting her head from side to side in an effort to release some of the tension in her shoulders. She rolled them back as she let her eyes flutter open.

Calm. Zen.

This would either be everything she'd ever worked for, or the crushing of a lifelong aspiration.

Either way, this was it. Her pivotal moment.

Despite her best efforts, she was still physically shaking with her nerves as she pushed her way into the office building, her bags echoing as they thudded through the doors behind her.

She'd barely taken three steps toward the lift, when the *one* voice she'd hoped to avoid practically shrieked across the foyer.

"Bennett, *what* the *fuck* are you doing here?"

She winced, sheepish guilt filling every muscle as she turned slowly to face the scolding and slightly baffled eyes of her best friend.

"I got a text from Amelia," she tried, her tone meek as Noah's dark eyes stared her down and he folded his arms across his chest.

"You're in the middle of the only fucking time off you've taken in *three years,*" Noah yelled, "and you're *supposed* to be in fucking *Cornwall,* and did you just say you got a *text?*"

Finley nodded.

Noah baulked.

"*Shit,* she *never* texts."

"*Exactly!*" Finley urged, her stomach swooping with her anxiety once more. "This is either very good or *very* bad and I need to know which one."

"Jesus Christ, you're intense, just *pick up the phone!*"

"She didn't answer!"

Noah raised a judgemental eyebrow, and Finley dropped her gaze, her cheeks flushing with the first flares of her embarrassment.

"So, you cut your holiday in half and travelled five and a half hours to appear in the office at 2pm because your boss didn't answer *one* phone call?"

Finley's blush deepened.

This was *exactly* why she'd hoped she wouldn't bump into Noah.

"Well, sort of…" she tried.

Then she huffed.

He knew her far too well.

She flicked her eyes back to Noah's face, groaning as he smirked knowingly.

"*No,* and you *know* I didn't."

"Then *why* are you *here,* Finley?" He grinned, shoving her shoulder lightly. "Amelia can wait until the *end* of your leave."

Finley bit her cheek. Her stomach was in knots, and her chest was tighter than ever now that her only excuse was being washed away.

This paper-thin excuse was the only thing holding together her sanity right now, and without it she would have to take a leap of faith that she wasn't sure she was brave enough for.

What if Sophie didn't want her?

"But I'm here now…" she mumbled.

"Yeah, and we both know that's not for Amelia, you useless lesbian," Noah scoffed, grinning impishly. "We all know work isn't the only thing you wanna *do* around here." He winked.

Finley wrinkled her nose.

"Never wink again."

"Yeah, just felt it." Noah nodded, his gaze dropping sheepishly. "Not a winky kind of guy."

Finley sighed.

"You really think I shouldn't meet Amelia? What if I'm losing my job?"

"Well, that's obviously not happening, and Bennett, she'll call back!"

"I-I left my phone on a rail platform in middle-of-nowhere Cornwall," Finley mumbled, scuffing the toe of her shoe against the ground in an almost childlike embarrassment.

"Your phone?" Noah repeated.

"Yeah."

"Your *phone.* The one…" He reached forward, his hand slipping into the rarely used front pocket of Finley's jacket, and producing perhaps the most infuriating thing Finley had ever had the displeasure of seeing. "The one sitting on your fucking chest?"

"Jesus *Christ,* are you *kidding me?*" Finley shrieked, lunging for the phone like some sort of bereft addict. "I have spent *five hours* trying to work out if I could perform a self-lobotomy with the edge of a credit card because I didn't have this, and it was *under my face?*"

"Get your *shit* together, Bennett!" Noah hissed. "You look insane! Like a tube rat addicted to rail fumes! And *go home!* Now. Before Amelia comes out here and sees you, and you're stuck here forever."

Finley darted her eyes around the office.

"Fin!" Noah gripped her shoulders, his voice softer and his eyes earnest as they searched Finley's. "Please, just…put your life first this time."

Finley's heart stopped.

The words wrapped themselves around every one of her nerves, anchoring her down until she couldn't find a single excuse.

Put her life first.

The *one* thing she'd told Sophie she'd do.

The one thing she'd told herself she'd do.

*"Shit.* Yeah. Yeah, you're right," she shook her head, her fingers gripping tightly over the handle of her suitcase, as if somehow, she could hold onto her resolve. "Thanks, Noah."

She gripped her phone tightly, steeling her muscles as she tried to bring herself to check her messages. After so many hours thinking, she *couldn't* get answers, she was now kind of afraid to check for them.

"Go!" Noah grinned, patting her shoulders as he released his grip. "I'm late for lunch with Cam anyway."

"We are catching up about this!" Finley insisted, her feet already carrying her backwards towards the door as Noah grinned cheekily. "Immediately!"

"Yep, as soon as you have your own juicy love story to share with me," Noah sang. "Get out!"

Finley was already practically running through the streets of London as she swiped the lock screen on her phone. Her stomach churned at the names on her screen, and she settled for least terrifying to most.

Bex: *Pub isn't open yet, where else is he gonna go?*

Finley grinned, shaking her head.

Amelia: *In meetings now. Call you back when I'm free.*

Finley exhaled heavily. Okay. That wasn't really an answer, but somehow just the name on her screen settled her nerves a little.

Her fingers shook as she opened the last message thread.

The oldest one.

The one that had come in first, just minutes after Finley had boarded her train this morning.

Sophie: *I'm at the Natural History Museum. That place is incredible! Have you seen the whale!* 😍

Sophie: *I can't stop thinking about Jack though. Or Bex. Or you.*

Sophie: *Are you really sure I can't come home? I really want to come home.*

Sophie: *Wait…I missed your call? I'm just listening to your voicemail….*

Sophie: *Holy shit!*

Sophie: *You're coming home?? Have you left???*

Sophie: *Oh my god, I think I'm having a nervous breakdown.*

Sophie: *Don't you dare turn round. Or get a hotel.*

Sophie: *Fuck!!! I'm so excited.*

Sophie: *And so nervous!*

Sophie: *I can't wait to see you* 😍

Jesus Christ.

Finley exhaled, her eyes welling and a laugh falling from her chest as six hours of anxiety dropped instantly from her shoulders.

She shook her head. Maybe Noah had been right. Maybe she *had* dealt with this a *little* intensely, but in her defence, she wasn't entirely accustomed to falling for someone from the other end of a phone, and she had no idea how one was *supposed* to deal with these things.

# Chapter Nineteen

Sophie paced the hallway between the bathroom and the bedroom of Finley's home, flat out losing her mind.

It was driving her *crazy* that Finley hadn't replied to her since her bombshell of voicemail in the early morning, and it was honestly embarrassing how hard Sophie had struggled to hold her sanity together since then. She'd paid zero attention to anything after Hope the blue whale skeleton, had walked into several exhibits because she was staring at her phone, and had spilled just about every drink she'd tried to consume all afternoon because her hands were bloody *trembling*. Like a *lunatic*.

She'd been trying fruitlessly to convince herself that Finley was simply driving Sophie's car up, and so she'd not been able to check the phone.

But the stark reality was that that voicemail had been over six hours ago now, so if Finley was really coming home, then she would be *really* close.

And that was both incredibly exciting and shit-your-own-liver *terrifying*.

What if Finley didn't like her?

What if she thought she was too short, or too skittish, or *smelled* weird or something?

But then *what* if it was every bit as goddamn fucking perfect as it had been from 300 miles apart, and *then some* with the woman she was falling for in the same room as her for the first time.

Sophie squeaked as her phone chimed.

Finley: *Yes, and yes.* 😊

Finley: *I've been having a nervous breakdown for six hours.*

Finley: *I can't wait to see you either.* 😊

Oh *god.*

Sophie had no idea how long she had until Finley arrived, but she was pretty certain it *wasn't* long.

She blew out a shaky breath, her socked feet slipping on the wooden floors as she scurried into the bathroom, spraying herself with perfume and tousling her hair into the waves that had dropped a little in the city's wind during the day.

She closed her eyes for a moment, flexing her fingers in an effort to stem the trembling nerves that rippled through her.

She replayed the words of the voicemail and the text messages in her mind.

Finley was nervous too.

Of course, she was. They both felt this.

Sophie huffed out a chuckle.

They both felt it, and Finley had felt it enough to jump in a car and close the gap between them without Sophie ever having to ask.

And that felt *incredible.*

If terrifying.

She panic-called Bex.

"Are you not having your swoon-fest union by now?" Bex answered, chewing noisily on a sandwich in her kitchen.

"I'm having a full-scale meltdown, is what I'm having!" Sophie cried.

"Why?"

"Oh *god,* what if she doesn't *like* me?" Sophie wailed, letting her head thud against the wall of Finley's bedroom.

"What if you don't like her?" Bex grinned.

*"Not* helpful!"

"What if you fall in *love?"* Bex wriggled her eyebrows, a glob of mayonnaise dropping onto her chin.

"Somehow even less helpful," Sophie grumbled. "What do I wear? Should I get changed?"

"How many times have you done that already?"

"Erm." Sophie glanced at the open wardrobe, and counted in her head. Then she blushed. "Six?"

"Then no."

"Auntie Sophie!" Willow sang, her little hands grabbing at the phone as she appeared beside Bex at the table.

Her mouth was as covered in mayonnaise as Bex's was, and Sophie chuckled fondly at the sight of them.

"Hi, Pickle!" she cooed.

"I miss you," Willow whispered.

Sophie's heart clenched, and her eyes burned suddenly with adoration and the very real threat of tears.

"Oh, I miss you too, honey," she breathed, forcing the tears to stay back. "I'll be home to see you very soon, okay?"

Willow nodded.

She pursed her lips, her eyes flicking down like they did when she was thinking.

"Are you gonna get laid when Finley gets to London?" she asked.

Bex snorted a laugh, spraying sandwich crumbs across the phone screen.

Sophie stared blankly; her brain unable to process the *really* abrupt about-turn.

"I-I'm sorry, *what?"*

"Mummy said Finley is gonna help you get laid if she goes home to London," Willow explained. "Now she's coming home so you'll be able to get laid."

Sophie closed her eyes for a moment, as if somehow when she opened them this situation would *not* be occurring.

"Uh...I..."

The knock at the door saved her, and for a moment she flooded warm with relief.

Until she remembered where she was and who would be the other side of the door, and her entire body froze.

"Oh my god," she whispered.

"Go!" Bex hissed, pulling Willow away from the phone. *"Go!* Go fall in love. Get laid."

Sophie, to be completely honest, wasn't listening. She was far too busy having the softest kind of panic attack known to man as she hung up the phone and crept in the direction of the door.

She felt the shivers grip her spine and her stomach as she reached the door, and she closed her eyes as she rested her forehead against the cold wood for a moment of composure.

She exhaled.

Then she stepped back, her fingers trembling as she grasped the handle, and pulled.

Sophie's mind blanked.

Oh *god.*

If Finley was gorgeous in photos and over video calls then she was fucking *celestial* in person. The dance of the afternoon sun in silky dark hair, and the way those deep eyes seemed to look straight into her soul. The way those lips curled instantly as her warm, mocha gaze met Sophie's. And *god,* that *smile.*

And she was *here.*

"Hey."

Finley beamed, and Sophie was gone.

Completely gone.

She could be in love, for all she knew.

*"Hi,"* she breathed.

The corners of her lips tugged shyly for the briefest of moments, and then her smile was spreading wide, and it was hurting her cheeks, and Finley was returning it with sparkling eyes and Sophie was powerless to hold back the giddy giggles as Finley stepped forward, pulling her into a bear hug.

A hug that felt *incredible.*

Incredible in the way strong arms wrapped just firm enough around Sophie's shoulders, sure palms holding her body just tight enough against her. In the way Finley's chest heaved against Sophie's, and the warmth of the soft skin of her cheek as it brushed against her own.

And *god* she smelled good.

Like jasmine, and cedarwood, and intrigue, and excitement, and butterflies.

Sophie clutched tightly at the back of Finley's shirt, desperately fighting the urge to bury her face in the crook of her neck.

For now.

"Your sheets do smell like you," she murmured.

She grinned as she felt Finley's chuckle before she heard it.

"And your car smells like you."

Sophie shivered as the murmured words ghosted the shell of her ear, Finley's breath hot against it as she pulled back.

She swallowed.

The voice that she had begun to crave in her ears this past week had been like a balm to her over the phone. Soothing, and reassuring. Calming.

Here, hushed against the sensitive skin of her ear, while her mind was swimming with the proximity and the warmth and the smell, it was gasoline. A fuse that sparked adrenaline, and butterflies, and goosebumps.

She shuddered.

Finley Bennett was *definitely* going to be her bittersweet end.

Sparkling sapphire eyes met Sophie's own, and she watched in awe as they searched her face, curiosity and reverence behind them, and something almost playful in that irresistible goddamn fucking smirk.

Finley's hands trailed lightly over Sophie's arms, her gaze flicking openly to her lips, and for a moment Sophie thought she might kiss her.

God, she *hoped* she might kiss her.

*So* bad.

But she didn't.

Finley shook her head in awed disbelief as she stepped forward, pushing Sophie back gently as she closed the door behind her.

"You look *beautiful,* Sophie Cedars," she whispered.

Sophie huffed out a laugh.

"Speak for yourself, Bennett!" She grinned. "How are you *so* much sexier in person?"

Finley chuckled, her cheeks tinting with the tell-tale signs of a blush that burned in Sophie's stomach and settled the nerves that had consumed her.

"I haven't lost any sexy points then?" Finley raised an eyebrow, grinning cheekily.

*"God* no," Sophie laughed. "Your eyes are even warmer in person, you smell even better than your sheets, and you've just travelled 300 miles to see me. Frankly you're more irritatingly attractive than you've ever been."

Finley laughed, her eyes flickering with something that made Sophie's stomach flip.

"Are you *flirting* with me, Cedars?" She smirked.

Sophie let her eyes trace the movement of Finley's lips.

"We've talked about that smirk, Bennett," she murmured.

"Mmmm. And I'm not even remotely sorry," Finley winked. "Come on then David Attenborough, tell me about the museum!"

Sophie grinned.

Finley was still *so* close, and her hands still roamed Sophie's arms, and Sophie was still clutching the flannel of Finley's shirt, and she was *completely* besotted with the proximity.

She had worried that things would feel different with Finley in front of her.

And she'd been right.

They did feel different.

In all the *best* ways.

Finley's cheeky charm, and the playful air between them was every bit as comforting and as alluring as it had been all week.

Except it was warmer. Magnified. *Real.*

"It was, um…" Sophie shook her head, her mind still struggling to process the very sudden turn of events in her day. She giggled softly. "I-I can't believe you're *here.* You came home to see me?"

Finley dropped her gaze, her lips curling shyly as something in the air shifted for a moment, vulnerability seeping through the cracks in the playful exterior.

"Yeah." She exhaled slowly, and Sophie could feel the hitch in the chest that was just centimetres from her own. "I just needed to know if…to see if it feels…"

Finley trailed off, wide, almost hopeful eyes flicking back to meet Sophie's. Sophie melted.

*"Yeah,"* she breathed. She swallowed thickly. "And, um…is…does it…?"

There was a long moment of pause.

Then that *something* shifted back.

Finley's eyes softened as they searched Sophie's, and Sophie grinned as a spark was lit behind them.

Playful. Easy. Familiar.

Sophie giggled.

They both felt this, and they knew it.

"Can I take you out tonight?" Finley smirked; her eyebrow raised in question.

"Oh, on a *real* date?" Sophie teased.

"On a real date." Finley grinned.

"You came all this way, Bennett." Sophie trailed her fingers over Finley's shoulders, closing them over the collar of her shirt. "You damn well better do."

She grinned as she finally backed away, giving Finley the space to settle into the flat. The eye contact and the playful tease between them lay thicker than ever with the heat of their mutual attraction, but the ease that they had built over the past week carried clear beneath the current, and Sophie felt elated that the connection still burned the same.

"So, where you gonna take me?" she murmured.

"Well, I figured we could have dinner, and then…" Finley's eyes were transfixed on Sophie's own even as she shed her jacket and followed her through the house, and the warmth behind them made Sophie's stomach flip. "You ever been on a ghost walk?"

"A what?"

"A ghost tour around London. They take you to all these places that are supposed to be haunted by historical figures," Finley explained casually. As if she wasn't explaining something right out of Sophie's dreams. "It might be a really stupid idea, but I figured since you like history, maybe…"

Sophie couldn't hold back the giddy squeal.

*"Seriously?"*

"If that's okay? We can do something more romantic if you'd rather? I just thought it might be something you haven't done yet."

Sophie bit back a sigh, her body melting more and more with every word that left this woman's mouth.

"Those sexy points are just piling up, Bennett."

Finley's cheeks reddened, her eyes dropping from Sophie's own for the first time as they flicked to her lips.

"Yeah?" she murmured.

"Mmmhmm." Sophie smirked, taking a brazen step forward. She slipped her fingers through the belt loops on the front of Finley's jeans, her stomach swooping at the subtle jump of the muscles beneath the waistband. "What should I wear?"

"Uh…" Finley cleared her throat quietly, her hands settling lightly over Sophie's waist. Her cheeks flushed deeper, and Sophie bit her lip with a smug kind of satisfaction at the obvious fluster behind those mocha eyes. "Whatever you feel most comfortable in."

Sophie's confidence surged under the intensity of Finley's gaze, and she took a cheeky little risk.

Where was the harm in a little flirtation with someone who quite clearly would not be adverse to it?

"So…" Sophie tugged on Finley's belt loops. "Not much, then?"

Finley's eyes flared and she groaned softly, her fingers flexing over Sophie's hips as if she fought the urge to pull her closer.

"You're a tease, Sophie Cedars," Finley muttered, blushing at her own groan.

Sophie grinned.

"But first things first…" Sophie stepped back, her smirk dropping as she remembered one particular detail that had niggled in the back of her mind since she'd heard Finley's voicemail. "Did I cost you your job?"

Finley shook her head.

"Let's put the kettle on." She grinned, gesturing for Sophie to lead the way. "I can explain how much you are *not* responsible for my career situation, and you can tell me all about Hope the blue whale skeleton!"

Sophie hummed as she forced herself to tear away from Finley's body and that goddamn smile. She was completely entranced, and she honestly had no choice but to turn her back on those dark eyes if she wanted *any* hope of getting anywhere near the kitchen. But she could feel Finley close behind her as she moved through the hall, and even just the knowledge of the proximity set her nerves on fire.

She headed straight for the coffee machine, needing to busy her hands just to keep them off Finley's soft forearms, or the spread of her shirt. She threw a glance over her shoulder, and blushed immediately as Finley smirked at her, watching carefully as Sophie moved about her kitchen.

"Sorry, I just…habit, already, I guess," Sophie laughed shyly, holding her hands up as she stepped away from the machine.

"No, please," Finley chuckled, shaking her head as she settled into a bar stool. "You look at home here."

Sophie shrugged shyly.

"I feel at home here," she admitted.

"I like it," Finley murmured, leaning her elbows on the counter. "You pottering about my kitchen."

Sophie raised an eyebrow, narrowing her eyes even as her entire body flooded warm, and her stomach tried for gold in the pole vault.

"Stop it," she scolded, turning her back deliberately away from those burning eyes.

"What?" Finley laughed.

"Flustering me while I'm trying to make you a drink."

Sophie shot Finley a glance over her shoulder, catching the tail end of a *very* cheeky grin.

"I'm just saying I could get used to being around you," Finley flirted. "You know, *within* three-hundred miles."

Sophie sighed, completely unable to stop the swoon as she fiddled with the buttons on Finley's coffee machine.

She had *just* managed to master this thing, but with its owner's eyes boring so warm into her back, Sophie could barely remember her own name, let alone which nozzle to twist or which switch to flip.

"Wait…"

Finley's hushed voice stopped Sophie in her tracks, and the hairs on the back of her neck bristled as she heard the barstool scrape along the floor behind her.

"No *way!*"

Sophie spun, frowning as she found Finley staring in bewilderment at the doorway to the living room.

Sophie followed nervously as Finley crossed the hall, unsure whether the confused look in dark eyes was a good thing, or whether Sophie was in trouble.

"That is *not* my parlour palm!"

Sophie laughed, her nerves falling away as Finley ran her fingers through the shiny green leaves of her only living houseplant. When Sophie had arrived here just over a week ago, this thing had looked decrepit. Browning, and droopy, and dryer than a stale kit-kat despite the fact that it had been drowning in an oasis of water.

Now, after a week in rays of actual sunlight, with an appropriate amount of water, and a little careful pruning, it looked like something fresh from a lowland forest.

"It just needed a little TLC, babe." Sophie winked, grinning smugly.

Finley let out a low whistle, rustling the leaves in awe.

Then those awestruck eyes were on Sophie, glinting with something she didn't think she'd ever seen before, but definitely *did* like. She wasn't sure if it was over the thriving houseplant, or the fact that Sophie had called her 'babe', but she was sure that it was making her stomach swim with an entire aviary of butterflies.

"I get the feeling you're good for everything you come into contact with, Sophie Cedars," Finley murmured, low, and hushed, and *way* too charming for Sophie's stomach to contend with.

Sophie blushed, and Finley smirked immediately as her eyes traced the reaction.

Sophie let out a frustrated growl.

"Good *god,*" she huffed, spinning Finley and pushing her back towards the kitchen. "Sit down and wait for your coffee, before I *climb* you."

Finley's stuttered, flustered reaction was everything Sophie needed to be absolutely damn sure that this was going to be the best date of her life.

# Chapter Twenty

Finley chuckled as Sophie bounced on the spot beside her, wrapped adorably in about five of her own layers, and at least three of Finley's.

She was completely and utterly enamoured by just how excitable Sophie was for the tour, and by the way her eyes sparkled and her lip clamped between her teeth in enthusiastic anticipation.

And Finley was just as enthused for the night, albeit for completely different reasons.

Meeting Sophie had been incredible.

The nerves that she'd felt as she'd rang the doorbell of her own home were unlike anything she had ever experienced in her life, and the way that they'd melted the moment those green eyes had crinkled into that smile had been almost euphoric.

Sophie was *impossibly* more beautiful in person.

It was almost painful, the way Finley's stomach and her chest had responded to Sophie's presence, and *god* she'd wanted to kiss her.

She'd wanted to kiss her more than she'd ever wanted *anything,* but she'd known that that would have been too much, too soon. So, she'd swallowed that need down; replaced it instead with words and soft touches, and she'd taken everything she could from the spark in Sophie's eyes.

And the late afternoon, and their dinner, had been so *easy.*

They had settled so quickly into their air of playful tease and comfort like they'd simply been together the whole time.

Like nothing was different.

*Almost* nothing, anyway.

The flirtatious back and forth had been stronger than ever with the addition of the physical pull between them, and the thicker air had been nothing short of intoxicating. Finley had been almost drunk on the touches; arms and hands and waists and teasing grips of clothing.

A tease, and a magnetism, but also just a subtle reminder that this was *real*.

Still now, Finley couldn't shake the goosebumps that prickled over her skin as Sophie's arm linked through her own, the warmth of her body close against her as they made their way out of the restaurant and onto the tube.

She wasn't even one complete date through with Sophie Cedars beside her, and she was already pretty certain she was falling.

~ ~ ~ ~ ~ ~ 🔥 ~ ~ ~ ~ ~ ~

Sophie was practically shaking.

The hairs on her arms stood on end, the skin beneath them rippled with goosebumps, and she was pretty sure every ounce of the blood in her veins had been replaced with the burn of adrenaline.

Largely at the frankly ridiculous attraction she felt towards Finley, that heightened with every second she spent in her company.

But predominantly because they were currently standing in the middle of a darkened church graveyard, listening to a man dressed as a Victorian soldier tell his third terrifying ghost story of the evening.

It definitely was not the most conventional date Sophie had ever been on, but she couldn't deny that it was absolutely the best.

She liked that Finley had picked something based on things that Sophie had said she was passionate about. And something a little different too. Not just the museums and the galleries that people usually picked when they heard her interests, without stopping to think that she'll have done those things time and time over.

"And legend has it that here, where the old church once thrived, the cries of Arthur Sattalion can still be heard when the winds blow North-West," the Victorian soldier whispered, low and dark and way too hammy, but somehow everything Sophie wanted to hear. "Hark! Listen now…"

The small group hushed, and Sophie listened.

"Convenient that the wind's blowing South now then, isn't it," Finley mumbled quietly, her hands in her pockets and her eyes darting around the church yard as she shuffled closer to Sophie.

Sophie smirked.

She also liked that Finley was puffing her chest out.

Metaphorically.

Literally, she was kind of hiding behind Sophie.

"Why?" she murmured; her lips quirked in a soft tease. "You worried we might hear old Arthur if the winds change?"

"No," Finley scoffed, shuffling a little closer into Sophie's side. "I'm saying this is bull, and if the wind had been blowing North-West, he'd have said East! We're on our third stop and he's had a convenient excuse each time."

The soldier wailed.

Loud, and long, and low.

Sophie jumped.

But Finley practically shat her own spleen.

She let out the most adorable half scream, her entire body tensing as she scrambled frantically into Sophie's side, her hands flying from her pockets to grip at Sophie's upper arm.

"Just kidding with you!" the soldier chuckled, his voice way too loud for the hushed churchyard and the group's racing pulses. "The wind blows the wrong way tonight. But that doesn't mean Arthur isn't around here, watching and waiting."

Finley huffed indignantly, though Sophie didn't miss the nervous sweep of wide mocha eyes across the graveyard, or the slight tightening of the hold on her arm.

Sophie grinned.

She chuckled softly, her chest warming as Finley instantly blushed, releasing her hold on Sophie's arm sheepishly. Sophie smirked. She nudged Finley playfully with her shoulder, linked her arm through the crook of her elbow, and then confidently slid her hand down and into Finley's.

The simple touch sent Sophie's butterflies soaring instantly into her throat, and she bit her lip to hold them inside as Finley's eyes glazed a little in surprised awe. Her lips curled into the softest smile Sophie had ever seen, and her tensed shoulders dropped immediately. Then she closed her fingers over Sophie's, giving them the lightest of squeezes, and Sophie's butterflies splintered into a goddamn aviary.

"Now, if you'll all follow me!" the Victorian soldier boomed, slamming the butt of his wooden rifle against the cobblestones, and performing an unnecessarily elaborate about-turn. "We shall make our way into the grounds of the Tower of London, one of the most haunted places in the UK."

"Come on, Scooby Doo," Sophie teased, tugging Finley into step alongside her. "Maybe we'll see a ghost in the castle."

"Great."

Sophie giggled openly at the tensed jaw and gritted mutter, but Finley's lips were still curled into a smile and her eyes still shone as she walked hand in hand beside her.

Sophie's head was entirely in the clouds as they made their way through the heavy iron gates and into the castle grounds. She was trying her absolute hardest to listen to the story of the ghost of a bear in the grounds of the castle, but Finley's body was pressed against her side, and her thumb was sweeping casually over the back of her hand, and Sophie was feeling it everywhere.

By the time they made it into the castle itself, Sophie was pretty sure she was made entirely of jelly, and liquid honey, and butterflies. The castle smelled damp, and it was cold, and a little creepy, but Finley smelled so good, and she was warm pressed against Sophie's arm, and Sophie couldn't help but nestle herself closer.

She was fairly certain her butterflies burst into flame when Finley confidently eased her hand out of Sophie's own, and slipped her arm instead around her shoulders, pulling her in.

"This room here is home to perhaps the most famous of all of our ghosts," the soldier whispered, low and hoarse once again. "And there are many."

The effect was impossibly more creepy in the echoey chamber of the castle, and Sophie felt Finley tense immediately beside her.

"For *this* is the great and terrible White Tower Dungeon," the soldier exclaimed. "The last walls seen by many tortured, pained and dying London criminals. Sir Walter Raleigh! Guy Fawkes! The White Woman herself, Anne Boleyn!"

Finley shuffled her feet nervously, and if Sophie hadn't been able to feel the quickening of her breathing, she'd have seen it in the little puffs of air in the cold, damp room. Finley was clearly a little on edge, and clearly had no desire to come face to face with Guy Fawkes, or Anne Boleyn, or the bear thing from the grounds. And Sophie's chest heated with an overwhelming urge of sudden affection for the fact that Finley had chosen this date for *her,* because she'd thought Sophie would like it.

Simple.

Not because it was a perfect date spot, or a cliche, or romantic, or something that Finley could show off doing and impress her date.

But simply because she'd thought it was something that Sophie would enjoy doing.

And that was incredibly endearing.

Sophie grinned.

What Finley needed was a distraction. Something to take her mind off the damp castle and the threat of the paranormal. And by the way Finley's eyes had lit up when Sophie had held her hand, she was pretty sure she had the power in her hands to create at least a little distraction.

She shuffled, slipping her own arm beneath Finley's jacket and around her waist, her fingers teasing the waistband of Finley's jeans. And the muscles beneath them tensed instantly.

Sophie smirked.

"It's said that many are still here," the soldier narrated. "Trapped, and screaming, and looking longingly at the narrow, high window."

Sophie trailed her fingers up, her nails tracing slowly over the back of Finley's shirt.

"Those who feel a presence will shiver when a spirit passes over them!"

Sophie dragged her nails down the length of Finley's spine.

Finley gasped; the tiniest of soft sounds, her arm tightening around Sophie's shoulders, and the spine beneath Sophie's fingers rippled as Finley shivered.

"Aha!" the soldier cried. "You see! We have a chosen one!"

Finley froze.

Sophie bit her lip, barely stifling a giggle as Finley's eyes shot wide, her cheeks flushed a deep shade of red, and the Victorian soldier began to hobble excitedly towards her.

"Tell us," he pressed, his eyes alight with excitement as they fixed on Finley's. "How did it feel?"

Sophie's entire body shook with the urge to laugh. She cleared her throat, biting her tongue to cover her giggles, the task only growing more difficult as Finley's arm around her shoulders squeezed.

"G-good?" Finley stammered.

The soldier arched an eyebrow.

"It felt good to be touched by the ghost of Anne Boleyn?"

"Uh…"

Sophie's giggles won.

She turned her face, burying her mouth in the back of her hand as Finley faltered beside her, and she could feel the eyes of every other member of their tour group watching them.

"It's uh…a little cold?" Finley tried meekly.

Sophie creased.

She giggled openly, leaning into Finley's side as the soldier turned bewildered eyes in her direction.

The soldier's eyes narrowed for a brief moment, and there was a long, silent pause.

Sophie felt Finley swallow beside her.

Then the soldier stood, very loudly and very abruptly, to attention.

"Very good!"

He slammed the butt of his rifle against the stone floor, and Finley jumped for the millionth time.

Then he about-turned.

"Onwards!"

Sophie giggled, falling easily into Finley's side as Finley exhaled hard, pulling her in close again.

"You're trouble, Sophie Cedars," she huffed, her eyes sparkling and her lips twitching in amusement as she shook her head. "That I *can* feel."

~ ~ ~ ~ ~ ~ (♪) ~ ~ ~ ~ ~ ~

Finley felt elated as they exited the ground of the Tower of London. And not just because they were finally free of the threat of a ghostly encounter. Sophie's fingers wrapped around her own as they made their way slowly in the direction of the tube station, and the simple touch heated Finley's skin beneath the chill in the breeze.

The evening had been perfect.

She couldn't even begin to recall any of the details of the event, but the way Sophie's eyes had shone and her smile had stayed and her fingers had consistently found Finley's had been exhilarating, and she was hooked.

And now that she'd been in a room with Sophie Cedars; now that she'd felt her hand in her own, and her breath on her ear; now that she knew that this felt *real*, there was just one niggling thought in the back of her brain that she couldn't fight.

And she needed to know.

"You're gonna stay, right?" she whispered, her voice trembling with her nerves as she flicked her gaze to Sophie. "F-for your trip. You'll stay the week?"

Sophie faltered in her step for a moment, her wide eyes glistening with something that made Finley's stomach swoop as they searched her own for a long, torturous moment.

Finley held her breath.

Then they flashed with something playful, and Sophie grinned.

"That depends," she murmured, nudging Finley softly with her hip as they walked. "Wasn't there something you wanted to do?"

Finley furrowed her brows.

That wasn't quite the reply she'd hoped for, and she pursed her lips as she racked her brains for the answer Sophie was expecting.

"On our video date," Sophie pressed lowly, her lips curled into a soft smirk. "And this morning."

*Oh.*

Finley huffed out a laugh, nodding softly.

Their steps slowed simultaneously, and Finley quirked an eyebrow, her stomach clenching at the hopeful uncertainty in Sophie's eyes as they watched her in anticipation.

"There were a *lot* of things I wanted to do, Soph," she husked.

She smirked as Sophie shivered; her eyes fluttering closed for the briefest of moments.

"I-I meant…" Sophie whispered.

Finley grinned.

She stopped walking, tugging Sophie's hand gently until she turned to face her.

She exhaled shakily as Sophie's eyes glazed, their usual green darkening as they mapped Finley's face. Sophie's lips parted, her breath shaky as her gaze settled on Finley's soft smirk, and Finley. Completely gone. She could be in love, for all she knew.

She tugged a little firmer, her adrenaline driving her muscles as she pulled Sophie's body against her own. She bit her lip as Sophie's breath hitched.

Finley's skin burned in all the places that Sophie was pressed against her, and she felt her eyes hood as the air around them seemed to thicken, the sounds of the city fading into the dull thump of her pulse in her ears. She wrapped an arm around Sophie's waist, her chest pounding at the slight tremble she could feel in Sophie's muscles as she searched misty eyes. She leaned forward, her nose just brushing Sophie's, and she smiled as she let out a soft gasp.

"You meant…?" she whispered.

Sophie inhaled sharply as she nodded, barely perceptible as her eyes fluttered closed, and Finley pulled her closer.

She closed the gap.

And holy god damn fuck.

She'd expected fireworks, but the moment her lips closed over Sophie's, her entire body erupted into crawling flames that she was sure could never be put out. Sophie whimpered, deepening the movements in barely an instant, and Finley's chest flooded with the almost terrifying realisation that she had *never* been kissed like this.

Had never *kissed* anyone like this.

So soft, and yet so *hungry*.

Like she needed every part of them. Like another part of her soul was being taken from her body with every swipe of Sophie's tongue, and fed back anew with every claim of her lips.

And maybe that was a little dramatic, but Jesus *God* Christ she was on fire.

Her whole body was in flames, and Sophie's hips were firm against her own, and her hands were tight in her hair, and the skin of her waist was warm beneath the fingertips that Finley had instinctively teased beneath the hem of Sophie's shirt. And they were in the middle of a sadistic historical landmark but Finley was powerless to hold back the soft moan that slipped from her lips as Sophie's fingers tugged a little harder in her hair, and her tongue swept just a little deeper into the kiss.

She had never been more ready to surrender to a person, and she was *really* regretting doing this in a public place.

She deepened the kiss impossibly further for just a moment longer, before pulling back, breaking away with a softer press over Sophie's trembling lower lip. She rested her forehead against Sophie's, her chest heaving as she fought to catch her breath.

"Yeah…" Sophie breathed, her lips quirking into a giddy smile. "I meant that."

Finley huffed out a chuckle. She couldn't resist, claiming Sophie's lips again in a softer kiss.

"To answer your question," Sophie grinned breathlessly as they broke away, her hands trailing teasingly over the spread of Finley's shirt. "If you keep doing *that,* it'll be impossible for me to leave."

Finley melted.

She grinned, connecting her lips once more with Sophie's. Her entire body felt drunk on the feeling of Sophie against her.

"Come on." Sophie giggled as she pulled back, her fingers dropping to link through Finley's own. "Take me home."

She tugged, taking a step backward along the path, her eyes sparkling with a dark kind of mischief that clenched in Finley's thighs.

Finley quirked an eyebrow.

"Are you propositioning me?" She grinned.

Sophie winked.

*"Absolutely."*

# Chapter Twenty-One

Sophie's stomach filled with butterflies as she turned onto the tiny path to Finley's door, the footsteps behind her making her feel almost dizzy. The air between them had been thicker than Sophie had ever known as they'd made the ten-minute walk back to the house, the adrenaline of their kiss alight with the glowing embers of the desire that neither of them were even *trying* to hide.

Sophie bit her lip, her grin almost giddy as she reflected over the evening, and over the way she hoped the next few hours would go. She had never felt such a raw, physical pull to someone before, and she had never been so sure of *exactly* what she wanted once she finally had her date alone.

And the devilish fire that had burned in Finley's eyes since their kiss told her she wasn't the only one, and the feeling was unexpectedly empowering.

She turned as she reached the door, leaning back against it as she watched Finley close the gap. There was something so purposeful in Finley's eyes as she stepped forward, that Sophie's breath hitched in her chest.

She pressed her palms against the wood, grounding herself as Finley's body moved torturously close to her own, her hips *just* far enough away to keep them from touching. The proximity and the scent of jasmine was almost overwhelming, and Sophie licked her lips instinctively.

Finley's dark eyes traced the movement and she smirked; that cocky, dirty smirk that Sophie was powerless to resist. She fought a shiver as Finley leaned closer, one hand pressing on the door beside Sophie's shoulders as she slipped the key into the lock.

Sophie swallowed.

*God,* she was in so much trouble.

Those eyes were *so* knowing; so playfully *teasing* as they flicked slowly and deliberately between Sophie's gaze and her lips. And that goddamn smirk was filthier than it had ever been as it hovered *just* close enough to Sophie's lips for the heat of Finley's breath to hit them.

Finley Bennett knew *exactly* how to stoke the embers slowly; how to build the fire into something completely uncontrollable, and Sophie was entranced.

She fisted her hand in the front of Finley's shirt as the lock clicked, pulling her in as the door swung back behind her.

She grinned as the door closed behind them and Finley instantly kicked her shoes off haphazardly, stumbling a little as Sophie pulled her backwards. Sophie kept her eyes trained on Finley's, toeing her own shoes off slowly as she basked in the open appreciation in her date's eyes. The spark behind the deep mocha was mischievous, *dark* with a visibly hungry arousal, and her lips curled in an amused smirk that was frankly *dangerous*.

Like a predator teasing its prey.

Sophie's thighs clenched.

She hadn't spent much time in her life thinking about how it would feel to be someone's prey.

But right now, she was starting to feel like she'd rather enjoy it.

Finley's tongue darted out to wet her lips, and Sophie smirked. She could almost *see* the words that hovered on Finley's tongue, and her stomach clenched at the thought that they might just match the hunger in those eyes.

The way Finley's voice had become her vice. Her poison. She felt the arousal pool thick between her thighs just to *think* of what that voice could do to her if it said the things those eyes were saying now.

"You look like everything you want to say is *filthy*, Bennett," she teased.

"Mmmm," Finley hummed, her lips curling into a dirty smile, and her eyes burning impossibly darker. She leaned closer, the husk of her words ghosting over Sophie's lips. "But *nothing* compared to everything I want to *do.*"

Sophie shivered, her skin prickling with the heat behind the gravelly words. She slipped her fingers through the belt loops of Finley's jeans, pulling her hips against her own as Finley's fingers closed over her waist.

"Then what are you waiting for?" she murmured, her lips brushing over Finley's as she spoke.

Sophie gasped as Finley tugged her hips forward, her lips dropping to tease feather-light over Sophie's jaw for the briefest of moments before she pulled back. She bit her lip through an almost sheepish smile, her eyes searching Sophie's face.

"Is it too soon?" She wrinkled her nose a little.

Sophie cocked an eyebrow.

Finley huffed out a chuckle.

"I *like* you, Soph, I don't want you to think this is just about sex."

Sophie smirked.

*Oh.*

Consent. *Empowerment.*

The words fuelled the fire hotter in Sophie's belly, and if there was one thing she knew right now, it was that this was *not* just sex. To *either* of them.

She let her lips hover over the skin of Finley's jaw as Finley spoke, feeling the tight pull of arousal in the base of her spine as the words got shakier.

"Or that I *expect* sex just because we're on a date. I just don't wanna rush you, or take…"

Sophie flicked her tongue over Finley's earlobe, pulling it into her mouth and biting down gently.

*"Advantage…"* Finley groaned. Her hands slipped firmly over Sophie's ass, tugging her roughly against her.

Sophie's stomach flamed low in an instant; the desire stoked way too hot to turn back.

"Whose *rules* are we following here?" she murmured, her lips brushing gently over Finley's. She let her hands trail over Finley's chest, wrapping them around her neck as she kept her eyes trained on hooded mocha. "You know I like you too. And I've wanted you since you called me from my own bathtub, and now that you're here, I don't wanna wait."

"Are you sure?"

Sophie grinned.

Finley's body was already pressed tight against her own, and she was already walking them back through the flat with a purpose that coiled tight in Sophie's core as she let herself be led blindly. She couldn't tear her eyes from the fire in Finley's gaze, and she gripped a little tighter around her neck, her nails dragging over the goosebumped skin.

She gasped as the back of her thighs collided with the edge of the sideboard in the living room, and Finley's hands gripped firmly over her ass as she hoisted her up onto it. Sophie wrapped her legs around Finley's waist, her eyes rolling back as Finley's hips pushed forward and her lips ghosted over her jaw and onto her neck, her hands trailing the tops of her thighs.

There was something *obscenely* sexy to Sophie about the fact that Finley's body had been so close to her own for so long now, the touches and the eye contact so *intimate,* and yet she hadn't *kissed* her since the Tower. Since the kiss that had quite literally changed Sophie's world.

Like she knew that as soon as she did, the fuse would be lit.

Like it would be that kiss that would break them.

And Sophie wanted *nothing* more.

"I'm *so* sure. I *want* you," Sophie groaned, her fingers gripping hard into the fabric over the back of Finley's shirt in an effort to keep her control. "But if you want to slow down, Fin, we can," she assured. "It isn't only me who has to consent here, you know."

Finley smirked against the skin of her neck, and Sophie held her breath.

She couldn't see the smirk, but something in it just *felt* like trouble.

Like a switch being flipped.

Finley's fingers dug into the curves of her thighs, her hips rolling fluidly as the soft brush of her lips pressed harder, and hotter, and Sophie felt the liquid heat of the open-mouthed kisses pool instantly between her thighs. She fisted her hand into Finley's hair, her head falling back under the slow curl of a tongue over her pulse point, and she was powerless to fight the soft moans that escaped her own lips.

Holy *fuck.*

She'd known this would be good. With the intensity of the heat between them, it had been inevitable, but *this* was already exceeding *every* expectation, and she couldn't quite believe, just how hot her body burned for Finley already.

"Of *course* I want you, Soph," Finley husked, low and gravelly. She punctuated the words with a curl of her tongue over the shell of Sophie's ear, and Sophie's jaw dropped open. Finley chuckled darkly, and Sophie's blood set alight. "And you have *consent* to do *whatever* you want to me."

Sophie was gone.

Completely gone.

Her skin was on fire beneath way too many layers of clothing, and she couldn't take another second of this.

Finley pulled back, her eyes meeting Sophie's for a long, torturously charged moment of electricity.

Then Finley smirked. That dangerous, hot as all hell smirk, and Sophie was done.

Sophie pushed both hands into dark hair, tugging hard as she finally pulled Finley into a kiss. The movements were slow, deep, practically animalistic in their lust fuelled hunger, and Sophie's hips ground forward instinctively as she lost herself in the unbearable heat of the kiss.

Finley's hands were *everywhere,* sure and firm, and her hips rolled tight against Sophie's in the *slowest* of movements that made Sophie's head swim and her spine tighten.

It was becoming a very feasible possibility that Sophie could come like this, and she was fast losing any ability to hold back.

She whimpered as Finley sucked her lower lip into her mouth, and she tugged once again in tousled hair. Finley's responding hoarse groan gripped hard on the hairs on the back of Sophie's neck, seeping *molten* through her heated veins, and pooling thickly between her thighs.

*Fuck.*

Sophie's clit throbbed, her muscles twitching and her entire body burning with the almost overwhelming need to make *that* sound happen again.

Preferably multiple times.

She growled, dropping her feet to the floor as she pushed forward with an unexpected level of strength, her hands not leaving Finley's hair as Sophie guided her backwards towards the sofa.

Finley huffed out a choked laugh as she landed on her back, her hands gripping harder over Sophie's thighs. Mocha eyes flared with both shock and deep arousal, following Sophie's every move as she straddled Finley's lap. Sophie bit her lip, the glaze of lust in those usually soft eyes making her confidence soar.

And she wanted to *ruin* Finley.

She wanted to break down that soft and playful exterior until she was unrestrained and unbridled. Wanted to unleash the fire she could see behind those *ridiculously* sexy eyes.

She pressed her hands over Finley's chest, pinning her down as she began to grind her hips, slow and firm over the seam of Finley's jeans.

Finley let out a shaky gasp, and Sophie smirked.

"Do you have *any* idea how *hard* it's been, wanting you from 300 miles away?" She murmured; her eyes trained on Finley's almost predatory gaze as she ground her hips.

"You *know* I do," Finley groaned.

"Knowing you were thinking about me," Sophie husked. "Knowing you were flustered and writhing in my sheets while I touched myself over you."

*"Sophie…"*

The low growl sounded like a warning, and Sophie's spine melted at the almost painful fire in Finley's eyes. The clear battle between the idea of taking the control that she so clearly loved back, and the idea of letting Sophie tear her apart.

There was something so intimate, and so sensual to Sophie about the fact that they were both still fully clothed; had barely touched each other, and yet she could see the flush in Finley's chest, hear the heave of her breath, and feel the way her hips stuttered beneath the grind of Sophie's movements.

*"Baby…"* Finley whispered.

"Mmmm?" Sophie closed her fingers tight around a fistful of Finley's shirt, dragging her nails over the skin beneath it as she rolled her hips in tighter, more deliberate movements.

*"Fuck."* Finley's eyes fluttered closed for a brief moment, her hips bucking softly as she gripped hard on the sides of Sophie's thighs. "Baby, I want to see you."

Sophie smirked. She pushed herself upright, her hips never ceasing their motion as she slipped her hands slowly beneath the hem of all…*eight* or whatever, of her own shirts. She trailed them over her sides, lifting the tight material up and over her head.

Finley's eyes dropped, hooding instantly as her lips parted in open appreciation.

Sophie trailed her hands back down her own sides, brushing the backs of her fingers over the curves of her breasts as she passed them.

Finley growled.

She pushed up immediately, her hands and her lips devouring every inch of newly exposed skin, and Sophie's entire body rippled with goosebumps at the unexpected sensation.

*This* was what she had wanted.

And it had barely taken a touch.

Sophie tugged frantically at the buttons of Finley's shirt, the need for skin to roll over skin becoming unbearable. But before her trembling fingers could ease the first button, Finley grunted, hoisting her up over her hips as she stood with a display of strength that flooded Sophie's already ruined underwear.

*"Fuck,* baby, what…?" She groaned as Finley's lips found her pulse point, her tongue and her teeth mercilessly working the sensitive flesh.

"Bedroom," Finley grunted, her hands gripping over Sophie's ass as she manoeuvred them effortlessly through the house. "I *need* you."

~ ~ ~ ~ ~ ~ 🔥 ~ ~ ~ ~ ~ ~

Finley's body pulsed, electricity coursing her veins as she pinned Sophie to the bed, their fingers laced together in a bind of Sophie's hands above her head.

Sophie's back arched, her skin flushed as she pressed into Finley's touch, and Finley groaned as she rolled her hips into the writhing body beneath her.

Sophie Cedars was a goddamn tease and she *knew* it, but there was something in the way she was watching Finley now that said she was *definitely* not averse to giving up the control either.

And Finley was more than willing to deliver.

She couldn't quite believe the way that things had turned around for her in just a day. Just hours ago, Finley had been alone in Sophie's bed in Polcarne, whispering the name of a girl she'd never met as her own fingertips brought her to orgasm.

And now.

*Now.*

She bit back a chuckle as she trailed a hand down the outside of Sophie's arm, her heart pounding at the goosebumps that rose beneath her touch.

*How* could the air feel so playful and yet so fucking *intense?*

She slipped her fingers over Sophie's jaw, just enough pressure to hold her still as she claimed her lips in a torturously soft kiss. She rolled her hips, holding the movement at the same speed and the same delicate pressure as the kiss.

Until Sophie whimpered, her hands gripping over Finley's ass in a pleading effort to increase the contact.

Finley sank down, slipping her tongue over Sophie's lips as she ground her hips down mercilessly, her fingers gripping harder over Sophie's jaw and the curve of her hip. She felt her muscles tighten, every inch of her skin burning with her arousal as Sophie's hand flew to her hair. Sophie clutched tightly, kissing Finley with a carnal intensity that made her throb.

Sophie moaned, the desperate heat in the vibrations seeping through the kiss and low into Finley's stomach.

Finley smirked. Sophie was putty. *Right* where she wanted her.

She pulled back, her hips and the pressure of her kiss feather-light once more, her tongue just barely teasing Sophie's trembling lips. Sophie whimpered in protest, her fingers tugging once again at the buttons of Finley's shirt, and Finley broke away with a devilish grin. She lifted her body entirely, her pulse racing in her ears as she watched darkened green eyes map her movements, and Sophie's tongue dart out to wet her lips.

"*Fin,*" Sophie whimpered, her back arching as she fought to keep the contact. "You're being a goddamn *tease.*"

Finley smirked. She couldn't deny that she was enjoying the tease, and the push and pull, and the slightly desperate glaze in Sophie's eyes, but there was something in the fire behind the lust-filled green that was making it impossible to hold back any further. She'd been enjoying the way that they'd worked each other so high without undressing, but under Sophie's watch now she felt *way* too warm, and her skin way too sensitive to handle the fabrics that pressed against it.

"*Fuck it,*" she chuckled, her resolve crumbling in an instant. She moved her hands to the hem of her own shirt, forgoing the buttons as she pulled it over her head.

Sophie grinned in triumph, her eyes darkening impossibly as she mapped her gaze over the newly exposed skin, her kiss-swollen lip trapped between her teeth. She reached forward, hooking her forefinger through the v of Finley's bra, tugging until Finley sank back down against her.

The kiss was *insane.* Finley had never melted into a kiss quite like this, and she was fast losing control of her desire. She rolled her body tight against Sophie's as she bit down on her lower lip, the responding low moans only spurring her on.

The sounds burned in her core, and the overwhelming need to *consume* blazed through her veins.

With one more hoarse groan from Sophie, Finley snapped.

She broke the kiss, tugging in Sophie's hair to pull her head roughly to the side. There was no light trail, no gentle tease this time. She let her tongue roam the length of Sophie's neck, sucking the flesh into her mouth every time she found a spot that made Sophie gasp.

"Baby, *please,*" Sophie whispered, her voice strained as she clutched desperately in Finley's hair, her legs wrapped tight around her rolling hips.

The plea was like gasoline, and Finley's core throbbed at the sound. She was *completely* entranced, utterly unable to tear her lips and her tongue away from the flushed skin of Sophie's neck, or her fingers from the underside of Sophie's thigh, or the silky auburn waves tangled around them.

Until Sophie's grip tightened almost painfully in Finley's own hair, pulling her forcefully back to meet her gaze. Finley growled, the force of the tug shooting straight between her thighs.

*Fuck,* the things she wanted to do to this woman.

And that *plea.*

She wanted to hear it again. She wanted Sophie to beg her.

She watched in an almost sinister amusement, her eyes hooded as a determined fire bled through the desperation in Sophie's gaze.

"Please wha…"

Sophie quirked an eyebrow, her fingers moving to the front clasp of her own bra, and Finley's words died in her mouth as her eyes followed the movement.

*Holy* god damn fuck.

She swallowed thickly, her arousal tightening into an unbearable lump in her throat as the material of the bra fell away, and she took in the bare curves of Sophie's breasts, and the hardened nipples that made her mouth water. She huffed out a harsh breath, her arousal gripping her every muscle.

It was frankly *ridiculous* how gorgeous Sophie was.

And it was almost *irritating* how much she *wanted* her, and something about it burned a fire in Finley that left her desperate to wipe that unfairly smug smirk off Sophie's face.

She sank down, her lips wasting no time in closing in around Sophie's nipple, circling the flat of her tongue hard over the sensitive bud. She smirked as Sophie gasped, and she sucked hard as Sophie's back arched into the touch. She trailed her kisses down, letting her fingertips tease over the inside of Sophie's thighs as she devoured trembling abs, and a writhing stomach, her tongue and her lips leaving no mercy.

She could feel the fumbling movements of Sophie's fingers beneath her, tugging frantically at the button of her own jeans.

Finley grinned.

She pulled back, her eyes finding Sophie's as she wrapped her fingers around her wrists, halting the desperate movements. She drew Sophie's hand to her own lips, slipping the fingers that had fumbled with the button into her mouth, her tongue gently teasing the pads.

Sophie's eyes rolled back, the muscles of her stomach visibly clenching.

"*Bennett,* you're fucking *killing* me," she whined, her head thrown back as she fought to control her heaving chest. She growled, tugging hard in Finley's hair. "Just *take* my goddamn clothes off, I can't take this anymore."

Finley chuckled darkly. She bit down gently over the flesh below Sophie's belly button, her eyes finding glowering green once more as she slowly worked the button and the zipper of Sophie's jeans. She teased the fabric down slowly over Sophie's legs, the gentle movement a stark contrast to the rough nips and kisses her teeth and her tongue littered over the trembling stomach and the tops of straining thighs beneath her. She smirked as Sophie brought a hand to her own mouth, biting down on a curled forefinger in an effort to hold back the frustrated growl that Finley could feel rumbling through her tightened body.

Finley was in her own nirvana.

Sophie was almost bare before her; the only remaining scrap of fabric visibly damp between restless thighs. Her skin was flushed and goosebumped, and her soft muscles were drawn tight in every area of her body as she writhed beneath Finley's teasing touches. Her eyes were wild; dark and predatory as they bore into Finley's own, and Finley was a thousand percent certain that she had never seen anything so fucking sexy in all of her thirty years on the planet.

She sucked hard over the sharp bone of Sophie's hip, and her stomach dropped at the ravenous *growl* that filled the air between them.

A *loaded* sound that flooded deep in Finley's core.

The carnal sound of Sophie's limit breaking.

Finley had absolutely *no* idea how it happened. The fierce pull in her hair, or the flip of their positions, or the rough and frantic hands that ripped and tugged at her own clothing until she was as bare as Sophie was, her head swimming and her muscles trembling under the merciless assault. She barely had time to process the silk and the heat of Sophie's body sinking down onto her own before her lips were claimed in the *filthiest* of kisses; hungry, and desperate, and animalistic.

Finley's mind was so clouded; so thick with her arousal and her lust, and the unbridled pleasure of Sophie's onslaught, that she was powerless to do anything but moan, her hands clutching at any part of Sophie's body she could reach.

And then those filthy kisses dropped down, the heat that burned beneath them growing hotter with every movement over Finley's neck and her chest. Unyielding lips tugged at her nipples and her abs and the soft curves of her stomach, and Finley whimpered as the ache between her legs grew unbearable.

Fucking *Christ,* how had she lost the control *so* quickly?

And so *completely?*

She sank back, surrendering to Sophie's touch entirely as insistent lips found her own once more, the kisses broken only by unbridled moans and gasps.

Finley whimpered into the kiss, her spine trembling as Sophie's hand slipped seamlessly between their bodies, her fingertips lightly grazing the crease of Finley's thigh. She broke away, her breath falling too hard and fast to focus as those teasing fingers trailed over the wet, swollen flesh either side of where she so desperately wanted them, still yet to slip into the heat that waited for them.

"Oh fuck, Sophie *please,*" Finley gasped, her hips bucking as those fingers pulled back slightly, nails dragging instead over the inside of her thighs.

*God,* Finley was a mess. She couldn't remember ever being as turned on as this, and she clamped her jaw shut in an effort to control her pleas as Sophie's lips trailed over the column of her throat. The way the touches of those goddamn fingers were *so* close, over the most sensitive of skin that she *knew* would be coated in the evidence of how much she needed Sophie's touch. It was almost physically painful, and the tease was beyond torturous.

Then Sophie's fingers trailed feather-light over her, and Finley's entire body clenched tight.

*Jesus.*

"Oh my god, Sophie you're too fucking much," she groaned, her hips writhing as they chased the movement of those *fucking* fingers.

"What do you want, baby?" Sophie smirked, biting down on Finley's lower lip.

Finley whimpered. The smug tone of that voice *should* have fuelled the fire to fight back; to reclaim her control. But she was too far gone. She needed the touch too badly, and instead the cocky push only made her more desperate.

"You. I want *you,*" she sobbed. She gripped Sophie's ass, her body rigid as she fought against the burning arousal pulling her under. *"Fuck,* Sophie I've never..."

She trailed off, blinking back tears of arousal and frustration as Sophie's fingers rested between her thighs, either side of her clit, and squeezed.

"You what, baby?" Sophie murmured, her tone nothing short of smug as she squeezed again.

Finley choked out a groan, her lips quirking into an amused grin despite the battle for her sanity.

*God,* she liked this woman.

"I've never *wanted* anyone like I want you," she husked. *"Please,* stop teasing me."

Sophie's eyes flared, her lips parting as she studied Finley's face.

The words hung in the air for a long moment, lacing through the tension and pulling it impossibly tighter.

Then Sophie smirked, dropping in to kiss Finley, slow and deep, and Finley's body sank back against the bed under the touch.

Then her fingers slipped lower, sinking hard into Finley without hesitation, and Finley dug her nails into Sophie's ass as she cried out into the kiss.

*"Fuck!* Sophie!"

She'd been expecting—and desperately fighting for—the touch on her clit.

This was *not* what she had expected, but the movement had her body tightening so hard she was in danger of coming on the spot.

She tried to keep her eyes focused on Sophie's, the dark fire in them intensifying with every thrust of her fingers. But under that lust-drunk gaze, and the irresistible lips that danced *just* out of reach, and the roll of her body into thrusts that were hitting her clit in exactly the way she needed it, Finley was completely losing her mind. She let her eyes flutter closed, her hands gripping at the sheets for something to ground her as the pleasure ripped her sanity to shreds.

Finley moaned as Sophie's lips claimed her own in those *unbelievable* kisses once more. She was on fire. She didn't know *what* Sophie was doing with her fingers, but it felt like she was *everywhere.* The relentless thrusts that curled against the spots that made Finley see stars, and the pressure of her palm over her clit, and the sporadic tease of the sensitive skin of her thighs and her stomach and her ass that Finley had *no* idea how Sophie was achieving. It was all too much, and the moans that the actions were ripping from Finley's chest were so husky and so gravelly that she didn't recognise the sound of her own voice.

Sophie's kisses trailed back down over her neck she dropped her weight onto one elbow, their bodies pressing impossibly tight together as they moved. Finley's hips began to buck up into Sophie's touch, and she clutched at the curves of her ass in an effort to increase the pressure.

"Can I make you come baby?" Sophie murmured, the words echoing through the column of Finley's throat. She bit down gently over Finley's pulse point as she curled her fingers forward. "I wanna make you come as hard as I came over you this morning."

Finley whimpered.

She wanted a smart response, but she was completely at Sophie's mercy and she was pretty sure she was one curl of those fingers away from her orgasm anyway, so she was in no position to be playing games.

She was completely ready to surrender.

*"Yes,"* she sobbed. "Baby, please make me come, I'm *so* close."

Sophie changed the angle, dropping her thrusts shorter and sharper as she drove persistently into the spot that made Finley delirious.

Finley sobbed. Her throat was hoarse with the gravel of her moans, her strained words fighting to tell Sophie how good she made her feel; how hard she was coming, but she wasn't sure the words were intelligible through the sobs and the moans and the cries that the pleasure ripped from her body.

Finley's vision blacked, her entire body shuddering with pleasure as her orgasm gripped her, and she clutched hard at Sophie's shoulders as she rode through her high. Finley's brain swam, but she was *just* aware enough to absorb the soft murmurs of reassurance in her ear, and the flick of a tongue over the flesh below it, and the gentle rake of soothing fingers through her hair.

The heat that had burned so stifling grew softer for a moment, and Finley's lips still trembled with her orgasm as Sophie claimed them in a languid, lazy kiss. Finley grinned almost giddily as she felt Sophie smile into the kiss, her nose brushing gently over Finley's.

Then Sophie sat back, holding Finley's gaze as she withdrew her fingers, bringing them to her lips without hesitation.

And the inferno was lit *immediately.*

Finley wasn't waiting any more.

She growled, gripping Sophie's waist as she surged forward. She flipped them effortlessly, hoisting Sophie's hips to the edge of the bed. She closed her fingers over the thin bands of Sophie's underwear, tugging them down as she sank to her knees.

Sophie gasped, her eyes flying wide as Finley gripped her thighs, pinning them open.

Finley smirked, her hooded gaze fixed on Sophie's as she trailed her tongue instantly between Sophie's thighs, closing her lips over her clit the moment she reached it.

Sophie cried out.

*"Shit."*

~ ~ ~ ~ ~ ~ 🦋 ~ ~ ~ ~ ~ ~

Sophie's legs trembled as she let herself slump into Finley's arms, her third orgasm of the night still coursing through her veins.

The heat between them still burned, completely insatiable in its intensity and its newness, but the afterglow of another high had left a little room for softer touches for just a moment.

Sophie couldn't deny that she *loved* the way that sex with Finley had been so *lust* fuelled. She wasn't afraid to admit that she hadn't ever had an emotional connection to someone quite like the pull she felt to Finley, and on some inexperienced level she had worried that a soft bond like that would always come with softer touches and a different kind of heat.

But Finley Bennett had well and truly proved her wrong. She had fucked her in the most carnal, animalistic way that Sophie had ever experienced, and the connection was only burning stronger as a result.

And *now,* after hours of unbearable hunger, the look in deep mocha eyes was softening to the warm glow that Sophie had expected.

Sophie pushed herself back, her chest swelling as Finley's eyes followed her movements.

She had never felt so wanted, and the reverence in Finley's face as she watched her was starting to feel a lot like something she never wanted to *stop* feeling.

She shuffled back, ignoring the screaming shake of her worn muscles as she straddled Finley's hips.

She moved slowly, her core still almost painfully sensitive as it ground over Finley's sweat-sheened skin, but it was impossible to care under the awed gaze of those *incredible* eyes.

Sophie was finding she was falling for a lot of things about Finley Bennett. Her easy humour, and her warm nature, and her stubborn determination. Her smile, and her laugh, and those full lips. Everything those lips did, and everything they said. The soft curves of her stomach, and that *ass.*

But more than anything, it was those eyes.

It was those eyes, and how *expressive* they were. And how they really seemed to *see* Sophie, and how sexy and smart and listened to and wanted she felt under their gaze.

And her muscles burned and shook, and her clit twitched with the oversensitivity of the grind of her hips, but Sophie was powerless to stop because she just wanted those eyes to keep looking at her like *that.*

"Tonight has been incredible, Finley," she husked, her spine tingling as Finley's hands found her hips.

"*You're* incredible," Finley murmured, her own hips beginning to circle to meet Sophie's.

"You make me *feel* it," Sophie moaned. "God, the way you *look* at me."

Finley's eyes misted, her lips tugging into a soft smile. She shook her head, something a lot like disbelief flickering across her face.

"Jude Law's got nothing on this," she whispered.

She blushed immediately, her hands and her hips halting their movements as she grimaced.

Sophie halted.

Then she laughed.

The reference, the blush, and the wrinkled nose were beyond adorable, and it only served to make her want Finley more.

"Touch me, Fin."

Finley's eyes fluttered open, the air shifting once again as she huffed out a harsh breath of arousal.

She inhaled shakily, her eyes hooded and her lips parted as she brought her fingers between Sophie's, groaning softly at the evidence of her readiness for her.

Still.

Again.

She sank her fingers in, and Sophie's entire body rippled with the immediate pleasure as she began to roll her hips over the touch.

She was transfixed, completely unable to tear her eyes from Finley's as she moved, the orgasm that finally splintered her bones more intense than anything she had ever felt, under that gaze.

And London was *definitely* seeming more and more appealing with Finley Bennett in it.

# Chapter Twenty-Two

"Do we *really* need to go?" Sophie groaned, pouting as she hauled herself from the bed, and away from the warmth of Finley's body.

She shivered a little, as she pulled open the drawer she had stored her clothes in, her body immediately aching to be back in Finley's arms. The burn of that dark gaze behind her was making it *very* difficult not to do exactly that, but they were on a schedule and they were now bordering on late.

And Sophie *hated* being late.

"No, absolutely not," Finley answered.

Sophie glanced over her shoulder at Finley still sprawled across the bed. She shook her head in amusement at the way wide eyes were glued to her naked ass, the pupils blown.

"You're *supposed* to say you've already bought the tickets and your friends are expecting us to come," she grinned. "Stop being a perv and get up!"

*"Noah* bought the tickets, and *you* agreed to it," Finley challenged, her eyes still tracking Sophie's ass. She wriggled her eyebrows, grinning cheekily as her eyes finally flicked up to meet Sophie's. "And *I'm* very *much* expecting us to come."

Sophie pursed her lips.

*"That* was fucking *dreadful,"* she teased.

She swayed her hips a little though.

Just to entice that gaze back to the curves of her ass.

"I can't be blamed, I'm *distracted,"* Finley murmured. She pulled herself up, crawling to kneel on the end of the bed, and Sophie felt her skin flame at the intent in teasing eyes.

She giggled as firm hands grasped her hips, tugging her back. Until Finley's lips began to trail heated kisses over her shoulders, then down over her spine, and the giggles petered quickly into soft gasps of anticipation.

They were already so late.

For this exact reason.

They *really* needed to get dressed and go.

And yet as Finley's lips and tongue teased at the curves of her ass; Sophie found herself pressing back into the touch.

She was putty; powerless to resist, and she knew it.

And *Finley* knew it.

"You're *insatiable,*" Sophie moaned, her head tipping back as Finley bit down on the goosebumped skin of her ass.

"Because you're *irresistible,*" Finley murmured, low and gravelly against Sophie's skin. She slipped her fingers between Sophie's thighs, trailing the tips softly through the pool of undeniable arousal. She groaned, her lips curling into a smirk that Sophie could feel against her ass. *"Oh,* and I'm not the *only* one who's insatiable."

Sophie moaned, her resolve instantly crumbling around Finley's touch.

"Just shut up and fuck me, Bennett."

*"Again?"* Finley teased; her sing-song tone smug. She drew her fingers back. "But baby, we have places to *be,* people to see."

Sophie growled.

*"You* started this, now you…"

She squeaked, her words dying in her throat as Finley's hands wrapped around her thighs, and through some feat of practically inhuman strength, Sophie found herself hauled onto the bed, looking down over the length of Finley's naked body as Sophie straddled her face.

"Holy *fuck,* that should be *illegal,*" she stammered, her arms flailing slightly in search of something to hold her shaking muscles upright.

Finley chuckled, the heated breaths that hit between Sophie's thighs pooling instantly into liquid desire.

Sophie shuddered.

And then Finley's irresistible lips were wrapped around Sophie's clit, and her tongue was doing that thing that Sophie could *not* understand, that made her entire body surge with megavolt electricity, and Sophie surrendered any hope of holding herself upright.

She cried out, letting her body fall forward. She caught herself on Finley's thighs, her fingers trembling as they gripped the curves tightly.

Jesus *Christ,* this woman was a *god* with her tongue.

Sophie whimpered, her hips rolling almost desperately as the pleasure cascaded through her veins, her arms beginning to tremble as she held herself over Finley's thighs.

She was aware, somehow, through the hazy fog of burning pleasure and arousal, of Finley's own hips bucking subtly below her, the muscles of her thighs rippling beneath Sophie's hands as she moved.

Sophie smirked.

She pushed Finley's thighs apart, and dropped down. The cry of shocked pleasure as she wrapped her lips around Finley's clit rumbled mercilessly through her stomach, pushing her dangerously close to the edge.

She sobbed, her hips beginning to grind down over Finley's face with purpose.

Sophie had always been a little uncertain about this position in the past. With men in particular, she'd always found it a bit gratuitous, and she'd never seen it as a particularly great opportunity for emotional intimacy, but *this*...

This was something else entirely.

The vulnerability, and the dual pleasure of giving and receiving simultaneously. Finley's moans against her, and the way she almost subconsciously seemed to guide Sophie to what she wanted with the movements of her own tongue. The way her fingers trailed Sophie's spine in a feather-soft contrast to the firm heat of her mouth, and the way they seemed to roll together in their movements as they chased their own orgasm as well as each other's. It all felt like a delicious extension of the strength of their connection, and Sophie was *desperate* for them to reach their highs together.

She wanted to speak. She wanted to ask if Finley was close, but she couldn't tear her lips from the pulsing heat beneath her, and she could barely think straight through the delirious pleasure of that goddamn tongue.

Then Finley's hips were shaking, her moans falling faster and shorter over Sophie's clit, and Sophie was tumbling headfirst into her own orgasm before she even had the chance to register Finley's cries.

She pressed her tongue firmly against Finley as they both rode out their highs, their hips jerking messily into each other as they fought to prolong their own pleasure.

Sophie collapsed over Finley's thighs, her chest heaving and her stomach somersaulting at the way Finley visibly clenched with her aftershocks.

She giggled.

If anything was worth being late, it was *definitely* this.

~ ~ ~ ~ ~ ~ ✍ ~ ~ ~ ~ ~ ~

Sophie's body practically floated through the ticket barriers to the music festival at Hyde Park, Finley's arm wrapped around her waist.

The park looked *amazing;* food and drinks vans lining the sides, and a huge stage across the back centre boasting hundreds of bright lights, and a woven kind of shrubbery wound across the metal beams, surreal in its effort to appear a part of the nature around it.

And the *sounds* were indescribable. Somehow both all-consuming and yet faded and muted at the same time. The low thrum of the music that almost vibrated along the grass of the park, and the hum of chatter from the thousands of people milling about the grounds. And distantly, the usual hustle and bustle of the city of London around them.

There were people *everywhere,* and Sophie was almost euphoric as the atmosphere buoyed her.

The atmosphere, and the way Finley's fingers stroked her side absently as they made their way through the crowds in the direction of the drinks van that Noah had told them they were waiting beside.

She was a little more on edge than she wanted to be. She had been for the past three days, overly aware of the shape of her phone burning against her thigh from inside her pocket. She hated the way it distracted her mind, from London and from her experiences, and from Finley. But she couldn't help it. She couldn't rid her mind's eye of the sight of her nephew in that hospital bed, with the white and the clinical blues around him, and the tubes in his veins, and the blood drawn from his face.

She knew he was okay, really. She understood enough about Diabetes, and she'd done a *lot* of research in the days since Jack's diagnosis, and she trusted her sister. Bex had cared for Sophie, and for their mum, and for her little family for most of her life, and Sophie knew she was more than capable. Far more capable than Sophie herself ever could be. But she also knew how tired Bex was. How tightly drawn the lines by her eyes were. And she wanted to be there for her. Pete was lovely. He really was, he was a wonderful husband, and a wonderful father.

But he also had the very frustrating tendency to be bloody *useless* in the face of emergency, and Sophie knew that Bex would always have to be the one to step up.

So, who was caring for her?

It worried Sophie, and it made her shoulders feel stiff, and her jaw feel tight, and her focus remain, constantly, at least half on her phone. And with her focus half on her phone, she was always one thought train away from packing her bags and fleeing back to the coast.

Which she didn't *want* to do. For all her insistence and her concern, deep down she knew she agreed with Bex. If she went home now, she would never leave again. And this city, this life, these people…Sophie wanted to entertain this for a while. She wanted to keep imagining the way she would feel if she woke in this city every morning. With the lights, and the bustle, and the opportunities.

And Finley.

It had not passed Sophie by that the only time her mind had *not* been on her phone and waiting for Bex's replies, was while Finley Bennett had her pinned to a mattress.

Or while she was straddling Finley. Or between her thighs. Or touching her in any way at all, frankly.

And Sophie didn't want to leave this. Not now. Not yet.

Not when she'd only just found it.

She grinned as she caught sight of the group of Finley's friends, the familiar faces of Noah, Harri, Kate and Zayan, all waving them over. Sophie pushed her thoughts down, ignoring the burn in her pocket as she leaned a little more against Finley's side.

"What time do you call this, Bennett?" Harri scolded, shaking their head as their lips pulled into a teasing smile. "First time we're seeing you in *months* and you rock up over an hour late!"

Sophie giggled as Finley rolled her eyes.

"Look at that *smile* though!" Kate sang, wrapping her arm around Harri's shoulder. "I think we can wait an hour if she shows up with *that* on her face."

Finley blushed.

Sophie grinned.

She wrapped her arms around Finley's middle, hugging her tighter as she leaned her head against her shoulder.

"Great to see you again, Sophie." Kate winked. "Bennett, come get the drinks in with me. I haven't seen you in an age and you *clearly* need to fill me in on a few things."

Finley grinned, shaking her head as she dropped her arm from around Sophie's waist.

"I won't be a minute babe," Finley whispered, pressing her lips softly to Sophie's temple. "What're you drinking?"

"A cider please." Sophie turned to face Finley, brushing her nose lightly over Finley's own. "Something fruity."

Sophie couldn't hold back her smile as Finley leaned in to kiss her, and the group around them erupted immediately into a chorus of whoops and cheers. Finley huffed out a laugh as she broke away, her cheeks flushing deep red with the tint of a blush.

"Guys, we're *thirty,* have I hit my head and woken up in primary school?" Finley grumbled.

"Look don't get grumpy just 'cause we dragged you from your sex cave," Kate chuckled, her voice carrying just enough to hear. "Number of hickeys under that collar, I'd say it's about time you came up for air!"

Finley's neck burned deeper, and Sophie giggled at the patches of red embarrassment spreading across the skin of Finley's chest. Sophie *might* have been embarrassed herself, but she knew full well she'd only left one distinguishable mark on Finley's body, and it was a *lot* lower down than the public eye could see.

Sophie beamed as she watched Finley shove Kate's shoulder lightly with her own as they walked towards the bar. She nodded her head to the music, feeling her body relax into the warmth of the sun. Despite her bubbling fears for Jack and her uncertainty about going home, Sophie knew her beaming smile hadn't left her face since the minute she'd opened the door to Finley yesterday, and she was having a very difficult time keeping a lid on just how much she liked this woman.

She jumped a little as Noah slung an arm around her shoulders, and she turned her head to face him.

*"So?"* he prompted.

Sophie smirked.

"So?" She quirked an eyebrow.

Noah sagged.

"Oh, *come on,*" he whined. "I've been awake *all night* waiting to hear how the big romantic meet went!"

Sophie bit back a giggle. The hopeful excitement in Noah's wide eyes, and the way his eyebrows were raised in anticipation were adorable, and she felt a sudden surge of affection for him for everything he had done. For the way he had gone out of his way to make her feel welcome in London, and for the effort and genuine excitement that he had shown for Sophie's budding romance with his best friend. It had felt *good* to know someone in the city was in her corner, and she was exceptionally grateful to him for it.

She beamed.

"Fine!" she giggled. "It was *everything.* I mean, you *saw* her kiss me, right?"

*"Yes!"* Noah exclaimed; his teeth gritted in visible excitement. "So Sophley is *on?"*

*"Sophley?"* Sophie wrinkled her nose.

"Finphie sounded stupid." Noah shrugged. "And you *cannot* be Bendars."

Sophie laughed.

"Well, *I* definitely hope that *Sophley* is on," she murmured, leaning her head against Noah's shoulder as she let her eyes wander to the drinks van, and the flash of familiar dark hair she could pick out in the crowd. "She's *really* amazing, Noah."

"I know," Noah hummed, and Sophie could feel the nod of his head. He nudged her shoulder slightly, and she lifted her head to look at him. "Got enough reasons to become a Londoner yet?"

Sophie smirked.

She was more than happy to admit that she had it *bad,* but she wasn't sure it was wise to have *this* conversation with anyone other than Finley at this point.

She patted Noah's chest in dismissal, and he huffed out a laugh.

"Kate was right, you know." He grinned, dropping his arm from around Sophie's shoulders as Finley began to pick her way back towards them. "I haven't seen Finley smile like that in a *very* long time."

And as Finley made her way back across the park, making a beeline for Sophie with her arms full of cider bottles and cardboard containers of steaming chips, and her face already spread into an adoring, excitable grin, Sophie wasn't sure she'd *ever* smiled like this.

The group settled themselves down onto the grass, close enough to the main stage that the low vibrating thumps morphed into clear beats and energetic melodies. Finley pulled Sophie between her legs, wrapped her own around her as Sophie leaned back against her chest. And Sophie had dated before. Obviously, she had. But she didn't think she could ever remember a time when it had felt so *easy* to be in someone's presence. So natural to seek their touch, and so comfortable to settle into it. She was aware of the glances that Harri, and Zayan, and Kate threw their way, and the little squees that Noah kept trying to hide beside them, and normally it might have made her uneasy. Embarrassed, or coy. But here, with Finley leaving kisses beneath her ear every time she stole a chip from over her shoulder, her free hand teasing soft patterns over Sophie's waist, it only made her feel more content.

Finley's friends looked happy.

Which meant Finley must be happy.

Which *definitely* made Sophie happy.

Sophie leaned back, placing a soft kiss on Finley's cheek, and her stomach filled with butterflies as the muscle raised with Finley's smile before she'd even pulled away. Sophie grinned. She placed another kiss beneath Finley's ear, her butterflies fizzing as Finley shivered.

Sophie smirked.

She buried herself a little closer back into Finley's body, and trailed her tongue over the shell of her ear. Finley gasped, her chest hitching against Sophie's back. Sophie grinned, wrapped her teeth around Finley's earlobe, and tugged.

Finley exhaled hard.

"You alright there, Bennett?" Harri teased. "You look a little hot and bothered."

"Finley Bennett, *please* stop forcing me to witness your sex eyes!" Noah whined.

"Put her *down,* Bennett," Kate laughed. "You are *not* a dog in heat."

"Wh…*why* are you acting like it's *me?"* Finley spluttered, her face burning red and her arms flailing in defensive gestures. "I didn't even *do* anything!"

Sophie giggled, grabbing Finley's flailing arms and wrapping them tight around her waist.

"Because Sophie is a picture of innocence," Kate goaded, grinning impishly at her flustered friend. "And *you* look like your head is full of filth."

Finley raised a brow, turning her face to look at Sophie.

Sophie smiled innocently, miming the shape of a halo above her head.

Finley rolled her eyes, but her lips curled into a fond smile.

"You can all fuck off!" she grumbled, burying her face in Sophie's neck. "Like I never have to endure any of you suck face."

"As the resident asexual," Zayan retorted, jumping to his feet. "I think I'm entitled to a responding 'fuck you', and to steal away your girlfriend."

He reached his hands out to Sophie, and she raised her brow in question.

She ignored the fizz in her belly, and the tightening in Finley's arms at the word 'girlfriend'.

That was *not* a conversation for now.

"Uh…probably should follow that up with an explanation of what for, bud," Finley replied.

Zayan rolled his eyes.

"To *dance,*" he exclaimed. "Obviously!"

Sophie grinned.

She'd been wondering how long it'd take them to make the most of this music.

She let Zayan drag her to her feet, planting a quick kiss on Finley's cheek as she passed. He led them a few feet forwards into the crowd, with Kate on their heels, and before they'd even stopped walking, Sophie found her muscles moving to the music. She *loved* live music. And it wasn't like Cornwall never had it. She wasn't from the stone age, and Newquay had bars and clubs and venues, but there was just something different about this. Something that felt *new,* and *exotic,* and exciting. Sophie let loose, her hips and her shoulders swaying to the beat, and she could practically *feel* Finley's eyes watching her every move. And something in it made her feel confident.

Powerful.

Unstoppable.

Things she didn't think she'd ever felt, in their entirety. Not before London, and before Finley Bennett.

She liked it.

She beamed widely as she caught Finley's eye, and she winked cheekily. She lifted a hand, beckoning Finley with a curling finger. Finley grinned, muttering something unreadable to Noah and Harri, and then she was on her feet.

The moment Finley reached Sophie, she pulled her into an elaborate, cheesy, hammy, adorable as fuck spin, and a little two step. Then kissed her so deeply that Sophie's head swam, and she swooned so hard her knees would have given way, had Finley's arm not been wrapped so tightly around her waist.

"You having fun?" Finley murmured into her ear.

"Mmmhmm," Sophie hummed. "But there is just one thing missing."

Finley frowned.

"What's that?"

Sophie grinned.

"I believe I was told you were the Queen of Magic Mike moves?"

Finley groaned. She tipped her head back, her ears tinting red, and Sophie giggled.

"And I *believe* I was promised a demonstration?" Sophie teased.

"You were promised a *private* demonstration, Cedars," Finley grumbled playfully. "This is the middle of Hyde Park!"

"You're gonna do it anyway though," Sophie grinned, her fingers stroking gently at the back of Finley's neck. "Aren't you?"

"Probably." Finley smirked, that dirty smirk that never failed to make Sophie's stomach clench. "I'm not sure I know how to say no to you."

Sophie grinned, and Finley wriggled her eyebrows.

She stepped back, her eyes glinting with mischief, and Sophie felt her stomach drop.

Then she did…*something* that Sophie wasn't sure she knew how to put into words. A spin, of sorts. With a kind of pop, and lock, and complete flood of sex appeal that for some absurd reason Sophie hadn't even *thought* to expect.

Then she dropped down, her hips rolling, and Sophie immediately regretted the decision to request this in public.

She swallowed thickly.

*"Yes!"* Noah yelped; his eyes wide with overjoyed surprise as he gawped at his friend.

Harri and Zayan whooped and cheered.

"She's *back,* kids!" Kate sang, jumping a little on the spot as the group circled around Finley.

Sophie giggled, but she couldn't tear her gaze from Finley and the ridiculous, extravagant, embarrassing, and yet supremely sexy dance moves. And the dark, smug, knowing eyes that watched Sophie at every possible moment.

Sophie licked her lips.

She was beginning to feel a bit on edge, her body itching with want to lie in the grass, and let Finley move her hips like that above her. Above her face, preferably.

She jumped as Noah leaned in beside her, his voice just loud enough for Sophie to hear.

"I haven't seen her like this with anyone else ever, Soph."

Sophie frowned.

"Dancing like that?"

"No, just…" Noah paused, considering his words for a moment. "Like *this*. Carefree. Affectionate, soft, happy."

"Not even with Jess?" Sophie whispered.

"God, no," Noah scoffed, shaking his head. "No. This is just you."

Sophie beamed.

Jealousy had never been her favourite trait. Neither had possessiveness. But she'd be lying if she said it didn't make her feel at least a little warm to think that she made Finley feel something no-one else could.

She smirked as Finley prowled towards her, cheeky, and mischievous, and sexy. Sophie reached out for her, wrapping her fingers over Finley's shirt collar, and pulling her grinding body in against Sophie's own.

She regretted it instantly.

They were at a family friendly event, in the middle of a circle of watching friends, and now Finley's hips were rolling over her own in a way that ripped the breath from her throat.

"God, okay, stop it," she groaned, low and quiet. "You've proved your point, now let me live."

Finley chuckled; her lips curled into a dirty grin as she pressed her palms into the small of Sophie's back. Her hips ground a little firmer, and Sophie gasped.

"Fin!" she hissed. "Please, we have an audience, and you are…"

Finley grinned, and Sophie blushed.

"I'm what, Soph?" Finley husked, far too cocky and far too knowing.

"Ruining my underwear," Sophie growled. "Now behave!"

She turned in Finley's arms, deliberately avoiding the fire in mocha eyes, and the way Finley's chest heaved a little heavier at Sophie's words.

She might have felt like a new woman in London, but she didn't think she was quite ready to become an exhibitionist. Or a criminal.

Both of which were dangerously possible if she didn't break herself out of Finley Bennett's Magic Mike spell.

Christ.

She relaxed back into Finley's body as they watched the band play on the stage, and Zayan and Kate danced flamboyantly around them. Finley's hips rolled a little into Sophie's ass in time to the music, and she planted frequent kisses over her neck, and her ear, and her temple, and Sophie would be lying if she said she wasn't getting a little hotter, and melting back a little more with every soft caress of those lips over her skin and fingers over her waistband.

She was completely besotted with the way it felt to be around Finley and her friends. How easily she slotted into the small group. How Finley still managed to make her feel like the most important person in the world, even while she caught up with friends she clearly hadn't seen in a while.

Finley Bennett was definitely a charmer, and Sophie was falling more by the second for London and all of its *charms.*

# Chapter Twenty-Three

Finley chuckled as Sophie's brow furrowed, her eyes flickering impossibly fast as she re-read the clues over her phone screen.

Finley had known the treasure-hunt-style Hidden London walks existed for *years,* but she'd never taken the time to complete any, and the way Sophie had so excitably picked apart the clues, a glimmer of unabashed self-satisfaction in her eyes at every successful turn, made her eternally grateful that she'd waited until now to experience them. Everything in the city seemed so much *brighter* with Sophie in it, and she made Finley want to experience things she hadn't strived for in a *really* long time.

Sophie was beautiful, and sweet, and sunny, and painfully skilled at flustering Finley into a useless pile of mush with a well pointed look and a few flirty words. But she was also driven, and determined, and fiery, and *just* the right amount of stubborn.

And smart.

*So* smart that it made Finley's knees weak, and she wondered, not for the first time, if it was possible to fall in love in less than two weeks.

She sighed.

*Fuck* she was a cliche.

"Under the right-hand arch, which body part can you see?" Sophie read the clue aloud, turning her gaze to the curved building of Admiralty Arch. She frowned. *"Body part?"*

Sophie practically skipped toward the archways, and Finley grinned, stumbling a little over her own shoes as she fought to keep up.

She chuckled as she came to a stop, Sophie's brow furrowed and her lips curled up in confusion.

"Is that a *nose?"* Sophie tilted her head as she looked up at the protrusion from the stone wall.

"Hoping for something more exciting?" Finley grinned.

"Honestly?" Sophie wrinkled her nose. *"Yeah,* I thought it might at least have been boobs."

Finley laughed.

"In the middle of Admiralty Arch?" she teased, wrapping her arm around Sophie's waist. "Perv."

Sophie scowled.

"Oh 'cause statues are always so *chaste?"* she retorted, narrowing her eyes in Finley's direction. She smirked, turning to twist both hands into the front of Finley's shirt as she dropped her voice to a low murmur. "Luckily for *me,* I have the *perfect* body to perv over anywhere I like."

Finley raised an eyebrow, her gaze dropping instinctively over Sophie's body as she tugged her closer.

*"Yes,* you do."

"I meant *yours,"* Sophie laughed.

"Mine?" Finley grinned, brushing her lips over Sophie's smirk. *"Anywhere* you like, eh?"

"Yep." Sophie's hands trailed up over Finley's chest and onto the collars of her shirt, her fingers hooking beneath the spread and pulling it back just enough to allow her gaze to drop beneath the material.

Finley laughed, gripping Sophie's hands and pushing her, giggling, back against the wall. She bit down on Sophie's lower lip, slipping her tongue hotly into her mouth for the briefest of moments before dropping down over her neck.

"This is a Grade I listed building, Sophie Cedars," she murmured. "Don't make me defile you against it."

*"Ooh,* talk architecture to me," Sophie husked, her eyes sparkling with playful amusement. "It's *very* sexy when you get all passionate."

Finley grinned.

Yeah.

Cliche or not.

She was pretty sure she was falling in love.

~ ~ ~ ~ ~ ~ ♪ ~ ~ ~ ~ ~ ~

Finley was halfway through a delicious vegan brunch with the most adorable date she had ever had, when her phone rang for the third time that day.

She suppressed a frown, trying her hardest to ignore the buzzing against her thigh as Sophie regaled her with stories of Trevor's cheese making ventures. She'd been aware of her phone, and aware of the calls that she'd been letting go to her voicemail. She'd been hyper aware of the anxiety in her stomach over the unheard messages, and the unanswered question that sat heavy on her chest. But she couldn't bring herself to answer.

Two days ago, she'd been ready. She'd been antsy, and buzzing, and raring to get her answers, storming brazenly into the office with her luggage in tow.

But now, she wanted to bury her head in the sand. Simply because Sophie was making her feel something she hadn't felt in a *long* time. Maybe even ever. And she didn't want that to end. She wanted to enjoy feeling free, and warm, and alive, before Amelia and her career dragged her back in.

"You okay, baby?" Sophie asked softly.

Finley frowned. She'd been trying to listen. She'd *wanted* to listen. But the buzzing in her pocket was clearly distracting her more than she'd realised.

"Yeah, it's just…" she sighed, pulling the buzzing phone out of her pocket, and laying it face up on the table for Sophie to see. "It's just Amelia."

"Amelia, your boss?"

"Yeah." Finley nodded.

*"Answer* it, Fin!" Sophie urged, her own brow furrowing in anxious concern.

"I…" Finley exhaled, the truth spilling from her lips before she'd even realised she thought it. "I'm scared."

Sophie softened.

"But surely it's better to know, either way?" she coaxed.

Finley smiled weakly, shaking her head.

"I'm not scared of what she's gonna say."

She wrinkled her nose as Sophie raised a brow.

"Okay, I am. I am scared of that, absolutely," she chuckled. She dropped her gaze, picking at the edge of the table as she let her confession fall softly. "But I'm more scared of what might happen to me."

"What do you mean?" Sophie asked.

Finley searched Sophie's eyes. That deep, sparkling green, that reminded her somehow of both the ocean and the forest. Of peace, and serenity, and freedom. That made her feel safe, to say whatever she needed to say.

"These past couple of weeks, Soph," she started, leaning across the table as she held those green eyes in her own. "The break, and Cornwall, and *you.*

They've done something to me. Something *wonderful*. I feel free, Soph. Alive. Like I've been sitting in the dark, and you came along and flipped the light on, and…and I'm scared that this phone call might make it dark again."

Sophie reached a hand across the table, closing it over Finley's own in a simple, soft, unspoken gesture that fizzed in Finley's belly.

"So, don't let it," Sophie stated.

Finley huffed a quiet laugh.

"That simple, eh?"

"It *is* that simple, really." Sophie shrugged, her fingers beginning to draw patterns over the back of Finley's hand and up over her wrist. "They can only take what you're willing to give, Fin. You can have both. You can work hard and still live. It doesn't have to be mutually exclusive."

On the table between them, the phone rang again, and Finley stared at it.

"Just go outside, call her back, and set your boundaries," Sophie coaxed, calmly but firmly.

No real room for argument.

Finley nodded, her fingers trembling slightly as she closed them around her phone.

"You're sure?" she checked. "I don't wanna just leave you in here, we're on a date, and…"

"Go!" Sophie insisted, leaning over to plant a kiss on Finley's cheek. "Call her back. I'll order us another coffee to go."

Finley leaned forward, catching Sophie before she could sit back. She kissed her, more passionate than was really acceptable in a busy cafe, but she couldn't help it. Sophie seemed, sometimes, to understand her more than she understood herself, and it made her entire body feel warm.

"Okay," she breathed, smiling against Sophie's lips as they broke away. "Thank you, baby. I won't be a minute."

Finley's nerves jittered hard as she paced the pavement outside the small cafe, her finger hovering over the call button. *Why* was this so hard? She'd been desperate to speak to Amelia just days ago, and now the idea was making her sweat. She took a deep breath, practically growled as she released it, and pressed her thumb down.

She swallowed thickly as she pressed the phone to her ear.

"Bennett. Jesus fucking Christ, woman."

Amelia's voice was sharp, both frustrated and relieved, and Finley winced the moment it hit her ears.

"I know," she breathed sheepishly. "I'm sorry, I…"

"I don't even need to hear it," Amelia huffed, cutting Finley's words off in her throat. "Just come in and meet me, I need to talk to you."

Finley's back bristled immediately, her brows creasing in the centre.

Not even thirty words in, and Amelia was already unravelling every moment of peaceful quiet that Cornwall had settled in her mind.

"I'm still on paid leave, Amelia," she replied, her voice still calm, but something colder laced beneath it now in her sparking irritation. "I'll be back in next week. Can't you just say what you have to say to me now?"

"I'd really rather not, Finley," Amelia insisted, frustration and something that sounded a lot like desperation forcing her words out harshly. "This is a face-to-face conversation, and I *really* need you to get your head out of your ass and come and hear me out."

Finley's thighs tightened, her body clenching with fear as her stomach bottomed out.

A face-to-face conversation wasn't good. Amelia's tone wasn't good.

Her stomach churned, anxiety and panic twisting together into something horrendously nauseating.

But also, she felt irritated. At the constant barrage of calls, when Amelia wouldn't talk to her over the phone anyway. At the demanding attitude, and the snappy tone, when Amelia was the one interrupting her annual leave. A fresh wave of anger at the way Amelia had so brazenly and unapologetically dismissed her for a promotion she *knew* Finley had wanted, once again, without so much as a word.

She glanced through the cafe window, feeling her resolve climb higher, brick by powerful brick as she watched Sophie fiddle with her phone as she queued for their coffees.

She smiled, her blood thrumming with something empowering as she turned her focus back to her phone call.

"No," she replied.

"N-no?" Amelia stammered.

The stammer bolstered Finley's determination, and she clenched her jaw, standing a little straighter.

"No, Amelia," she replied. "I'm not available, and I won't be until next week. If you have something urgent to talk to me about, then tell me now. Otherwise, it can wait until I'm back."

Finley closed her eyes, holding her nerve together with everything she had as Amelia faltered.

"Bennet," she tried, "I really think…"

"I'm not going to budge on this, Amelia," Finley sighed. "So, if you aren't either, then I think it's best we end this conversation and pick it up again on Monday."

"You're really serious?"

"I'm serious," Finley stated. "See you Monday, Amelia. Take care."

Finley didn't wait for a response before she hung up the phone, shaking, and weak, and anxious, and annoyed, and stressed.

Everything she'd feared she would be if she let Amelia penetrate her vacation.

But also, she felt kind of proud.

Her whole life, she'd been determined not to answer to anybody but herself. And somehow along the way, that determination to reach her successes had pushed her onto a path with the exact opposite requirements. She'd done nothing *but* answer to Amelia, and to Oak Hills, and to Bryce Ridge, and to the thousand other clients she had in her inbox and on the other end of her phoneline.

And she knew now that she had it all backwards.

She didn't need to be alone, but she did need to take control. And today, she'd done that. She'd set her boundaries, and she'd set her principles, and she'd stamped them down hard.

So why did she still feel *so* on edge? Why was she still shaking so hard, and why was her phone still burning so hot against her skin?

She pushed her phone back into her pocket and made her way through the doors, into the cafe, and in Sophie's direction.

The moment she reached Sophie, Finley wrapped her arms around her, and tugged her into a tight cuddle. And as Sophie's arms closed around her own shoulders, Finley's chest eased immediately.

"Baby?" Sophie breathed.

Finley considered holding it together. She considered brushing the anxiety off, and simply telling Sophie that she'd done it. She'd stood up for herself, and laid down her law.

But Sophie was Sophie. She understood Finley like nobody she'd ever met before, and the gentle caress of her hands over Finley's spine was so comforting and empowering at the same time, and Finley broke before she realised it was coming.

"Shit, I really think I've fucked up, Soph," she whimpered, burying her face into the crook Sophie's neck.

Sophie stiffened, and Finley held her tighter.

"Are you gonna let me apologise to her yet?" Sophie murmured; her voice strained against Finley's ear.

"No!" Finley pulled back, meeting Sophie's gaze. "This is not your doing, baby. She stormed my home; you were *well* within your rights."

She rubbed a hand over her face, as if she could wipe the stress and the well of tears away with trembling fingers.

"This is because I gave her staff member a black eye, then disappeared off the grid for two weeks with less than twelve hours' notice, and have outright ignored her fifty times since. I'm not confident that's something that many bosses would overlook."

Sophie blinked.

"You...you gave her staff member a black eye?"

Finley winced.

"During a dramatically embarrassing failed one-night stand," she admitted sheepishly, glancing up at Sophie coyly from beneath her eyelashes.

Sophie snorted a laugh.

"Her loss, my clumsy little gain," she teased, reaching her hands out to wrap around Finley's shoulders, gripping gently at the muscles there as she massaged them.

Finley grinned. Her muscles relaxed under the touch, and Sophie's soft eyes. But her stomach still churned, and she still vibrated with apprehension.

"What did she say?" Sophie asked.

"Bella?" Finley wrinkled her nose. "Not a lot, her nose was bleeding, and..."

"Amelia, you ridiculous Casanova," Sophie laughed.

"Oh!" Finley grinned, feeling her cheeks heat in a blush. Then she sighed. "Also, not a lot. She won't tell me unless I go and meet her face to face."

"So, are you going?" Sophie asked.

"No. It's my annual leave, I'm spending it with you. She doesn't get to rip me out of it like this." Finley growled, bringing both hands up to rub at her face.

*"God,* it's so infuriating, *why* couldn't she just have left me to lick my wounds for two weeks?"

Sophie watched Finley quietly for a moment, her fingers still squeezing softly at the tense muscles of her shoulders.

When she spoke, they were the last words Finley expected to hear.

"If it's eating you up baby, then go. It's just one meeting."

Finley's chest hitched.

She had expected to be praised for sticking to her principles. To be told she'd done the right thing to say no, and to be scolded softly for feeling so agitated by it. She couldn't help the smile that tugged at the corners of her lips as she searched Sophie's eyes for any signs of irritation, and found none.

"Seriously?" she breathed.

She felt her entire body sink with relief as Sophie nodded. Somehow, despite every line that Amelia had crossed, Sophie knew that this was the right thing for Finley. Knew the right thing to say. *God,* the *very* right thing. The way the words had seeped relief and reprieve through her veins immediately. The way Sophie sounded so *sure,* and so *understanding,* without even the first trace of mockery or bitterness.

"You don't have anything to prove to anyone but yourself here, Finley," Sophie assured, stroking her thumbs over the back of Finley's neck. "It doesn't need to be about principle. Yeah, Amelia shouldn't be hounding you on your leave, but she has and now we're here. Acting on principle is only hurting you."

Finley's eyes filled with tears, and she couldn't stop them as she pulled Sophie into her and buried her face into auburn hair.

In her thirty years, Finley had never met anyone who simply accepted her and what was important to her the way Sophie did. Had never met anyone who didn't expect something different, or something more.

Her mind flashed instantly to Jack, and to Bex, and to the anxious way Sophie's hand would often fly to her own phone in the same way Finley's did. Was this what she should be saying to Sophie? Sending her home, to settle her heart and her mind?

"It's not the same," Sophie whispered.

"What?"

"I can *feel* you thinking about me. About Jack," Sophie chuckled softly. "It's not the same. *Go,* baby. And come back to me when she's said what she has to say. It doesn't mark the end of your leave."

336

Finley laughed openly, shaking her head as she pulled back to meet Sophie's gaze.

"Are you real?" she blurted.

Sophie giggled.

"I think you might be a mirage, frankly," Finley teased, brushing her thumb gently over Sophie's lower lip. "No-one is this perfect."

"Finley?" Sophie whispered.

"Yeah?"

"Go!"

~ ~ ~ ~ ~ ~ (♪) ~ ~ ~ ~ ~ ~

Finley shook her hands out, her body almost trembling with her agitation as she watched the glare of the sun over the glass doors of her office building.

She had been hovering outside for well over five minutes, her feet catching like treacle every time she tried to take a step towards it.

God, she was nervous.

In part, because she still didn't understand what Amelia wanted with her, and she wasn't entirely convinced she wasn't losing her job, but mostly because her time off had been *amazing*.

Especially these past few days with Sophie.

And despite every assurance from Sophie, and every assurance she told herself, Finley still couldn't help but worry that going into the office today would burst her bubble, and send her back into the headspace she'd been in when she'd left for Cornwall.

*Before.*

Before the tiny Cornish town that had changed her life.

Before she'd understood.

Before *Sophie.*

She almost turned around. Almost ran; the urge to be back in her bubble with Sophie almost physically lifting her feet in the opposite direction, but she knew she needed to do this. She wanted to enjoy the last few days she had with Sophie before she was due to go back to Cornwall, and she didn't want *this* uncertainty hanging over her head and distracting her thoughts for a moment longer.

She took a deep breath, steeling her nerves as she pushed her way through the glass doors and trod the familiar path to her boss's office.

The sounds were almost deafening. The familiar sounds of phones, and clacking keyboards, and murmured phone calls, and clicking heels. All sounds that Finley would never have noticed two weeks ago, but today they sounded *dark*. Threatening, and ominous.

She shot an awkward, guilty glance in the direction of Bella's desk, exhaling heavily in relief as she found it empty.

She made a mental note to smooth things over on Monday morning.

If she still had a job.

She reached the closed door of Amelia's office, closed her eyes, and knocked before she could talk herself out of it.

"Yeah?"

Finley rolled her eyes at the snapped tone.

Always so *abrupt*.

Her nerves intensified as she closed the door behind her, and something in Amelia's eyes shifted as she realised who had entered.

"Bennett!"

Amelia seemed to tense, somehow, and she brushed the non-existent wrinkles awkwardly from her pristine skirt as she stood to greet Finley.

That in itself was uncomfortable enough. Amelia never *stood* on Finley's entry.

"Please, sit."

Amelia's voice was softer than usual, but clipped somehow, and Finley instantly recognised the shaky sound of nerves hidden behind the short command.

She swallowed.

If *Amelia* was nervous, surely this couldn't be good.

"How's your holiday been?" Amelia sat back; her eyes almost wary as they watched Finley's face.

Finley exhaled softly.

Perhaps this was her fault.

Maybe she wasn't getting fired, but maybe Amelia simply didn't know what to say to the dedicated employee who had abruptly disappeared off the face of the earth for ten days and ignored every one of her phone calls.

Perhaps it was down to her to settle this.

"It's been good." She grinned, fighting her own nerves in an effort to ease the uncomfortable atmosphere. "Been harassed by my boss a little, but I've gotten pretty good at ignoring her calls." She winked.

Amelia scowled, her lips quirking a little as she visibly relaxed. Finley chuckled.

"Missed me?" She smirked.

*"Yes,* and *not* sentimentally," Amelia retorted, her grin growing bigger. "Bound to happen when my best architect fucks off without notice for a fortnight just as her biggest project is tying up."

Finley blushed.

"I'm sorry." She smiled sheepishly, picking at the edge of Amelia's desk in her guilty embarrassment. "It was just a…a series of things, and it was either run to Cornwall and hide in a country pub, or have a breakdown."

Amelia nodded, her eyes softening. She paused for a moment, her lips pursed as she considered her next words, and Finley felt her stomach swoop at the shift in the air.

"Look, Finley…" Amelia's voice shook subtly, *just* enough for Finley to notice. "Maybe I haven't handled this well."

Finley held her breath.

The shaky voice, the use of her first name, the words…none of it was doing much to calm Finley's own racing nerves.

Her eyebrows shot up as Amelia reached beneath her desk, and pulled out two bottles of beer, offering one to Finley.

"Have these always been there?" Finley huffed out a surprised laugh.

Amelia smirked.

"How do you think I cope staying so late every day?"

Finley chuckled.

She relaxed back against the chair as Amelia popped the caps on the beers, and both took a sip to calm the ripples of nervous energy that coursed the room.

"I owe you an explanation," Amelia started, her eyes apologetic as they watched Finley. "I got my head stuck in my own ass, and it didn't occur to me how this would look to you, but there's a reason I didn't give you the principal role, Bennett."

Finley frowned.

Her stomach tightened, the butterflies growing smaller until the fluttering turned to something gnawing. She still had no idea if this was a good thing or a bad thing, and now that she was about to find out, she wasn't entirely sure she wanted to. At least not knowing wasn't knowing, she was fired.

Amelia watched her, unmoving for a moment.

Then her lips quirked softly, and she took a swig of her beer.

"Opal Arches has made a new acquisition, Finley. I want *you* to head up the transition. Manage the new offices."

Finley's stomach dropped.

Her eyebrows flew up, and any words she knew caught in knots on her tongue as she stared for a moment, her brain struggling to process the information.

*"What?"* She blinked. "A-a new…*really?"*

Amelia nodded, her smirk growing.

"It's all still under contract negotiations right now, and I don't have a full job description or a full business case or ATRs for your team, which is *why* I haven't made you an offer yet, but…" Amelia chuckled, shaking her head in amusement. "But when that *firecracker* you have in your apartment told me I was keeping you static, I realised I couldn't keep the plans from you anymore, or I might lose you."

Finley laughed. The mere mention of Sophie, and the way she had worried—was *still* worrying—that she had cost Finley her job, when it was actually starting to sound a lot more like she might have saved it, was enough to spark the warmth in her chest and the ache of a smile in her cheeks.

She certainly was a firecracker, and Finley felt almost searingly proud of her.

"I-I don't know what to say," she chuckled, shaking her head in disbelief. "Where is the acquisition?"

There was a long pause.

Amelia studied Finley too intensely, for just a moment too long, and Finley's heart dropped to her stomach.

*This* was what was making Amelia nervous.

And that was enough to make her own stomach clench.

She held her breath.

Amelia exhaled hers.

"Dubai."

Finley's heart sank.

"I'd…I'd have to move to *Dubai?"*

Amelia nodded.

"F-for how long?" Finley stammered.

"Indefinitely. I'd need you on the ground there."

Finley's throat felt tight, the words wrapping around her lungs and pooling nausea in the pit of her stomach.

Dubai.

She'd wanted this job for so long. She'd worked so hard for it for *so* many years. She'd sacrificed her time, and her life, and her relationships, and her friendships.

But *Dubai?*

*Now?*

She closed her eyes for a moment, her brow furrowed as she fought to clear her head. If she'd been offered this two weeks ago, would she have gone? Left London? One city for another? She let her eyes flicker open. She likely wouldn't have even batted an eyelid, and she knew it. But now? Now that she was falling in love with London again? Now that she was falling in love with her city, and her life, and her friends, and...

She swallowed, her gaze dropping to her beer bottle as she picked at the label.

"When do you need my answer by?"

"You've got time," Amelia assured. "I'll have a full offer to you in three to four weeks, and you can review it then." She grinned, tilting her beer in Finley's direction. "Just don't *leave* me in the meantime, okay Bennett?"

Finley nodded, a half laugh escaping her lips.

She had *no* idea what she felt.

She felt elated that she hadn't been overlooked, and a little smug that fucking Dan Myles hadn't been considered for this role.

But also, she felt more than a little irritated that this hadn't been put to her before. She had wanted the principal position, and Amelia had given it away under a *very* bold assumption that Finley would lift her life to a city five thousand miles away. And she'd done so before Finley had ever been given the chance to make an informed choice, and now it sounded like it was Dubai or nothing.

*Static.*

But also, she was so goddamn *proud* of herself for finally hearing the words she'd wanted for so long, and so grateful to Amelia for believing in her enough to offer this.

But also, more than a little sick about what this would mean for her.

Her mind was swimming with conflicting emotions, and she felt overwhelmed with the sudden burning need to be away from this office and its sounds of doom, and back in Sophie's arms.

The silence was deafening for a moment, until Amelia nodded softly, and Finley was grateful in the moment for her boss's unexpected ability to read the room without her having to say anything.

"This is all I needed to say right now. Go boat the Thames or whatever it is you do when you're not here." Amelia smirked. "Enjoy the rest of your leave, and I promise to leave you alone now until 8am on Monday morning."

Finley bit her cheek, shaking her head.

"Make it nine," she deadpanned.

Amelia raised her eyebrows, folding her arms across her chest, and Finley grinned.

"Thank you, Amelia." She fixed her eyes on her boss's as she stood to leave, hoping that Amelia would see the earnest gratitude within them. She grinned, grabbing the glass bottle from the table and tilting it in gesture. "And thanks for the beer."

"See you Monday," Amelia tilted her own bottle.

Finley exhaled slowly as she turned away, hoping her boss couldn't see the tremble in her hand as she reached for the door.

"Oh, Finley?"

Finley turned.

"The firecracker…" Amelia smirked. "Is she available?"

Finley narrowed her eyes.

"No."

# Chapter Twenty-Four

Sophie hummed contentedly as Finley's arms wrapped a little tighter around her waist, her lips brushing gently over the back of her shoulders.

They had spent the rest of the afternoon in the city, with Sophie dragging Finley around the small and quirky museums she had found on a Google list the night before. But then the skies had opened somewhere between Dennis Severs House and The V&A Museum of Childhood, and they had gotten drenched. And so, they had swapped their afternoon gallery plans for tea, sweats, the sofa, and the *best* goddamn cuddles Sophie had ever had in her life.

Finley's legs were either side of Sophie's own, her body was warm pressed against her back, her lips soft against the back of her neck, and her fingers were trailing nonsense patterns over the skin beneath the hem of Sophie's hoody. Sophie was in heaven.

And she was also a little nervous.

She'd seen an advert, in one of the small museums.

*Assistant Archivist Wanted.*
*Apply within, or online.*

The application form sat open on her phone screen, the account created and the basic details filled in while Finley had showered.

The thought of *telling* Finley made her far more nervous than she had anticipated that it might.

And she didn't know why!

This was *why* she was here. It had been why she had come to London in the first place, before she'd ever known Finley Bennett was anything more than a name on a home-swap website, and yet something about telling Finley that she wanted to move here felt like an admission of something that was *way* too big for someone she had only just met.

It wasn't like it would be *for* Finley.

But she *definitely* made the idea a *lot* more appealing, and Sophie was terrified that an admission along those lines would make Finley feel pressured. And the last thing she wanted, four days into this thing, was to scare her away.

*Especially* not when the trail of those kisses over the back of her neck were starting to reach the sensitive skin beneath her ear, and the spots on her jawline that made the heat flood her stomach.

She shivered.

She grinned as Finley chuckled against her neck, and she turned her head to catch those wandering lips in her own. It never failed to amaze her just how warm Finley could make her with the *softest* of kisses, and she shuffled herself around on the sofa in an effort to increase the contact.

She groaned as Finley's phone rang, the vibrations audible somewhere beneath the cushions.

*"No,"* she whined, wrapping her fingers around Finley's neck in an effort to halt the fumbled search of the offending vibrations.

"It's Amelia," Finley sighed, her voice a little shaky as Sophie nipped along the column of her throat.

"Thought you said she was leaving you alone until Monday," Sophie grumbled, her lips vibrating over Finley's pulse point.

"She was, but I asked her to call me," Finley whispered, her head tilting to the side in betrayal of the effect Sophie's lips were having on her composure. "I had some…*conditions* I wanted to discuss with her for this job offer."

Sophie sighed. She pulled herself back, allowing Finley the space to reluctantly drag herself and her phone up from the sofa.

"I won't be a minute, baby." Finley murmured against her lips, before kissing her hotly.

Sophie smiled softly as she watched Finley leave the room.

Finley had been almost physically shaking when she had arrived home from her meeting, and she had told her with trembling hands that she'd been offered a better job than the one she'd been hoping for. Sophie had instinctively been ecstatic, but the reserve in mocha eyes had given her pause, and she hadn't quite known what to say when Finley had told her that she wasn't entirely sure whether or not the role was the right choice. When Sophie had pushed for why, Finley had told her it sounded like it wouldn't give her the freedom to live her life any better than she does now, and had promptly distracted Sophie with frankly *mind-*

*blowing* sex before she'd had even been able to form the thought processes to hold a coherent discussion about the ins and outs.

And so, Sophie hadn't pushed anymore. It wasn't her business, really, so long as Finley knew she could talk to her if she needed to.

She dragged herself from the sofa, moving quietly as she headed for the bathroom, so as not to disturb Finley's phone call.

She absolutely, one-hundred percent did not *mean* to eavesdrop, but Finley's voice carried clear along the hall, and the words wrapped around Sophie's muscles instantly, running her blood cold and freezing her in her spot.

"I *wouldn't* let you down, you know I've worked all my life for this, but you sprung moving to Dubai on me out of *nowhere.*"

Sophie's stomach clenched, her muscles tightening painfully.

Moving to Dubai?

*That* was the condition?

Sophie felt sick.

She willed her feet to move, willed her ears to shut off, and allow Finley her privacy, but her head was spinning and she just couldn't find the strength.

"Am I even *safe* there?" Finley's exasperated voice continued. "I'm *gay* Amelia!"

Sophie took a shaky breath.

She felt winded. Her chest ached, her vision swam with spots of heated black, and she needed, desperately, to get air into her lungs.

She needed to calm down.

This made sense, now. It made perfect sense as to why Finley had been so shaken, and it made even more sense why she hadn't wanted to talk through the finer details with Sophie. If Sophie was nervous to tell Finley she wanted to move to London, then she could only imagine the crawling anxiety that Finley must feel over telling Sophie she could be moving to the *fucking* United Arab Emirates.

300 miles was one thing.

Four and half *thousand* was another thing altogether.

Selfishly, she clutched hard onto the reassurance that Finley clearly had her reservations over this, but she both hoped it *was* and hoped it *wasn't* because of *her.*

She absolutely did not want to stand in the way of Finley's dream, but also, she *really* wanted to mean enough to her that she would be considering her as a factor.

Which was ridiculous, and she knew it.

But she also knew that however fast it may be, she was falling for Finley, and she just *really* wanted to believe that this was mutual.

Really wanted Finley to feel the way she did.

"I *know* it's a fantastic career opportunity, and *you* know I want it," Finley sighed, the low sound almost bordering on a growl of frustration. "I-it's just…"

She trailed off, and even from the opposite end of the hall, Sophie could feel the shift in the air. Something tighter, less certain.

Something almost defeated.

"It's just that I've…"

Sophie held her breath.

"Well, what would I do with Peanut?"

Sophie's heart sank.

She wasn't stupid. She could read between those lines, and she could hear everything she felt in her own chest reflected in Finley's dejected voice.

And it made her stomach churn.

She *couldn't* be the downfall in something Finley had worked for all her life. She couldn't be the reason Finley stayed.

But she knew, in the ache that gripped in her chest now, that she couldn't take the rejection if she wasn't.

*London* was Sophie's dream.

And she'd belonged. Every minute for almost two weeks, she had belonged.

But suddenly she felt like she was a hurdle. A catalyst in the lives of those she'd met, and the feeling sat like acid in the pit of her stomach.

She loved London, and really, if she was honest, she knew she loved Finley.

But right now, she wanted nothing more than to be in Polcarne where she was a big fish in a little pond, and everything felt safe and familiar, and she couldn't ruin any dreams, and nobody had the power to break her heart.

# Chapter Twenty-Five

"Am I even *safe* there?"

Finley ran her hand through her hair, her tone betraying her exasperation.

"Why wouldn't you be?" Amelia replied.

"I'm *gay* Amelia!"

Finley rolled her eyes at the heavy sigh that echoed through the phone, as if somehow *she* was the one causing problems here, not the boss who had asked her to uproot her life out of the blue and now refused to hear her out.

"Bennett, I know this is a lot to take in and you've got time to think things over, but this is a *fantastic* career opportunity," Amelia's irritatingly calm voice continued. "I thought you'd *want* this!"

"I *know* it's a fantastic career opportunity, and *you* know I want it," Finley sighed, the low sound almost bordering on a growl of frustration. "I-it's just…"

She trailed off, her throat burning with the first signs of her emotion as she considered what she had to lose in this decision.

Whichever way it swung.

"It's just what, Finley?" Amelia pushed.

"It's just that I've…"

Finley trailed off again. She swallowed, her mind swimming with the words she wanted to say. There was no sane way she could follow this up with *'I'm falling in love and I want to see where this goes'*.

She couldn't say that out loud.

Not yet.

Not while things were so new, and she was still processing her feelings herself.

It was too personal, and it was *definitely* not Amelia's business.

She sighed, wincing at the resigned lull in her voice as she gave the first excuse she could think of.

"Well, what would I do with Peanut?"

"Who, or what, is Peanut?" Amelia retorted.

"My cat…"

"Weird thing to call a cat," Amelia huffed.

"Her nose looks like a peanut, she's all sort of out of shape, and…anyway, I can't just leave her."

Amelia paused. When she spoke again, her voice was a little softer.

"Finley, what is it that you want me to say?"

"I *want* you to tell me I can take this role from *here,*" Finley practically cried, the burn spreading from her throat to the back of her eyes. "I want you to tell me I can do this with video calls and technology, and regular shorter trips to Dubai." She took a deep breath, determined not to let her emotion break in her voice. "I want you to tell me I don't have to choose between my career and my *life,* Amelia."

"I can't do that, Bennett. The job is in Dubai."

Finley's heart sank.

The burn sparked, the worry and the anxiety flaring into something hotter. She slammed her eyes shut as the anger washed through her.

"God, *why* didn't you *talk* to me about this *before?" She* hissed, fighting the urge to shout. "You gave the role I *wanted*—the role I worked my *ass* off for— to Dan Myles because you just *assumed* I would give up *everything* for you at the drop of a hat."

"I assumed you'd want the best I could…"

Finley shook her head. The anger was too strong now, and she couldn't hear these excuses any more.

"Whatever defence you're about to give me, you still *assumed,*" she snapped. "You didn't *ask* me. You just assumed I would drop my whole life, to move to a country that *flogs and kills* people of my community, and in making that assumption you gave away the thing I've been working for since the *day* you met me."

"Finley, you're the best I have." Amelia's voice was soft. Weak. Almost resigned.

Finley's shoulders sank.

"Then *treat* me like it!" She whispered.

"I'm trying to."

The pause was stifling.

Finley's stomach was in knots, and her heart burned in her throat at the understanding of what the silence meant, and at the words she knew she was going to have to say.

At the fact that after *everything,* she was going to have to do this.

She took a deep breath.

"I can't move to Dubai, Amelia."

"Yeah," Amelia sighed, defeated. "Yeah, I know."

This time the silence felt a little less stifling. Finley's chest hurt, but her shoulders felt a little lighter.

Pain, and frustration, and grief for the dream she'd had to turn down…but also relief.

That she wasn't going to fucking Dubai.

"Can you just…" Amelia started, the nervous break that Finley had heard in her voice just hours ago when she'd first mentioned this clearer than ever in the words now. "Just give me some time? Please don't do anything rash just yet?"

Finley swallowed.

There was something in those words. Something in the nerves behind them. Something in the way her boss had played this whole thing out. There was *something* that lit a spark over Finley's head, and she realised, for the first time, that she'd already achieved everything she'd worked for.

She was invaluable.

She was the best at what she did, and Amelia needed her. And that put her in a position to take some control back over her career and her life, and it was high time she used it.

Maybe Dubai wasn't her opportunity, but she was *definitely* not going to lie down and take her *static* stature back with open arms.

And she could do that while living in *England.*

Where her life was.

Where Sophie was.

~ ~ ~ ~ ~ ~ ⟨♪⟩ ~ ~ ~ ~ ~ ~

Sophie's fingers trembled as she pushed her suitcase back under the bed for the third time.

She closed her eyes, pacing the room in a moment of insanity.

Then she dropped to her knees, pulling the suitcase back out.

Again.

Her mind was a hazy mess of every emotion she knew it was possible to feel, and she couldn't pick one coherent thought from another.

She *knew* she couldn't just leave.

She wasn't that cruel.

She knew she needed to just *talk* to Finley, but she was absolutely, stomach-through-her-asshole goddam *terrified* of what she was supposed to say.

And even *more* so of what Finley might say back.

"Soph?"

She jumped back as she heard a light knock on the bedroom door, and Finley's soft, unsuspecting voice calling through the thin wood of the door.

"Yeah?" Sophie managed; her voice strained.

She *had* managed to ignore the prickle of tears behind her eyes. She had managed to keep them from falling.

But the moment the door opened and her gaze landed on warm mocha eyes, they filled her own with a hazy film that she knew Finley would see.

"I'm sorry, that took a little longer than expec…"

Finley halted, her brow furrowing as she searched Sophie's face. She stepped forward, her hands reaching for Sophie's arms almost instinctively, and the soft gesture pushed the tears over the edge.

"Baby, what's wrong?" Finley frowned, her eyes darting around the room. She froze, her eyes widening a little as they landed on the open suitcase on the floor, half pushed under the bed. She dropped her hands. "Were…a-are you gonna leave? Is it Jack, did something happen?"

"No, Jack's okay. I assume. It's…I…" Sophie sniffed, wrapping her arms around her own chest. "I don't know. If I'm gonna leave."

Finley swallowed; her eyes visibly pained as her brow creased a little.

The pause was deafening, and Sophie bit back the urge to run to Finley as she sat tentatively on the bed, her hands trembling as they gripped the edge.

"Why?"

Finley's voice was so small, so confused and yet so undemanding that Sophie could practically feel her heart break.

She exhaled shakily, willing her voice to stay steady.

"Because I can't be the reason you turn down this job," she whispered. "But I can't watch you leave either."

Finley's eyes widened, and her brows arched a little in surprise.

"Baby…" she started.

Sophie couldn't bear it. The words formed on her lips before she could even think them through, and they cut off Finley's own as they tumbled into the stifling air between them.

"Finley, I know this is insane," she rushed. "I know that this is the last thing you'd expect to hear so soon, a-and maybe I'm crazy, and maybe to you this is nothing more than a *really* unconventional holiday fling, but to me this is *everything.* I'm falling harder for you in two weeks than I ever have for anyone, and I *can't* watch you get on a plane to Dubai. I can't."

Sophie took a sharp breath as she finished, her hands starting to shake with the adrenaline of her confession. She bit her lip, her eyes searching Finley's face in anxious anticipation.

Finley was quiet for a long moment, wide eyes fixed unmoving on Sophie's. Sophie felt her stomach flip and her chest clench as those wide eyes glazed; something almost awed in them.

She held her breath.

Then Finley's lips tugged at the corners, the most subtle of smiles that Sophie wouldn't have even noticed had she not been watching so closely. Had she not been *so* on edge.

"Y-you're falling for me?" Finley whispered.

Sophie huffed out a laugh.

She wasn't quite sure what she had expected Finley's takeaway from her rambling to have been, but the fact that it was *that* was surely a *very* good sign.

"Of *course,* I am," she breathed, her own lips quirking into a shy smile. She shook her head, almost in disbelief. "I mean, you're *here,* right? You're feeling this?"

"*Yes!*" Finley sighed, her grin growing wider. She pushed herself from the edge of the bed, taking a tentative step toward Sophie. "Which brings me to my next question."

Finley cocked an eyebrow, flashes of her usual tease *just* dancing behind the sincerity in warm eyes.

Sophie's stomach flipped.

"In *what* world would I be seeing this as any kind of *fling?*" Finley chuckled, closing the gap between them. She brought her hands to Sophie's hips, resting just firm enough to keep Sophie grounded.

"I-in the world where you have to move five thousand miles away?" Sophie mumbled.

"Sophie, I'm not going to Dubai."

"But that's even *worse!*" Sophie cried, breaking away from Finley's hold and taking a panicked step backward. "I *can't* hold you back from everything you've worked for like that!"

Finley shook her head, her eyes calm and her voice steady.

"My career is important to me…"

"I *know,*" Sophie interrupted, her voice strained with her emotion. She paced the floor slightly, desperate to keep her body moving for fear it would shut down if she didn't. "That's why I have to…"

"Baby."

Sophie halted.

There was something so *calm* in Finley's voice. Something so earnest, and so easy in that one word, that it wrapped its way into Sophie's chest and soothed her nerves for just a moment.

For just long enough for Finley to reach her again, those grounding hands finding her hips once more.

"Baby, my career is important to me but I'm *good* at what I do," Finley started, her voice low and reassuring, and her eyes honest. "I've worked hard for a *long* time, and this will not be my *only* opportunity."

Sophie swallowed, her eyes filling once again with tears as she searched Finley's face.

"But…"

"I *can't* move to Dubai, Soph." Finley cut her off. "And yes, it *is* because of you, but it's also because of *me.*"

Sophie's shoulders dropped, and she exhaled slowly as she felt the first of her resolve crumble around the words and the soft tone of Finley's voice.

Finley grinned, tugging her a little closer.

"I've spent so long giving up everything to reach what I thought were my dreams, but it turns out a suit and a salary aren't the *only* things that make up my life," Finley explained. She laughed softly. "It took me forever to realise it, but your tiny little country town, with its people and its ridiculously narrow roads, and its fucking *satanic* badgers taught me that I need to slow down. I need to make time for the things I really want. And that I don't need to be *alone* to stand on my own feet."

Warm mocha eyes showed nothing but genuine, earnest honesty, and Sophie felt her body melt as she processed that this was *okay.*

This decision was Finley's to make, and to make how she saw fit.

And she was making it.

And not because of her. Not solely, anyway.

And with *that* anxiety out of the way, Sophie felt nothing but sheer relief.

And elation that Finley did care enough to stay for her. Did feel the same.

"And what I really *want…* " Finley grinned, her eyes sparkling with mischief as she brushed her nose over Sophie's. "Is you."

"Cheeseball," Sophie giggled, her eyes misting once again with unwanted tears of a *totally* different kind. She grinned, her hands wrapping around the back of Finley's neck. "I *really* want you too."

Finley beamed, her eyes crinkling at the edges as she tugged Sophie into a soft, lingering kiss.

"So, you'll put that suitcase away, right?" she murmured, her lips still brushing Sophie's. "For a few more days?"

"Mmmm." Sophie kissed her again. "For a few more days."

"And uh…" Finley pulled back, the tips of her ears tinting red as her eyes dropped bashfully for a moment. "Then what?"

Sophie felt giddy.

And with everything that she felt reflected back at her in Finley's eyes, she felt the familiar air of playful mischief begin to settle over her.

"What do you mean?" she teased.

"Uh, I…" Finley pursed her lips, *just* biting back a smirk at the knowing tone in Sophie's voice, despite the deepening of the blush over her cheeks and her ears.

Sophie grinned.

"Yeah, you know what, I'm just gonna shoot my shot," Finley laughed, shaking her head. "Sophie, I don't *want* to be five thousand miles from you. I don't wanna be three *hundred* miles from you either. I don't care how soon it is, honestly. I want you, I want this, and I want *all* of it. So, if you still want to come to London then I'll wait for you, as long as you need. And if you don't, then…"

Finley trailed off, her eyes drifting as she considered her next words, and Sophie's chest hitched in anticipation.

"Well, I *guess* I could see myself tending to Trevor's chickens every morning." Finley grinned. "Stashing rum in your cupboards with Bex. Maybe I'd learn how to make a vegan cheese."

Sophie blinked.

"Are you telling me you'd move to Polcarne?"

"Yeah, if that's what you wanted." Finley nodded; her smile shy again. "I know how much your family means to you, and I want to be with you. So, it's London, or its Cornwall, right?"

Sophie flicked her ear.

*"Ow,* what was *that* for?" Finley huffed, her brow furrowing and her lip jutting into a pout as she rubbed at her ear. "I thought I was being cute!"

"I wasn't prepared to be the reason you didn't go to Dubai," Sophie scolded, "you think I'm gonna be the reason you move to *Polcarne?"*

Finley frowned.

"Well, granted I was *hoping* I wouldn't have to, but I thought maybe with Bex, and Jack, and…"

"Despite *lots* of things that suggest the contrary, this is not some holiday romcom, Finley," Sophie huffed, her lips curling at the adorable confusion in Finley's eyes. "We are not the American cliche where the person with the successful career drops it all to move to the ass-end of podunk nowhere, where there's no potential and no phone signal."

Finley laughed, her brow relaxing as she understood what Sophie was saying.

Sophie grinned.

"I know your career is important to you, baby," she continued. "I would *never* ask you to give that up. And yes, I'm spine-curlingly terrified of leaving Polcarne, and of missing Bex, and Jack, and Willow, and of not being there when he has his lows and…well, all of it."

She trailed off, her eyes welling with tears and her throat closing with emotion at the thought of the five-hundred miles between her own two feet, and the family she loved so much.

But she'd made her decision. She knew she had. And it was time Finley did too.

"I'm terrified of all of that, and I'm just as terrified of London, and the tubes, and of how fast and how hard I'm falling for you, but I *want* it." She exhaled heavily, blinking through the tears as she beamed at Finley. "I want you, and I want here, and I want this new life. And we are *not* going to be sacrificing it all to be with each other. We don't need to! Honestly, it's time I chased my own dreams."

Finley kissed her, short and sweet, and Sophie melted a little further into her arms. She grinned as she pulled back, the open adoration in mocha eyes making her bones melt.

"I'm in London because I want to *stay* in London," she finished softly. "And maybe *you* are just the push I need to finally bite the bullet."

She whimpered in surprise as Finley kissed her again, a little hotter and a little more urgent, her body pressing tighter against Sophie's own.

"So that suitcase can just go right back under that bed then, yes?" Finley murmured, barely pulling back enough for her words to be audible.

"For now. I can't just *never* return home." Sophie chuckled. "I have things I need to sort out, and also, we may be cliché but we're not *that* cliché, I'm not assuming I'll be moving in here, Bennett."

"Hmmm that's fair." Finley nodded, her lips beginning to trail over Sophie's jaw, and her fingers teasing under the waistband of Sophie's sweatpants. "Although *I am* enough of a cliché that I feel a *little* disappointed by both of those things."

Sophie grinned.

"But I *am* moving to London," she gasped, the words strained as Finley's lips worked over her neck.

*"Yes!"* Finley hissed triumphantly, the words vibrating over Sophie's pulse point.

Sophie moaned.

"And until then," she murmured, "five and a half hours isn't *that* far."

"And we've always got video calls," Finley mumbled, her lips and her tongue very much otherwise occupied.

"Plenty of ways I can tease you." Sophie smirked.

Finley chuckled, her lips making their way back to meet Sophie's.

"I'm in so much trouble, aren't I?" She grinned.

"Oh, you have *no* idea."

# Epilogue

"What's the latest on Oak Hills?"

Amelia's voice rang out through Finley's laptop, the screen filled with her stern face.

"They're due to finish building the first wing in six weeks, and so far, they've been pretty much on schedule," Finley replied, leaning back in her chair in an effort to stretch her stiff muscles.

This was her fourth video call of the morning, and she hadn't even had a chance to make herself a coffee in the past two and a half hours.

And she was *distracted* this morning.

The first three meetings had been important, and she had had to force herself to focus, but this one was merely a catch up and her mind was beginning to wander.

To Sophie, and to what today meant for them.

"Was Jonah happy enough to take the day to day over from you?"

Amelia's voice brought Finley's focus back to the laptop screen, and she shuffled slightly in her seat in an effort to keep her energy trained on the call.

"You kidding? He practically snatched it from under me!" She grinned, shaking her head at the memory. "How's Dubai?"

"Fucking *warm,*" Amelia exclaimed, her eyes rolling back a little as she fanned herself with her hand.

Finley laughed.

"But it's beautiful, I love it." Amelia grinned. "I guess I have to thank you, really!"

"You definitely do *not* have to thank me," Finley scoffed. "You literally gave me your own job and fucked off to the Emirates because I turned down an offer."

Amelia's eyebrow shot up.

"Hey, I did *not* give you my job, I'm still your boss!" she retorted.

"Sure, so you *think.*" Finley grinned.

Amelia rolled her eyes.

"I was getting *bored* in London. It was my *static.*" She winked, and Finley cursed herself for the blush that heated her cheeks. "When you turned this job down, it got me thinking!" Amelia shrugged. "Anyway, are we still scheduled for the global town hall at 4:30pm GST?"

"No can do, Noah is leading that for me today."

"You've been managing the place five minutes, and you've hired an assistant manager and delegated to him already?" Amelia laughed.

"Yeah, share the load and all that." Finley wriggled her eyebrows cheekily. "I'm finishing early today, my girlfriend is moving to the city!"

"Oh shit, the firecracker?"

Finley grinned.

"You're a lucky woman, Bennett." Amelia shook her head, her tone deliberately wistful.

"Don't I know it," Finley sighed. "Right, I've got another call in ten and if I don't get a coffee before then I might start ripping heads off. I've got to go. Don't keep my staff too late in the town hall, I don't want them locked in!"

Amelia scowled.

"Your whole *'office locked and phones off by 6pm'* rule is a pain in my ass," she grumbled.

"Yeah, well *you* were a pain in *my* ass for too many hours of the week, and I don't wanna do the same thing." Finley winked.

"Asshole," Amelia mumbled. "Catch you later."

Finley bit back her shit-eating grin as she hung up the call, and finally dragged herself to her feet, making her way out into the kitchen.

It had been three months since Sophie Cedars had crashed into her life in the most unconventional of ways, and Finley had spent *way* too many hours on trains since then, but today was *finally* the day that her girlfriend was due to arrive in London.

For good.

She was *so* proud of Sophie for chasing her dreams, and Sophie was due to start her job as Assistant Archivist at one of London's tiny museums in just a week's time. And *today* she would be moving in with Noah and Zayan in their three-bed bachelor pad.

Which Finley wasn't jealous about.

Obviously.

Not at all.

For now. One day she'd convince Sophie to move in with her. But even she could accept it was maybe a *little* too soon for that just yet.

She sighed; her eyes practically glued to the clock on the kitchen wall as she flicked on the coffee machine.

Two hours, and she could leave.

Two hours, and Sophie would finally be a Londoner.

~ ~ ~ ~ ~ ~ 🎵 ~ ~ ~ ~ ~ ~

*"But she caught me on the counter!"*

Sophie pressed her face against the cool glass of the van's window, trying her hardest to tune out Bex's relentless singing as her older sister drove through the busy streets of London.

The singing hit a particularly screechy note, and Sophie turned her head to face her sister, shaking it in bemusement.

Bex didn't even blink.

She simply sang louder, pointing her index finger at Sophie, her eyebrows raised in a wordless demand for her sister to join in.

Sophie cocked an eyebrow.

"Wow, you're no fun," Bex mumbled, shovelling a handful of Haribo into her face.

Sophie rolled her eyes.

"Bex, we've been in this van for five and a half hours and this is the seventh time you've played this song."

"It's timeless," Bex retorted, her mouth full of sweets.

"Is it even old enough to be considered timeless?"

"It doesn't need to be, Shaggy is the man, and it will absolutely be timeless," Bex scoffed. She softened a little as she glanced at Sophie, and the incessant twisting of her hands in her lap. "How are you feeling?" "I'm nervous!" Sophie groaned, throwing her head back against the seat.

"Of course, you are, it would be weird as all fuck if you weren't," Bex chuckled. "You're gonna do *so* great, kiddo. I'm so *proud* of you."

"Thank you." Sophie whispered. Unexpected tears threatened in the back of her eyes, and she blinked them back stubbornly. "I'm gonna miss you *so* much."

This had been the *one* thing that sat in the pit of her stomach every time she thought of London, and her impending move. For three months she'd felt elation, and excitement, and intrigue, and giddy enthusiasm for what the move would bring for her, but the thought of being 300 miles from Bex, and Jack, and Willow made her feel sick.

Jack was coping well. He had a pump now, to manage his insulin, and he was more organised than Sophie and Bex put together with his carb counting, and his little phone alerts. He was profoundly interested in the science behind his condition, and he'd spent hours poring over his pamphlets and the internet, and the books Bex had bought him.

Astronaut or not, they *definitely* had a scientist on their hands.

But still, it had been hard to leave him. And Willow.

"Hey," Bex soothed, her hand reaching out to close over Sophie's knee. "The way you make this place sound, I'd put money on us moving here ourselves in another three months!"

"Don't tease me," Sophie groaned. "I'd *love* that!"

"Maybe we'll all move in with Bennett." Bex grinned. "She seems like she'd make a good roomie."

Sophie smirked.

"I wouldn't, I hear her girlfriend's *really* loud in bed."

Bex baulked.

*"Christ,* Sophie!" She screwed her face in disgust, her hand flying off Sophie's knee as if it had been burned. "Jesus, do you *wanna* see my Little Chef bacon painted across this dashboard?"

Sophie giggled, shaking her head.

She took a deep breath, her nerves flaring high through her veins as Bex turned the van onto a small side road, and the map system declared it Chapman's Court Road.

Her new home.

"This is it up, on the left!" She pointed at the now familiar apartment block, with its barely-there front garden and its slate steps, and its iron railed fence.

Sophie's nerves warmed, excitement replacing their pulse through her muscles as Bex pulled the van up along the kerbside, and both sisters jumped out onto the London street.

The building looked older in its architectural style than Finley's apartment block did; almost golden brick at the top, and white wood cladding at the bottom.

But it looked almost exactly the same in shape and size, and Sophie already knew that its layout was an almost exact mirror.

Bex let out a low whistle as she scanned the building, leaning back against the van as Sophie fumbled with the keys that Noah had given her when she last visited Finley.

"How the fuck are you affording *this* place on a starting salary?" Bex challenged, her tone almost bewildered.

"*Charming,*" Sophie shot, narrowing her eyes as she turned back to face her sister.

Bex quirked an eyebrow.

Sophie blushed.

"Noah owns it. And I'm pretty sure he's charging me a *lot* less than he should," she grumbled. "And a lot less than he charges Zayan. Come on, I'll give you the tour."

Sophie felt her excitement peak as she showed her sister around her new home, her chest surging with pride at the impressed look in awed green eyes. There were even more gadgets in this place than there were in Finley's, and Sophie chuckled as Bex's eyes widened a little more at each one. At the lights that dimmed by an AI assistant, the robo-hoover, and the curved smart TV that took up most of the living room wall.

The flat was smart, and clean, but it was very much a bachelor pad, and Sophie couldn't wait to put her own stamp on it.

By the time she managed to drag Bex away from the electric roller blinds, Sophie was itching to get her things inside and unpacked, and make this place feel like home.

She had done her very best to pack up the van with her larger furniture items nearest the door, so that she would be able to unload those first, and get the room set up before she brought in her stacks of boxes.

And up first, was the wardrobe. Sophie was *very* glad that Noah lived on the ground floor, because she had a pretty strong feeling that Bex was about to be incredibly useless.

"You think *we're* lifting this thing?" Bex raised her eyebrows, her thumb gesturing between herself and Sophie.

"Why not?" Sophie huffed, jumping up into the van and wriggling her way behind the wardrobe. "Pete and I got it in here."

Bex blinked.

"You're about four feet tall, and I'm ninety percent Haribo right now," she argued. "I'm *really* not convinced we're a furniture-shifting dream team."

"Remind me again why I brought you and not Pete?" Sophie mumbled.

"Rude!" Bex scoffed. "You're my baby sister, I couldn't let you galivant off to London without checking the place out for myself!"

"And the guise for that was *helping me move,*" Sophie grunted, shifting her torso against the wardrobe as she manoeuvred it to the edge of the van. "So put your Haribo hands on the top of this fucking wardrobe, and take the weight while I tip it back!"

*"Alright,* so *pushy,"* Bex grumbled, her eyes widening in surprise.

She placed her hands under the top of the wardrobe, and Sophie breathed a sigh of relief as she tipped it back and the item was met with resistance.

For about three seconds.

"What the *fuck,* Sophie, it's getting *heavier!"*

Sophie growled.

"Yes, because you're *taking its weight,* now just..." she grunted as she crouched down, wriggling her own hands beneath the base. "Get ready cause I'm gonna lift my end. On three, two, one..."

Sophie pushed with her thighs, hauling her end up and into her arms.

Bex screamed.

The top of the wardrobe plummeted.

Sophie stumbled, her heart soaring into her throat as she fought to catch her footing before she, too, plummeted face first into the tail end of her own wardrobe.

"What the *fuck* Bex?"

"My fucking *hands* are trapped *under* it!" Bex wailed.

"Well, *lift* it the fuck *up* then!"

There was an almighty grunt.

Then a wobbly moment.

And a few whimpers.

And then the top of the wardrobe was airborne once more, and Sophie's hold steadied with two people holding the thing level. Bex managed to hold her own as they carried the wardrobe to the steps leading up to the front door, then the fumbling started again as they began to climb.

"There's nothing to *hold,"* Bex whined, her voice panicked. "It's like a 90s barber shop up in here."

*"What?"*

"It's…it's all slippery?" Bex explained, her tone almost sheepish. "Like too much gel?"

Bex moved her hand, waving it around her head in a gesture that Sophie *might* have interpreted to mean *too much hair gel,* had she not been far too preoccupied with the crushing weight in her chest of the wardrobe that her sister was now deciding *not* holding her fair share of the weight of.

"Bex *hold the fucking wardrobe!"* she rasped.

*"Wow,* the Chuckle Brothers reboot is a lot *swearier* than I expected."

Sophie twisted to the source of the familiar voice, her whole body igniting with the urge to run to the owner she had *not* seen coming.

Unfortunately, that was not a move that bode well with holding ninety percent of the weight of a heavy oak wardrobe.

Fortunately, Finley was by her side, her hands firm beneath the oak, before the furniture could even begin to slide from her grip.

"Hey, baby," Finley murmured, her lips spreading into a wide, beaming grin.

*"Hey,"* Sophie breathed.

She didn't know what it was.

Whether it was the fact that it had been two weeks since she'd last seen Finley in person, or whether it was that this time she knew she was staying here, or whether it was the heroic save, or the sudden unexpected close proximity to the woman she'd fallen head over heels and then some for, and the familiar scent of jasmine that invaded her senses…

But whatever it was, Sophie felt utterly giddy, and she could barely think straight as she searched the warm mocha eyes she'd missed for two weeks.

"I missed you," Finley grinned, pressing her forehead briefly against Sophie's.

"I missed you too," Sophie whispered.

She couldn't take her eyes off her girlfriend, and she was completely unaware of her surroundings as Finley leaned in, connecting their lips in a short, soft kiss.

Until the wardrobe shifted, knocking them back, and Sophie's surroundings came flooding back to her faster than the arousal had pooled in her underwear.

"Oi!" Bex yelled. "Ninety percent Haribo over here, remember?"

Finley chuckled.

"I've got this end." She grinned, gesturing toward Bex with a nod of her head. "Go rescue Wreck Armstrong over there before your wardrobe ends up smashed across the pavement."

Sophie beamed. She kissed Finley hotly once more, before scrambling up the steps to relieve Bex.

"*Wreck* Armstrong?" Bex spat through a half laugh. "*Wreck? And you thought Fidget Jones was bad? That was fucking abysmal,* Bennett."

Sophie grinned at Finley's scowl as they pushed past Bex and into the building.

"Nice try, Punny Bravo, but you can stick to being the brawn in this relationship and leave the wit to me, k?" Bex called after her.

"You and I are not *in* a relationship," Finley grunted. "And we *both* know I'm neither the brains *or* the brawn in my *actual* relationship."

"So, what *do* you bring to the table?" Bex challenged, leaning against the wall of the hallway, chewing yet more Haribo.

Sophie smirked.

They just made it *too* easy.

"Orgasms," she deadpanned.

Bex choked on her Haribo.

Finley dropped the wardrobe.

~ ~ ~ ~ ~ ~ ⟨♪⟩ ~ ~ ~ ~ ~ ~

Finley couldn't wipe the smile from her face as she laid the cutlery out on the dining table in Noah and Zayan's place.

Noah and Zayan and *Sophie's* place.

She shook her head, the elation threatening to overwhelm her.

Sophie was here. In London. To *live.*

And Finley had never been so happy about anything in her life.

They'd been working for most of the afternoon, but the van was now empty and Sophie's room looked homely. Bex was planning to move into Sophie's house in Polcarne, and as Noah had most stuff set already, most of Sophie's bulkier things had been left behind, but there were already soft furnishings and candles and photo frames around the place that felt like her. Finley couldn't help the warm surge of adrenaline that she felt at the little snippets of her time in Polcarne that now surrounded her life in London.

She grinned as the front door latch clicked, and the sounds and the scent of Noah and Zayan arriving home with the Chinese takeaway floated down the hall.

She laughed, leaning back against the dining table alongside Bex as she watched her girlfriend greet her best friend, both wriggling their hips in a mirrored dance she'd never seen either of them do, but was clearly familiar to them.

She felt her chest inflate, swelling with adoration for her girlfriend, and for her best friend, and for the fact that they clearly had a bond that went well beyond her.

"Welcome to London, Sophie!" Zayan popped a champagne bottle, shouting above the whoops and cheers that rang out around him. "It's gonna be so great living with you."

As they sat down to eat, introductions to Bex over and the group already jostling and bustling and talking over each other like a family, Finley felt the unexpected prickle of tears hit the back of her eyes.

Sophie's hand landed over her thigh, and Finley blinked the tears back as she met her girlfriend's gaze, grinning widely.

She couldn't quite believe her luck.

Three months ago, Finley had been the loneliest she'd ever felt, spending her nights eating Bella Collins' sandwiches in her darkened office, and closing the doors on the sounds of her city at every given opportunity.

And now, thanks to Polcarne, and to Sophie Cedars, Finley had never felt so at *home.*

Sitting around a dining table at 6pm on a Thursday night, with the love of her life and her best friends, the late September air carrying the sounds of the city through the open windows, Finley Bennett knew she had it all.

### THE END